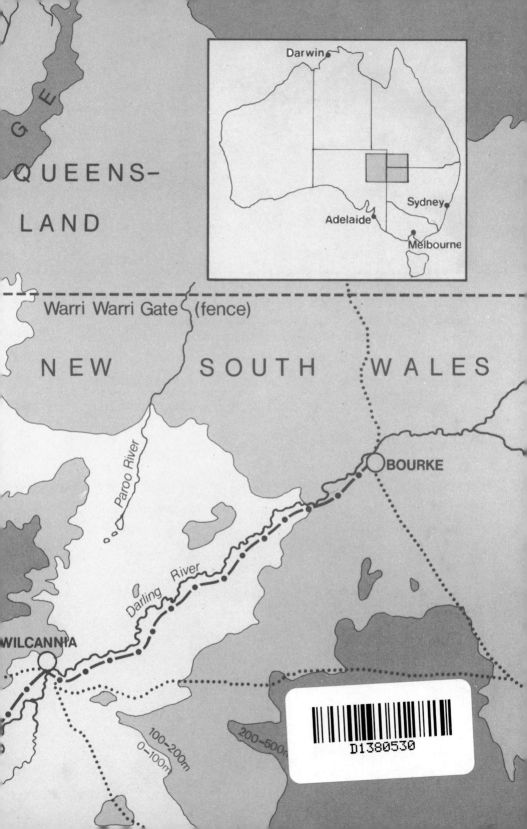

THE BUSH SOLDIERS

By the same author

JACOB'S SEASON

THE
BUSH SOLDIERS

John Hooker

COLLINS
London and Sydney
1984

William Collins Sons and Co. Ltd
London · Glasgow · Sydney · Auckland
Toronto · Johannesburg

The publishers acknowledge permission to reproduce the lyrics
of the following songs: *The Honeysuckle and the Bee* © 1901 Sol Bloom;
reproduced by permission of Francis Day and Hunter Ltd.
Ain't We Got Fun © 1921 Remick Music Corp.
Reproduced by permission of B. Feldman and Co Ltd.
Carolina Moon © 1929 Benny Davis.
Reproduced by permisssion of the Lawrence Wright Music Company
Ltd.

BRITISH LIBRARY CATALOGUING IN PUBLICATION DATA

Hooker, John
The Bush soldiers.
I. Title
923[F]   PR9619.3.H6/

ISBN 0-00-222649-9

First published 1984
© John Hooker 1984

Photoset in Sabon by Centracet
Made and printed in Great Britain by
William Collins Sons and Co. Ltd, Glasgow

For Jake,
and thanks to E.S.

All the business of war, and indeed all the business of life, is to endeavour to find out what you don't know by what you do.

Arthur Wellesley,
1st Duke of Wellington

Contents

1	To Bourke	1
2	1917	16
3	Bourke	33
4	1919	49
5	Bourke	69
6	1925	98
7	Bourke	122
8	1932	140
9	Wilcannia	171
10	1934	199
11	To Broken Hill	220
12	1939	248
13	Broken Hill	276
14	1941	298
15	To Tibooburra	332
16	To Four Mile Well	364
17	To Innamincka	387
18	Cooper's Creek	407

· I ·

To Bourke

GEOFFREY SAWTELL woke six times during the cold, black night and reached for the Hollis shotgun. But each time there was nothing. No sound. Frank Counihan was getting back under his grimy blankets and the fire had been built up. Sawtell watched the flames burning within the prehistoric rocks. There were ghostly trees of stone, the Southern Cross shining brightly, the Milky Way. There was a huge white moon, ant hills, one falling star, eternal puzzles, the firmament and the beginning of the world. He watched Counihan, listened to his shallow breathing and went back to sleep. At nights in camp, Sawtell kept the shotgun very close. He always had the feeling that someone was watching them.

In the grey morning, Sawtell woke to see the infinite horizon: he listened to the sounds of the crows, the parakeets and the laughing jackasses. Another river line stretched west, about ten miles away. A big male kangaroo was watching them at about fifty yards from the edge of the creek bed, its paws clasped loosely in front of its chest. Sawtell stared back; he thought of picking up the Lee Enfield, then changed his mind. Why eat roo when there was plenty of mutton on the way? Frank Counihan was up, kicking at the fire. The big army boots, the battered slouch hat, the police and fireman's braces and the St Christopher medal hanging from his neck. He was bending and blowing

1

at the ashes. Fragile sticks and leaves, a delicate spiral of smoke and the black billy. The leaves of the ghost gums hung down still, and the earth was red. Sawtell lay there in his blankets and looked at Counihan's strong, narrow back; the long, ragged greatcoat, the webbing, the cartridge belt beneath and the Colt .45 revolver in the open holster. He listened to Counihan's song:

> It was there for the sake of five hundred pounds
> I was sent across the main,
> For seven long years, in New South Wales,
> To wear a convict's chain.

A friend of Sawtell's father used to sing that song many years ago.

They had continued to follow Colonel Madigan's orders; there was nothing else they could do. In the last two weeks, they had fired two petrol dumps at Nyngan, smashed the telephone exchange at Byrock, poisoned the wells with sheeps's carcasses at Trafalgar station and blown the signals and points on the railway. They had started fires in the wheat fields and done their best to deny the enemy, who remained unseen. The destruction had been complete. Sawtell had seen to that: he was a very efficient soldier.

'Jesus Christ,' Frank Counihan said, scratching his black beard, 'I'm getting sick of this. It's been over four months now. I'm sick of looking after the fires and I'm sick of this country.'

He stood up very fast and threw a rusty jam tin at the rabbits.

'Bastards,' he said. 'Bloody furry bastards.'

'Steady on, Frank,' Sawtell said. 'We both have to do it. They'll have matches at Bourke.'

He got up from the blankets and stretched in his long filthy underwear, pulled on his trousers and looked at the packhorses and the gear. He was a big, powerful man. He stared again at the dead horizon, the huge early-morning sun, the crows crouching on the staggering fence posts. The land had gone back badly since the war, but he still loved the country. It was his.

'Your saddlebag needs mending,' Sawtell said. 'We've got an awl and thread somewhere.'

Counihan, crouched over the fire, did not reply.

Sawtell strapped on the .45 Service Webley, broke open the Hollis, removed the cartridges and cleaned the barrels with the ramrod. He put the shotgun carefully back in the gun bag and then cleaned and oiled the Lee Enfield. The dust had got into everything. He pulled on his boots, rubbed his eyes, picked up the bag of oats and walked along the creek bed and over the stones to the horses at the picket line. Once again, he caught the smell of the strong billy tea. Sawtell examined the horses' feet and fetlocks. Two horses would need shoeing when they got to Bourke. Counihan would do it. He checked the ammunition cases, the cans of petrol, the sticks of dynamite and the water in the canvas bags. Everything was okay. He considered the dry creek, listened again to the laughing jackasses and the crows; he looked at the rabbits at the water hole and the flat, brown horizon. A wedgetail eagle soared and then hung still in the morning sky. He untethered the horses, led them to the lagoon and pissed on the ground as he watched them drink. When he had fed them, he tethered them again and went back to the fire.

'Oh Jesus, and what do you want this morning?' Counihan said as he took the old wicker fishing creel down from the branch. He stood up, stiff and cold. 'You have a choice, me old mate, cold mutton or cold rabbit.'

'I think this is a morning for rabbit.'

The two men crouched before the fire and ate. Sawtell drank his hot tea, ate the dry flesh, picked at the tiny bones of rabbit and spat them into the ashes. Again, he looked

3

south-east across the dry country where they had travelled, but there was nothing. No plumes of dust and no sound of motors and armoured equipment. He got up and listened, then went back to the fire. Counihan poured some more tea into the pannikins and they drank silently. He tossed his rabbit bones into the fire.

'We need fresh vegetables or we'll get sick.'

'We're okay, we're in fine form,' Sawtell said. He stood up suddenly, pulled the Webley from the holster, cocked it and, with both hands, aimed at a gum tree. 'I could do with a bloody big drink, a bloody big Johnnie Walker, and a tailor-made cigarette.' He squeezed the trigger of the Webley and took a branch away. Echoes and echoes sounded in the vast hinterland.

'Jesus,' Counihan said.

'Target practice. For Christ's sake, Frank, they've never been out this far.'

'They'll be here.'

'Bullshit, not this far, not in this country. The jungle, yes, the desert, no; they can't maintain their supply lines. We'll get some fresh tucker tonight at Bourke.' Sawtell looked again at the sky. 'This sure is the dry season. There'll be rain on the coast.'

'I thought I heard someone last night,' Counihan said. 'Those little yellow bastards could creep up anywhere.'

'There was nothing,' Sawtell said. But he was uneasy and thought of the German engineers muttering in the dark tunnels. 'I listen all the time, even in my sleep. I can hear the enemy, I learnt when I was a young man.'

'You can never tell,' Counihan said. He pulled out the Colt revolver, broke it open and checked the rounds.

'Bullshit, maybe it was the roos, or the rabbits or a dingo, or the rats, or some thieving blackfellow. They can't get this far, they've got the coast and that's all they need. We've got the rest.' Sawtell laughed. 'Jesus, let's get out of here. Have you finished?'

4

'Okay,' Counihan said. 'I've finished. What time is it?'

Sawtell stroked his beard, felt in his waistcoat and took out his gold hunter.

'Six o'clock in the spring.'

'What day do you think it is?'

Sawtell laughed again. 'For God's sake, Frank, I can't remember, you know that.'

'How many days since Dubbo then?'

Sawtell took the date-stick from his saddlebag and counted the notches.

'Twenty-four.' He pulled out his sheath knife and carved the twenty-fifth.

'Twenty-four days in the saddle,' Counihan said. 'Me arse is sore and me balls have turned to leather. We should be drinking cold beer and going to the football.'

Sawtell thought of the great days when he played centre-half forward for Richmond. 'You're right, Frank.' He tore a page from his prayer book. 'We're up to Psalm 60: *Deus, Republisti Nos*.' He smiled and read: 'O God, thou hast cast us out and scattered us abroad.' This was the best use of his prayer book now. They rolled their cigarettes carefully in the rice paper from the prayer book and lit them from the fire.

When they had finished smoking, Counihan smothered the last of the fire with dirt and sand. The two men went forward and threw their blankets and saddles on to the station horses. They tossed their belongings into their saddlebags. When that was done, they began loading the gear on the packhorses. They did this methodically, adjusting the loads with great care. The horses were valuable. They tightened the girths of the packframes and Sawtell looked at the sky. There were no clouds and the whole country lay exposed. It was going to be another hot day and he could not remember when it had last rained. Three months maybe?

'Do you reckon Bourke will take us?' Counihan said.

5

'They sure will, they'll take us. We can identify ourselves, we'll get that whisky. We've got the dynamite, petrol and ammunition, they'll want all that. We've got the Brens, the Thompsons and the Lewis. We know what we're about. They'll love us.'

Sawtell walked over the stones and gave Counihan the lead rope of his packhorse. 'Take this horse and be thankful, there'll be no trouble. We can rest up at Bourke and enjoy the hospitality of Major Jackson.'

'Major *St John* Jackson, get the name right, a double-barrelled English bastard, one of the buggers that let us down.'

'Any port in a storm, Frank. At least he's meant to be a professional, a regular army man.'

'Oh yeah?' Counihan blew his nose into the dirt, picked up his Luger submachine gun and mounted his big grey horse. Sawtell, too, swung up heavily in his greatcoat, wound the hunter, put the date-stick back in his saddlebag and looked at the desert vermin running through the dead trees. There was a big flock of emu moving west about half a mile away. He took off his slouch hat and wiped his forehead.

'They'll take us.'

Counihan kicked at his gelding and moved off a little in the dust. His packhorse followed.

'There must be a bore still going at Bourke,' he said. 'I could do with a bath.'

Sawtell rode up alongside and looked at his friend's long dark hair and beard, the blue eyes and the lean body, the Luger submachine gun over Counihan's shoulder. God help the English Major. Counihan had fought strongly at Newcastle and Sawtell could ride with no better man.

'They say that St John Jackson fought at the Somme and was decorated.'

'That's what they say. You know the English better

6

than I do. You fought with them, and you say they're bastards. They don't like Australians, do they? What's Churchill done for us?'

Sawtell brushed the flies away from his face.

'Okay, Frank, they're bastards, they put us to death in the Great War, Haig, French and Kitchener, the public school generals.' He remembered the red-tabbed officers on their thoroughbreds, trotting on the bullring, and the rumble of the artillery. 'But we've been told he's a professional, and that's what we want. We're professionals and that's what he wants.'

'Well,' Counihan said, 'I won't take orders from a bloody Englishman.'

'You won't have to. We work for Colonel Madigan.'

Counihan laughed. 'Madigan? Where's he now?'

'It doesn't matter where he is, it doesn't matter if he's captured or dead. He said to delay and deny, and that's what we're doing. There's nothing else.' He sat on his horse.

'We never stood a chance,' Counihan said. 'It was bloody hopeless. I never thought it would come to this. Where were the bloody Yanks? I still can't believe it.'

'You've said all that before, Frank. You say it every day.'

'Okay, okay, we're wasting time. Let's see what this English bugger's like. Let's see what he's made of.'

Sawtell thought of his father drinking and arguing about politics with his mates at the Mountain View. He thought of Jack Hanrahan playing the harmonica and singing *Bold Jack O'Donohoe*. His father had been right when he said Australia should not fight other people's wars but defend itself. That seemed a long time ago. They would follow Colonel Madigan's orders to the letter. He had no doubts about that.

A sudden wind gusted, the dust flew and the horses started and snorted. Sawtell looked up and saw the eagle in the sky. The red kangaroo was still watching them. He looked at the broken land, the vermin and the pestilence.

7

The bush rats ran and he remembered the trenches. He swung around, big and uneasy on his horse. He listened. He was sweating now, around his neck and under his arms. At least there were no lice. Was that the sound of motors and machines? Then he heard the sound of an aircraft. They looked up and saw it flying north-west. It was too high to identify.

'I don't like this,' Sawtell said.

Counihan scratched at his beard. 'Okay, let's go then. It's a full day's ride and it's going to be hot.'

'Yeah,' Sawtell said. 'There's a wireless there and maybe there's some news.'

'News? Maybe the war's ended and we've been forgotten.'

Sawtell kicked at his horse, wheeled around in the dust and said: 'Of course we've been forgotten.'

Counihan, in turn, used his boots. His horse reared and turned. 'Did you pick up the prayer book? We'll be needing that.'

'I've got it, and the glass.' Sawtell kicked at his horse, and the packhorse followed. 'Yah, yah,' Sawtell shouted. 'Yah, yah.' He looked again at the country very hard, but there was no sign of pursuit.

Counihan rode quickly down the creek bed. The horses stumbled over the soak and the stones and they topped the other side into the saltbush. Counihan took a fix with the hand compass. He pointed due west, saluted Sawtell and raised a smile. The rabbits, rats and goats ran across the dry country and the hot wind blew. Counihan kicked at his horse again and took the lead as the two men started away. The bushflies settled down black on both men's backs.

After four hours, they got to the main road. It was very hot now. Counihan was a quarter of a mile ahead, riding steadily, his horses throwing up sand and dirt. Sawtell could hear his thick voice, singing the familiar song:

Then come, my hearties, we'll roam the mountains high.
Together we will plunder, together we will die.

Sawtell glanced back down the road, but there was no pursuit. Nothing. Sometimes when he was alone, he thought of Marcia. She was in the West and safe maybe? He still missed her, despite what she had done. The land had gone back badly: no sheep, no fences, no beef on the run. Where were the blackfellows? Not that it mattered, they were treacherous and unreliable. Sawtell watched Counihan on the road ahead and rode easily. He pulled his hat down over his face and dozed. In the heat, he dreamed again of the salient, of men up to their waists in mud; the whizz-bangs; of killing the battery horses with the shotgun as they drowned, dragged down by their limbers; of the mines he had laid and the tunnels he had dug; of old professional soldiers weeping. He woke and saw Counihan still ahead and riding steadily with his packhorse. Counihan sat tall and straight in his stock saddle like some cowboy in a Hollywood picture. But maybe he looked more like Ned Kelly. Sawtell felt in his waistcoat pocket and consulted the hunter. He thought of his dead father. Was his mother alive? It was ten past eleven. So, he thought, it is ten past eleven on a spring day in the Year of Our Lord, 1943. I am riding with my mate Frank Counihan, I have lost my wife, but I have valuable possessions and skills and I shall join the Englishman, Major St John Jackson, to see what shall be done. Like Counihan ahead, he started to sing:

We'll wander over mountains and we'll gallop over
*   plains —*
For we scorn to live in slavery, bound down by iron chains.

They rode all day without stopping, and a little after five that afternoon they saw smoke. They slowed and finally stopped. Sawtell pulled at his beard, took off his hat and raised dust and foam from the flanks of his horse. Everything smelt of sweat. He pushed on the butt of the Lee Enfield in the scabbard.

'Aha,' he said. 'Aha, Bourke.'

'You slept all day,' Counihan said. 'All day. How can a bloke ride and sleep?'

Sawtell squinted into the western sun. 'Aw, for Christ's sake, I followed you, me old mate, I followed you.'

They rode on slowly and watched the smoke from the fires. It was very quiet and the rabbits ran. They saw a windmill turning and then some corrugated-iron outbuildings through the gum trees. Counihan pulled the Colt revolver from the holster and pushed it under his belt.

'There could be a man on the road in,' Sawtell said. 'Who rides out, you or me?'

'I'll ride out,' Counihan said. 'It's my turn.' He turned around on the dusty road and gave Sawtell the lead rope of his packhorse. He grinned and said: 'You be careful, I'll see you later.'

'Okay,' Sawtell said, and watched him ride over the low ridge. He took the Hollis out of the gun bag. He looked through the trees. Counihan was gone. He rode on slowly towards Bourke. What had happened to his mother? She, too, must be dead by now.

At half past five, Sawtell saw the man sitting on his horse in the shade of the she-oak, his hat over his face. Sawtell squinted into the sun and knew the man was not asleep. He was young, eighteen maybe, wearing an army shirt, Akubra hat, braces and moleskin trousers. He gathered himself in very quickly, sat up straight in the saddle and watched Sawtell approach with the packhorses. The young man looked tough and rangy and had a rifle cradled in his arms. Sawtell was close enough now to see it was a Winchester pump-action .22. He brushed the flies from his face and kept moving in. The horses snorted. There was no

10

sign of Counihan. Some rabbits ran across the road and the dust rose, but the young man sat quite still in the saddle and watched Sawtell coming in. The crows screeched and took off from the gum trees. There were burnt stumps everywhere. Sawtell held the Hollis in his right hand, then put it on his shoulder. He stopped about thirty yards from the man. A sharpshooter, he thought, a young clever-dick bushranger. Was he with St John Jackson? He licked his lips. Everything was still. Was Counihan there?

'Well, mate,' the young man said. 'Where do you think you're going?' He looked at Sawtell from under his hat, at the laden packhorses and the petrol cans. He gazed at the Brens and the Lewis.

'I'm going into Bourke,' Sawtell said, and smiled.

'Oh yeah?'

Sawtell saw the young man's hands move down the stock of the Winchester and said, 'Major St John Jackson is there.'

'Oh yeah? I never heard of Major Jackson? Nobody goes into Bourke unless there's a special reason.' He looked at Sawtell's long, grey hair and beard. 'And it looks like you ain't got no special reason.'

'I've got a reason.'

'Oh yeah, old man, what?'

Sawtell raised the Hollis and saw the man stiffen. He pointed at the Lewis, the Brens and the cases on the packhorses.

'That's the reason.'

'What's in them cases?'

'That's none of your business,' Sawtell said. 'I'm going into Bourke. Stop buggering me around.'

'Listen, mate, don't bullshit me. Bourke's a restricted area, any old bastard like you just doesn't come wandering in. Where are you from?'

Sawtell sat still on his horse and glanced around. The young man seemed to be alone. He thought of that big

11

whisky and began to lose patience. The boy was young enough to be his son.

'Dubbo,' he said.

'Oh yeah? Dubbo was took a year ago.'

Jesus, Sawtell thought, should I just take his bloody head off? He suddenly felt very tired. Twenty-four days in the saddle, no matches, no booze and a daily diet of cold mutton and rabbit, the routine of destruction and watching for the enemy. And now, outside Bourke, a smart little bastard with a Winchester pop-gun.

'Listen, son,' he said. 'I know Dubbo was taken a year ago, but that's where I'm from. I'm an officer in the Volunteer Defence Corps, I've come to join Major St John Jackson. Any more bullshit and I'll blow your bloody head off.'

The young man looked again at the equipment and his sharp eyes gleamed.

'That's good gear you got there, ain't it?'

Sawtell threw down the lead ropes of packhorses, kicked hard at his own horse and wheeled out to the side of the road. The dust flew, and the young man brought up the Winchester. Jesus, Sawtell thought, and released the safety catch on the Hollis, but the boy was very fast.

Counihan watched from behind the big gum tree, held the Colt revolver in both hands and shot the stranger dead centre in the right shoulder blade. A thousand crows screamed and flew from the branches. The horse reared, the young man fell to the ground and lay there. Sawtell squeezed the front trigger of the Hollis and shot him in the middle of the chest. The crows shrieked and wheeled and flew. He watched the bright red blood pump from the torn shirt. Bugger the young bastard, bugger him. Sawtell put down the Hollis. He thought of that big whisky.

Counihan came strolling down the bank, leading the horse and looking at the body. 'I meant to take him alive,' he said. 'What did you do that for?'

12

Sawtell rode up and dismounted. He took off his hat and wiped his face. 'I don't know, he went for me and I'm tired. And he called me "old man". Only my friends can do that.'

'This could be serious,' Counihan said. 'We've killed one of Jackson's men. You and that bloody shotgun.'

'It's saved your life before this,' Sawtell said.

The boy's chest was wide open and the guts pumped from the smashed ribs and broken bones. The bushflies buzzed and settled.

'We've taken one of Jackson's men,' Counihan said. 'What'll he think of that?'

'If he *is* one of *St John* Jackson's men, all he's lost is some trigger-happy larrikin. Christ knows who he is, the country's full of hooligans and riffraff. At my age, I'm not going to be bushwhacked by some illiterate young bastard. Let's give him to the crows.'

Sawtell went through the dead man's pockets. There was a filthy handkerchief and a crucifix in the back pocket of the moleskin trousers. Nothing else and no identification. Counihan went back to the station hack and rifled through the saddlebags. In one, he found a packet of Capstans. There were six cigarettes and a box of wax matches. In the other, there was some ammunition for the Winchester — forty or fifty rounds which he put in his webbing pocket. He also found tins of camp pie and an old bone-handled sheath knife. The horse was a lean and bony station hack and the stock saddle was old and battered. There was the usual stuff: a billy, a tin plate, knife and fork, a bag of flour, some sugar and tea, a cuttyhunk fishing line and some hooks stuck in a cork. The young bugger obviously lived by the river. Sawtell should not have killed him, but such was life. The saddle wasn't worth keeping and Counihan undid the girth straps and heaved it into the saltbush. He put the sheath knife carefully under his belt.

Sawtell waited as Counihan moved around the horse, then turned back to the body. The blood was quite thick now and starting to cake in the heat. The flies crawled and buzzed and Sawtell stepped back and wiped his hands, but the blood was already dry between his fingers.

Counihan came back, picked up the Winchester and said, 'At least we've got some cigarettes and matches, and a good pump-action.' He put the tins of camp pie into the saddlebag. 'The saddle was junk, but we'll take the horse.'

'Good,' Sawtell said. 'Let's get this mess into the ditch. The ants and crows can have it.'

Together they dragged the body across the road. Sawtell then went to one of the packhorses and got the shovel. They covered the body with dirt and leaves. When they had finished, Sawtell walked over to his horse, took down his water bottle and washed his hands. He felt the young man's crucifix in his trouser pocket, stood silently for a moment, but said nothing. It was getting dark by now and the smoke from the fires drifted heavenward over the tops of the trees. The birds had returned and they heard them calling and chattering. Counihan came up with the packet of Capstans in his hand and said: 'Do you want a tailor-made?'

'Why not?'

Counihan lit them both and gave one to Sawtell, who dragged the smoke down deep. They crouched on their haunches at the side of the road and listened to the sounds of the bush.

'Most unfortunate,' Sawtell said. He drew out the crucifix. 'And he was a Catholic.'

'He was a larrikin. These are bad times for us all.'

'Well, that's that,' Sawtell said, grinding the butt of his cigarette under his boot. 'Let's get on into Bourke.' He swung up on his horse. 'There may be some more bloody fools on the way in. Do you still want to keep riding out?'

'Sure,' Counihan said as he mounted. 'I'll keep riding out. See you later.'

For the second time that day, Sawtell watched Counihan

14

disappear. It was getting dark very fast now. This was strange, bad country. He held the shotgun in his left hand and consulted the hunter. It was seven o'clock. He touched his horse with his boot heels and went back for the packhorses. He wanted somewhere comfortable to sleep tonight. He put the crucifix next to his father's watch in his waistcoat pocket and rode on into Bourke. The country looked all burnt out, it didn't seem to belong to anyone any more. These were hard times, but he would make sure they survived.

At half past seven in the dark, Sawtell heard the sound of a wind-driven water pump and expected to be challenged by soldiers, but there were none. This was strange, but you could count on nothing these days. He rode slowly along the dirt road and got out the Webley as he saw the outlines of houses and buildings in the moonlight. Counihan came up from the other end of the street; he had the Luger submachine gun cradled in his arms.

'There's no bastard here,' he said. 'The place is deserted.'

Then beyond the town they heard the sound of distant laughter and saw the glow of fires.

'That's Abos,' Counihan said. 'I can smell them anywhere.'

Sawtell said nothing and they continued down the street past black, empty houses and the ghostly shapes of peppermint trees. At last they saw a light gleaming from the windows of a small house and Sawtell could smell the river.

'That's it, Frank,' he said. 'God knows what's happened to this town, but that's where we'll find the Major.'

· II ·
1917

IT WAS SEPTEMBER. It was still raining that dark morning and they had waited two hours on the firestep, ready to go over the top. Someone had called it another stunt. He had also been told that the battle had started in June and nobody seemed to know what it was about. It had rained for two months and a lot of men had been killed. Whole battalions wiped out, so they said. In the trench, Geoffrey Sawtell could see nothing, and it was very cold. They had been told to take off their greatcoats because they impeded progress. There was nothing but the eternal thunder of howitzers and 18-pounders from the Allied lines. Where were the trees? Where was the countryside? Where was No Man's Land? The heavy rain fell and the noise was appalling. They were glad they weren't getting it. The Corporal had said the British had 4000 guns, one gun for every six yards. Two young officers were laughing and talking and smoking cigars.

The trench seemed very crowded with overburdened men and dirty weaponry. The older soldiers were very quiet; they had wrinkled faces. There were discarded tin helmets, splitting sandbags, mess tins, spades, bayonets and strange bones. It was the tenth day of the bombardment and the Company Sergeant Major had told them that they would be able to walk over to the German lines, that after all the Germans would be dead and the wire blown away. He said there would be no worries. They had been told that the plan was for them to advance ten minutes after the creeping barrage came down. Geoffrey Sawtell leaned on his Lee Enfield; it seemed to make sense. He was only eighteen, and the officers must know what they were doing.

The flies crawled over scraps of bully beef, grimy sticks and stones, mud and broken basketry. There was the smell of sweat, chlorine and tobacco. Dead rats floated between the ancient duckboards. The ground heaved and shook. A lot of the men looked very tired. There were explosions deep inside the earth, strange shrieks and the rumble of French .75s and archetypal gunnery. Geoffrey Sawtell drew his father's gold hunter from his cardigan pocket. It was seven o'clock. Next to him, Smith stood like a stone and said nothing. There was a barrage balloon and sad trails of rain clouds in the sky.

Ten yards up the dog leg, there was a Lewis gun and big stocks of heavy ammunition. Soldiers were standing by with bags of cartridge pans; others were asleep. Geoffrey had heard that these machine guns jammed alarmingly if there was mud about. He looked down the traverse; some of the men were standing in mud up to their knees. When the time came, how would they jump over? The old soldiers looked pretty awful: white faces, eyes of glass. They looked broken and some of them had grey hair. One man was bent and giggling as he unwound his puttees. He looked like a hunchback, like a cripple he had known at school. The rain fell, the guns thundered and Geoffrey Sawtell glanced back at the crumbling wall where small trickles were forming. Why was it not repaired? There were also three Stokes mortars, clumsy sticks of bombs and hand grenades. He hoped he wouldn't have to throw one. The tripod for the Maxim gun was broken and it lay upended in the bottom of the trench. Things didn't look too shipshape. In the unearthly din, one old soldier with a cigarette filed behind his ear was picking at his nose.

17

Earlier in the week, he remembered, an old soldier in the communications trench had told him that in the spring there had been honeysuckle growing, larkspur and forget-me-nots. He had thought of his mother in Melbourne and her sunny front garden, weeping roses on chicken wire and sprays of flowers for Mothering Sunday. He had felt in his side pocket for the crucifix.

Smith shouted suddenly: 'Why aren't we going over now? It's getting too bloody late. Soon be time for morning tea.' From time to time, Lieutenant Atkins peered through the periscope. Geoffrey Sawtell leaned on his Lee Enfield in the rain, his right hand clutching the crucifix, and thought of the forget-me-nots, his mother's front garden, the climbing roses, the hot Australian summers, the best Sunday bone china and cups of milky tea. Matins on hot, breathless mornings and cicadas singing. He would write to her soon. There must be no Germans left by now.

Sometime earlier that week, they had waited a long time at the railhead. They had been carefully watched by the officers and the NCOs. Some men had complained that their packs were too heavy; but his was not. They were formed in fours in platoons in company and at eight o'clock the brigade had finally moved up the Menin Road. Geoffrey had never seen so many men together before, and was impatient to be off. Maybe he would see Ypres. It was supposed to have lots of fine old buildings and churches and there was the Cloth Hall he had been told to see. All the soldiers were sunburned and big boned. He liked the march; he had been good at military drill at school; he had learned how to fire the Lee Enfield. He remembered saluting the flag and the morning trumpets.

I love God and my country, I honour the flag, I will serve the King and cheerfully obey my parents, teachers and the laws.

When he had joined up, his mother had wept but said she was proud of him. His father had said nothing, had left the house and gone to drink with his mates at the Mountain View.

The soldiers marched fifty minutes in the hour, and at stand easy they were allowed to smoke and talk. Geoffrey didn't have a mate, and he didn't smoke, so he said nothing, but some of the men around him talked, and one old man played *Waltzing Matilda* and *Australia Will Be There* on the harmonica. Geoffrey had liked the march: the sound of the hobnailed boots on the *pavé*; all he owned was on his back and he was going somewhere. The landscape was different from home, but it was a bit like walking up a winter country road in Victoria. And when the men sang again, he finally joined in, learning the words of a new song and marching in time. He wasn't lonely; this was a great adventure and he had some new mates.

There were avenues of bare poplars and beech trees, chalky ploughed fields and silent women and children watching. They wore clogs and smocks. It was a bit of a ramble up the Menin Road, and the older men sang songs of home. He didn't mind being a footslogger. And as he marched with the men, he remembered his mother, gently be-hatted and silk-scarved, lying neatly in the back of a rowing boat on Sundays after church while his father pulled the oars, sweated and sang *Cruising Down the River*, dying for a drink. Some men dropped out, but Geoffrey didn't see them. It was a shadowy, wet, rolling landscape with stone houses, medieval churches, thunderclouds, massive stone barns, domestic pigs, geese and poultry. There were crucifixes in stone shrines and the peasants were hoeing some strange crop in the muddy fields. There was no corrugated iron in Belgium.

After lunch, the rain had started again and there was the sound of gunnery. They had marched ten miles, the *pavé* had ended, the braces of his pack bit into his shoulders and

19

he felt lice in his armpits. He adjusted his Lee Enfield, and sang the patriotic songs. The trees were shattered, and as they got closer to the front, there was the smell of mildew, decomposition and chloride of lime. In the afternoon light, smoke rose from braziers as old soldiers huddled, puffing Woodbines and drinking mugs of billy tea. There were no cheers as they passed, and suddenly he heard the sharp, distant sound of machine-gun fire; the sky was lit with apparitions and mysterious flashes. The earth shook with the thud of howitzers. At one ruined farmhouse they heard the sound of a steam saw, and as they passed, they saw some Belgian peasants making wooden crosses. The soldiers marched by steadily and no one said anything. It had stopped raining.

At four, they stopped at an assembly point and Geoffrey looked at the unfamiliar northern light and the long avenue of plane trees. He took off his pack, and with the other young soldiers, gazed upon the encampment. It was a small, muddy, pitted plain, rising gently to a line of smoke and earthworks. Some nurses in grey uniforms and carrying black bags went into one of the tents. They looked tired. Some soldiers were digging in a vegetable garden. The constant sound of thunder rolled. He looked at the ammunition dumps, bales of hay for the horses, sandbags, bolts of timber, reels of telephone cable and vast nests of barbed wire. There were pack mules and lines of dirty men marching. Engineers were laying waterpipes and he saw some British brewers' trucks and two London buses. Dead horses lay on the bare ground, Crossley motor ambulances stood stalled and men stretched spread-eagled on filthy stretchers. He heard some crying. There were six large army tents, and bearers were carrying men in and out, their arms and legs dragging on the earth. Some soldiers were rolling shells down planks. He gazed upon the shattered lines of limbless trees, heaps of grey masonry, the devastated terrain, the long shallow landscape, the hinterland of

20

broken stone buildings, deserted fields and the sky palely gleaming. Sawtell started to shiver and the old soldier next to him said:

'Gooday, son, my name's Smith, I've been up here before.' Sawtell shook his strong, bony hand.

'How old are you?' Smith asked.

Sawtell said: 'I'm eighteen. Our whole street joined up.'

Smith leaned on his Lee Enfield, his hair was turning grey, he looked at Sawtell and said nothing; he looked a bit like his father. Then the platoon had to take off their boots and socks and sit cross-legged while Lieutenant Atkins and the CSM examined their feet.

At six o'clock, the battalion was formed into an open square, and a colonel Sawtell had never seen before rode up on a dappled mare. Other officers were standing around the colonel on his horse. They all wore red tabs on their shoulders and carried brass-tipped canes. Their brown riding boots were very clean.

'Here's the bloody news all right,' Smith said.

The sergeant major stood them easy. The colonel spoke to them through a megaphone and said they were going into battle the day after tomorrow, that they were a fine outfit that Australia should be proud of and that he expected every man to do his duty. The guns echoed and flashes lit the sky. The men stood very quiet and puzzled and Sawtell thought of being head boy at school and playing football in the finals. The men were as still as glass as they listened to the colonel, who said that they were going to attack from the salient, that the sound they could hear was our guns softening up the Germans, that they were fighting the forces of evil, that they must save the Empire and their loved ones back home, and that God was on their side. A chaplain was standing with the officers. Some big explosions shook the ground and Sawtell saw the chaplain turn and cross himself and gaze at the lights and flashes from the front. The colonel's mare snorted and

21

shifted on her hind quarters nervously, and from one of the big grey medical tents came the sound of men screaming. It was getting dark now and the watery moon was rising behind the beech trees. They could smell cordite and mustard and the colonel said that they would have tea and then proceed to the front line under cover of darkness. It wouldn't be too difficult, he said, as long as they obeyed orders. The colonel dismissed them, and they moved toward the field kitchens where they were given warm mutton stew and mugs of black, sweet tea. The food was nourishing and tasted good. When they had eaten, they all lay around on the earth and Sawtell saw Smith go over to some old soldiers and give them money.

Smith came back, sat down and said: 'Just spreadin' it around so's the bloody crows don't get it.'

Sawtell didn't understand and said nothing.

'I've made me will,' Smith said. 'The missus has got it all.'

Then the NCOs ordered them up and each man was given an extra one hundred and eighty rounds of rifle ammunition and two Mills grenades. The NCOs shouted as they filled their water bottles. Geoffrey wished he could have talked to the chaplain, but he had disappeared and Smith was shoving him down the line. The colonel and the other officers left the parade ground in a car. It was almost dark now, and a full, dead moon had risen in the rainy northern sky. They were formed into twos, and to the sound of mounting pandemonium and flashing star shells, they set off for the front.

It was bad going up to the line and the men kept on passing back messages Geoffrey did not understand. It was a black night of awful sound and thunderous confusement, of blasphemies, star shells and Very lights. There were ceaseless warnings of insuperable obstacles, of holes and craters and pits of death, ancient entanglements of steel, ruined constructions and nests of barbed wire. The warm, muddied, broken bodies of dead soldiers lay spread-eagled in *cul-de-sacs*. Blood-and-iron was in the night. Someone had said they had to go five miles in the dark and that they were allowed ten minutes rest every hour. He picked at the lice in his armpits as he crouched in the mud, the pack breaking his back, his sodden greatcoat bearing him down upon the earth, his entrenching tool tangled with the webbing, his tin helmet falling over his face. At last, Geoffrey managed to get out the hunter; he peered in the light of the flashes. Somewhere a man cried out, but he could not see the time. It seemed that the noise would burst his brain, that his body would explode, that he would be torn to pieces and hurled into fathomless pits of everlasting fury. Then Smith got up. Geoffrey clutched Smith's great-coat, staggered forward, avoided the pitfalls, re-shouldered his grinding pack, gripped the Lee Enfield, repeated the messages, cursed the blackness, tripped, fell, was blinded by the gun flashes, heard men shouting, smelled corpses, crawled and plunged his hands into putrefaction, clapped his hands to his ears against the roar of the bombardment, of field guns, howitzers and thumping mortars, and crying, fell. Smith picked him up from the mud and shouted:

'Come on, you'll do. Never mind, I done this before.'

Almighty God, Father of our Lord Jesus Christ, Maker of all things, Judge of all men; We acknowledge and bewail our manifold sins and wickedness, Which we, from time to time, most grievously have committed, By thought, word and deed, Against thy Divine Majesty, Provoking most justly thy wrath and indignation against us.

The sound of howitzers roared as the bombardment continued, but in the morning at six, they took Holy Communion in a small ruined space behind the front line. A green hill far away. Somehow God had preserved some grass and they knelt upon it thankfully, their packs and

23

burdens gone, their bodies eased, their helmets off and their weaponry discarded. It was a small gathering. There was a poplar tree on the edge of the field. The rain had gone, it was late winter and the leaves had gone. It was six o'clock in the morning, but Geoffrey did not know what day it was. He knelt on the yellow grass and Smith knelt beside him. The chaplain looked a kindly old man. He had one arm missing and wore a white surplice and polished brown cavalry boots. A slight wind carried the smell of gas, and the poplar tree trembled. The altar was made of old stretchers and somebody had found an upright piano. Smith knelt next to him, his head bowed, his face covered with his stained hands. He had taken his puttees off and had shined his boots. He had combed and oiled his grey hair. The dun-coloured clouds flew, and suddenly there was the sound of enormous thunder and a few spots of heavy rain, which ceased. Behind the lines, the big guns rolled. Chlorine hung in the heavy air. Geoffrey Sawtell uncovered his face and looked at the chaplain and the poplar tree. The soldier at the piano was young and sallow and thin. He had a big, black moustache, and as he played, all the men got up and sang.

> God moves in a mysterious way
> His wonders to perform;
> He plants his footsteps in the sea
> And rides upon the storm.

A lot of the older men, Geoffrey had been told, had made their wills, written letters to their loved ones and had divided their money among their pals. Nobody had told him what to do, but he was sure he would be all right, and after the show was over, he would write to his mother. He would place his body in God's keeping and go into battle with His name on his lips.

Within the sound of shells whining overhead, and dreadful lights in the early sky, the chaplain stood before the

24

altar and consecrated the bread and wine. He took the paten into his hand and awkwardly broke the bread and took the cup. They all got up and moved toward the stretchers, and Smith tripped on the stony path and fell. Geoffrey helped him up, and they proceeded as the rain started to fall. The chaplain laid his hand upon the vessels, turned towards them, blessed them, and knelt and, as they crossed their hands, offered the Host and said:

Take and eat this in remembrance that Christ died for thee, and feed on Him in thy heart by faith and thanksgiving.

Geoffrey took the wine, took the bread and prayed for himself and his mother and father. Smith knelt next to him, also prayed, crossed his hands and took Holy Communion.

In the trench there was a great deal of noise. The British bombardment continued, the debris fell on the ditches and smoke bombs exploded in No Man's Land. The old soldiers suddenly stoked bombs down the mortar and some men came up with bales of barbed wire on their backs. They were dirty, overladen and weary and threw their loads on to the duckboards. Lieutenant Atkins cursed them and peered through his periscope. The bombardment had ended and the barrage had started. Smith suddenly turned round and gazed at Geoffrey Sawtell.

'It's about time,' he shouted, 'but the buggers are late. I hope they get on with it.'

It was 7.30 and all the men knew it was time to go, but there was no sound of the whistle, no caps fell, and they all hung about in the fire trench.

'Jesus,' Smith shouted, 'there's the 18-pounders and the mortars. It's time we went over.'

A huge explosion deafened them and the morning sky was choked with mud and debris. Along the traverse, one soldier fell and the wall of the trench collapsed. There was a great deal of noise, one shell exploded near the parapet, the sandbags flew and burst, and one man Geoffrey didn't know was badly hit. His back burst and he was carried up the traverse, screaming, blood and sinew writhing and pumping from his neck and shoulders. Mortar bombs landed and the Maxim gun crew were taken out, it seemed, quietly, but Geoffrey was not afraid then, just irritable, it was his first time, why didn't the whistle blow? Where were the orders from the company HQ? Then a runner dashed up to Lieutenant Atkins, who blew his whistle, and the first wave climbed the ladders with Lee Enfields, bayonets, packs, Mills bombs, wire cutters, loads of barbed wire, gasmasks, and went over the top.

It was raining heavily and there was no cover in No Man's Land; but he and Smith walked steadfastly into smoke and Spandau fire. Lots of men were falling but Geoffrey Sawtell walked through the rain towards the German trenches and the broken wire, his eyes streaming with water, gas and cordite, his bayonet at the ready, into the rattle of machine-gun fire behind the creeping barrage. All the men looked very small as they clung to the earth. He could see the German pill boxes. The landscape seemed quite flat and exposed like a country football ground. Suddenly he fell, and in the crater, hands and faces, wire and helmets protruded from broken walls of chalk. He was confused and waded through discarded equipment, dead rats, offal, excrement and tin cans, climbed out and ran after Smith. There were floods and bushfires, burned stumps, he fell and fell again; he saw sodden, screaming men staggering and clutching at their chests, their tin helmets falling; they were stumbling into flooded, bloody streams and howling as they died. He trudged through the mud toward the deadly frontier of ruined emplacements and insuperable wire fences. From the Allied lines, their bombardiers were laying smoke and Geoffrey Sawtell walked steadily now, feeling quite remote. Then Lieutenant

Atkins ran up, brandishing his Webley revolver in the rain and fire; he followed him towards the burning prehistoric fire traps, deadly fire holes and smoking cancerous growths bursting from the earth.

There seemed to be Spandau fire everywhere; mysterious deadly confusion, lethal potholes, ankle-jarring stones and tricky crevices, but he ran after Lieutenant Atkins towards the German lines. It was a vast rubbish dump of treachery and death: twisted metal, unexploded mortar shells, wire growing from the earth and clutching at his boots, slimy ponds and pools, arms, legs and ravaged torsos, helmets, rotting food and the detritus of war. But somehow he was moving and racing after Lieutenant Atkins, he was miraculously untouched and free, he was expert at leaping the craters and fiery traps, he ran like a fox across the shaking landscape. They reached the German line, turned and ran parallel, trying to find a way through the unbroken hedges of wire. The rain fell. He thought he could see grey German helmets bobbing above the broken ground; the sharp sound of a thousand engines crackled, the endless chatter of lethal industry; then the shattering explosions of enemy artillery firing point-blank at the centre of No Man's Land. All around him, men screamed, staggered, ran back and forth, searching for a gap, were butchered, beheaded, smashed to pieces and fell. It was like some silent moving picture that Geoffrey could not understand. Suddenly, Smith came through the noise and smoke and the three of them dashed further down the wire. Then Lieutenant Atkins was hit, his tunic blazing with fire and bursting entrails; he was blown away in the rain. There was the endless, unbroken wire, the Spandaus, mortars, bodies, violent machinery, clouds of dust and shuddering blows. He felt Smith grab his arm, saw him shout, and together they turned and ran like pursued wet animals back to the line.

Shaking with fear and cold, he crouched in the forward

sap, up to his knees in muddy water. After the late-afternoon bombardment, all was astoundingly quiet. The rain fell softly now, smelling of sulphur, alcohol and corpses. Geoffrey Sawtell looked heavenward and saw nothing. Where was the North Star? Where was the Great Bear? Where was the Star of Bethlehem? All he had been taught at school of the Northern Hemisphere and now could not recognize. He quietly picked at the lice under his armpits, his sodden greatcoat undone and gaping. He kept shaking, for he was very cold and very afraid. No sound came from the German trenches or his own front line. After a while, rain stopped falling and the vast, obscene maze of restored wire in No Man's Land became clear in the pale moonlight.

Geoffrey stopped picking and took his father's gold hunter from his cardigan. He squinted: it was half past two, half an hour to go, then back down the connecting trench into fire-bay to report to the Company Sergeant Major. On the other side of the sap, he could see Smith very clearly, huddled in his greatcoat, motionless, dead, it seemed, made of stone.

A small animal, puffed and blown, floated at Sawtell's feet. Smith was quite visible in the moonlight. Surely someone could see him now? Geoffrey wanted to warn him, but he knew he could not. He held the hunter very hard in his hands, then put it back into his cardigan pocket. There was a zephyr of breeze and the smell of death. He tried to stop shaking, but could not. He thought of his mother and prayed, as he had been taught to do:

Almighty and most merciful Father, we have erred and strayed from Thy ways like lost sheep. We have followed too much the devices and desires of our own hearts.

The battle had continued and it had been a bad day. He and Smith hadn't had to go over the top again; they had

28

stayed in the trenches clearing up. They had filled sandbags, reset the duckboards, carried drums of water and repaired the parapets. And they had seen the stretcher bearers stumble, fall and crawl in with the wounded. He had seen inexplicable mutilations: one medical officer had prised a soldier's hands apart and yards of intestines fell on to the duckboards; another had been castrated and another had lost his nose. Dogs had been sent into No Man's Land to search for the wounded, and when they had been found, they were taken to the regimental aid posts. Their wounds had maggots crawling in them. They had tried to amputate the leg of one man in the trench, but he had died. Someone had told him that Lieutenant Atkins was a public-school boy: he had been to Melbourne Grammar; that public-school boys were the cream of the nation. Rats ran in the trench in broad daylight; they were big and black, with bright eyes and wet, muddy hair.

For lunch they were given bully beef and black sweet tea, and a British soldier who had lost his way sat down and talked. He said he had heard that the Germans took corpses from the battlefield at night and that they were made into tallow in factories behind the line. The Tommy also looked directly at Sawtell, at his blue eyes and fair hair, and said:

'They've been crucifying the Canadians. They've got it in for young colonial lads like you.'

Then later in the afternoon, they had been drinking mugs of tea and another bombardment was started. Fifty yards down the traverse, a young, plump-faced major whom Sawtell had seen earlier in the day got a direct hit, so it seemed, and his body exploded into meat; it was like a heifer being butchered in some country abattoir. More shells came in and the back of the trench had collapsed and Smith had put his arms around him and covered him with his greatcoat. It lasted about two hours, and when it was over, Smith had looked rather tired and said:

'Come on Geoff, get up and forget about that bloody Tommy. Maybe there's a biscuit and a cup of tea.'

The air in the trench had smelled of rum and blood.

Very carefully Geoffrey Sawtell raised himself above the level of the sap and gazed upon the wire, but there was no movement, no sound. He looked up: God was in His place and the stars were in the heavens. On the other side of the sap, Smith seemed quite comfortable and had not moved at all. Geoffrey once again took out his watch. Fifteen minutes to go, then the comfort of the dugout, he could watch the men playing pontoon and have a cup of tea. He crouched and held his Lee Enfield and thought of home as the quiet east wind blew. Then, in the moonlit darkness, Smith began to sing:

> Nobody knows how tired we are,
> Tired we are, tired we are, tired we are,
> Nobody knows how tired we are,
> And nobody seems to care.

A Very pistol flashed, the sap was lit up, the muddy water shone and there was the sound of rifle fire. In the clear light, Geoffrey saw Smith's head explode and the body pitch into the water, his old greatcoat gaping as he fell headlong. The dirty water heaved and splashed over Sawtell's boots. All was silent again. Geoffrey crouched, trembling like some young hare. Then he grabbed the Lee Enfield and ran down the connecting trench to the line, to the traverse, the dugout, over the sleeping remains of young friends. His mouth was dry. He wanted to be safe, underground and have a cup of billy tea.

A hurricane lamp burned in the chaplain's dugout; he was reading a newspaper and drinking Queen Anne whisky and the bottle stood beside the brass cross. He was reading the *Daily Mail* and there was a big soldered food-tin from

Fortnum & Mason on the table. From without, came the sound of French .75s and the battle continued. A prayer-book lay on the dirt floor and the chaplain sat drinking. There was a spare canvas chair, but Geoffrey was not asked to sit down. He stood before the clergyman.

'What can I do for you?' the chaplain said. 'Do you need help?'

He rummaged in the food-tin with his left arm and ate some fruitcake. Geoffrey stood still and said: 'I've just lost a friend, sir.'

> Come unto me all that travail and are heavy laden, and I will refresh you.

'We all lose our friends,' the chaplain said. 'I saw you at Communion, what Parish are you from?'

'St Stephen's, Richmond, sir.'

'I don't know it,' the chaplain said. 'I don't know it, I'm from New South Wales.' He drank his whisky and the prayer book lay on the dirt floor. Outside in the trench, some soldiers went by, laughing and blaspheming in the rain. Geoffrey said:

'I've just lost my friend, sir, I can't understand, is it God's will?'

'God moves in a mysterious way. The Germans are the forces of evil,' the chaplain said. 'That's why we are here. They threaten the Empire, if we don't win this show, they'll invade Australia.'

He flourished the *Daily Mail*. 'Read the papers. What's your name?'

'Geoffrey William Sawtell, sir.'

'Well, Sawtell,' the chaplain said, 'you run along, and I'll expect you at Holy Communion. I've been in a war before. That time it was the Boers, the same people.' He reached for the glass and the food-tin. He drank once more and ate the fruitcake.

Geoffrey went out into the traverse, tripped and fell over

31

a sleeping soldier. It was still raining; he took the wrong trench and got lost in the dark mazes of mud and black confusion. All the men were asleep, so it seemed, and there was nobody there to help them.

My God, my God, look upon me; why hast thou forsaken me?

But Geoffrey Sawtell was young and strong and lucky. He had another nine months to go, was transferred to the First Divisional Engineers and made a corporal. The Germans didn't have it in for him.

· III ·

Bourke

MAJOR FRANCIS ST JOHN JACKSON, Commander of the Military Area of Bourke, sat before the fire reading the *First Epistle General of St John*:

> *If we confess our sins, He is faithful and just to forgive us our sins, and to cleanse us from all unrighteousness.*

He coughed and swallowed some more whisky. A cold draught blew under the front door. A rat ran across the floor boards. John, the gracious gift of God. The night was still, and he thought of his long evenings as a student in the library at Marlborough. He listened for any sound, got up and went over to the table for the bottle of Queen Anne. It was below the half-way mark; another outback station would have to be foraged in the morning. He topped up his glass and drank. He listened again. Sergius Donaldson would be back at nine, after his evening walk. Thank God for him. He coughed once more, lit another Capstan and smoked in the dark room. Tonight, dammit, he would have a bath. He would have to light the furnace.

Earlier, at about seven, he had heard the sound of distant rifle fire, but he had decided to do nothing. As usual, there would be no action. It was 2000 hours. He went to the battery wireless and tuned into the usual frequency. He put on the earphones and listened. It was the familiar recording from Sydney:

33

*Australian soldiers of the Volunteer Defence Corps,
give up the impossible fight, go back to your farms and
workshops, promote your businesses and care for your
wives and children who are missing you ... the
Japanese rule is best of all ... the Emperor of the Great
Empire of Nippon has given orders to the strongest
military force in the world to rescue all innocent
Australians suffering from the cruelty of England and
the United States of America ...*

Major St John Jackson never ceased to wonder what the
Australians thought of all this. The military collapse had
been complete: he had never seen such a shambles, it was
far worse than the capitulations in Malaya and Singapore,
and those had been a disgrace. Darwin had been unbeliev-
able and heaven knows what was happening in the Western Desert and Europe. He was alone and God had
forsaken him. He wished for the sounds of regimental
bands and hoarse commands on smart parade grounds. St
John Jackson then went slowly across the rest of the dial,
but there was nothing except the time bands and scrambled
Morse code he could not understand. He switched off
quickly to save the power from the car batteries, put the
earphones down and went back to the small table. He took
up the glass in his small, colonial house with its shabby,
blackened, pressed-tin ceilings and drank the whisky
carefully. He considered the walls of cracked plaster and
corrugated iron. This was a far cry from his comfortable
bungalow in Meerut. No hunting trophies hung on these
walls. This was very unfamiliar architecture, and the
materials had been transported four hundred miles on
bullocks' drays from the coast. It was a grand Victorian
township he was living in by the river. The main street was
twenty-two chains wide; it was a boulevard lined with
ancient pepper trees, with a monument to the Great War, a
customs house, wharves and all the facilities of river
commerce. There were three fine churches here, a Masonic

Temple, ten pubs and three sunken paddle steamers. There was much iron lace on the Shire Offices and ornately carved sandstone. But the river was not the river he knew. There were no lock gates, and there was no fresh water running. He had come to the oldest place in the world, but it revealed no visible signs of its antiquity. The brown river barely moved and the leaves of the gum trees hung down; there were no people here, and in the country around, there were no signs of any occupation. The nights were cold and the stars shone brilliantly.

St John Jackson went over to the upright piano, sat down at the keyboard and played a few bars from *HMS Pinafore*, hummed as he played and thought of his golden days before the Great War in the Thames Valley, of his father standing proudly outside the greenhouse where all kinds of exotic plants and flowers grew. His father had been a stalwart man, a squire, but there was no stalwartness here, and certainly there were no squires. He played a few more familiar bars of Gilbert and Sullivan. Here there were no mountains, no treacherous rocky passes, no hostile tribesmen and no morning trumpets on dusty parade grounds. He played a few bars on the upright and a rat, with bright eyes, ran across the broken floor; he watched it disappear. St John Jackson thought of the smell of the blood and rum in the trenches in the Somme, the odour of cold dormitories, Kennedy's *Latin Primer* and old housemasters in dressing gowns. Now he was in Australia. He tossed another piece of river gum on the fire and riffled through the old code books. Where were the standing orders? He wished he was back in India; that was a place he had come to love and understand. There was nothing for him here: only loneliness and disgrace. He had not played polo for four years, but he would go for his usual ride in the morning on his chestnut mare through the unfamiliar landscape. He looked at himself in the small broken mirror nailed to the wall. Every night, St John

Jackson saw his face and raised his glass and drank. There was still the neat, grey moustache, the clipped sideburns, the pale blue eyes, the ancient suntan and the straight military shoulders. What was Winston Churchill doing now? He felt his stomach muscles. Had the Russians been defeated at Leningrad? What was happening in the Western Desert? And where was General Douglas MacArthur? The Japanese said he had betrayed the Australians and had gone to New Zealand, that he had evacuated the US 41st Division. The Americans had always been poor fighters, lacking grit and discipline. He had seen them fight in the Great War at Meuse-Argonne. The same questions every day. He sat down before the fire to have his last whisky and to wait for Sergius Donaldson. He knew he would have to move from this town soon. This was no country for an English officer to be fighting in, this was one place he could not understand. He consulted his watch, sat in the gloom and read his Kipling.

There was the sound of men, horses and equipment outside his door. St John Jackson picked up his Webley from the table, cocked it, walked over, opened the door and gazed upon the threshold. Two soldiers were standing in the street, men he had not seen before, and laden packhorses. He saw the Lewis gun and Brens. A red moon glowed in the black sky and he caught the smell of the bush. The blackfellows' campfires burned and the unfamiliar men stood at his door. There was a silence, and the big grey-bearded soldier said:

'Major St John Jackson?'

The other man stood very still in the darkness. St John Jackson saw he was carrying a Luger submachine gun and he, too, had a thick beard. He smelt smoke from distant fires and heard the sound of drunken laughter. The blackfellows must have found some more drink somewhere. He would inspect the camp in the morning.

The big man stood at the door in the street and said: 'I'm Captain Geoffrey Sawtell and this is Lieutenant Frank

Counihan. We're soldiers in the Australian Volunteer Defence Corps.'

The grey-bearded man was wearing a slouch hat and a Webley Service revolver, and he was carrying a Hollis shotgun. He stared across the room and saw the upright piano and the bottle of whisky. He stood in the doorway and said:

'We've come a long way, Major.'

St John Jackson stood his ground at the door. The kerosene lamp gleamed. The big Australian's eyes were hard and as blue as ice.

'You have some identification, I presume?'

Sawtell thought of Dr Livingstone and they produced their plywood identity discs. St John Jackson shook their hands and said:

'Gentlemen, please come in. Welcome to Bourke.'

Sawtell and Counihan crossed the floor and it creaked beneath their boots. Sawtell looked at St John Jackson and saw the red shoulder tabs and the officers driving away in their cars; he remembered the clean-shaven faces and the shining cavalry boots. Here, once more, was the clipped, public-school accent of authority; the colonel on the dappled mare. Sawtell watched Counihan looking at the bottle of whisky on the table. He also saw the upright piano and the sheet music: it was Gilbert and Sullivan, one of his mother's favourites.

'We've run out of matches, Major,' Counihan said as he took out the last of the dead man's cigarettes. 'Can you oblige?'

'Certainly.' The Major considered his two unexpected guests, went to the shelf above the fireplace, found a box and tossed them over. He stood, small and erect, in the centre of the room.

'Would you gentlemen care for a drink?'

'Nothing could be better for two thirsty diggers,' Counihan said. He put the Luger submachine gun down on the table next to St John Jackson's bible.

37

'That's a fine German weapon, Mr Counihan.'

'Yeah, I reckon it's better than the Thompson.'

'It's a long time since I've seen one of those.' The Major found glasses and put them down by the bottle. 'Please help yourselves.'

Sawtell poured out two large whiskies and passed one over to Counihan. The two men drank and the whisky tasted good. The Major, Sawtell thought, looked small and tough like his father. He was a veteran and could have been on the Menin Road.

'Where are you gentlemen from?' St John Jackson said as he poured himself a drink.

'Victoria,' Sawtell said, 'and then Newcastle.'

'You fought there?'

'We did, it was a catastrophe, we never stood a chance.'

'So I've heard, and after that?'

'Maitland, Singleton, Bathurst,' Counihan said, 'and then Orange, Wellington, Dubbo and Nyngan, each place a bloody shambles.'

'And where are the Japanese now?'

'We last sighted them in Dubbo,' Sawtell said. 'That was a month ago, they've got supply problems.'

St John Jackson smiled and lit a cigarette. 'Haven't we all? Who's your commanding officer?'

'Colonel Madigan.'

'Ah, Madigan. I've seen his instructions.'

'To harass, deny and destroy,' Sawtell said. 'That's our mission.'

'Indeed. Where is Madigan now?'

'God knows. The whole military command's non-existent,' Sawtell said. 'What have you heard?'

'Nothing for some considerable time.' St John Jackson passed over the bottle. 'And other units of the VDC?'

'We seen a few,' Counihan said, 'but they were rabble, so Geoff and me decided to go it alone.'

'What's on the wireless, Major?' Sawtell said.

38

'The same blasted propaganda: "Australian soldiers of the VDC, return to your farms and workshops, your wives and families are missing you . . ."'

'So nothing has changed?'

'No, Mr Sawtell, nothing has changed. It's the same damned message night after night.'

The rat ran from a cupboard and Sawtell watched it go. He felt tired and thought about unloading the packhorses.

'All we have is Colonel Madigan's orders and we're doing our best to carry them out.'

Counihan got up, went over to the door and looked out into the night at the packhorses. The distant fires burned, he heard the sound of laughter and a bottle smashed somewhere. There was no one about and he wondered how many men the Major had under his command. He could see no other lights shining in the town. So far, so good, he thought, the Englishman wasn't as bad as he had expected; but where were his men and what was going on here? Counihan closed the door, went back to the table, touched the bottle and said:

'Do you mind?'

'Not at all, Mr Counihan. I have another bottle – the last, I'm afraid – and then we shall have to forage.'

'What strength do you have here, Major?' Sawtell said.

St John Jackson coughed and looked at the two bearded Australians. He hoped they weren't the same as those under his command previously; Sawtell looked tough and dangerous and Counihan was obviously bog-Irish, mean and touchy, a man who did not like the English, but then neither did most colonials. He had found them an insubordinate lot and, after Darwin, any respect he had held for them had gone. But he remembered Singapore and General Percival.

'I have no strength, Mr Sawtell. There were fifty-odd men here six months ago but, as you Australians say, they've gone bush.'

There was a silence, and then Frank Counihan said:
'You've got no one?'

'At present, Mr Counihan, I have two men: a Padre who has been with me since Singapore and a young Australian lad who comes and goes.'

'You were at Singapore?' Sawtell said.

'I was, then at Darwin. Please excuse me a moment.'

Jesus Christ, Sawtell thought, what had they come to? He watched the English Major get to his feet and go out into the kitchen. Counihan looked at Sawtell, but said nothing. Then Sawtell got up and strolled around the room; he noticed the Church of England prayer book and a cloth-bound volume. He picked it up: it was the collected poems of Rudyard Kipling. The Major appeared with another bottle of whisky and placed it on the table.

'Gentlemen,' he said, 'our last. We might save some for Sergius Donaldson when he comes in from his nightly walk.'

'Sergius Donaldson?' Counihan said.

'The Padre. What equipment do you have?'

'With respect, Major,' Sawtell said, 'perhaps we can give the inventory to you tomorrow. We should unpack the horses.'

'Of course, please forgive me, do you require any help?'

'It's okay,' Counihan said, getting up and swallowing his whisky, 'we can do it ourselves.' He looked at Sawtell who was still holding his glass. 'You stay here Geoff, I'll make a start.'

'There's a vacant house across the street, Mr Counihan,' the Major said, 'you can use that.' He laughed. 'They're all vacant.'

'I'll see you later,' Counihan said, and closed the door.

'Someone tried to bushwhack me on the way in,' Sawtell said. 'I had to kill him. I wonder who he was.'

'What was he like?'

'A boy, in his twenties, carrying a Winchester Repeater. I hope it wasn't your lad.'

'My lad?'

'The young Australian lad who comes and goes.'

'It's unlikely. He's not the bushwhacking type and, as far as I know, he has no weapon.'

'I wonder who it was.'

'I've got no idea, Mr Sawtell, the country's full of riffraff, there are brigands everywhere.' St John Jackson coughed. 'It was unfortunate, *c'est la guerre.*'

Sawtell thought of the deserted town, the Major, and the Padre he had yet to meet. He felt the crucifix in his trouser pocket; he had killed one of his own kind: a wild colonial boy. He looked at the suntanned face of the English regular army officer from a public schoolboys' battalion and felt tired. There must be no more mistakes. He got up again, and St John Jackson watched him as he walked around the room. Sawtell saw there were several faded photographs pinned to the timber frames. One was of a tiger-hunting party, of British soldiers with their trophies and shotguns. The other was of a group of polo-playing officers in riding boots and spurs. Sawtell recognized the Major, moustached and sitting in a wicker chair, the polo sticks carefully posed for the camera. There was another distinguished, bearded man in a Panama hat with a child wearing a pinafore seated on his knees. Two guns stood in the corner of the room with their cases nearby. One was a sporting rifle and the other a shotgun. Sawtell went over to the weapons. There was much to be learnt about men from their guns. He pointed to the shotgun and said:

'May I, Major?'

'By all means.'

St John Jackson watched Sawtell as he picked up the shotgun.

It was a Purdey custom-made and the Australian knew it.

'This is a fine weapon, Major. Snipe?'

St John Jackson smiled. 'Indeed.'

The other was a BSA sporting rifle with a Lee Enfield

41

action; both were in excellent condition. The Englishman knew about guns and this seemed a promising start. The fewer men the better: less to go wrong. Sawtell realized he should not underestimate this British officer.

'Which regiment in India did you serve in, Major?'

'The Fifth Gurkha Rifles.'

'Very pukka.'

'You might say so. Where did you serve, Mr Sawtell?'

Sawtell knew what the Major was asking: veterans recognized each other; it was their faces. 'Passchendaele, and you, sir?'

'Loos, Arras, Messines; and after that, as you have seen, I served in India.'

'Loos,' Sawtell said, 'the gas balls-up?'

'Indeed.' St John Jackson recalled the men retching and falling, poisoned by their own chlorine in the trenches. 'We had 50,000 casualties there. Mr Counihan, I take it, did not serve?'

'He missed out. What outfit did you fight in at Loos?'

'The 25th Brigade, 2nd Royal Berkshires. And you?'

'The 6th Brigade, 2nd Australian Division, then I was transferred to the Engineers.'

St John Jackson looked at the Australian, thought and said:

'Would you care to eat later? We have some meat and vegetables here.'

'Thank you, Major, may we leave it for a while? I must go and help Counihan.'

'We also have hot water if either of you wants to bathe.'

To bathe, Sawtell thought, to bathe and to cleanse us all.

'Yes, Major. If you would, please light the furnace.'

Sawtell downed the rest of his whisky and went out into the night. St John Jackson drank the dregs and thought again of his schooldays in Marlborough when he had played rugby. Men like Sawtell had held the pack together; they had also been found wanting.

42

The wind was in the ghost-gums; there was cloud across the moon, but no sign of rain. Counihan had moved the horses across the road to the empty house and Sawtell saw him unloading the packhorses and carrying the gear inside. A hurricane lamp gleamed. He glanced around the street: there were many small houses, outbuildings, piles of junk and water tanks lying on the ground. As he crossed the street, Sawtell saw the horses standing in front of the house. Their heads were down: they, too, were very tired. He lifted an ammunition case from his packhorse as Counihan came back.

'What do you think, Frank?' He put the case down.

Counihan laughed and pulled the saddle and blanket off his horse.

'You tell me, you know how to deal with a bugger like that. I don't.'

'He ain't so bad, he gave us his Scotch and he says there's food and hot water for a bath.'

Counihan thought as he stood in the dark with his gear. He was too buggered to eat, but he could do with a bath. It seemed he had been dirty all his life. He thought of the draughty parish schools in Ballarat and his apprenticeship on the railways. 'I could do with a bath.'

'Okay, he's lit the furnace.'

They lugged the guns, the explosives, the food and the packsaddles into the empty house, and stood in the light of the lamp, the worn gear all around. Counihan lit a cigarette.

'Who was the man you shot, not one of his men?'

'No, thank God.'

'Not the boy who comes and goes?'

'No.'

'That's good, I'd better water and feed the horses and two of the buggers have cast their shoes.'

Sawtell thought: I have shot a boy young enough to be my son. Maybe they should go back and give him a decent, Christian burial.

43

'As you say,' Counihan said, 'any port in a storm. The Major sure knows his guns.'

'You saw them?'

'Yeah.'

'Tiger hunting, snipe and polo,' Sawtell said. 'Jesus.' He knew the Major was probably a potential drunk and a failure, but why not? His faith might bear him up.

'Let's get the rest of the gear in,' Counihan said, 'the horses are buggered.'

They worked slowly and carefully in the dark and, at last, all the equipment was inside the house. There was a trough beneath a water tank by the Major's house and Counihan watered the horses, fed them and led them into the yard for the night. He checked the rails and the gate. He, too, felt very tired. There must be a smithy here, where he could shoe the horses.

'You have your bath, Frank,' Sawtell called from across the street. 'I'm going to doss down. He's an English gentleman who plays Gilbert and Sullivan and offers hospitality to strangers. He might even draw the hot water for you.'

Sawtell went into the house by the light of the hurricane lamp and sat down on an ammunition case. He considered the gear they had taken 500 miles: his guns, Frank's submachine gun, the dry and cracked packsaddles, the water bags and all the shabby baggage of war. Sawtell wished he had been an officer; he wished he had played polo and ridden thoroughbred ponies; he wished he had worn the red tabs of authority, shining cavalry boots and spurs. The Major's good whisky lay in his gut, God bless him for that. Purdey shotguns, tiger hunting and smiling children in pinafores, his father raising his glass in the Mountain View and his mother singing by the piano in the front parlour on those temperate Melbourne nights. There were piles of old newspapers from Sydney on the floor and Sawtell laid his blankets upon them. He went back to the

44

door and saw Frank Counihan standing by the yard rails, waiting for the Major and his bath. They would stay here for two or three weeks and see what they could do with the Major, the Padre and the boy. A force of five was better than a force of two. They should be thankful for small mercies. He lay on his blanket and wondered about Marcia, his mother, Jack Hanrahan and the working men he had drunk with. Sawtell lay on his blanket and thought of the southern coastline and the salmon running in the deep blue trenches beyond the reef. *To bed, to bed, to rest your head.* He thought of his room in Rotherwood Street, his cricket bat, his .22 rifle and stamp album. The house smelt of dust and death, and outside the wind blew in the trees; there were strange animals in the night. The wind blew and something moved in the room. His body ached, and he remembered his mother kneeling beside him with the old book of Victorian nursery rhymes as he lay beneath the eiderdown and the winter nights closed in, dark and cold.

> *My pulse is the clock of life;*
> *It shows how my moments are flying.*
> *It marks the departure of time,*
> *And tells me how fast I am dying.*

Frank Counihan stood in the main street of Bourke and waited for the English Major. He could see the ghostly shapes of the pepper trees, the familiar outline of the post office, the small houses and the gum trees on the river. He had heard it was an important river port with wharves and paddle steamers. The street was empty, nothing moved and he saw the fires gleaming from the blackfellows' camp. Jesus, he thought, those black bastards could learn nothing; they were incapable; the place had been invaded and they were on the piss. At least the Major had kept them

45

where they belonged. He bet it was hard to keep the thieving buggers out. All the drink had obviously gone. The Abos had to be dealt with, or they'd take over all these outback towns. He saw a light flickering in a shed at the back of the Major's house, sat on the front step and waited. The stars gleamed.

Counihan lit his last tailor-made and thought about the Major. Sawtell sure knew how to deal with blokes like that, one of the advantages of having served in the Great War. Now he was by himself, Counihan wasn't quite sure how to handle the Englishman. He hadn't met a British regular army man before. He looked in his late fifties and had that accent. If they went further up-country, how would a man like that get on? He and Sawtell had found it hard enough. At least the Japs weren't here and there must be something of value. Then he saw the Major coming down the path by the side of the house. He was carrying a kerosene lamp and there was someone with him. As the men came down the path, Counihan saw that the other one was wearing a dog-collar and was in officer's uniform.

'Ah, Mr Counihan,' said St John Jackson, 'the furnace is going in the back shed and you should have hot water very soon.' Counihan was grateful, stood there in the dark and said nothing.

Then he said: 'Thank you, sir.'

St John Jackson held up the lamp. 'This is my colleague, Padre Donaldson. Padre, a new comrade-in-arms, Mr Counihan.'

The clergyman stood, tall and thin, under the pepper tree.

'Good evening, Mr Counihan, welcome to Bourke.' They shook hands. 'As Major St John Jackson has, I believe, told you, we are somewhat light on the ground, so you and Mr Sawtell are at least part of an answer to a maiden's prayer.' He coughed and laughed in the dark. Counihan wondered if they had Catholic priests in the

English army, but decided not. This man must be Protestant. He tried to see his face in the pale light of the lamp. The Padre looked old, in his late fifties maybe, gaunt and old. What use would he be?

'Pleased to meet you, Padre, I must get to me bath.'

He walked quickly up the path to the small shed where a light was gleaming. The two Englishmen watched him go.

'My God,' Sergius Donaldson said, 'he looks a rough one.'

'Wait until you see Sawtell. They've come prepared for something: explosives, a Lewis, Brens, Thompsons, and Counihan has a Luger submachine gun. God knows what they intend to do. I must say their horses are in fine condition and they know the country. The Australians,' St John Jackson laughed. 'You know what they're like. We fought with them once before.'

Sergius Donaldson paused at St John Jackson's front door.

'Counihan is a Roman Catholic, obviously.'

'Yes, Frank or Francis Counihan, but God knows what Sawtell is, he gives nothing away. He's an observant man, he noticed my guns and made the India connection. He fought at Passchendaele, it's in his face.' They went inside and sat by the dying fire. 'They've drunk most of my whisky, but there's enough left for a nightcap.'

'It's in all our faces,' Padre Donaldson said.

'Ah,' St John Jackson poured the drinks, 'you'll meet our new friend, Mr Sawtell, in the morning. He seems to have retired unwashed.'

'Life in the trenches, we both know all about.' The Padre had conducted many last rites during his career. He drank and wished he could leave this place which he hated and could not understand.

The Major went over to the piano and put away the sheet music.

'They've been riding three weeks from Dubbo and

47

Wellington, they fought at Newcastle and I imagine they've been laying waste ever since. Scorched earth like the Russians, since we heard, the whole country is in a shambles.'

'The whole country?' Sergius Donaldson said. 'I don't know what the whole country is. Are there any cities? I haven't seen them. Are there any cathedrals? I haven't seen them. I sometimes think God has forsaken this place, it's like no other country I've ever known.'

He went to the door and looked out into the night. The stars shone and he smelt the river and the blackfellows' fires.

'If you will excuse me, Francis, I'm going to turn in. I've had my usual nightly walk and we shall meet these men properly in the morning. Sleep well.'

Sergius Donaldson put down his glass and left, shutting the door behind him.

St John Jackson stayed by the fire until it burnt out. He considered his room, the photographs and the sporting guns. He thought of Sawtell's inspection and cleaned his teeth in the enamel basin. His mouth washed, he went once more to the small mirror, regarded himself, thought of the two Australians and the boy they had killed, and went to bed.

Outside the house, in the township of Bourke, the blackfellows' fires burned and the smoke rose through the gum trees. In his room, Sergius Donaldson consulted his ecclesiastical calendar and said his prayers. He thought of the advent of the two strange travellers. *Come unto me all that travail and are heavy laden, and I will refresh you.*

· IV ·
1919

HE HAD FORGOTTEN what a grand Victorian city Melbourne was. It seemed there were ten thousand people on the pier. The sun shone and Geoffrey Sawtell heard them shouting and screaming, as the tugs pushed the *Ballarat* closer to the dock. The bands were playing *Land of Hope and Glory, Auld Lang Syne* and *Australia Will Be There.* There were working men waving their caps in clinker-built dinghies and sailing boats everywhere. The smell of malt and hops from the breweries was in the air.

It was a very warm morning; he had never felt so hot before, his uniform was heavy and he leaned on the ship's rail and looked at the masts and rigging and the spars of the sailing ships. He saw, beyond the warehouses, the tall, ornate, smoke-blackened buildings of Melbourne: there was the familiar sight of Coop's shot tower. Brick factory chimneys were belching smoke in spirals into the clear Australian sky. He had never seen it so blue and it startled him. Most of the soldiers around him were shouting, laughing and whistling and trying to see their loved ones; but some looked glassy-eyed and others were grim and silent. Geoffrey thought he knew how they felt. He tried to shout, but could not, and looked hard at the crowds on the pier. He tried to see his mother. Everything looked bright and clean and the smell of fresh fish was on the air. The sea was calm and a school of mullet flashed as they broke the water.

The *Ballarat* edged closer and the sailors threw the ropes to the watersiders on the pier. He saw plumed draught horses, decorated beer wagons, cabs and motor cars. There was the sound of sirens and ships' hooters and the noise was tremendous. On the wharf there were lots of pretty young women wearing long white dresses and flowery hats and many of them were holding European parasols to protect their faces from the sun. The women looked pure and untouchable; some wore veils, others were dressed in sky-blue and carrying large posies of flowers: jonquils, daffodils and spreads of maidenhair fern. The hot wind blew their hair and moved their fragile dresses. The men wore grey three-piece suits, stiff white collars and felt hats. Their black boots shone. The north wind blew and he could smell the bush and looked at the men and women on the pier. They all looked healthy and unreal. Why had all these clean-shaven young men in their three-piece suits not been in France? How had they escaped the War?

The southern sky was clear and brilliant, and as the *Ballarat* was being tied up, Geoffrey looked at the hand-some young men. He thought of the broken, bloodied bodies and soldiers dying in the mud, the roar of the howitzers, the whizz-bangs and could understand nothing. What were all these people doing here? Some of the young men were wearing straw deckers; he had forgotten all about summer. He looked very hard but could not see his mother. There were Union Jacks flying everywhere: ten thousand tearful, beckoning faces. He could not bear the sight, he leaned on his Lee Enfield and turned away. He felt old and tired in his threadbare khaki uniform and his battered slouch hat. He thought of France and he thought of home. He had not counted on these crowds of laughing, cheering people and they frightened him.

It had been a long voyage on the troopship from Southampton and Geoffrey had thought they would never get home. A lot of the men were sick in the heat of the Red

Sea, and every night they gazed south-west for their first glimpse of the Southern Cross. Then one evening, when they had almost given up hope, they had seen it shining. A cheer went up and the boys knew they were on their way to Australia.

The previous evening as they had steamed up the bay, and gazed upon the Australian hinterland, the Company Sergeant Major had told them to look spick and span in the morning, to polish their boots, adjust their puttees and clean their rifles. He said that when the ship tied up, they would file down the gangplank, meet their loved ones on the pier, then form into platoons in the company and march to the Melbourne Town Hall. He said that they should look their very best and that all Australia would be proud of them. He said there would be speeches and prayers of thanks, that the Prime Minister would tell them they had saved the Empire. Many of the men stayed up all night, drinking beer, singing and playing pontoon. Then they had gone to the quarantine station to be checked for flu and inoculated.

The gangplanks still had not come aboard and the soldiers laughed and waved and whistled. Some of the younger women were doffing their flowery hats and their long, unpinned hair floated in the breeze. Suddenly Geoffrey's heart lifted at the sight of them and at finally being home. He thought of his fishing rods, the trout rising, and playing football; and some of the young women looked very beautiful. He looked once more at the faces on the pier and saw his father, short, dark and unsmiling. He was wearing a cloth cap. His mother was not beside him. The crowd milled and his father disappeared. Many of the men were drinking openly, bottles of beer raised to their lips and shouting. They were obviously drunk and Geoffrey thought of the smell of the rum in the trenches and the Chaplain with the whisky. His father had gone.

Then the gangplanks were shoved aboard and the limb-

51

less, the gassed and the blind were carried down. Geoffrey and his mates watched them go into ambulances and be taken away to the repatriation hospital. Some of the women were weeping as they saw their sons disappear. Sawtell wondered how soon those men would be forgotten. Thank God he had not been wounded like some of the soldiers he had visited in the hospital in Berkshire. He knew he could not forget, whatever happened. He looked around at his mates and wondered what they would do.

Then the bands started playing, and the soldiers, stiff and proud and carrying their rifles, descended. The crowd engulfed them, shook their hands, hugged and kissed them, passed them bottles of beer, the children ran, the bands played, the sirens bellowed, the north wind blew and the young women cried, their white dresses billowed and hats were thrown into the air. He still could not see his mother, or his father. It all seemed unreal. Then his mother was beside him, her arms around his body, her clean white dress and straw hat, her blonde hair pinned up, her breasts smelling of attar of roses, her blue eyes filled with tears, her lips on his face, her voice saying:

'Dear God, thank you, thank you, Geoffrey, you're back, you're back.'

Then his father appeared from the crowd, shook his hand and said: 'Welcome home, son, welcome home.'

His mother would not let him go. It seemed it would never end.

'Thank God,' she said, 'thank God.'

Her silk scarf floated around him and his father shook his hand again. But at last, they were ordered into platoons by the Company Sergeant Major, ready to march to the Town Hall.

'I'll see you after the march,' Geoffrey said. He kissed his mother and shook his father's hand.

As they marched off the pier, on to Flinders Street,

past the bluestone stock and station houses, over Princes Bridge and on to Swanston Street, thousands of people clapped and cheered. The military band played *Waltzing Matilda*, and *Australia Will Be There*. The soldiers marched stiff and strong in the bright sunlight, the drums rolled and the Cameron pipers played, their boots rung on the pavement and the avenues of English trees were very green. From the dockside, they could still hear the ships' hooters and sirens. The children waved small Union Jacks and some of the little boys wore military uniforms. Mothers carried babies in their arms, other young women ran after the soldiers down the long lines of shadowy trees and threw them kisses. There were no peasants making wooden crosses, no calvaries, broken churches and strange crops in muddy, pitted fields.

The soldiers marched to the Town Hall, and the drum majors hurled their batons and the trumpets blew. The army was on the march. The soldiers' eyes lay deep under their slouch hats, their rising-sun badges shone and the officers' buckles gleamed, the bands played and Geoffrey Sawtell felt proud. Thousands of civilians were shouting. The soldiers glanced neither right nor left as they marched, they looked straight ahead down the avenue as if fixed upon some terrible enemy, as if peering over a shattered ground of craters, pits, holes and trenches. It seemed like going back down the Menin Road after the Armistice and they spoke no word. Their faces looked lean and unmoving under their hats, their uniforms looked dusty and decayed. The regimental horses stamped and pranced upon the pavement and the crows screeched and flew from the trees. The soldiers marched up Swanston Street, they looked dangerous, they were veterans and they had been where most men had not. Geoffrey remembered Smith singing in the dark and Lieutenant Atkins being blown away. The young women threw roses, the young men cheered and all the children ran. But some soldiers' heads were filled with awful, secret memories and the hawsers for the cable cars hummed beneath their feet.

His mother's garden had not changed: pink weeping roses climbed the fence; daffodils, forget-me-nots and gladioli bloomed. Beside the crazy-paving path, freesias and bluebells grew abundantly and the plum tree was thick with green fruit. There was larkspur growing, and violets and passion fruit vines clambered on wires around the wooden verandah posts. The lawn was green, the magpies swooped from the gum trees and the cicadas droned in the heat. His mother had kept her garden well watered. The old gelding was still grazing in the paddock opposite, where as a boy he used to play. There, still, were the ruined apple trees and the draughty pines. Down at the creek, watercress and wild hyacinth grew, crows sat on fence posts and frogs croaked in the reeds. Someone, many years ago, had planted a row of hawthorn trees: he remembered the blossoms in the spring, the convolvulus and the fennel. Geoffrey walked up the path behind his mother, and his father followed. The Australian sun shone and the street was quiet. His mother, dressed in pure white, kissed him once more, stepped on to the verandah, helped him up, opened the front door and the three of them stepped into the cool, dark hall. He was home.

The house was silent and he walked down the hall. Geoffrey looked at the black-framed family photographs: his mother and father at their wedding (she fair-haired and beautiful, he short and unsmiling), his dead younger brother Henry, his mother's parents and their daughter picnicking by the river at Walton-on-Thames, himself in the under-nineteen Richmond Football Team. His mother's hooked wool carpets lay on the linoleum and he almost tripped and fell. He passed by the front parlour, then the door of his room and his mother said:

54

'I'm going to make us all a cup of tea.'

Outside, the cable trams rattled up Bridge Road and the bells clanged. After the bands, the young women, pipes and speeches, the house seemed very quiet.

The house was cool and Geoffrey followed his mother into the kitchen; he unloaded his military gear and sat at the table. The black and white cat watched him from the window shelf but did not approach. There were poppies in vases. Geoffrey looked at the familiar signs of home: the grandfather clock and his gollywog sitting on the mantel-piece next to the small marble Ionian cross. *Bless This House.* He watched his mother take the woodchips from the cast-iron trivet and light the coal range; she went to the sink, filled the kettle and put it on the stove. He watched her back bend. Then she went to the cupboard and took out her best willow-pattern cups and saucers. She had also prepared a big jug of barley water which she put on the table. The kitchen was dim and polished, but the sunlight shone in shafts through the windows where the wisteria grew. The grandfather clock ticked and suddenly chimed. It was four o'clock and the cicadas still droned. His mother poured the boiling water into the pot and waited for the tea to draw. His father, cloth-capped and silent, stood by the kitchen door, reached for his buckskin pouch, lit his pipe and said:

'Mary, I think Geoffrey coming home calls for some-thing stronger than tea.'

'If you must, Angus,' his mother said. 'If you must.'

Mary Sawtell laid the hand-embroidered cloth upon the table and got the milk jug from the ice chest. There was a plate of date scones and sliced fruitcake. Geoffrey's father said nothing, went to the drink cupboard, took out the whisky bottle and got out two glasses. The house seemed very clean. His mother leaned across the table and kissed her son once more; she ran her hands through his un-washed hair; she smelt of Cashmere Bouquet soap and

55

there was a Spanish comb in her long, blonde hair. She touched his arm and said:

'There's been a drought here, it hasn't rained for months, heaven knows how my garden has survived.'

Geoffrey thought of the eternal rain of Belgium, the flowers in the trenches, the vegetable plots behind the lines and the green hill far away. The light from the afternoon sun was blinding him through the window; his mother pulled down the blinds and the three of them sat in the dark. She poured the tea and his father drank the whisky. There was no sound.

'There's some epidemic,' his mother said. 'They say there are millions dying in Europe and it's come here. It's come on the troopships. Were you inoculated?'

Geoffrey felt diseased and thought of the limbless men being taken down the gangplanks. He looked at his mother and father in the dark, clean kitchen and the flowers in the vases.

'I'm very tired Mother,' he said. 'I'm very tired.' He looked at the glass of whisky on the table before him.

'There was a chaplain I met once, he drank Queen Anne and ate fruitcake sent to him from London. He had lost one arm and had trouble with the Host.'

His mother and father did not reply and the kettle steamed on the stove.

'You have a lovely garden, Mother, I had forgotten how beautiful it is.' He drank the whisky very fast. It was better than rum. Then he said to his father, 'I'll have one more if I may.'

His father tipped the whisky into his son's glass and they both drank it down as his mother went to the stove to freshen up the pot. Beyond the kitchen, the cicadas sang and the garden grew and the cable trams rattled up Bridge Road, their bells clanging and the subterranean cables running. Outside in the street, children laughed and played.

'If you don't mind,' Geoffrey said, 'I'll go to my room and have a rest.' What could he say to them? He had been to a place where they would never go.

'Don't you want some fruitcake? Don't you feel well?' his mother said, but he had left the room. He was inoculated.

The Chums' Annual, Puck of Pook's Hill and *The Jack Harkaway Stories*. Geoffrey rummaged through his bookshelves. He touched the books and there was dust on his fingers. The western sun shone brightly into his room. This was his childhood, his bookshelf, these were the books that had made him what he was. He opened his stamp album: Togoland, Pitcairn, the Sudan. Something had changed now, since the Great War. He riffled through copies of *The Boy's Own Paper*. He looked at his young, hard face in the mirror on the oak wardrobe and laughed. He thought of another Scotch. What was his father doing in the kitchen? What was he talking about? Then he heard the sound of her voice raised and quick footsteps on the wooden floor of the hall and on the verandah. He lay on his bed where he had spent his childhood and thought of Smith and the Very pistol. *Nobody knows how tired we are.* He heard his mother crying in the garden. There was a knock at his bedroom door, his father came in and said:

'I'm going to the Mountain View. Do you want to come? It closes at six.'

Geoffrey raised himself from the bed, the books and the memories and said, 'Yes, I'll come.' He looked at his father and followed him down the hall.

Like his mother's house, the bar at the Mountain View was dark; the kegs of draught bitter were on the counter, the spigots were turned and the men sat drinking beer and portergaffs. This was his father's pub; he had been coming for years, ever since Geoffrey could remember. When he was young, his father had said:

'Baking's very thirsty work, you do it day in and day out, and that calls for a drink.'

There were framed pictures of Melbourne Cup winners and the Richmond Football Team hanging on the varnished walls. The smell of beer and tobacco was in the air and the working men sat quietly talking and drinking. There was the sound of cable trams but no thunder of guns. Geoffrey still had his uniform on and all the men looked up when he came in with his father.

'Gooday, Angus,' the publican said, 'and here's young Geoff back from the wars.' He grinned and shook Geoffrey's hand.

'Jesus, mates,' the publican said loudly, 'here's young Sawtell back from the wars.'

All the men got up, gathered around him, slapped his back and shook his hand. Angus suddenly smiled: he was proud of his son.

'Jesus,' said the publican, 'young Geoffrey Sawtell. Well I never. What do you want, son? It's all on the house. You're back from the wars.'

The men all crowded around him, pushing and shoving and laughing. They banged their glasses on the counter. Geoffrey was very popular; he was strong and had been a good footballer at school and many of them thought that if it hadn't been for the War, he would have played for the Seniors. Now he was home, he still could.

'Well, I never,' the publican said, 'what do you want, young Geoff, what do you want to drink?'

'I'll have a whisky,' Geoffrey Sawtell said. He had not been in an Australian pub before. The men still kept shaking his hand. The publican couldn't work the spigots fast enough and called for help.

'Hey, Mary,' he called, 'come and help, young Geoffrey Sawtell's home.'

This was a big friendly Saturday crowd of men and Geoffrey thought of France and his mates. He thought of

Smith. It was a bit like being in the army; all the men had working boots on and they all wore old felt hats and grimy open waistcoats; they looked like soldiers with their grey, lean faces. Some of them still had Irish accents for this was a Roman Catholic pub, but they didn't mind Angus because they all voted Labor.

'Jesus, Geoff,' the publican said, 'you've filled out. A bit of training and you'll get straight into the Seniors.' He took down the Dewars and poured him a nobbler.

It was five o'clock now, an hour to closing, and more men came into the pub. The air grew thick with tobacco smoke, shouting and talking, more glasses banged, the publican served the beer and someone had started to play the old bar piano. They sang all the old songs: *It's a Long Way to Tipperary, Pack Up Your Troubles* and *Mademoiselle from Armentieres.* Geoffrey joined in; he remembered the marching songs on the Menin Road, and the games of pontoon; he joined in, he felt his father take his arm and he sang with the men until a quarter past six when two policemen arrived and the doors were closed.

They sat drinking after hours in the small back room, the three of them: his father, the publican and Geoffrey Sawtell. The singing and shouting had stopped and it was quiet. There was a picture of Daniel O'Connell on the wall. This was the back room where friends of the publican drank illegally. The ashes of last winter's fires still lay in the grate. The publican rolled a cigarette from his old tin and passed it over to Angus; he took up the bottle and poured three large whiskies. He looked directly at Geoffrey and said:

'What was it like, the War, what was it like?'

The publican was a man with grey hair and nicotine-stained fingers; he had lost all his teeth and looked like an old soldier; his hands were shaking as he raised his glass. His name was Jack Hanrahan and his father had known him for a long time. Over the years, his father had spent a

59

lot of money at the Mountain View. It was a very small room and smelt of plug tobacco and fried onions; Geoffrey thought of the tunnels and dugouts, the mines and shafts where candles flickered and men spoke in whispers, their breath bad and their bodies reeking of sweat and death. In the crypts of Catholic churches, the soldiers had played pontoon and the rats had eaten their food beneath their tables.

He look back at the publican and said: 'It was all right. I got through. I've still got my father's watch.'

His father started to speak, but Geoffrey Sawtell got up, opened the door, groped down the long, dark passage and tried to find the outside privy. He could not find it and pissed on the piles of beer crates. It was a hot night and the yard was piled high with slabs of timber and junk. It looked like a battleground. *Pack Up Your Troubles*. He thought of his mother waiting at home and weeping in the garden, and went back to his father.

Jack Hanrahan was rolling another cigarette and said: 'Ah, gooday, young Geoff, what was it like being in the War?' Geoffrey sat down next to his father and said: 'I got through all right, I'm back safe and sound.'

'This is the first time you and I have been in a pub together,' his father said. He reamed his pipe and looked uneasy. Jack Hanrahan reminded Geoffrey of Smith and the other diggers. He had a face carved from an old tree. His father's face was the same. They were both workers: hard labour in the bakery and hard labour in the pub. Even though neither of them had been away, they were veterans of a sort. He hadn't realized that before. His father belonged in this small back room with his mates, as he belonged in the Army. His mother had always said that his father went about with Holy Romans because they drank; but it was more than that. He drank some more whisky, raised the glass and said: 'I got the taste for booze in the trenches.'

'They didn't give you whisky?' Jack Hanrahan said.

'The officers had whisky, we had rum. A lot of the boys were drunk when they went over the top.' He looked at his father,

'I think I told you: our Chaplain drank whisky.'

'There's nothing wrong in that.'

'No,' Geoffrey said, 'but he was a bit short on spiritual advice.'

He laughed and laughed, nearly fell off his chair and grabbed his father's arm. 'The Chaplain was one of the New South Wales ruling class and had never heard of St Stephen's, Richmond. It takes all sorts.'

Jack Hanrahan shifted on his chair and said: 'I was always against that bloody war, what did it do for the working man? We're all still in the same boat.' He waved his arm. 'Those fat bastards out there made all the money, guns and uniforms and supplies for the troops.'

'That's all right, Jack,' Angus Sawtell said.

'That may be true, Mr Hanrahan,' Geoffrey said, 'but I've been there, and nothing will change that. I'm not going to discuss it any more if you don't mind, but me and my mates have done something that you will never do.' *They've got it in for young colonial lads like you.* He looked at his father and Jack Hanrahan. 'All I want to do now is play for the Seniors and put the War behind me.' He stood up very strong and tall. 'I want to get out of this uniform and play for the Seniors.' But as he made to leave, his head was filled with confusion and he sat down for another drink.

'How many were killed?' Jack Hanrahan said as he rolled a cigarette from the tin.

'Millions and millions,' Geoffrey's father said. 'Nobody knows, they say seventy thousand of our lads alone, and then there's the wounded, what will they do with them?'

They'll hide them, Geoffrey thought as he drank his whisky, they'll hide them, just like they'll have to hide me.

61

But he said nothing and listened to Jack Hanrahan and his father talking.

'It was a trade war,' Jack Hanrahan said. 'It was the capitalists. If the working class had've united, it need never've happened.'

Sawtell drank his whisky and listened in the dark back room; it was like a burrow and the walls seemed very close. It smelt of old food and poverty. He thought of those silent lines of young men, cheaply uniformed, carrying heavy loads, trudging forward across No Man's Land through the mustard gas and Spandau fire. Nothing had been done about it. Such was life. But he had come through and, he thought, he had been away from his mother, the kitchen and the garden. Now, somehow, he had been cast out and thought of the men and women on the quayside, waving and shouting at the troopship and the soldiers. They were his countrymen, but now he could not understand them. Something dreadful had gone wrong. He wanted to go to the bush, the paddocks, the pines and the country streams running, where he had spent his boyhood. He hoped that had not changed. He listened to Jack Hanrahan and his father talk and felt powerless.

'I don't care if it was a trade war or not,' Geoffrey Sawtell said. 'I don't know what a trade war is.' He drank his whisky down and looked at Jack Hanrahan and his father. 'It was our war, us and the Huns, we all belonged to it; it was what we all did and there's no going back; the war was itself and we all belonged to it; it was ours.'

Jack Hanrahan coughed and said: 'You're a hero, Geoffrey, you've come home unscathed and we're proud of you. It was the wrong war, that's all. What do you think, Angus?'

'It was the wrong war.'

Geoffrey drank and looked out of the small window at Bridge Road and the cable cars rattling. His father drained the bottle, his hands shook and he filled his pipe. The three men sat in the dark back room of the Mountain View and discussed the Great War and Geoffrey wanted to be in the countryside by the familiar stream where the brown trout swam silently by brown, mossy stones. There had been the river and the geese had been flying home. He stood up again, glass in hand.

'Look Dad and Mr Hanrahan, I don't understand what you're talking about: it was our war, it's made us what we are.' He stood up and made to go home to his room, his mother and her garden.

'Come on Geoffrey, sit down,' his father said. 'We won't fight on this, your first night home.'

Jack Hanrahan changed the subject, got out his harmonica and played *Botany Bay, Bold Jack O'Donohoe* and some other Australian songs. They all drank more whisky and later that night, Geoffrey and his father staggered silently home under the corrugated-iron verandahs of Bridge Road. The gas-lights gleamed and the big moths fluttered.

'They're going to close the pubs and churches down because of the epidemic,' his father said. 'I don't mind about the churches, but not the pubs.'

It was very dark and his father almost fell, but Geoffrey caught him.

'We've missed our tea,' Geoffrey said.

But his father said: 'You don't come every night from the war; we should have had a party, but your mother wanted you to herself.'

Geoffrey felt sorry for his mother, waiting alone in the front room. She had probably gone to bed. He would go to church with her in the morning. It was the first time he had got drunk with his father, and there was nothing wrong with that.

The hot north wind blew and the smell of bushfires was on the air. They went from Rotherwood Street, past the wood and brick cottages, through his mother's garden and into the house. There was a full red moon and the tree-frogs were croaking in the reeds of the paddock over the road. His father wished him goodnight and slipped quickly into the front bedroom. Geoffrey went to his room, took off his uniform and climbed into bed. In the dark, he could smell his boyhood books and magazines; it was a pity there was no one to pass them on to. Through the wall, he heard his mother and father arguing. He listened to the sound of the trees rustling and bending in the garden and, at last, went to sleep.

Almighty God, to whom all hearts be open, all desires known, and from whom no secrets are hid: cleanse the thoughts of our hearts by the inspiration of thy Holy Spirit

He knelt next to his mother in St Stephen's Church. When he had been young before the War, he had been an altar boy and had assisted the Vicar with the sacrament. It was another hot, sunny day and there was a large congregation, but no other returned men. Richmond was a Roman Catholic stronghold and Geoffrey thought they must be at St Ignatius' next door. The familiar service proceeded: the Confession was made, the Creed was said, the Responses sung and the Communion delivered to all of them, meekly kneeling upon their knees. Then they sang hymn number 373: *God moves in a mysterious way, His wonders to perform.* The pipe-organ trilled and boomed, the Vicar thanked God for allowing so many boys to be brought home, safe and sound. He said that the War had purged them all and saved the nation from degeneracy and moral decay; that the Australian Imperial Force had brought together the finest body of young men in modern times. Then, for the thousands of those that had fallen, the Vicar said:

They shall not grow old, as we that are left grow old: Age shall not weary them, nor the years condemn.

At the going down of the sun and in the morning,
We will remember them.

Geoffrey Sawtell looked at the marble font, where he had been baptized and the side-altar where he had been confirmed. With his big frame, Geoffrey looked like a national hero, but he could not forget the inexplicable mutilations. *And there is no health in us.*

The sun blinded him as they left the Church and the strange young Vicar, smiling, and in his surplice, shook Geoffrey's hand and welcomed him back to the Parish. Many other parishioners also shook his hand. The men looked ruddy with good health and wore three-piece suits and bowler hats. Their watch chains gleamed. The sky was blue and cloudless and the children shouted and tumbled about on the grass under the oak trees and spreading pines. His mother's friends gathered about her in their long white frocks of silk *crêpe-de-chine*. They opened their parasols against the sun and congratulated her on her son's coming home. The young Vicar, balding and suntanned, was still shaking hands. Geoffrey stood to one side and watched the people. He could now understand only two things: he had been in No Man's Land, and there was no God. But how to tell his mother? He still had her crucifix in his kitbag.

The children laughed and shouted and Geoffrey stood, waiting for his mother under an elm tree. What would he do now he was back? As it happened, most of his mates in the army were in the country in Victoria and New South Wales. They had gone back home and he doubted if he would see them again. He was glad to be home, but he already missed the men and the comradeship of battle. He knew he would never be the same.

He sat with his mother in the garden. It was a beautiful January afternoon; the English trees and flowers grew, the birds sang and it was very quiet. A cable car bell sounded

65

far away. Geoffrey drank some barley water and looked across the street at the paddock and the pines. He was wearing an old striped shirt without the collar and a pair of his father's trousers. He had grown and they were too short for him.

'We'll have to take you to Foy & Gibson's and get you some new clothes,' his mother said. She was knitting and the ball of fine, grey wool lay on the grass at her feet. Her son's face was white. 'The sun's strong, don't you want a hat?'

'No, Mother.'

'You didn't write much for the last six months.'

'No, I couldn't find the time. It was all a bit awkward.' He put his hands under his braces and stretched them.

'Awkward?'

'There was a lot going on.' What could he say to her? Tell her about the endless noise, the French .75s, the rats, the rum or Smith singing in the dark? What was the point? It would take too much explaining and would take too long and she would lose interest; he would have to start right back at the Menin Road, or even military drill at school, and that would be too exhausting. He drank his barley water. She would become bored. His father and Jack Hanrahan had become bored. The War wasn't necessarily a secret by itself; it became one because it was too hard to explain. Only with the fellows could you talk about things that had happened and not have to explain. It was like poetry.

'We were very busy,' he said.

'Did you go to Holy Communion?'

'When I could, it was difficult sometimes.'

'Who was the minister? Was he from Melbourne?'

'He was from New South Wales, he was a nice man.'

'What was London like?'

'You know it, Mother.'

'That, my dear, was a long time ago.' Mary Sawtell

66

gazed at her English garden as the crows and the magpies swooped.

'Well, it was very big, there were lots of old buildings and soldiers on leave. We walked around Piccadilly and Leicester Square and I went to Berkshire to see a friend.'

'Berkshire? You didn't tell me that.'

'I've only just remembered.'

'Who was your friend?'

'One of the fellows. He got hit and I went to see him in hospital.'

'Where was the hospital? I know Berkshire.'

'I forget. We went by train.' Should he tell her about all the limbless soldiers and their new mechanical contraptions?

'Did you go to Walton-on-Thames? It's on the way.'

'No, Mother, we may have gone past it on the train. I can't remember.'

'I wish you had, you could have seen where I was born and the lovely Norman church. I wish you had.' She knitted his cardigan.

'Do you realize that tomorrow would have been Henry's twenty-third birthday?'

Again, he had forgotten and wondered what to do. He wondered what the time was, but he had left his father's watch in his bedroom.

'Henry would have been twenty-three.'

His brother, he thought, would have been a prime target for a German sniper or potato masher; the young Vicar could have given a sermon on Henry's death. *We shall remember them.* Geoffrey got up.

'If you'll excuse me Mother, I think I'll go for a walk.'

'Must you Geoffrey? We haven't talked, you've been away for two years.'

Been away. He had been away, he wanted to leave the shadowy garden and the English flowers.

'I won't be long,' he said, 'I just want to stretch my legs.'

67

'Don't forget your hat.'

He didn't reply, walked down the gravel path, opened the gate and disappeared. His mother sat in the garden with her knitting. He had not kissed her since he'd been home. She got up, pierced the ball of wool with her needles, put her knitting into her bag and went inside to prepare tea.

It was four o'clock and there would be nobody in the Mountain View until half-past.

'Gooday Geoff,' Jack Hanrahan said, 'what can I do for you?'

'Gooday, Mr Hanrahan. I'd like a whisky.'

'What would you like it with?'

'Soda.'

Jack Hanrahan, tall and thin, leaned across the bar and gave Geoffrey his whisky.

'You didn't used to drink.'

'I couldn't, Mr Hanrahan, I was under age.'

'Ah, but you didn't look the drinking type.'

'I suppose things have changed.'

'That was a bad war, and it's brought an epidemic, they might close the pubs.' Geoffrey laughed: his mother would be pleased; the three of them could sit by the piano in the front parlour and listen to her sing. He drank his whisky down and put another shilling on the counter. 'I'll have the other half, if you don't mind, and wait for my father.'

'All right Geoff,' Jack Hanrahan said as he reached for the bottle, 'do what you like, it's a free country.'

Geoffrey had the other half, sat by himself by the window and waited for his father.

That night, Geoffrey Sawtell sang old songs, got drunk after hours, vomited and was taken home by his father. His mother had eaten her tea and gone to bed. In the morning, his mother did not speak to him, and he did not know what to say. He wished he was back on the Menin Road.

· V ·

Bourke

IN THE MORNING, Sawtell strolled across the street and through the back yard to the Major's shed. He looked at the sky for aircraft, but there were none. The garden was littered with timber, rusting water tanks and forgotten machinery. There was an old Reo truck with grass growing through its wheels, its cabin doors open and the bonnet raised. Sawtell looked at the vehicle: it had not moved for years. Wild flowers were growing. He walked through the ruined garden, past staggering tank stands, clothes lines and deserted fowl houses. This was the junk of generations, the dead weeds stood high and sunflowers grew. He thought of his mother's garden in Rotherwood Street and the smell of the damson plums rotting on the ground, the passion fruit vines clambering on the front verandah. The fences were down, the palings were stripped from the posts and the doors wrenched from the outside privies. Here, there were no dogs barking and children playing on green grass under oak trees. Sawtell kicked at the dry earth of the vegetable garden, there could be old spuds in the dirt, then went next door to the shed. He would wash himself and his filthy clothes. He looked out for the Major, but there was no sign. Then he saw the orange and lemon trees and his heart lifted. The bright fruit grew abundantly and they would have some for breakfast. He thought of Marcia, of picnics and the old apple orchards in the countryside of

Victoria. Inside the shed, Sawtell stripped off; the water from the boiler was still hot and he let it run over his body for a long time. He washed himself very slowly and made the most of it. Then he washed his clothes. When he had finished, he felt like a new man and he thought of his married days, of steam in the bathroom, Marcia's body, talcum and her strong arms around him after they had loved on quiet, still Sunday mornings. Sometimes they had stayed in bed until mid-afternoon when they had gone to the beach to walk until dark and watch the yachts, schooners and yawls beating close-hauled up the bay, sails set for the comforting navigation points and lights of home.

Frank Counihan had the coal range going in the kitchen; he made some damper, put it on an old tin tray and shoved it in the oven. It would be as good as bread. Then he made some billy tea and put it on the stove. He sat on the floor, watched the billy boil and waited for Sawtell. Three of the horses needed shoeing: he would have to find a smithy. The time by Geoff's hunter was half past six but, as usual, he could not remember what day it was. The month, he knew, was August. Soon it would be summer. The billy was boiling and he made the tea. The house was quiet and nothing moved. He wondered who had lived here; people who worked on the river probably. They must go to the warehouse and see what was there.

Jesus, this place was a turn-up: an army of two old Pommy officers and a boy they hadn't seen yet. He poured some tea into his enamel mug and drank. Such was life. One thing was certain, the Japs wouldn't want to come here. If they did, they were welcome to it. It was bad not knowing what was happening. His mother had probably gone to Mildura, the bloody Nips couldn't be everywhere, Australia was a big place – as big as Siberia, he remembered. What was going to happen? Wars didn't last for ever, somebody must come to the rescue. England or

70

the Yanks? But both those buggers had let them down. The only thing to do now was to take each day as it came and get on with it. It was all like a bad dream. Maybe they should have stayed in Newcastle, but what good would that have done? They would have been taken prisoner and now doing forced labour or dead. Anyway, Colonel Madigan and other big-wigs had told them to go into the bush and fight, and that was what they were doing. The Japs couldn't handle the bush but, by Christ, the Australians could.

Sawtell came in and stood in his long-johns, his hair and beard dripping, and smelt the tea. He tossed Counihan an orange.

'There's a whole tree-full outside, at least this place has got something and it solves the food problem.'

Counihan cut the orange into quarters and sank his teeth into the fruit. The juice ran down his chin and into his beard.

'There's lots of oranges in Mildura, acres of them. Do Japs eat them?'

'Buggered if I know, they live off rice and the smell of an oily rag. What about getting some?'

'Okay,' Counihan said, 'there's some damper in the oven, and there's some tea.' He grabbed his haversack and disappeared. Well, thought Geoffrey Sawtell as he poured the billy tea, life looks up: damper, oranges and tea. What more could a man want? There must be some drink in this town somewhere. The blackfellows obviously had it, but it was probably cheap booze. Tokay or Muscat, perhaps? They would look at the camp later in the day. The damper tasted almost like bread; he ate it with his mug of tea and put the rest back in the oven for Frank. Then he got up and scouted around the house. It only had four rooms and there was nothing but old newspapers, cobwebs and ratshit. The windows were broken and he peered into the street. On the way back to the kitchen, Sawtell found an

71

old paperback book lying on the floor. It was an Ellery Queen mystery and he put it in his haversack for the trip ahead. He sat on the floor by the coal range and had another mug of tea. It was a small house and the walls were made of corrugated iron. He had heard that iron was cheaper to transport than brick. They only used brick for churches, pubs and town halls.

Frank Counihan came in with his haversack full of oranges and put it on the floor. A few rolled out and Sawtell caught them. 'What do you think, Frank, a great find? We'll take what we can with us, it makes a break from mutton.'

'Yeah, the trees are loaded, just like the old days. How's the damper?'

'Good.' He laughed. 'You should have been a baker.'

They both drank their tea, and outside a gentle breeze blew. It was an enjoyable breakfast, the best for some time. But outside the house was the sound of the crows as they fed off the carcasses of abandoned livestock and dead animals that lay in paddocks and in country stockyards.

'I found a book,' Sawtell said.

'Yeah?'

'Ellery Queen.'

'I never heard of her.'

Sawtell ate some more damper and began to peel an orange.

'Did you ever read a book, Frank?'

Counihan banged shut the door of the oven. 'Not really, a few, F. J. Thwaites is good, and the newspapers. You know, I left school when I was fourteen and went to work on the railways like me Dad. I haven't fought in the Great War like you and the Major. As I said, the battle of life. Jesus, I'd like a tailor-made.'

'We'll go foraging,' Sawtell said, 'and we'll find some. The blackfellows can't have got everything.'

'I didn't get much time to read books,' Counihan said, 'I

spent most of me time playing hookey or being bashed up.'
He got up and stared out the window at the ruined garden.

'It wasn't much of a start, everyone hated Tikes in them days and I suppose they still do.' He came back from the window and sat on the floor. 'Do they have Catholics in the British Army?'

'Catholics?'

'Priests.'

Sawtell thought. 'They have Anglican priests, I met one once, so I suppose they have Catholic ones.'

'I met Padre Donaldson last night, what would he be?'

Sawtell laughed and said: 'He would be a Protestant, why do you worry? You haven't been to Mass for years.'

'Just wondering.'

Sawtell thought again of Marcia, her lover, her books and her politics. He thought of his father at Labor Party meetings with his black notebook and Jack Hanrahan listening.

'My wife used to read a lot, all kinds of things, politics and novels, her father was a schoolteacher.'

He remembered her by the stream and in the dry country, her body and her hair blowing in the breeze on the beach, as the sea ran. He had loved her.

Counihan picked up the Luger submachine gun and worked on it, oiling it carefully. He removed the snail magazine, checked the rounds and replaced it.

'Why did she leave you then?'

'She wanted to be by herself. It's taken me a long time to understand.'

'Not for another bloke?' Counihan looked at him directly.

'No, I've told you, for herself.'

'That's funny, there must have been another bloke.'

'No, there wasn't.'

'That's what me mother would call a mortal sin.'

'What, leaving for yourself?'

73

'Leaving a marriage.'

'Maybe, but my wife didn't believe in that sort of thing. She was an atheist.'

'What?'

'Someone who doesn't believe in God.'

'Ah.'

'You do, you're a Catholic, you're worrying about the Padre.'

'I never thought about it much. The nuns used to drum it into us at school in Ballarat with a bloody great stick. Religion's for women.' Counihan carefully put the Luger back in its bag. 'Anyhow, you had no kids and that's turned out good, seeing what's happened.'

Sawtell did not reply; he was still thinking of Marcia.

'The best school, Geoff,' Counihan said, 'is the school of life. That's what I've had and it's done me no harm.'

'Why didn't you ever get married, Frank?'

'Aw, I was always too busy working on the railways, the Port Pirie line, you know that. I was up and down the country, then the Depression came and I lost me job, it didn't seem like a good thing. I've always been on me own, you're the first regular mate I've had. Then I used to send money to me Mum, there wasn't much left over. Anyway I've always preferred me own company.' Counihan picked his teeth and spat out the orange pips. 'Do you want any more tea?'

'Have you ever had a woman? I've never asked you.'

'Aw, here and there, I've never had much use for them.'

'You've worked hard, haven't you, Frank?'

'Yeah, that's true. Hard work never killed anybody, and know your enemies, like that bloody Englishman. He'll bring us down, you'll see. Ned Kelly never trusted anybody except his family.'

'Do you trust me?'

'Yeah, we've been together a long time now. I know a man I can trust. I remember the first day I met you in camp, you played for Richmond.'

There was someone at the door.

'Ah,' Sawtell said, 'here's the Major. Good morning Major. Would you care for a cup of tea?'

Jesus, Frank Counihan thought, why was Geoff so polite to these bastards? There was another man at the door. He was tall and thin and wore a dog-collar. He, too, was an officer.

'Padre Donaldson,' St John Jackson said, 'you've met Mr Counihan, this is Mr Sawtell.'

Geoffrey Sawtell looked at the familiar figure of an army chaplain, the comfortable dugout behind the lines, the words of comfort and the prayer book lying in the dirt.

'Padre Donaldson,' he said, 'I'm pleased to meet you. Would you care for a cup of tea? Please excuse my dress.'

'I do excuse your dress.'

'Right then.'

He poured out two mugs of tea and gave one to the Englishmen. Well, Sergius Donaldson thought, here's a man I can do something with. He looked at the big body, the hard face and the blue eyes. He had seen many young men like him twenty-five years ago in the trenches. He had seen them crouching on the firestep, waiting to go over the top, and he had served them Holy Communion on makeshift altars in muddy fields.

St John Jackson tasted his tea. It was not Darjeeling. He looked again at the Luger submachine gun lying on the floor by Counihan's haversack and webbing.

'Have you shot anyone with that weapon, Mr Counihan?'

'Yeah, Japs at Newcastle and Dubbo.'

There were flies in the room and the Englishman brushed them away.

'We know all about weapons Major,' Sawtell said.

'I'm quite sure you do, and so do I, and so does the Padre. That means we have one thing in common.'

'We have two other things Major. We are all soldiers and we have a common enemy.'

75

'I didn't know priests killed people,' Counihan said as he sliced another orange.

'They do, Mr Counihan,' Sergius Donaldson said, 'when faced with the forces of evil. Onward Christian Soldiers.'

'What weapons can you use, Padre?' Sawtell said.

'Army chaplains are supposed to administer to soldiers' spiritual needs first, but I can use a shotgun.' Donaldson sat on the floor and faced Sawtell. The Padre looked lean and fit for a man of his age, Sawtell thought, and his accent was impeccable. 'My father taught me to shoot grouse before the Great War.'

Sawtell remembered the military hospital in Berkshire, the limbless soldiers and the distant sound of shotguns over the downs.

'There's lots of ducks on the river,' he said. 'You can have a go at those.'

'I've done so already. You intend going down the river?'

'We've got plans.' Sawtell stretched his legs on the floor. The morning was getting warm now and the flies buzzed in the kitchen.

'How long have you been here, Major?'

St John Jackson remained standing. 'Since August last year. Darwin was, as they say, evacuated.' He coughed. 'As you no doubt know, it was a shambles, a disgrace.'

'Worse than Singapore?' Counihan said.

The Major turned and looked at Counihan. 'Much worse, it was disorderly, a rout.'

'We didn't march into prison camp, we didn't let our cobbers down.'

'True, Mr Counihan, you didn't march into prison camp.' He laughed. 'Or maybe you did, this place is hardly any more than that.'

'Is there any more of that excellent tea, Mr Sawtell?' the Padre said.

'There is, Padre.' Sawtell got up, took his mug and gave him some.

'I can't excuse Percival at Singapore,' St John Jackson

76

said. 'God help me, I was there. I know the disgrace, but Darwin was a catastrophe, the civilian population were terror-stricken and the VDC acted abominably. Furthermore, some damned fellow stole my mess kit.'

'Stole your what?' Counihan said.

'My mess kit.'

'What's your mess kit?'

'Look Major,' Sawtell said. 'There's no point arguing about past defeats. As you know, Frank and I fought at Newcastle and that, too, was a catastrophe. Dive-bombing, a naval bombardment, landings all over the place, Port Stephens, Tweed Heads, Coff's Harbour, the Hawkesbury, Sydney's northern beaches, you name it. We didn't stand a chance, the people panicked and ran. They say over 300,000 Japanese troops landed, all seasoned men from Thailand and Burma.'

'We didn't march into prison camps.'

'Come on, Frank, it was bloody terrible: old men with country shotguns and reject stuff from the Great War, boys with air rifles, and women and children screaming, suburbs being bombed, we've never been invaded before. Christ, you and I pissed off.'

'Under Colonel Madigan's orders.'

'And you men still intend to harass, deny and destroy?' St John Jackson asked.

'This place is big,' Sawtell said. 'They can't occupy it all, and we intend to lay waste to everything of value to the enemy.'

'Do you intend to destroy this town?'

'What we can.'

'And what is that?'

'We've got Colonel Madigan's list,' Counihan said. 'You've seen it, and it goes from mines and power stations to wells and homesteads.'

'These are drastic measures, gentlemen,' Sergius Donaldson said. 'To destroy one's own country.'

'What would you do, Padre, if your country was invaded?'

vaded?' Sawtell reached for the gold hunter from his tunic and held it by the chain.

'God knows, the Germans could be in England now, but I should try to preserve.' Sergius Donaldson thought of his father's eleventh-century church at Hungerford, the brasses, the stones at Avebury, the Downs and the haymaking. His father had owned a white stallion, wore a top hat and rode to hounds with the best of them. He remembered Combe gibbet and the commons of bracken and heather. He lit a cigarette and Counihan saw it was his last one.

'I can't conceive of destroying Westminster, the Royal Observatory or my father's church.' He watched Sawtell playing with the hunter. 'That's a fine watch you have there, Mr Sawtell.'

'It belonged to my father. There are none of those buildings in Australia. We don't have any Royal Observatories and we don't have any sixteenth-century pubs and thatched cottages. All we have is this house, corrugated-iron towns, the river and the bush. We have war memorials in every main street, boys killed for fighting for England. All we have is somewhere to go.'

'And where is that?' Sergius Donaldson asked.

'Out there,' Frank Counihan said. He waved his arm. 'Out there in Australia.'

'I'm not sure I understand.'

'I'm sure you don't, Padre,' Sawtell said.

'You intend to go out there?'

'We do, to the north-west.'

'I understand it's difficult country.'

'It is,' Sawtell said. He suddenly thought of the explorers, Burke and Wills, the epic of his schooldays, their bad luck and death. 'But it's all we've got.'

The Major walked over and squatted by Sawtell. 'What military news do you have, Mr Sawtell?'

'I told you last night Major, we have none. We found a paddock full of mutilated corpses at Nyngan. We heard

78

that sixty people were machine gunned in a tennis court at Wellington. We've heard that there's forced labour in the steel works at Newcastle, that there are bushfires in Victoria and that the Prime Minister, Mr Curtin, is dead. God knows where the home army is and what's happening in the Desert or Europe, I don't know.'

There was a silence and Sawtell looked at the English Major. It was his turn to fight a foreign war.

'The Japs are at Broken Hill,' Frank Counihan said, 'and they're working it with forced labour. We heard that at Wellington and other places on the track.'

'That's the big mining town,' Sergius Donaldson said. 'Silver, lead and zinc. Eldorado, you might say.'

'That's right Padre,' Sawtell said. 'It's Australia's biggest mine and the Japs have got it.'

'And what is your plan, Mr Sawtell?' St John Jackson asked. He now thought he knew why these two Australians had come so far. This, at least, was some kind of courage. He again considered them both; they looked like the trees of the landscape, like the gums that clung to the sides of the river. The big Sawtell, the lean, dark Counihan.

'We've got a plan Major,' Sawtell said, 'we've had it since we left Wellington.'

'And what is the plan?'

'To sabotage the Zinc Corporation Mine at Broken Hill. It's a prime military target.'

'Isn't that what the Americans would call a tall order?'

'Aw, I don't know,' Frank Counihan said, 'at least we won't march into prison camp.'

'Your plan, Mr Sawtell?' St John Jackson got up and walked around the room. The flies were annoying him. What could these two Australian rough-riders do? But Sawtell had fought before. Had he been decorated?

'We intend to ride from here, down the Darling to Wilcannia, to Menindee and then to Broken Hill.'

79

'How long will it take?' Sergius Donaldson said. He, too, was interested. The deserted town of Bourke was not the place for him, either as a clergyman or as a soldier. The blackfellows were past help and there was no work for him here.

'We've looked at the maps,' Frank Counihan said. 'It's about 400 miles from here to Broken Hill and the trip will take us about four weeks. We've got gear and the horses and we can do it easy.'

'I take it that you have experience as a saboteur, Mr Sawtell?' St John Jackson thought of the officers' mess in Meerut, the drill on the bullring, the route marches to the north, the fine Scotch and the familiar smell of the Indian countryside. Sawtell thought of the broken villages in Belgium, the mine-shafts and galleries he had helped build, the charges he had laid and his work on country bridges in Victoria.

'I was a sapper in the Great War and a civil engineer after that. Frank Counihan also has some experience of explosives and has worked on the railways.'

'What explosives do you have?'

'We've got dynamite,' Sawtell said, 'fuses and petrol, and what we haven't got, we can make. I've worked at the mine we intend to destroy. You are, Major, as the Americans say, checking us out?'

'I've always believed in thorough preparations.' The Major thought of the bloody catastrophe at Loos where over half his Brigade had perished. 'There's nothing worse than military incompetence. I know, I've suffered from it in both this war and the one before.'

Sawtell smiled and said: 'And I, too, Major, have suffered from gross incompetence, and I've seen some of my best mates die because of it.'

Sergius Donaldson listened to all this, and his pulse quickened. This was a chance for retrieving honour, for courage and for striking back at evil and bestiality; this was a chance to atone for Singapore and the years of inactivity since the Great War.

'What's the boy like?' Sawtell said.

'What boy?'

'The young Australian boy. What's his name, Major, and where is he?'

'His name is O'Donohue, Kevin O'Donohue, he's been here for about a month, good with horses, about nineteen, he forages, he comes and goes. He's a drifter.'

'And the other men? How many were there and what happened?'

'We came down from Darwin in lorries, the terrain was bad, it took us weeks. The men, shall we say, kept dropping off, they were rabble and by the time we got here, there were only about seventy left.' St John Jackson coughed. 'I had some difficulty with discipline; every pub was ransacked, there was endless drinking and fighting, disgraceful scenes, violence, and thank God, eventually they all went away.'

Sawtell smiled. 'But you kept a stiff upper lip?'

'Indeed.' St John Jackson also smiled. 'One might say that British phlegm kept the Padre and me here.' He smiled again.

'A good soldier never leaves his post.'

'You may find this hard to believe, Major, but I've always believed in British phlegm.'

'Four weeks' riding, you say, Mr Sawtell. I think we can manage that. Are you asking us to join you?'

'Yes, Major, we're asking you to join us, five men are better than two.'

'Five?'

'There's the young Australian boy, if he comes back.'

'I should imagine, Mr Sawtell, that he'll be back.'

Any port in a storm, Counihan thought as he looked at the two Englishmen. A polo-playing Major from India who's lost his mess kit and a bloody old clergyman. Jesus Christ.

81

'Can you ride a horse Padre?' Sawtell said.

'I can. Again, my father taught me.'

'It's not exactly like fox-hunting on the Berkshire Downs, Padre. It's different here.'

'I'm sure it is, Mr Sawtell. Later this morning, if you wish, I shall ride a horse for you.'

'We'll take you up on that Padre,' Counihan said.

'And I shall be delighted to accept.'

'We shall give you our answer this evening, Mr Sawtell,' the Major said. 'It's a matter of preparation and logistics.'

'And dedication.'

'And dedication.' St John Jackson smiled.

Sawtell suddenly thought of playing football and the crowds cheering. 'Well,' he said, as he got up, 'I'm going to get back into my uniform.'

Sergius Donaldson watched him go. Sawtell's back was scarred. Was it shrapnel?

Kevin O'Donohue was at the saleyards. Sawtell and Counihan were exercising their horses there. Some of the rails were down and the dust rose as the stock horses ran. Kevin O'Donohue was dark-haired, lean and rangy and rode very well. Sawtell watched him come up. O'Donohue was riding a big, black horse about sixteen hands high; it was covered with sweat and he had worked it very hard. Counihan looked at the horse as O'Donohue approached: it was bright-eyed and in good condition. It was a warm morning now, the dust rose and the horses trotted around the saleyard. The young man rode up and dismounted in front of Sawtell and Counihan. He grinned and said:

'Gooday, I'm Kevin O'Donohue.'

'Gooday,' Counihan said. 'I'm Frank Counihan and this is Geoff Sawtell.'

'Youse came in last night?'

'Yeah, how did you know?'

'Aw, the Abos, they don't miss a trick.'

'Treacherous bastards, they're always watching,' Counihan said.

'Yeah.' O'Donohue was wearing an old slouch hat with white galah feathers in the band and had cold sores on his lips.

'Jesus Christ,' he said, 'I could do with a beer, but there isn't any.' He looked at the horses in the yard, the three packhorses and the two geldings.

'What do you call your horses?' he said. They looked strong.

'We don't have names for them,' Counihan said. 'They're just our horses and we look after them.'

'I can see that.' O'Donohue picked his nose and waved at the flies.

'Where have you been?' Sawtell said.

O'Donohue put his thumbs behind his old, patched-up braces.

'Aw, round and about, nowhere special. Do you know what's in them saddle bags? Two bottles of whisky. I don't go for the hard stuff meself, but I thought the Major and the Padre would like it.'

'Did you get any tobacco?' Frank Counihan said. He wanted the whisky.

'Yeah, you're in luck, it's pipe but you can rub it if you want a fag.'

'How long have you been here?' Sawtell said.

'About three weeks, I've been all over the place, I come down from Longreach.' He grinned. 'A bit of a ride but me and my horse did it. No worries.'

'Have you seen any Japs?'

'Nah, not a one.' He looked around. 'But who can tell? I ain't seen the bastards.'

Sawtell looked at O'Donohue's horse. 'What do you know about horses?'

'Aw, a bit, we ran them on me father's place near Mount

83

Parnassus at Gundagai before the war and I've worked on stations since I left home.'

'Why did you leave home?'

'Trouble.' He laughed and spat in the dust. 'It was a bit tough.'

'Where have you worked?' Counihan said.

'All over, Longreach, Mount Isa, Ivanhoe, Balranald, everywhere.'

'How old are you, Kevin?'

'Eighteen.'

'Religion?'

'Catholic. Don't go any more.'

'Take him, Frank, he's all yours,' Sawtell said, 'he's a Holy Roman.' He laughed and walked away in the dust to look at the horses. He looked at the sky and the clouds, he thought of St John Jackson and Padre Donaldson. Christ, he thought, needs must when the devil drives. He could see the river and the warehouses, the water towers and the big trees on the river line. He walked away. He felt better after his bath and the hot water upon his body. No doubt the boy would give them one of the bottles of Scotch.

'Can you shoot, Kevin?' Frank Counihan said.

'Aw yeah.'

'What have you shot?' Counihan looked at the clear, open face and the cold sores. O'Donohue had two teeth missing and his moleskins had worn at the knees. There were old spurs on his boots. He looked like a bushranger, one of the Kellys.

'Rabbits, roos, goats, things like that.'

'Did you ever shoot a man?'

'Nah, not yet, but I'd give the Nips a go.'

He looked, Counihan thought, a very strong boy. 'What sort of guns did you have?'

O'Donohue leant on the broken stock rail. 'Little pop-guns, .22s and things like that. The last one I had was a

84

Winchester pump-action, a good gun but some bugger stole it. I was good with that.'

Counihan watched Sawtell moving around with the horses and waited for him to come back. Some of the horses sneezed and snorted and two of them needed shoeing.

'Hey,' O'Donohue said, 'two of your horses need shoeing.'

'We know that,' Counihan said. He spoke to Sawtell, coming up.

'This young bugger says he can shoot. A Winchester pump-action.'

'Yeah? We've got a spare one. What can you shoot?'

'I've told Mr Counihan, rabbits and roos.'

'That'll do. What do you think of the Major and the Padre?'

'Aw, pommies, not one of us, but I seen the Major shoot and, Jesus, he can shoot with that fancy shotgun. Ducks. Him and the Padre can bring them down.'

'Have you seen the Padre ride?'

'I've been away. I suppose he can. Why don't you ask him?'

'I have. He says he can.'

'Well then.'

'When he comes, choose him a horse.'

'Okay,' Kevin O'Donohue said, grinning, 'no worries.' He rolled a cigarette and gave the tin and papers to Frank Counihan.

'Where are youse going?'

'To Broken Hill.'

'What for?'

'We're going to blow up a mine.'

'Why?'

'The Japs are there.'

'Get away.' Kevin O'Donohue studied the horses as they trotted around the yard. Sawtell was amongst the horses

85

again, standing and crouching in the dust. There was a light north wind blowing and Kevin O'Donohue thought Mr Sawtell looked old but big and strong. He thought Frank Counihan looked like a bushranger. Like Ben Hall or one of the Kellys.

O'Donohue picked at the cold sores. 'Do youse want any help?'

'Aw yeah,' Counihan said. 'We could do with a horseman.'

'I'm your man then. Horses is my speciality, I can manage the bastards.'

'What about one of them bottles of Scotch?'

'No worries.'

'How far west have you been?' Counihan said.

'West? Aw, a bit. I been west to Menindee and over to Broken Hill.' He considered. 'I been west of Laidley's Lakes and over the highway. It's okay if you look after yourself.'

Counihan watched the young man. 'What highway?'

'The Silver City to Broken Hill.'

'What's it like from here to Wilcannia?'

'Aw, dead easy, just follow the river. There's overflows to the north, but the south side's dead easy. You give me the horses and I'll look after them.'

'You want to come then?' Counihan said.

'Too right, I'll give it a go.'

Sawtell had come back and listened. 'Right then,' he said. 'Where's the smithy?'

'Just down there.' O'Donohue pointed. 'When do you want to do them? I'll give youse a hand.'

'Okay,' Counihan said. He climbed the rails and jumped into the dust. He blew his nose with his fingers.

'Got any shoes?' O'Donohue said.

'Yeah, a selection back with the gear. Odds and sods, but we can bang them into shape.'

Sawtell remained leaning against the rails and squinted.

There were two station hacks, a mare and a big waler he hadn't noticed before. They were on the far side of the yard. He pointed.

'Whose are those? Who owns the chestnut mare?'

'The Major,' O'Donohue said. 'That's his horse. The Padre ain't got a regular.'

'What about the waler and the hacks?'

'Aw, nobody. I picked them up at a station a week ago.'

'We could use them.'

'Yeah, they're strong bastards, they'll go a mile or two.'

'And you've seen no Japs?'

'Nah, aeroplanes, but no Japs. I reckon they can't get out this far. Sometimes I reckon the invasion is bullshit, but every bugger's pissed me off.' O'Donohue waved his arm at the buildings of Bourke, at the empty street and the vacant houses. 'There's no bastard here, so it must be true.'

'It's true all right,' Counihan said. 'Geoff and I fought at Newcastle, they're here all right, they're as far west as Dubbo and they got Sydney, Melbourne and Canberra. No bugger knows where the government is.'

'Shit, how do you know?'

'Aw, for Christ's sake, Kevin,' Sawtell said. 'It's on the wireless.'

'Okay,' O'Donohue said, 'it's hard to believe when you haven't seen the bastards.'

Frank Counihan suddenly climbed the rail and jumped back.

'Here comes the Padre,' he said.

'Ah, Padre,' Sawtell said as he stepped away from the rail, 'you've come to ride?'

'I have indeed.'

Sergius Donaldson smiled and looked at the three Australians: the big, grey man, Sawtell; the lean and hungry Counihan; and the boy, O'Donohue. The horses snorted and ran around the stockyard. Two Irish Holy Romans, he

87

thought, and the unknown Sawtell, the man who had yesterday killed a boy, a man who led others through the bush and who wanted to harass, deny and destroy. The sun was high in the gum trees and the windmills were immobile. Sergius Donaldson placed his boot on the stock rail and looked at the horses. Which one would they choose for him? Frank Counihan was rolling a cigarette from a tin of pipe tobacco and Sawtell was gazing toward the river. There was the sound of crows and parakeets. The Padre thought of his father, straight-backed and well mounted, riding about his Parish on his big, white stallion before the Great War. Those were the good years in the English countryside. He thought of his father, teaching him how to ride, and remembered the hounds, the stone walls, the brambly hedges and the bloodied fox running for his life. His father's Parish had been extensive; there were few roads, the tenants' cottages were far-spread and remote, and a clergyman had to ride well on country tracks to give comfort and administer the Holy Sacrament.

'I would like to ride a horse, Mr Sawtell.'

Geoffrey Sawtell looked at Sergius Donaldson's military boots. He looked around the yard and squinted in the sunlight and dust.

There were many stock horses in the yard. There were the station hacks and now Kevin O'Donohue was riding with them. It was a dry, dusty day. The sun was high now and O'Donohue was riding with the horses. He worked them like a Trojan. The brumbies, the station hacks and a big waler ran.

'O'Donohue,' Sawtell shouted, 'bring Padre Donaldson a horse. He wants to ride.'

Frank Counihan smoked his cigarette and watched. O'Donohue acknowledged and brought up the tall grey waler. He stopped before the clergyman. The horse was a big bugger, Sawtell thought, it was about sixteen hands high and looked irritable and nervous.

'Here's your horse, Padre,' O'Donohue said. He dismounted and tethered the waler to the top rail. He walked off, came back with an old army blanket and Australian stock saddle and threw them over the fence. Sergius Donaldson climbed the rail as the Australians watched him; he looked carefully at the waler for less than a minute, touched its nose, threw on the blanket and stock saddle and tightened the girths. The horse stood still and Sergius Donaldson mounted it and rode quickly around the yard. He rode properly and straight-backed as his father had taught him, twice around the yard. Sawtell, Counihan and O'Donohue watched from the rails. Then Sergius Donaldson and his waler leapt the broken fence and rode away down the river line.

Sawtell saw Sergius Donaldson disappear into the ghost gums and she-oaks and said: 'Well, Kevin O'Donohue, what do you think?'

'He can ride a horse, Mr Sawtell.'

'I think he can. I think he's going for his constitutional.' He thought of the young vicar at St Stephen's and the children laughing and tumbling under the oak trees.

The five men met at the stockyards in the late afternoon. Most of the horses were drinking at the water trough. Each man carried his saddle and blanket. Counihan and Sawtell made for their geldings. O'Donohue saddled up his big black horse and Sergius Donaldson had no trouble with the waler. St John Jackson saddled his chestnut mare very quickly and rode up to Sawtell. The Major was obviously an expert horseman: it was those years of playing polo and riding on the plains of northern India. He was wearing his topee and was carrying his Webley high in its holster on his left side, the lanyard around his shoulder. As always, he had shaved, his riding boots were clean and Sawtell thought the Englishman looked formidable, enough to frighten the guts out of any native or private soldier on the bullring. Frank Counihan and Kevin O'Donohue rode up carelessly and the Padre followed, upright, on his waler. Sawtell stood by his gelding in the dust. Counihan was carrying a sledgehammer. The big sun was behind the trees. 'Right, Mr Sawtell,' St John Jackson said, 'if you're ready, we shall go and see the blackfellows.'

Sawtell swung up on his gelding, looked north-east at the fires and said: 'Yes, Major, I'm ready, we'll go and see the blackfellows.' They rode from the yard.

To Frank Counihan, this was just another Abo camp, he could smell it. They had seen several on the road to Bourke. There would be filth and treachery. These Abos, he knew, were in league with the Japs; they drank, pilfered and stole and would stab you the moment your back was turned. They rode slowly along the track toward the fires. The two Englishmen, he thought, rode well, he had to admit that. The topee was a bit of a joke, but that's what they wore in India. He now thought they might make it to Broken Hill.

Sergius Donaldson rode alongside Frank Counihan, the Australian bushranger. He wondered why he had the sledgehammer. When he had first arrived at Bourke, Sergius Donaldson had visited the blackfellows' camp on a number of occasions, but had always returned baffled and defeated. He had not been trained as a missionary, but thought it his duty to see to the needs of native peoples when the occasion arose. He had been told that the Australian blackfellow had no formal religion like the Hindus and the Moslems and that, because of this, they were more receptive to the Christian doctrine. He had heard that, in the north, there were many successful Protestant and Catholic missions. However, from his brief experience with these natives, he could not see how they had succeeded. He seemed to recall that someone, some English explorer, had called the Australian blackfellows

90

the most miserable race on earth; and he was right. They were, he was sure, doomed to extinction; it was tragic, but there it was. Unlike the Indian natives, the blackfellows had no civilization, they had no common language, they had no crops and no domestic animals. There were no signs of any places of systematic worship and he believed they had been cannibals. But, above all, the blackfellows seemed to lack any fighting spirit. The Indian sepoys were good soldiers even though they had mutinied and the Burmese and even the Malays were worth something in a scrap. God had created the Australian blackfellow, but why, Sergius Donaldson could not fathom.

The fires burned in the saltbush and the smoke rose in the still afternoon air. Sawtell saw the inevitable humpies, over-thrown water tanks, motor car bodies, broken bottles and collapsing tin sheds. The Abos were sitting on the ground; there were old men and fat lubras with piccaninnies covered with dirt and flies. The empty wine bottles shone in the sun and broken toys lay upon the earth. Even the blackfellows' dogs did not bark and slunk away as they approached. Then he saw two young black men watching them from the shade of a she-oak. They were wearing filthy shirts, torn moleskins, riding boots and slouch hats. They were stockmen obviously, and they would have to be careful of them. Counihan had seen the young men too, and looked for their sheath knives; those bastards could maim a horse before you could blink your eyes. He looked at the windmill turning slowly. There were three brumbies drinking from a trough. He could see no other well, so they all used it: the animals and the blackfellows. Sawtell rode up before a group of old men sitting on the ground before a fire. He remained on his horse and said:

'My name is Sawtell, I am an officer of the Australian Volunteer Defence Corps and we have orders to destroy everything of use to the enemy. Do you understand?'

The two old men sat by the fire and said nothing; they

looked neither up nor down. There were flies crawling on their lips and faces, but they did not brush them away. Sawtell sat uneasy on his horse.

'Jesus, Geoff,' Counihan said, 'they're too bloody stupid to understand.' He wheeled his horse around, scattering ashes, tins and dust, but the two old men stayed silent.

'The natives have been like this ever since I arrived,' St John Jackson said. 'They're odd devils and I kept them out of town.'

'They know their place,' Counihan said. 'They know their place. They're in league with the Japs.'

'Is that so, Mr Counihan? I've no evidence of that. It seems to me that they're poor, harmless creatures. Drink and a lack of fighting capabilities seem to be the main problem.'

'They're from the North where the Japs are from.' Counihan waved his arm. 'They're all from the same place.'

St John Jackson shrugged his shoulders. 'What do you intend to do, Mr Sawtell?'

'I'll talk to those young buggers, they're stockmen and they should understand.'

Sawtell rode over to the she-oak. The two young black-fellows looked up as he approached. Unlike the older men, the taller of the two looked him straight in the face. He was a sinewy black boy, wearing moleskins, riding boots and an old Akubra hat with cockatoo feathers.

'What's happening boss?' the young blackfellow said.

'We're officers in the Volunteer Defence Corps. Have you seen any Japanese troops?'

'No boss.'

'Where did you last work. What station?'

'Aw long time ago.'

'How long?'

'Aw nine months.'

'Where?'

'Boogah, Dirranbandi; they all went away. There's no work, boss.'

'Where have you been since?'

'Around here boss.'

'Do you have any weapons, rifles, shotguns?'

'No boss.'

Sawtell knew they were lying. There were flies on the young blackfellow's face and he brushed them away. He lifted his old Akubra hat and still looked straight at Sawtell.

'Well,' Sawtell said, 'we have orders to destroy anything of use to the enemy.'

'What are you going to do boss?'

Sawtell pointed to the windmill slowly turning. 'We're going to destroy that pump and take out every bore and well in Bourke we can find.'

'What about the old people and kids?'

'You'll survive, you've got the river, we can't destroy that.'

'Okay boss.'

The other young blackfellow stood under the she-oak and said nothing. The flies settled on Sawtell's face and he brushed them away. The day was getting cooler now and the afternoon breeze was rising. He would have liked to stand for a moment under the she-oak. They had better get the job over.

'Okay Frank,' he called, 'smash the pump.'

He saw Counihan get down from the gelding, take the sledgehammer, walk over to the bore and smash the pump. For good measure, Counihan went to the trough, smashed the supports and the water poured into the dust. The brumbies snorted with fear and Counihan shouted and scattered them into the saltbush. The piccaninnies and the women ran towards the trees. The old black men sat on the ground.

'We're destroying every bore and tank,' Sawtell said.

'You'll have to use the river.' He looked at Counihan with the sledgehammer. 'Use the bloody river.'

'Okay boss.'

Sawtell turned his horse and rode back to St John Jackson and Sergius Donaldson. The old men still had not moved.

'That's that. They've got the river.'

'Right then,' St John Jackson said, 'let's get back to town, we have much work to do.' He pulled his topee over his eyes against the sun. Sawtell noticed that Counihan had given the sledgehammer to O'Donohue. Sergius Donaldson said nothing and they rode out of the camp. The two black stockmen watched the white men go, and Frank Counihan, his military work done, looked forward to that whisky. That would teach the thieving, black bastards.

The fire was burning and they had eaten a good dinner of roast mutton and potatoes. It was the best feed for some time and reminded Counihan of his mother and home. There had been no sound of aircraft and the evening breeze had died away. All was quiet in the small town. Beyond the windows, the blackfellows' fires still burned. Let them have the river. St John Jackson stood before the fire; Counihan looked at the Purdey shotgun and Kevin O'Donohue sat on the floor. Sergius Donaldson rolled a cigarette from the tin of pipe tobacco and Sawtell wondered about the piano and sheet music. He suddenly wished the Major would play a few bars from *HMS Pinafore*. The Major's house, too, smelt of dust and death. The tin ceilings were black and the windows were broken. *This is my father's house.* Sawtell looked at the black wood stove and remembered his mother's back bending, the cat on the window ledge and his father at the drink cupboard. He wondered how a pukka officer coped with a place like this. At seven, they had turned on the wireless receiver, but nothing had

94

changed: it was the same Japanese propaganda from Sydney. Counihan remembered Kevin O'Donohue saying that the invasion was all bullshit. Maybe it was all a bad dream and they should go back east and give the whole thing up. But there had been Newcastle, the bombing, the fighting, the women and children shouting and screaming; it had been like a Movietone newsreel of the war in Spain. He would never forget that. It now all depended on the Volunteer Defence Corps. He thought of the size of Australia and took heart: it could never be occupied, it was too big. They would get to Broken Hill and blow the bastards up.

The Major, still wearing his Sam Browne belt, stood before the fire. He held his glass of whisky and said: 'Gentlemen, Padre Donaldson and I have decided to join you.'

'Good,' Sawtell said. 'We'll drink to that.'

'Indeed,' Sergius Donaldson said, 'indeed we shall.'

'Furthermore,' St John Jackson said, 'I propose that in these unusual circumstances, you command this expedition.'

Counihan looked up and smiled.

'With pleasure sir.' Sawtell looked at both the Englishmen. 'I've no doubt we shall all get along; these trips can be as hard on the mind as on the body.'

'I've no doubt we shall, Mr Sawtell, providing we all exercise self-discipline.'

Counihan drank his Scotch down. Here it comes, he thought, the old school tie. These pommy bastards were all the same, him and Geoff would outride them and outlast them in the bush; they would ride them and walk them to death.

Sawtell got up and said: 'Frank, have you got the ordnance maps?'

Counihan produced them from his haversack and spread them on the floor.

'Right,' Sawtell said, 'I'll show you the route.'

The five men squatted in the centre of the room. Sergius

95

Donaldson looked at the maps, the vast, unfamiliar territory, and his pulse quickened.

'Here's the route,' Sawtell said. He traced the road on the south side of the river. 'We'll have to ride three days and rest one. We shall arrange between fifteen and twenty miles a day, depending on the country, stops, foraging and so on. How far down the river have you been, Major?'

'Not far, down to a place called Louth, a small river town, it was burnt out and derelict.'

'And no further?'

'I was otherwise occupied.'

'So from here to Wilcannia,' Sawtell said, 'is ten days. We can stop and forage there, providing the bridge over the river is up. If it's down, it could be difficult, but we can probably find somewhere to cross. Kevin, you've been there?'

'Yeah, the original one-horse town, eight pubs, it depends who's there. If it's like this, just Abos. There's wharves and things, old paddle steamers and that. There's also a big bond store.'

'We can take the Abos out,' Counihan said.

'Okay,' Sawtell said, 'let's hole up at Wilcannia for two or three days, and then on to Menindee, that's about five days.'

'What's at Menindee?'

'Aw, smaller than Wilcannia, two pubs, the railway to Broken Hill and wharves. Then there's the lakes, they go for bloody miles, there's lots of birds, good food.'

'Then,' Sawtell said, 'it gets tougher. We go north-west to Broken Hill, I reckon that's about ten days. It's dry country. Have you been up there' Kevin?'

'Yeah, I told you, I been west over the highway.'

'That's good,' Sawtell said, 'I know the country too, I've been up from Mildura. It's tough, all saltbush and bad feed, but there's some stations. Christ knows who's there now, but they'll have tanks and wells. Then we cross the main road and come up on Broken Hill from the south.'

'And sabotage the mine,' St John Jackson said. 'You have a precise target?'

'We do. If you remember, it's the Zinc Corporation Mine, the largest in Broken Hill. I worked there once. If we blow up the winding house and the tower, it's out of action for months.'

'And then?'

'We go north. I've been as far as a place called Tibooburra, there are stations on the way, we can hole-up there.'

St John Jackson insisted. 'If we're pursued, what is the country like?'

'It's dry,' Sawtell said, 'but we know it. We're on home ground.'

'It seems that the whole of Australia is dry,' St John Jackson said.

Sawtell laughed. 'This country is ideal for cavalry, Major, but the trouble is we can't see the enemy, there are no waiting lines of horsemen and no trumpets. There's no Light Brigade.'

'Ah, the cavalry,' Sergius Donaldson said. He had loved India, but hated Burma, where the cavalry could not charge. There were too many trees.

'The three of us fought in France,' Sawtell said. 'This is easier ground to fight over.' He thought of the mud and the death of the trenches, of running like a fox along the wire of No Man's Land, of the battery horses and mules drowning in the quagmires, the endless rain and the drowned fields of the Somme.

Frank Counihan listened very carefully to all this and thought: we know this country and we'll run the bastards down. Of course the Australian was right, thought St John Jackson, wars were won on movement and action; he had hated France, it would be good to ride a horse and attack the enemy again. He had not done that for years. His spirits lifted. God indeed moved in a mysterious way.

· VI ·

1925

AFTER THE TALK, they all got up and crowded around the speaker. His name was Frank Anstey and he was a Labor Member of Parliament. Geoffrey had been told that Frank Anstey was very influential in the party, and some of his father's Labor mates from the Mountain View had come along to listen. At question time, there was a lot of argument about Marxism versus social change and what they should do at the forthcoming elections and Geoffrey had grown restless: he didn't care about social change, and the fellows at the Returned Soldiers' League said that the Australian Labor Party was full of Bolsheviks and Irish Nationalists who wanted to overthrow the Empire. If you could judge a book by its cover, Frank Anstey looked all right, Geoffrey thought. He looked strong, tough and capable. He looked like a sportsman. Someone had asked Mr Anstey a question about the Japanese and Australia. There was a British seamen's strike on and people were saying that the Reds were subverting the country and that they were financed with foreign gold. Most people seemed to agree that the Reds wanted to destroy Australia; that was what the newspapers said.

Throughout the talk, his father listened intently, craning forward on his seat and making notes in his little black notebook. He was out three times a week at Labor Party meetings, and then at the Mountain View with Jack

Hanrahan. His mother had said that his father was never home, so after tea Geoffrey had kept her company. He was working for his father at the bakery, but when he started night school, he too was out three nights a week and again she was left alone. He felt sorry for her, but what could he do? Sometimes she played the piano in the front parlour and sang songs by Victor Herbert and Ivor Novello. *The Italian Street Singer* was one of her favourites. She had a fine soprano voice and played the piano well. Sometimes when his father came home, say, Sunday evenings, he wanted to sing songs by Harry Lauder; but his mother did not approve, saying that they were the songs of drunkards. His father then left the parlour and went to bed or out to the back shed to read his books and drink the whisky which he kept there. It seemed that his mother and father had no mutual friends, and no one came to Rotherwood Street. Things were not too good at home, but Geoffrey stayed: he had little money and nowhere else to go. He had bought a second-hand Indian Scout and sidecar to hold his rods and guns and went to the country by himself at the weekends. The fishing had been good this spring and he usually came home in the evenings with three or four brown trout. He was looking forward to duck-season. Sometimes, though, the country he knew so well, disturbed him when it should have made him happy. The rocks in the paddocks often looked like unexploded mines and he thought he saw troops moving through the dead trees. He had told nobody of this. On Friday night, he went to the Returned Soldiers' League, drank beer and played pool. He was the club champion. There, they mainly talked about tennis, cricket and football. Geoffrey had had a couple of games for the Richmond Seniors at half-back flank this season, but he wasn't that good these days, not since the final in 1921. Being big and strong isn't good enough, the coach said, you've got to show more endeavour, and they put him in the Reserves. He might get a game in the Seniors next season. He was going to church less often, but hadn't told his mother yet. What was the point of upsetting her?

The hall was big, varnished and draughty and pictures of Keir Hardie, George Bernard Shaw and Sidney and Beatrice Webb hung on the wall. The Union Jack and the Eureka flag were also there, and on several small tables by the door lay piles of pamphlets about socialism. The trestle tables were covered with butcher's paper and women were carrying in plates of food from the kitchen. There were hot pies, sausage rolls, jars of pickles, butterfly cakes and sponges on fancy plates with paper doilies underneath. The women were also bringing in bottles of beer and steaming urns of tea. They set big jugs of milk upon the tables. Geoffrey moved away from his father as he didn't know what to say to Mr Anstey or the other men who were gathering around. He didn't know anyone at the meeting, but felt hungry and wondered about getting some food from one of the tables. Nobody seemed to be eating; they were all talking. He looked at the elm trees through the windows. The glass was fogged, it was spring and the nights were still cold. At the weekend, he would ride the Indian Scout, ride north to the quiet, hidden streams and go for the brown trout. That was his country.

Then a young woman, whom Geoffrey hadn't noticed before, came up.

'I'm Marcia Smith,' she said. 'Who are you?'

She was tall, dark and big-boned; she wore a long, white cotton frock, a plain straw hat and glasses. She had big teeth, her eyes were green, and her long black hair was pinned up under her hat. She looked at him square in the face.

'I've been watching you,' she said. 'You don't know anybody here, do you?'

'No, I don't, except my father.'

The men were moving toward the tables. Some of them

100

were arguing and waving their arms. They were opening the bottles of beer and passing the glasses to their mates.

'Who are you?' she said.

'I'm Geoffrey Sawtell.'

He was surprised to find a young woman at the meeting.

'And what do you do?'

'I'm with my father, he's a member.'

She pushed her glasses down her nose and looked at him, laughed and said: 'I didn't ask you who you were with, I said what do you do?'

His father was talking to Mr Anstey and drinking beer; the other men were laying into the food and the women were serving out cups of tea.

'Oh,' Geoffrey said, looking at her as the other men laughed and talked, 'I'm training to be an engineer.'

'Engineering what?'

She was dark and strong and mischievous.

'The Country Roads Board, building bridges and roads.'

'Men, money and machines,' she said.

He could not understand her, and was nervous and puzzled.

'I travel around a lot with maintenance men and go to night school. Richmond Technical College. My father's a member here. I'm not, I'm his guest.' He stood awkwardly as the men laughed and talked. 'What do you do?'

'I work in the State Library.'

Geoffrey said nothing: books did not interest him.

She pushed her glasses back up her nose, fiddled with her straw hat and said: 'Would you like some food?'

'Yes,' Geoffrey said, 'but I'll get it.'

'Oh no you won't,' Marcia Smith said, 'I've got two good legs, I'll get it. You stay here.'

He watched her as she plunged into the crowd of men at the table, her pinned-up hair, the nape of her neck and her broad back. He waited, and she came back quickly with a plate of sausage rolls and pickled onions, two glasses and a bottle of Abbot's Lager. She put the plate of food on the varnished floor, gave him the glasses and poured the beer.

'Tip,' she said, 'or it will be all head and no drink.' She bent and picked up the plate from the floor. 'Have a pickled onion.'

Geoffrey saw his father reach for the whisky bottle; he was telling something to Jack Hanrahan, who was looking old and tired and had contracted tuberculosis.

'Are you ashamed of your father?' she said.

He was angry and said: 'No, not at all, I'm just not a member.'

'Why aren't you a member?'

'Because I'm not interested in politics. My father is, and he invited me. I'm not interested in politics, I don't care what they do.'

He was very tall, fair-haired and strong-looking. He looked like a hero. She touched his arm and said, 'I didn't mean to offend you.' She looked into his face. 'Were you in the Great War?'

'Yes,' Geoffrey said, 'I was, and so were millions of others.' She looked like one of those young women on the pier who were blowing kisses at the soldiers. Someone had wound up the gramophone and it played the *Internationale*.

'Oh God,' she said, 'it's stupid playing that. Why aren't you interested in politics?'

'Because I'm not. Let them do what they want to do. I've done my bit.'

She drank her beer; she seemed to be the only woman in the room. He considered her hair: it was falling down around her neck and throat. She brushed it back from her face and passed him the plate of food.

'Gallipoli?'

'Passchendaele.' He remembered. 'I spent a year in the salient.'

'Oh my God,' she said, looking at his face, 'I understand.'

'No, you don't.'

She blushed and fiddled with her glasses. 'No,' she said, 'I don't.' She was ashamed. 'None of us can, I made a mistake.'

Geoffrey, too, was embarrassed. 'It's just that my father and his mates keep talking about the War and they weren't there. I'm not saying they should have gone, they just weren't there.'

'It was the War that changed everything?'

'Yes, it changed everything.'

Marcia Smith stood in front of him, and looked at this blond, handsome young man. He was well built and wearing a gold watch chain in his waistcoat.

'You're a sportsman?'

'I am,' he laughed. 'I sometimes play half-back flank for Richmond Seniors. That's a No Man's Land position, and the coach says I lack endeavour.' He lacked endeavour, but it seemed there was not much he could do about it.

Frank Anstey was now leaving at the door with a group of men around him; his father was one of them. They were pushing and shoving and trying to shake his hand. Jack Hanrahan was rolling a smoke and sitting on a chair, and the gramophone was playing *Waltzing Matilda*. Geoffrey saw the dark night through the windows. Marcia Smith was beautiful, but he didn't speak to her any more. He wanted to be with his father and took out the gold hunter.

'If you don't mind,' he said, 'I'll just see what my Dad is doing.'

She smiled at him and said: 'You do that. The salient, of course I can't understand.'

He thought of the tired nurses, carting the bodies into the grey medical tents. She could have been one of them.

'I must go and see my father.' He, too, smiled and then plucked up his courage. 'I might see you next time, perhaps.'

'You go and see your father.'

103

Geoffrey Sawtell bowed strangely, and Marcia Smith watched him go.

Geoffrey sat by himself in the Fitzroy Gardens beneath an oak tree; the spring leaves were pale and green. It was Saturday, and he was on his way into town. His mother had said he needed some new shirts. She had turned the collars twice and the cuffs were fraying. A gardener was working in the flower beds, among the crocuses, jonquils and daffodils. The gardener was an old man in his sixties, but from the way he moved between the rows of fragile plants, and from the way he weeded the spring flowers, Geoffrey knew the gardener was a veteran. The gardener had secret skills and knew the rules, why they worked, and when they could be carefully broken. The spring flowers were beautiful, their scent was upon the air, and he thought of his mother working in her garden. He watched the lovers strolling arm in arm beneath the oak trees and down the narrow, winding path to the greenhouse and the strange, imported, tropical plants from Honduras and Brazil. Geoffrey sat beneath the oak and heard the sound of Melbourne's traffic: the sound of the omnibuses and tram cars; the horse-drawn drays and the clatter of the motor cars. He watched the gardener weeding the bluebells and freesias; the gardener was a craftsman and had been apprenticed to a man wiser than he. The lovers walked and Geoffrey watched them. It seemed that the girls were beautiful, wearing their new short dresses, cloche hats and drifting silk scarves. They walked on slender legs through the flower gardens. The men looked very young and sported moustaches, pressed grey suits, felt hats and Fair Isle pullovers. They had not been to the Great War.

He sat beneath the oak tree and watched the gardener and the lovers; he smelled the spring flowers. But now the noise of the traffic seemed unfamiliar and menacing and he could not see the oak trees and Canadian pines properly. A tram bell clanged and he started from the seat and walked quickly down the grassy slope towards the greenhouse and the strange plants. He was unsure where he was going and the stone path seemed tricky; the gentle, ornamental stream ran and he crouched and missed his footing. He felt someone was watching him and he must hide himself. At last, he faced the rockery. What had gone wrong? A gentle wind blew and he saw the loving couples walk through the iron gates of the garden and disappear. He walked to Spencer Street and caught a cable tram.

'Hullo, Geoffrey Sawtell,' she said.

Marcia Smith got on to the Bourke Street cable tram and held on to the rail as the tram rattled down the slope. She had a new frock on – it was at her knees – and a cloche hat, but her dark hair flew and tumbled in the wind. He got up immediately but she said:

'Heavens, no, I'll stand for an old soldier.' She laughed, pushed at her glasses and said, pointing to the oak trees, the maples and the blue sky:

'Isn't it a lovely day?'

They were by the gripman, his hands big with gloves, the huge cogs meshing and the brakes grinding. She continued to stand and the conductor cheerfully demanded their fares. The young men and the urchins clung to the side-boards, some dropped off without paying their fares, and the buildings and trees flashed by; there were gigs and cabs and horse-drawn wagons and motor cars and men and women promenading; the sun was shining, people were strolling. It was indeed a lovely day. Geoffrey got up suddenly at Elizabeth Street and said:

'I'm getting off here, do you want to come?'

She let go the rail as the cable tram stopped. 'Of course I'll come.'

They stepped down together and walked up Bourke
Street past the Myer Emporium past the maple trees and
the patriotic flags. Marcia took his arm; Geoffrey was
surprised but very pleased.

'There's a coffee place here somewhere,' he said.

'Yes, I know it, I'll take you there.'

She thought he looked smart in his suit and starched
collar. They walked along the block and then through the
elegant arcades, stocked with fine and expensive merchandise. She still held his arm and he was proud of her. They
stopped before the window of a grocery store; there were
tins of Twining's tea from China, India and Ceylon,
pressed meats and crates of smoked cod from the North
Sea.

'I've got an Indian Scout and sidecar,' Geoffrey said,
'and I go to the country every weekend, sometimes I go
fishing, do you want to come?'

Marcia grinned at him and fiddled with her dark hair.

'Of course I'll come.'

Geoffrey left the motor bike chained to an old gum tree,
and they walked down country roads, past market gardens
and Jersey cows grazing in paddocks. They looked back at
the buildings of Melbourne: the terracotta roofs of the
bungalows and the brick suburbs baking in the sun.
Groups of Chinese workers were bent double, hoeing rows
of lettuces and tomato plants; white leghorns picked and
poked beneath the hedgerows of hawthorn in full bloom,
and crows stood on blackened stumps. The road was
rutted and pot-holed and Marcia left him, delighted, and
splashed through a puddle. She pointed to the apple
orchards and shouted:

'What a great place for boys, trees to climb, apples to
steal, mysterious roads to ride your bike.'

She ran back to him, her boots sodden and muddy. 'Girls

aren't allowed to come to places like this, except with their parents on picnics. I was, because my father let me; but most have to stay at home and learn to sew and practise the piano.'

She ran away and laughed and shouted. It was a sunny day; there were no shadows here.

On the way out to the countryside, they had passed by gangs of working men laying rails for the new electric trams. The underground cables for the old cars were being torn from the ground by huge, steam-driven machines and the severed, muddy wire lay twisted on the ground. Big men were working with picks, crowbars and shovels. They wore cloth caps and had their shirt sleeves rolled to their elbows. Long lines of horses and drays waited for the rubble and the spoil. The horses were eating from their nosebags. Rusted iron was growing from the ground and braziers were glowing for their morning tea. Old kettles steamed, and some of the men were smoking briar pipes. There were piles of wooden road blocks and stacks of sleepers on the road and the men were bolting up the new rails with huge spanners. It was heavy work and it looked as though the working men were soldiers, and the place was the war.

They came to a broken frontier of wooden houses, corrugated-iron outbuildings and staggering fences. The clouds flew high, her dress blew in the wind and the crows watched them from the gum trees. The paddocks were studded with boulders which seemed to have come from the moon, and long grass grew beneath the post and rail fences. There was the smell of fresh cow manure on the breeze. Suddenly, she took his hand and they walked up the long country road toward the distant row of pines. The crickets sang in the grass and the frogs croaked in the hidden, reedy pools. An old steam traction engine lay rusting in the weeds. He saw her look up at the geese flying west in the clouded, steaming sky. She still held his hand and said:

'You're a big, handsome man, Geoffrey Sawtell, but you don't say much, do you?'

He was embarrassed and said: 'I used to ride my bicycle out here before the War.'

Geoffrey didn't know what to say to her. It wasn't only because she was beautiful and strange: there were calvaries in his mind, and already here, there were monuments to the soldiers at intersections, parks and in the main streets of country towns. *Our Glorious Dead*. He had become a riddle to himself. What would his mother think of Marcia, splashing through puddles, wearing short frocks and going to meetings of the Victorian Labor Party?

'Look,' he said, 'I'll show you something, a place where I used to fish when I was a boy.'

Geoffrey jumped the barbed-wire fence, went to help Marcia, but she had jumped over too. Together, they ran through the long, dry grass where the crickets sang. There were weeping willows ahead, borer-ridden stumps and thorny wild roses. They ran and he stopped her at the brink. There was the creek: the mysterious, deep pool reedy and black, with the willows overhanging. He pointed at the dark water.

'That's where I used to catch eels,' he said.

The small, black stream flowed. He looked into the water, but there was nothing. Then Marcia touched him lightly on the face. He didn't seem to notice and said:

'There's an old bridge further down where you could get brown trout. I'll show you that, too.'

He barged off through the long grass, leaving her behind; and she ran after him, her long dress wet with the water from the reeds and her straw hat tumbling from her hair. She bent, picked it up and ran.

They sat by the bridge, where the black water swirled around the piles and flowed over the green stones. There were dragonflies on the wing and grasshoppers at their

108

feet. The starlings chattered on the old trees. Geoffrey looked again at the water and then at the willows.

'How did you catch eels?' she said.

'With big grubs from rotten logs. It was easy, they would always take them.'

'What did you do with them?'

'I cut their heads off and left them to die. Nobody eats them. There's a saying that eels never die until dawn, but I don't know.'

She was surprised, but said nothing. 'And the trout?'

'They were harder, that's real fishing, I learnt to cast a heavy flyline on the water. It's hard in a small pool like this with all the reeds and trees. But I caught them, I caught them with grasshoppers early in the morning.'

He remembered and was happy. 'You get the hoppers in the dew and put them in a jar before they can jump.'

'And what did you do with the trout?'

He looked surprised. 'I took them home in a sugarsack on the handlebars of my bike for my mother to cook for tea. She used to bake them with potatoes in the stove.'

'Is your mother a good cook?'

'I think she is, she preserves vegetables and fruit, she works hard. We've never gone without.'

'You and your father.'

'Yes,' he said, 'me and my father. I had a brother but he died from infantile paralysis.'

'And it broke your parents' hearts?'

'My mother's. My father's got other things.'

'Has she lost you?'

'Yes,' he said, 'she lost me eight years ago, but I haven't told her yet.'

'What would she think of me?'

'Do you believe in God?'

'I'm a free thinker, so is my father.'

'You would disturb her.'

Marcia lay on the grass by the dark pool, her straw hat

109

over her eyes, her frock spread over her knees and muddy boots. The birds sang. She watched Geoffrey as he looked carefully at the paddocks and the trees. Somewhere, a farmer was cutting wood with a steam-saw.

'What are you looking for?'

'Wooden crosses,' Geoffrey said. 'When we marched past the farm houses in Belgium, the peasants were making crosses.'

'And you've not told your mother?'

He did not reply. The birds sang in the hawthorn trees and a wedgetail eagle hung still in the sky.

Marcia lay upon the grass, but he didn't look at her at all, but went back to the water and watched it flow. He walked away, alone, under the bridge, where it was dark and silent. There was a small brown trout swimming close to the bottom of the pool; it was feeding in the gravel. He wished he had his rod and line. He moved carefully beneath the bridge and searched among the reeds for deep pools and quiet places where big fish might be. The creek looked barren, and there was nothing to be seen. He put his hand in the cold water and the sullen stream flowed. An old gum had fallen across the creek and rotting weed flowed from its branches. He looked up, over the bank. What was beyond that row of pines? He crouched in the hollow water, he was in a crater and seemed powerless. But this time, he had a friend with him and he was safe. He wanted to tell Marcia about the landscape in his mind, and the hedges of wire. She would understand. He ran from the bridge and up the bank. But Marcia had gone. He looked for her around the countryside and didn't know where to find her. He lay on the grass, thinking about her, the breeze blew and the sun shone upon him and he fell asleep. The bushflies buzzed and settled on his clothes. He dreamed of Smith in the sap and the sodden greatcoat falling. A big brown trout swam under the bridge and around the piles and rose to take a fly from the dark water, but Geoffrey did not see it. He slept upon the ground for some time.

Then Marcia was back, opening the picnic hamper, she touched his body and said:

'Geoffrey, I've got some sandwiches, do you want some?'

Her eyes were green and there were tiny pearl buttons at her wrists, she was on her knees, pushing her glasses up her nose with her long, strong fingers. He smiled at her, took a sandwich and ate it. The corned beef tasted good, and he took another. She took off her hat and unpinned her hair, and she laid her hands upon her knees.

'Where have you been?' Geoffrey said.

'Oh, I went for a walk. You were down at the bridge.' He said nothing and looked at her hair and the pearl buttons at her wrists.

'Your father's a socialist,' she said.

'He's dedicated, a dreamer,' Geoffrey said. 'He was born in Glasgow and came out here when he was a child. His father was a slaughterman, he's a baker and works long hours. I should know, I worked for him after I left school. Like you, he's a free thinker. I think you'd like him.'

'And your mother doesn't approve?'

'No, she doesn't, she's very religious.' He thought of the Mountain View and the working men, the spigots, Jack Hanrahan and the songs. 'And it's also his mates and the drinking.'

'She doesn't approve of his politics or his mates?'

'Both, but I suppose it's his mates and his drinking. They're all Holy Romans, Irishmen who opposed the War.'

'Why doesn't your mother leave your father?'

'Leave? She can't, they're married, what would she do?'

'Married women can leave their husbands, you know,' Marcia said.

'Not in my book.'

'You think marriage is for ever?'

'I hadn't thought about it. What does your father do?'

He saw some geese flying low and wished he had his shotgun. Marcia ate her sandwich and said: 'He's a teacher at a small school; like your father, he's a free thinker, he's not very popular.' Marcia delved into the hamper. 'I love him; he's given me what wisdom I have, and he let me ramble in the countryside and didn't make me stay at home and learn sewing.' She offered him the last corned beef sandwich. 'He's made me strong, he's made me self-reliant, just like a man.'

Geoffrey thought of the dark, moving water and said:

'Well, he's like my father then.' But he knew that her father was not. Her father wouldn't drink at the Mountain View with people like Jack Hanrahan in small back rooms.

'And your mother?' he said.

'My mother's dead.'

'I'm sorry.'

She shrugged her broad shoulders. 'You needn't be. I never knew her, she died having me.'

Geoffrey thought of his mother kissing him at the pier when he had come home, of never letting him go, of his father standing silently in the dark kitchen and getting out the whisky. He looked at Marcia, hunched up by the creek, eating her sandwich, and wanted her, but didn't know what to do. There were grey moths fluttering through the grass. He consulted the gold hunter and said:

'It's four o'clock, it's time we were getting back.'

'How old are you, Geoffrey?'

'Twenty-seven, and you?'

'Twenty-three.'

'Have you ever had a girl friend?'

'Aw, yes, there was an English girl in London once during the War, but it didn't come to anything.' He looked her in the face. 'I think you're beautiful.' He picked up the hamper.

'It's time we were getting back.' The shadows were lengthening from the gum trees and hawthorn hedges, the sun shone through the willow trees and it was getting cold. Marcia looked up and saw the geese were flying home over the hills and far away. She got up from the grassy bank, smoothed her dress, picked up her bag and said: 'I think I might love you, Geoffrey Sawtell, I'm quite sure my father would approve.'

Geoffrey shivered. What should he do? His father would be at the Mountain View and his mother would be getting the tea.

'Do you play tennis?' she said.

'Yeah, I do, I play like Jean Borotra.'

'Next Saturday?'

'Next Saturday.'

'And golf?'

'Golf too.' He grinned. 'I'll give you a game on Sunday.'

Together, they left this strange place and set out down the road to the Indian Scout. He would drive Marcia home. He glanced at the countryside as they walked. Sleeping tonight would be difficult, and it would be too late to have a whisky with his father and Jack Hanrahan.

It was a brilliant Saturday afternoon, the land birds were flying high; they had played three sets of tennis and he had won, narrowly. Geoffrey rode the motor bike north to the red, stony plains, she in the sidecar and he driving to the endless Australian hinterland. This time, they went further: there was no sign of the city and no sign of cultivation. Her hair flew in the wind, and they drove north to broken fences and fields of stone. At last they came to a rocky place, a small gorge on the high plains with strange trees from prehistory and a stream flowing over a vast, shallow bed of stone. The early summer sun shone upon them. Geoffrey looked across the country for livestock, but there was none. Only the rabbits ran. Marcia took off her goggles and got out of the sidecar. She put on her straw hat, shaded her eyes and gazed at the landscape, the dry paddocks, the bent trees and the boulders from the moon.

She walked down to the stream, sat upon a rock and raised her tennis dress above her knees. She squinted and saw Geoffrey coming down the narrow path to the river stones and reeds. There was dirt on the knees of his white flannels and his face was already tanned by the sun. He sat beside her and looked at the water.

'You do play like Jean Borotra,' she said, as she took off her sandshoes and wriggled her toes in the grass.

'Well, you ain't too bad yourself. Do you want another game next Saturday?'

'Yes,' she said, 'I do.'

Nothing more was said, and they looked at the dry stone walls and fences. A dead sheep was hanging in the wire and the crows waited patiently on the posts. The small stream flowed.

'Would there be fish in this river?' she said.

The fresh was on and there was mud in the water.

'No,' he said, 'there's no fish in this stream.' There was no life in the water. 'Come on, put your tennis shoes back on and we'll go for a walk.'

Together, they walked the high, lonesome road that meandered across the plains. The earth was pitted with stones, and to the north lay the flat-topped mountains. Hand in hand, they walked and considered the earth: the rocks piled against the fences, the ash from black fires and the ramparts of iron. They gently talked of tennis, the weather and country affairs, and walked through the droughty paddocks. Suddenly, on the high plateau, he took Marcia by the waist and kissed her on the lips and smelt her body. He looked down upon the stream and said:

'This was once a river, but now it's come down to this.'

She smiled at him, and they walked down the hill, through the boulders and outcrops toward the barren stream. There were mullock heaps and the remains of antediluvian machinery where Victorian miners had worked. The rabbits ran and prehistoric thistles grew

114

among the tailings and discarded machinery. It had rained recently, fresh grass grew, and God had tried to make this place beautiful. They reached the water and a lone duck swam on the dark and tranquil surface, where nothing lived. Not one bird sang as they walked carefully across the aged rocks, where forgotten cables lay and trees stood dying. Marcia gripped his hand and said:

'This is bad country, it's all been worked out.'

The plateau and the plains had been besieged by ancient winds.

'It can be brought back,' Geoffrey said, but he knew it could not. There was a soft, grassy spot and they lay upon it; she kissed him, the sun shone, and they lay together upon the grass while the barren stream flowed.

'I suppose I should meet your mother,' Marcia said.

'And I should meet your father.'

'I've told you, my father would approve, he plays tennis and golf. What's your handicap?'

'I play off twelve.'

'Christ, you *are* good.'

Geoffrey took her hand and said: 'I told you, love, I'm a sportsman.'

'Should we get married?'

'Aw, I don't know, it's a bit soon, let's wait a bit and play more tennis. We could get engaged.'

'Good Lord, Geoffrey,' she said and laughed, 'people are either in love or they're not.'

'Okay, I love you, and you'd better meet my mother, I shall tell her all about you.'

'Yes,' she said, 'you tell her all about me.'

He thought of his mother's flowers decorating St Stephen's on Mothering Sunday and said: 'I shall.'

Marcia stood up and said: 'I don't believe in God, and my father doesn't either, you'd better tell your mother that.'

'I shall,' Geoffrey said.

115

But he remembered his mother weeping in church on Palm Sunday and the little, faded, flax cross in his prayer-book.

'Can you ballroom dance?' she said.

'A bit, I'm not quite like Borotra.'

'Let's go to the Menzies.'

'The Menzies? What for?'

'Dancing.'

'When?'

'Next Friday.'

'Okay then.' He laughed and hugged her. 'Okay then.'

Marcia Smith, big-boned and strongly cheerful, got up and faced the landscape. She pushed her glasses back up her nose, kissed him and said:

'I don't believe in God and the Holy Trinity, I don't believe that marriage is for ever and I'm a socialist, but I love you.' She stalked off, and he watched her go as she disappeared behind some rocks. He saw a wallaby in the distance, watching him.

He waited for her and wished she would come back. But it was twilight and getting cold when she did.

He met her at the tram stop on Bridge Road and they walked down Rotherwood Street. She was wearing a long frock and her straw hat, and they walked past the paddock where the old apple trees grew, and the pines. The early evening was still and the frogs at the creek croaked. Geoffrey looked at the hawthorn trees, and the flowers had turned to berries.

The blackbirds and starlings flew between the thorny branches. Marcia ran over the street to the fence.

'That's a fine paddock, and there's a creek at the bottom, and apple trees.'

'You can't eat them,' Geoffrey said. 'They're all dry and woody.'

116

'Most old things are.' She laughed and kissed him on the lips. Hand in hand, they walked down Rotherwood Street. He opened the gate and they strolled through his mother's garden to the verandah where she was waiting. She watched the two of them come up the wooden steps.

'Mother,' Geoffrey said, 'I'd like you to meet Marcia Smith.'

Marcia bowed and Mary Sawtell was pleased to see she was wearing a long dress.

'Please sit down next to me,' she said, 'it's such a pleasant evening. I'm afraid Geoffrey's father isn't home yet, he apparently has work to do.'

There was a silence and the evening birds fluttered in the oak trees and the pines. Geoffrey looked at the two women sitting on the seat. Marcia looked at Geoffrey as he sat on the verandah fence, his strong body and his legs swinging.

'You have a lovely garden, Mrs Sawtell.'

'It reminds me of home.'

'Home?'

'England, I was born there.'

Like Geoffrey, Mrs Sawtell was very handsome. The cicadas sang and Marcia looked at Mary Sawtell's pale blue eyes, her fair skin and her long, pinned-up blonde hair. She sat in her long white dress on her seat on the verandah and waited for her husband to come. She looked a lonely, but determined woman who would not give up easily what she thought was hers. From what Marcia knew, Geoffrey's father and mother had little in common and now her other son was about to leave her: he had memories he could not tell her about and had fallen in love.

Geoffrey glanced at Marcia sitting on the seat next to his mother and listened to the cicadas. He knew his father was drinking with Jack Hanrahan and his mates, and that quite soon tea would be spoiled, but he didn't care. He wanted to leave home and marry Marcia. At last, he saw his father coming down Rotherwood Street; he opened the front gate

117

and mounted the steps. He looked cheerful, raised his hat at Marcia and said:

'Good evening, I'm Angus Sawtell, you're George Smith's daughter?'

Marcia had seen Angus Sawtell before at Labor Party meetings; he was a small, dark man, most unlike his son, but she liked the look of him. 'Yes,' she said, 'I am.'

He came up to her and held out his hand; she took it and smelt the whisky. Mary Sawtell stood up and smoothed her dress.

'Now we can have tea,' she said, 'before it gets spoiled.'

The house was spotless, the linoleum shone, the vases were filled with flowers and there were family photographs on the walls.

'Please sit in the front parlour,' Mary Sawtell said, 'while I serve the tea.'

Geoffrey and Marcia sat on the sofa, but Angus went to the door and shouted down the hall: 'Have we got time for a lager?'

'No,' came his wife's voice, 'we have not.'

'Never mind,' Angus said to Marcia and Geoffrey, 'we can have some later. We might sing around the piano.'

Marcia looked around the front room: this was an orderly house, nothing was out of place, but no one was happy here. She was glad she lived with her father where all was confusion. There were several photographs of Geoffrey and his brother: two of them when they were choir boys, a family portrait with both boys in smocks and another of Geoffrey by himself in military uniform in 1915. He was smiling and full of confidence. She had been fifteen when Geoffrey had fought at Passchendaele, and could remember the casualty lists as they grew longer in the paper every day. It seemed that the Great War would stay with Australia for ever.

'Well, Marcia,' Angus Sawtell said, 'who's going to win the election?' He had used her first name and asked her a political question. She liked him for that.

'The National Party,' she said. 'There's a Red scare on.'

'That's what the boys at the RSL say,' Geoffrey said.

'What?'

'That the bolsheviks are behind the seamen's strike.' He grinned.

'Oh, Geoffrey.'

He got up and put his hands on her head, and Angus Sawtell smiled. He liked Marcia Smith and knew he could talk politics with her. They might get married: he hoped they would. Then Mary Sawtell called and they went down the hall to have tea.

Mary Sawtell served roast mutton, potatoes, cabbage and mint sauce. His father carved the roast and passed the plates around. Geoffrey's mother had worked hard, the food was good, the grandfather clock ticked and chimed and the cat sat on the window shelf, watching them as they ate. The western sun was strong and his mother had lowered the blinds. Little was said, and Marcia thought that this was a silent family: there was no laughter and lively conversation here. She didn't mind, she ate her food and Geoffrey was beside her. Mrs Sawtell asked her what she did, and she said she worked at the State Library. This seemed to please her, but she didn't ask why she was alone, she didn't ask about her mother and father. Mrs Sawtell was a polite, strong woman and she would no doubt ask Geoffrey these questions after she had gone. Angus didn't mention politics again and Geoffrey went into his shell. Marcia wondered about marriage, if this was what it became, maybe you were better off by yourself, but what could be worse than a life of spinsterhood? Then during dessert, Mrs Sawtell asked her what church she went to. Marcia thought for a bit before she answered, and finally she said she didn't go at all. Angus looked up, Mary Sawtell fell silent and Geoffrey said:

'That was a nice tea, Mother, can we help you wash up?'

'No,' she said, 'Angus and I will do it. You go and sit in the front room.'

Marcia and Geoffrey left the dining room and went down the hall to the front verandah. It was dark now and the moon had risen. There was a gentle breeze and the frogs croaked in the paddock over the road. They sat on the seat and held hands.

'She had to know,' Marcia said.

'Oh God, it's not that important.'

'It is, to her. You're all she's got.'

'Not any more, I want to get married definitely, do you?'

'Yes,' she said, 'I do.'

Geoffrey kissed her on the lips, the breeze blew and smelled of the bush and they went inside.

After Geoffrey asked her, his mother agreed to sing and he accompanied her. Angus sat beside Marcia, drank his lager and watched them both at the piano. Geoffrey played very well and they both sang songs from *Naughty Marietta*. Marcia was delighted at Geoffrey's gentle baritone voice; she had not heard him sing and play before. They sang three or four songs and Angus got a fresh bottle of lager. He offered a glass to Marcia and they drank together and listened to the music. This, she thought, was the best part of the evening and their voices drifted through the house and sometimes as she sang, Mary Sawtell put her hand on her son's shoulder. Then Angus asked his son if he would sing a solo. Geoffrey was embarrassed, but finally agreed and sang *The Honeysuckle and the Bee*. Marcia saw Geoffrey's mother sit very still as he sang, then she went to the kitchen to make another cup of tea. It got to half past ten and Marcia said it was time for her to go. She thanked Mrs Sawtell for the evening and Angus shook her hand on the verandah and said he hoped she would come again.

'I'll take you home in the Scout,' Geoffrey said.

'No, I'll get a tram. I don't need looking after.'

He walked with her to the tram stop at the top of Rotherwood Street, saw her get on and wave and smile through the window. Geoffrey watched the tram rattle

120

along Bridge Road, then walked back home. When he got inside, he wanted to talk to his mother about Marcia, but she had gone to bed and the house was still and silent. His father was still sitting in the front room with a glass of whisky in his hand.

'That's a nice girl,' he said.

Geoffrey considered having a whisky with his father, but decided not.

'Yes,' he said. 'If you don't mind, I'm off to bed.'

'I suppose you should talk to your mother,' his father said. Geoffrey did not reply and closed the door.

In his room, Geoffrey Sawtell thought about Marcia, her walking with hin on the stony plain, of their tennis and her running across the street to the old apple orchard. If nothing bad happened, he could live with her for ever. He sang to himself.

You are my honey, honeysuckle, I am the bee,
I'd like to sip the honey sweet from those red lips, you see;
I love you dearly, dearly, and I want you to love me,
You are my honey, honeysuckle, I am the bee.

Marcia and Geoffrey were married on 21 January 1926. They were married in the Registry Office and Mary Sawtell did not attend. Marcia's father was ill and could not go, but Geoffrey's father went with Jack Hanrahan and some mates from the Mountain View. They spent their honeymoon at the seaside town of Queenscliff and stayed in an old rambling hotel by the sea. The weather was hot and clear; they swam, sailed a clinker-built dinghy, played golf and tennis and went on moonlit cruises in a steam boat across the Bay. It was a good time, and the summer seemed it would never end.

· VII ·

Bourke

THE KETTLE BOILED on the wood stove and Sawtell made the tea.

'I've prepared a list of essentials,' he said. 'But what's the food situation?'

'Very satisfactory,' St John Jackson said. 'There's one warehouse still intact, under lock and key, that's where we shall get our supplies from. It's not quite Fortnum & Mason.'

'You mean there's no Dundee marmalade or smoked salmon?'

'I'm afraid not.'

'There's nothing better than marmalade with billy tea.'

'Indeed, Mr Sawtell.'

'What's in the warehouse?'

'Bran and oats for the horses, sugar, salt, bully beef, rice, tea and tinned vegetables.'

'Enough to get us down the Darling and on to Broken Hill?'

'If your calculations are correct, more than enough.'

'Right, we'll get that together tomorrow. Here's the essentials. Counihan and I have everything except binoculars and matches.'

'Let me see,' St John Jackson said. He sat down at the table, poured the tea into enamel mugs and read Sawtell's neat handwriting in the notebook. This man was thorough if nothing else.

'We've also lost our dividers,' Sawtell said.

'We can manage all that. I've got some excellent Zeiss binoculars, but one question, Mr Sawtell, what about explosives?'

'We've got dynamite, petrol and fuse, and with respect, Major, you can leave that to me.'

'With pleasure, Mr Sawtell, I have a limited knowledge of the subject. And spare horseshoes?'

'Counihan and O'Donohue are down at the smithy now. The boy's chosen five packhorses and they're hot shoeing. We'll have two spare sets for each horse. Counihan can make shoes out of almost anything.'

St John Jackson looked at Sawtell. 'And the pack saddles?'

'O'Donohue's been scrounging, he and Counihan will work out something that won't break their backs. The boy's good, Major, he's only eighteen but been on stations all his life. His father taught him well.'

'Mr Counihan is a very versatile man, is he not?'

'He is, Major, he is.'

'How long have you known him?'

'For almost a year now. As you know, we fought together.'

'Your best friend?'

Sawtell considered and drank his tea. His friends had been few and far between. There had been Smith, Marcia, his mates at the War and his father, and he had liked Jack Hanrahan.

'No, Major, in my life I've had better friends than Frank Counihan, but you have to narrow your choice in times like these.' He thought about asking St John Jackson about Sergius Donaldson, but decided not.

'He doesn't care for British officers?'

'No, he doesn't. His parents were Irish Catholics from

123

Dublin and he's carrying on the battle. Counihan is a plain-minded man, or what you might call a provincial: in this country, Major, we're all provincials.'

'I spent one year in Dublin before I went to India.'

'You know the story then.'

'I do.'

But, thought Sawtell, did the Englishman know what rebellion was about? However, he knew he would need him: he was a thorough, professional soldier. It wasn't his fault that the *Prince of Wales* and the *Repulse* were at the bottom of the South China Sea.

'And you, Mr Sawtell?' St John Jackson said. 'You don't care for us either?'

'To be frank, Major, not particularly. I think you know: the Great War. We lost more men than any other country per head, the British treated us like dirt, and I agree with Frank Counihan about Malaya and Singapore. Look, Major, I don't intend to get into a discussion about the Australians and the British. All I know is that, this time, it's my country that's been invaded and it's your turn to fight for the Empire on unfamiliar ground.'

'Unfamiliar ground? It seems I've always fought on unfamiliar ground: France, India, Ireland. The Irish, Mr Sawtell, were traitors.'

'Not in Frank Counihan's book.' He remembered the endless discussions in the bar of the Mountain View. 'So were the Scots once.'

'You know your history, Mr Sawtell.'

'A bit. All I want to do is blow up that mine at Broken Hill. It's on Colonel Madigan's list.'

'Do you trust anybody, Mr Sawtell?'

'Very few people, sir.'

St John Jackson smiled. 'That squares it away then. I shall perform to the best of my abilities. You have my word on that. In our own ways, we are both soldiers.'

Sawtell looked at the Englishman, the neat haircut, the

moustache and the clean-shaven chin, the poems of Rudyard Kipling and his father's Purdey shotgun. He thought of Frank Counihan, working on bankrupt stations and the Port Pirie railway, the remote boarding houses and his old deserted mother. There had been no one to tuck Frank into bed and to recite to him Victorian nursery rhymes. The School of Life. Counihan did not wear his father's signet ring.

'Yes, Major,' Sawtell said, 'we're both soldiers, and you might find Frank Counihan is too.'

They considered each other and drank their tea.

'Where on earth are the Americans?' St John Jackson said. He, too, felt a sense of betrayal.

'I think I've told you, Major, the last we heard they had gone to New Zealand. General MacArthur seems unable to return.' Sawtell got up from the table, took out his tobacco tin and rolled a cigarette. He didn't care where the Americans were. One day at a time, get to Broken Hill and blow the Zinc Corporation Mine. Madigan's orders made sense. It was like the Depression, there was no sense arguing about it, just get on with it and do the best you can. He moved around the room and looked out of the window. There was still the smoke from the blackfellows' fires. They could have the river. The Major had been cleaning the Purdey, and the ramrods and brushes lay neatly on the mantelpiece. It was a very fine shotgun and he wondered if the Major might let him use it. He thought not.

'What school did you go to, Major?'

'Marlborough.'

'I went to Richmond Technical College. We didn't study the classics there, it was a place for the sons of working men to improve upon the lot of their fathers.' He thought of the navvies, working with their crowbars on the Melbourne tramlines.

'What's Padre Donaldson's experience, Major?'

'His experience?'

'His military experience.'

'Ah.' The Major, too, took up Geoffrey's tobacco tin and papers. 'May I?'

'Go ahead.'

The Major rolled his cigarette expertly. 'Donaldson fought at Loos, where I first met him, then on the Somme. The latter, you and I know well.'

'Fought?'

'Helped, administered, soldiers do need help, you know.' Sawtell laughed.

'As far as I know,' St John Jackson said, 'Donaldson never took up arms, but he's a courageous man, I can vouch for that.'

'Courageous?'

'Yes, Mr Sawtell, courageous, he got me out of a spot at Loos, front-line stuff.' St John Jackson coughed. 'That is why I admire him.'

Oh God, Sawtell thought, the English public schoolboys, but there was Lieutenant Atkins from Melbourne Grammar. Their education was in their faces. Then he thought of the clergyman from New South Wales in the dugout and the prayerbook lying on the dirt floor. *You run along, and I'll expect you at Holy Communion.*

'Tell me, Mr Sawtell, where did Counihan get that Luger submachine gun?'

'In Ballarat from some old soldier. It uses the same ammunition as the Sten, 9mm, it's an unreliable but terrifying weapon.'

'That I know. And he used it at Newcastle?'

'With great effect, there's nothing like Great War machinery, especially German.'

'Tell me, Mr Sawtell, do you believe in God?'

'No, sir, I do not. My mother did, but I do not.'

'And Mr Counihan?'

'He's a Roman Catholic like young O'Donohue.' His

mother had said that the Holy Romans always reverted to form, that being a Catholic was easy.

'And you, Major?'

'Belief in God is essential.' St John Jackson rose from the table. 'This list does not include liquor, which I should have thought is also essential.'

The rum for the other ranks and whisky for the officers. Sawtell smiled and said: 'I agree, Major, and so would Frank Counihan, and so, I think, would Padre Donaldson.'

'That liquor is essential.'

'That liquor is essential.'

'That, Mr Sawtell, is one thing we have in common.'

'It is, sir. We shall have, as you say, to forage.'

St John Jackson thought of the gins and tonics in the officers' mess at Meerut, the pegs of whisky, of riding next morning on the plains and the games of violent tennis. India was a soldier's paradise, the escape to the hill stations in the summer. Those were the days. He looked at his watch: it was twelve noon, in India the day would be over.

'I take it that you've inspected the hotels in this town, Major?'

'Inspected? They were ransacked by your countrymen, there's not one drop left in the township. As you know, young O'Donohue is our supplier, he seems to have the knack.'

Sawtell said: 'I think Counihan could find something.'

'I'm sure he could. Do you drink port, Mr Sawtell?'

'Port?' He laughed. 'We Australians drink anything, you know that.'

'But mainly beer?'

Sawtell thought of the kegs of draught bitter at the Mountain View and Jack Hanrahan's back room, the smell of onions and sad tunes on the harmonica. He thought of the half whiskies at Wrigley's on Victoria Street and the muscat with the men by the fire at Deep Lead. Those were the days.

127

'My father drank whisky, he was the son of a Scot from Glasgow.'

'Indeed, and did you learn to drink from your father?'

'I learned to drink where you did, Major, in the trenches.'

Sawtell rose to leave the room, to go and see Frank Counihan at the smithy, but St John Jackson said:

'There's one other matter to discuss, and that is the destruction of Bourke.'

The door opened, and Padre Donaldson walked in. He had been riding and was soaking with sweat.

'Good morning, Padre,' Sawtell said, 'would you care for some tea?'

'I would indeed. Gentlemen, I have some news: I have just sighted two enemy aircraft.'

'You're sure they were enemy?' St John Jackson said.

'Absolutely, they were Zeros, flying low from the southwest.'

'They wouldn't see much,' Sawtell said. 'Only smoke from the blackfellows' fires and the smithy. I wonder if young O'Donohue saw them, it would convince him that the Japanese are here.'

The Major walked to the window and looked down the main street. Nothing moved.

'All the same, Mr Sawtell, this is not good news.'

'It's not. Where were you when you saw them, Padre?'

'About five miles down the river.'

'What's the range of a Zero?' Sawtell said. 'There's an aerodrome at Broken Hill, they could have come from there.' There was no reply. 'Well, Major, if you agree, we'd better get on with it. I'd like to be away the day after tomorrow.'

'I agree, Mr Sawtell. This time, I've got *my* list.'

'List?' Sergius Donaldson said.

'Items of destruction, Colonel Madigan's inventory.'

'I hope it won't be an orgy.'

'Don't worry, Padre,' Sawtell said, 'there's only five of us, we'll divide the work up. Do you want the job of shooting the horses?'

'I would prefer not.' He looked at Sawtell and did not like the man.

'What's on your list, Major?'

'The fuel dump, telephone exchange, the railway, bulk food supplies and livestock. And there's the bridge which, I fear, could present a problem.'

'There's no way we can take the bridge out,' Sawtell said. 'We haven't got enough explosives, but we'll do our best.'

They divided the work, and the destruction of the town was planned. When they had finished, Sawtell went down to the smithy.

Kevin O'Donohue was working on the anvil. He was a strong young man and the sweat ran down his arms.

'Where's the Padre?' he said. 'I want to shoe his nag.'

'He's been out riding, he'll be down shortly. Old habits die hard.'

'What habits?'

'British officers always go riding in the morning.'

'What's he been doing?' Counihan said. 'Hunting foxes?'

'He's seen two aircraft, Zeros.'

The two men stopped working, and O'Donohue was excited.

'We heard nothing,' Counihan said.

'They were five miles away, in the south-west. We're leaving the day after tomorrow.'

Sawtell looked at the packhorses. He inspected their hocks, tendons and fetlocks and looked for cuts, lumps and old scars. O'Donohue had chosen well: they were sturdy and high-withered and, if looked after, would go a long way. There were three packframes lying on the smithy floor. O'Donohue left the anvil and joined Sawtell.

Counihan worked the bellows and the fire glowed. O'Donohue had found grain bags and kerosene cases for the pack frames. He had also found some old army blankets and saddlebags.

'It's all a bit makeshift, but it'll have to do.'

'It looks okay to me. What's the feed situation?'

'We've got oats, pollard and salt, the country's poor where we're going.'

Sawtell went up to his own horse, looked at its fetlocks and feet. He stroked its nose; it was a good, strong animal and had served him well. It would be hard if he lost it, and he hoped that wouldn't happen.

'What's to do?' O'Donohue said.

'I wish you'd seen those Zeros, then you'd know the Japs are here.'

'Aw, Christ, I know they're here, it's just funny to be fighting somebody you can't see.'

'Most wars are like that. In the Great War I never saw a Hun for a year.'

'Go on?'

Counihan came over, wiping his hands. He rolled a cigarette.

'Well, that's that, two spare sets for every horse. When the old bloke comes over we've finished. Does he think we're his bloody servants or something?'

'Patience, Frank, Donaldson will have his uses.'

'What uses?'

'Don't underestimate him, that's all. We've all got to get along in the next five weeks.'

'Aw.' Counihan sniffed and blew his nose into the dirt. Sergius Donaldson arrived, his big grey waler was shod, and later that afternoon, they lifted their food from the warehouse and the destruction began.

Occasionally as they worked, they looked up at the sky, but there were no aircraft. They worked all next day and by the evening, little of any value remained. The fires

130

burned and the smoke climbed high. If a thing was worth doing, it was worth doing well: the telephone exchange was smashed, bores and pumps disabled, wells poisoned with creosote, as many taps as they could find were left running and the water flowed down the gutters. The points at the railhead were blown, the Victorian station building set on fire and the valves and compressors smashed in the dairy factory. As far as they could manage, everything of use to the enemy was destroyed or made useless. The Englishmen were impressed by the Australians' ingenuity. At the fuel dump, Counihan opened the sludge valves and ignited the tanks with oily waste; and at the warehouse, Sawtell had slit and poisoned the bags of flour with linseed oil. O'Donohue pitched sheeps' carcasses down wells and smashed the cylinder heads of tractors. Counihan used his sledgehammer and broke up carts, buggies and sulkies: it was an efficient inventory of destruction. It took them all day; there were explosions, the fires burned and Counihan's sledgehammer rang. They did their best to scorch the earth. All the pubs were searched, but not a drop was found. They did, however, find some tobacco in a grocery store, and for that small mercy, they were grateful. O'Donohue left that afternoon and made one last search for liquor, but came back empty-handed. They had two bottles of Scotch to last them ten days unless they found something at a station on the way, and that would have to do. Counihan slaughtered one of the steers they had shot, so they had fresh meat for a couple of days. Meat would be no worry as the country was over-run with wild sheep, roos, rabbits and foxes. There would be water-fowl on the river. They finished at seven and, as the fires burned, Sawtell was dying for a cold beer; but there was none. No one suggested they open the whisky: that would be needed on the track. Little was said; the Major and the Padre retired to their house and O'Donohue dossed down with Counihan and Sawtell. It grew dark quickly and the smoke obscured the moon. There had been no sign of the blackfellows since they had knocked out their tank. Maybe they had gone.

In his room, Sergius Donaldson prayed that God would assist them in their best endeavours, read the 41st Psalm, cleaned his shotgun and opened his Communion case. He held up the small chalice: there was no wine, but he had a few wafers left. Maybe Francis, at least, might want the Holy Sacrament.

The Padre fingered his father's crucifix and put it back in his tunic pocket and thought about the big waler they had given him. The stock saddle was uncomfortable, but if luck was with them, they might pick up a cavalry saddle on the way. That could be a blessed relief in the wilderness ahead. Counihan had shod the waler well and there was no doubt the Australians knew how to care for their horses. He thought of his father riding his big mare to visit the parishioners on the glebe when he was a boy before the Great War, and that pleased him. What would happen at Broken Hill? It didn't matter, at least they were on the move. The Australians might be uncouth, but at least there was a military objective in view. He also thought about St John Jackson's decision to allow Sawtell to lead the party. Was that wise? He supposed it was, as the man knew the country. He and Francis had had bully beef and tea for supper. There was little conversation and they did not discuss the Australians; there was no need to, they had seen them at work and knew what they were like. At least they were more disciplined than the rabble that had come down from Darwin; those had been terrible days. The looting and the violence had been unbearable and thank God they had gone. This seemed to be a disastrous war, the Americans had betrayed them and God knows what was happening in Europe. Like the Great War, would it go on for ever? Sergius Donaldson took up the chalice once more and thought of the church services in Meerut and Singa-

132

pore. It was a strange party: two Roman Catholics and three Protestants. He laughed, there were two active Christians; they were in the minority, but that had always been the way. Sawtell was a strange fellow: he had watched him shoot the remaining horses at the saleyards. Counihan had driven them up the race, one by one, and Sawtell had shot them between the eyes with his Lee Enfield. It had been quick and efficient, like the boy Sawtell had killed on the way in. He thought. Needs must when the Devil drives. Donaldson looked out the window at the smoke from the fires, gathered up his belongings, said a silent prayer and went to bed. He would shave and bathe himself in the morning.

St John Jackson took his photographs down from the wall and put them in his saddlebag with his Bible and the sheet music of *HMS Pinafore*. He put the Purdey in the gun bag and the cartridges in the ammunition pouches. He had smashed the wireless and had considered the upright piano, but decided that a piano was of no military value. It had been a satisfactory day and there was no doubt that Sawtell was an efficient soldier. They would now have to see what happened on the expedition. He fiddled with his father's signet ring, worked the bolt of the BSA and looked at himself in the mirror. Did the Japanese, he wondered, play pianos? He thought not. This was indeed the strangest war he had been in, a bad dream, but Donaldson's sighting of the Zeros yesterday had put paid to that. He started to pack and did it very neatly: spare underclothing, tunics, boots, his scarf, socks, puttees, needle and thread, gun oil and medical kit. He placed Kipling's poems next to his Bible, took out his toothbrush and cleaned his teeth in the enamel bowl. It was now quite dark and the paraffin lamp gleamed. He placed his cut-throat and shaving brush on the table; he would rise, wash and shave at 0500 hours. The paraffin lamp was extinguished, and the Major, very tired, went to bed.

After he had packed his gear for the morning, Sawtell

133

went for a walk down the main street to survey their handiwork. The fires at the petrol dump, the warehouses and the woolstores burned. The smoke billowed and Sawtell thought this had been a satisfactory day. Counihan and O'Donohue were playing pontoon in the small kitchen and he had left them to it. Cards bored him, and as he walked, he thought of the bushfires he had fought at Rubicon and of Marcia leaving him. *I have a lover.* The barren stream and the dead sheep hanging in the wire. He laughed to himself, rolled a cigarette and walked towards the fires. He passed an old tennis court where the grass grew, rank and tall, and the wire netting sagged. *I play like Borotra.* In the darkness of smoke and fire, Geoffrey Sawtell walked towards the river, but he knew there would be no mossy stones and brown trout swimming there. He looked upon the lifeless water. When he returned, Counihan and O'Donohue were still playing pontoon. Sawtell said goodnight, tossed his mutilated prayer book into his saddlebag and went to bed.

They left Bourke at seven o'clock and rode down the main street past the old bond stores and woolsheds. The fires still burned and the smoke drifted into the opaque sky. They rode down the main street, past the war memorial, the five soldiers, each with his packhorse, as the smoke rose and a light north wind blew. Not one windmill turned. They rode south-west towards the river where the trees grew in the water and the hulks of Victorian paddle steamers lay stranded on the mudbanks. As he rode wearing his topee, St John Jackson looked north-west; he rode easily and looked at the dark and ugly ranges, the saltbush, the flat-topped hills and the wild hollyhock growing by the river. This, he thought, would be a formidable trip: it was a long way to Broken Hill and the mine. The river road was red and dusty, the ancient leather creaked and the flies clung to their bodies and he watched Sawtell beside him roll a cigarette. Sawtell's slouch hat was down over his face as he rode, and he looked set for a long ride, his packhorse with the Brens and the explosives following. St John Jackson looked at the big Australian and thought that this man could ride through the landscape for ever. He looked like a Boer farmer: that was one campaign they had lost. Sawtell, he thought, was a most efficient soldier: he had obeyed Colonel Madigan's orders and nothing at Bourke of any value remained. Counihan worried him, and he would have to be more careful. He thought of the Luger sub-machine gun. St John Jackson looked at the gum trees as they rode by the river; this was indeed a most dismal countryside. The river was nothing more than a ditch and there were no villages here. Where were the mountains and the glacier-fed rivers? The soldiers rode south-west, the saddlery creaked, and they left the fires of Bourke behind them. They passed a dog-leg fence and a slab hut; there were dead foxes hanging on the wire. St John Jackson wished he were back in India, there would be no villagers beneath the banyan tree tonight. He consulted his watch: the time was 0800 hours. It would be a long day, the first of many. The Australians would try to outride them, he was sure of that. He looked back at Sergius Donaldson on the big grey station horse and raised his hand. The Padre smiled and returned the salute.

Kevin O'Donohue knew this country well. It was tricky, with re-entrants, billabongs and lagoons. There was good hunting here, loads of ducks and geese, fresh-water crayfish, and wild cattle. They would live off the land; there were no worries until they left Menindee. He liked Frank Counihan because he had worked with him at the forge and knew how to shoe horses; he didn't say much but he knew what he was doing and was a craftsman. As for Mr Sawtell, he was the toughest man he had ever met; he wished he had seen the Zeros and fought at Newcastle. But

135

that didn't matter, at last he was a soldier and with fighting men.

They rode until six o'clock and the countryside had not changed. It was still hot, the horses and men smelt of sweat, the sun was getting low and shone through the box trees. The old river moved and the galahs were settling down on the branches for the night. Sawtell stopped, wiped his face with his scarf and said:

'I think we should walk the last hour, it will do our backs and the horses good.'

Nothing was said and they dismounted, eased their backs with their hands and walked around in the salt-bush. Counihan walked through the bush to the road and looked back toward Bourke. There were no plumes of dust and no sound; it was the same as the trip up, nobody was following them. Then on the way back, he looked to the west across the river and thought he saw men on horseback through the trees on the other side. He stopped, looked again, saw nothing and must have been mistaken. The crows screeched and he walked back to the horses.

'Where do you intend to make camp, Mr Sawtell?' the Major said.

'We'll walk an hour, we want a safe place by the river. Did you see anything, Frank?'

Counihan thought and said: 'Nothing.'

'Okay then let's walk. We'll doss down in an hour.'

The shadows lengthened and Sergius Donaldson walked through the saltbush with the big waler and his packhorse. He proceeded carefully as the ground was pitted with rabbit holes and broken timber lay all around. This was to be the routine for a long time, he thought. Sawtell would lead, measure the hours of the days and choose the campsites. He would plan the destruction of the mine at Broken Hill. Francis had given him command, how long would it last? But when in Rome, they must do as the Romans do. And after Broken Hill? Only God knew that and he would place himself in His keeping.

After an hour, Sawtell stopped. He walked through the bush, kicked at the earth and looked around for a spot to make the campfire and sleep. They should not be seen from the road and they should try to keep the glow of the fire hidden. St John Jackson waved away the mosquitoes and looked at his watch, it was getting dark and the time was almost 1900 hours. The moon was coming up through the trees and he was feeling cold. At last Sawtell found a pleasant, dry creek with gums overhanging toward the river. There was a big log they could all sit on, and trees for the picket line.

'What do you reckon, Kevin?' Sawtell said.

'It's okay.'

Sawtell waved his arm and the others came up.

'We'll camp here, they can't see the fire from the road.'

'They?' Sergius Donaldson said.

'Anybody who might be around.' Sawtell thought of the boy on the road to Bourke. 'We don't want to be bush-whacked on our first night out.'

Counihan listened to Sawtell and the Padre and looked across the river. O'Donohue started to unload the pack-horses. He placed his gear carefully on the ground, then the packframe and the saddle from his horse; he took out the rope, moved through the trees and strung up the picket line. St John Jackson was about to ask O'Donohue to unload his packhorse, then remembered: there were no bearers here. He had avoided his first mistake. They all unloaded their packhorses, saddles and gear and Sawtell came back, looked around and said:

'Our first night out, I think this calls for a drink when the unloading is done.'

He quickly took the kerosene-cases of explosives, the Brens and the Lewis from his packhorse and put them neatly on the ground, unsaddled his horse and led both animals to the river. Frank Counihan, Sergius Donaldson and St John Jackson followed him. The stars came up and the moon shone upon them. When the watering and feeding was done, Sawtell lit a fire and they all sat around. The night sky was clear and Frank Counihan rolled a cigarette; he would have to tell Sawtell about those riders across the river.

'What's for supper, gentlemen?' St John Jackson said.

'Aw, I reckon we could use them mutton chops,' Kevin O'Donohue said.

'Okay,' Sawtell said. 'Chuck them on the grill and we'll all have a drink. Would you bring out the bottle, Major?'

St John Jackson did as he was bid and the bottle of whisky was produced. It was passed around and each man drank then wiped the neck of the bottle. The smoke and the smell of the mutton chops drifted through the trees and the men drank the whisky. Counihan got up from time to time and moved down the river. Sawtell watched him go and wondered what was up. It didn't take them long to finish the bottle and Sergius Donaldson knew that now there was only one left.

He drank and shrugged, they might pick something up at the river port of Louth. Sufficient unto the day is the evil thereof. Then the mutton chops were ready and Kevin O'Donohue handed them round with some bully beef; he put the billy on the fire. The Padre ate his dinner and when he had finished, he took up his shotgun, broke it open and examined the cartridges. He took out the ramrods. Tomorrow they might have wildfowl for dinner. He remembered the roasted snipe in the officers' mess in India with pleasure. Sawtell watched the clergyman cleaning his shotgun, then got up and followed Counihan down to the river. He found him gazing across the water.

'What's up, Frank?'

'Christ, I don't know, I thought I saw some bastards on horseback on the other side of the river when we stopped

138

at six.' Sawtell looked at the tangle of trees on the other side. The moon shone on the water and the frogs croaked in the billabong.

'You're not sure?'

'No.'

'Come on, let's go down the bank for a bit.'

They went carefully down the river, and after half an hour they saw the tell-tale sign: the glow of a fire on the other side of the Darling.

'Jesus,' Counihan said, 'who can those buggers be?'

'Blacks, swaggies, anybody, let's get back and keep it dark for the moment.'

When they got back to the camp, the others had turned in. Counihan picked up the whisky bottle, but it was empty. They rolled their cigarettes and sat and smoked by the fire. Then Sawtell stood up and ground his cigarette butt under his boot.

'I'm going to doss down,' he said. 'I'll see you in the morning.'

'Okay.' Frank Counihan rolled another cigarette and looked into the night.

Sawtell took off his trousers and got under the blankets, his head resting on his saddle. He watched Counihan sitting in the dark and wondered about the strange campfire down the river. Whoever it was, using the west bank was smart. And they were being followed. He was sure of that.

· VIII ·

1932

THE SOUND OF ten thousand boots rang on the pavement and people waited for the men to appear. It was a bitter winter, the oak trees were bare and the cold wind blew. The mounted policemen waited in their black raincoats and helmets at the top of Bourke Street, their horses snorting and stamping nervously. They carried their truncheons. Smoke rose from the steam trains in the yards at Flinders Street and the policemen waited. Somewhere, far away in the dark city streets, came the sound of a tin whistle and a drum, and the boots thumped nearer. It sounded like thunder. The south wind blew and it began to rain. The pigeons warbled and fluttered from the stone buttresses of the Town Hall, the crows called in the damp and silent parks and the gulls wheeled and flew. The sound of the boots, the tin whistle and the drum grew louder and the rain fell. There was a storm out to sea.

The people waited and stood beneath the ornate verandahs and sooty porticoes. The smoke flew high from Victorian factory chimneys and the shop keepers stood outside wearing their aprons, black jackets and sturdy shoes. There were Tin Lizzies, errand boys on bicycles, horse-drawn wagons, Essex Tourers and Ford trucks. The men in felt hats waited at the kerb, the shops this day were empty of customers, the women raised their black umbrellas against the rain and the urchins ran along the magnificent, shabby boulevards. The smell of charcoal was in the air, and the commercial buildings rose tier on tier into the wet afternoon sky.

There was a lull. Then the men appeared over the top of the hill and came marching down Bourke Street, their thick boots thumping on the bluestone, the tin whistles and the drums playing. There were five thousand of them, and they wore cloth caps, felt hats and overcoats; some were old men with beards and gold watches and chains on their waistcoats; others were returned soldiers, wearing their greatcoats and medals. Their heavy dole boots thundered. The signs and trade union banners staggered and fell in the cold wind. WE WANT WORK. The men marched, their faces were lean and hard: they were veterans. The women and children marched too, with their men, and Marcia Sawtell marched with them. Many of the men were pushing their bicycles, and all were silent as they went over Elizabeth Street, past the Post Office where the Union Jack and the Australian flag flew, and up the hill to the State Parliament and the policemen on their horses who were waiting there. The cable cars and trams had stopped and trading had ceased.

Marcia Sawtell was proud to march and wished Geoffrey was with her, but he was not. He was at work. Next to her, the women marched with their children in perambulators and billy carts, their eyes and noses streaming in the wind. Tom Cobbler's cold, Marcia kept thinking, Tom Cobbler's cold. Her sad nursery rhyme. She thought of Geoffrey and looked at the women next to her and she was proud. And all over the city of Melbourne, the dark clouds streamed, the rain fell, the gulls wheeled and the pigeons flew. They were going to march to the Parliament and demand jobs: that was their right and that was what they were going to do.

Marcia thought of her dead father: she wished he was here. The men marched over Swanston Street, twenty

141

abreast; they were quiet and ominous and looked very powerful. Many unions were present: timber workers, coal miners, farriers, waterside labourers, slaughtermen. There were carpenters, iron workers, tinsmiths and shop assistants. They all seemed big and strong and purposeful. Something terrible had happened in Australia and there was no work for them; many had been evicted from their homes and their belongings had been taken away. They had worked hard and their savings had been lost for ever. Others had been locked out from their factories and mines and their children had turned to scavenging for fish heads, firewood and dog's meat in the streets; returned soldiers were humiliated and tramped from door to door selling home-made articles which their wives had made. Thousands were bankrupt and soup kitchens had been set up. It was puzzling: there were plenty of goods to buy, but no one had any money to buy them; farmers were ploughing in their crops, but people were starving. There was a sense of shame. They had been told to tighten their belts and make sacrifices, but nothing had improved. The Archbishop of Melbourne had said that their salvation lay with God and that they should wait on Him. Governments came and went, there were many plans and meetings, but it was obvious that nobody knew what to do. All that was left to them was to march to the State Parliament, see the Premier and ask for work. That was their right. At the top of the hill, the mounted policemen waited as the rain fell and the cold wind blew.

Marcia knew that the Depression was world wide; that banks had closed in America and Europe; that in Germany, money was worthless and there was violence from the Nazis; and that the Fascist, Mussolini, had come to power in Italy. Some said that in Australia, it was the migrants' fault and cheap goods from Japan. It was said that many returned men belonged to a secret organization called the New Guard and there were stories that they trained with weapons in the bush in case the Socialists took over. Houses were vacant, but there was nowhere to live. There seemed little anyone could do except to go to meetings of the Socialist Party and march in the streets. So far they had been lucky: Geoffrey had kept his job as an engineer with the Country Roads Board. He worked hard and built bridges in the country and took no interest in politics; as he said, he left that to Marcia and his father and Jack Hanrahan. Things were very bad in Richmond; it was a working-class suburb and had always suffered more than most; the poverty there had always been considerable, but now the people were starving, the factories closed; there were strikes and violence and ragged children ran in the streets. Marcia did what she could and, after the Library, worked at the Unemployed Girls' Centre; she was very strong, worked hard and enjoyed the company of other women; and they liked her. She was very popular. It was difficult for women: if they worked, they only got half as much as the men; and many of them supported entire families because they were cheaper to employ.

But now the drums rolled, the tin whistles played in time to the marching feet, and at last the procession reached the steps of the State Parliament where the line of mounted police stood. The men waited with their banners and signs as the leaders talked to the officers. Then they heard the message: the Premier would not see them and would not let them in.

The crowd surged and moved restlessly at the foot of the steps for some time, and then somebody shouted:

'Come on boys, let's go in.'

The drums sounded again, the people shouted and they moved forward up the steps. It seemed there were all five thousand of them; the banners waved and fell; the horses reared and snorted as they were ridden into the crowd; a policeman fell, bottles and bricks flew, batons were drawn and beatings started.

Marcia started up the steps towards the big oak doors and the Grecian colonnades; she saw a chestnut horse go down, the policeman's helmet tumbling; children cried and screamed; the men swore and shouted profanities; the batons struck, heads were broken and blood flowed. Now it seemed to Marcia, it was some kind of hell and she wanted to get out, but could not. Prams and billy carts jolted down the steep steps; the policemen rode their big horses into the crowd and people fell; the red blood streamed from their faces and many of them lay on the ground as the horses stamped and the policemen rode expertly; someone grabbed her arm and she was pushed up the stone steps; she tripped and fell and then got up, she fell again; five thousand people milled, screamed and shouted; the police truncheons fell upon their heads and bodies as they tried to gain the steps. The boots clattered, another horse went down, the men shouted, the children cried, but they could not enter the citadel. There was blood on Marcia's blouse, her glasses were broken and she could not see; more policemen on horses came and the crowd broke up and ran down the steps, and she, sobbing, ran after them. Bodies were lying on the stone steps, limbs were broken, the banners were down and it seemed that in that bloody pouring rain, men and women lay dying. It was a battlefield and Marcia ran down the steps into Spring Street with the others. She ran like a fox and kept running.

'You're mad,' Geoffrey said, 'quite bloody mad.'

He looked at Marcia as she sat before the small coal fire in the front room. Her face was cut and bruised and she could not see without her glasses. 'You could have been killed or gone to gaol, but you're built like a bloody tree.' He did love her.

'It's my body,' she said.

'I happen to love your body.'

144

'It doesn't mean you own it.'

'Oh, for God's sake, I know that.' He drank his lager and smoked a cigarette. Then he got up and shovelled some more coal on the fire. The night was black and damp. 'These marches don't achieve anything.'

Marcia leaned from her chair, took his cigarette and had a puff. The evening newspaper lay at his feet, he had been reading the sports pages. The football season was in full swing and his team was in trouble.

'They do, you know.' She thought of the women and children on the steps of the State Parliament, the police horses snorting and rearing, the tin whistle and the sound of the dole boots. She didn't mind his not being there with her.

'What will they say at the Library?' he said. 'They'll think I've been knocking you around.'

'But you haven't.' She smiled at him. 'That's the last thing you would do.' The night was cold, it was raining heavily and the water drummed on the tin roof. She pulled her chair closer to the fire. 'Would you be a sport and make another cup of tea?'

'Of course I will.' He got up, kissed her on the back of the neck and went out into the kitchen. The hall was a mess and he almost fell over his old bag of golf clubs. He picked up his tennis racket and swung it in the dark. There were piles of books everywhere. They must tidy the place up, but he loved the muddle; it was not like his childhood at Rotherwood Street.

'It's almost nine,' he called, 'turn on the wireless for the news.'

Marcia sat by the fire listening to Geoffrey moving around the kitchen. She heard the familiar complaint.

'I can't find the tea.'

'It's on the shelf above the gas stove, and the milk's in the ice-chest.'

'Okay.'

She listened to him whistling and rummaging in the kitchen, found her old glasses and picked up the paper. Her face and neck were sore, she was still a bit shaken and she shivered. There was a picture of Captain von Papen and Herr Hitler on the front page. The report said that the Austrian ex-corporal might be the next President of Germany. She looked at the pictures of the crowds in the streets of the German cities. The Jews and the bolsheviks were being blamed for the collapse. Geoffrey came back with the tray and put it at her feet.

'You didn't switch on the wireless and we've missed the news.'

'This man Hitler is the news.'

'Who?'

'Adolf Hitler, the leader of the National Socialists.'

'Him? He's a trumped-up little squirt, like the Kaiser. I don't know why you take him so seriously, my father's carrying on about him. He's like Charlie Chaplin, except Charlie's funny. The Germans are too sensible, they're efficient and good fighters, they'll work their way out.'

Marcia drank her tea and poked at the fire. She looked at Geoffrey; she had known him a long time now, and he was still strong and sensible. One day at a time.

'That's your solution, isn't it? Working your way out.'

'I never thought about it, I suppose it is.'

'What about the Japanese in Manchuria?'

'The Japanese where?'

'Manchuria.'

'For God's sake, love, that's thousands of miles away. We've got enough to worry about at home – without getting bashed up.'

'But something has gone wrong?' she said.

There were always children, Fuller Brush men and returned soldiers at the door; they were trying to sell you something: clothespegs, bootlaces, pots of jam and even holy pictures. Everywhere in Melbourne, there were signs saying *No Vacancies*, and men tramped the streets all day looking for work.

'Yes,' Geoffrey said, 'something has gone wrong. I don't know what it is, I'm a practical man, I just do things; maybe you and my dad know, I don't.' He got up from his chair and put his arms around her neck. 'I'm sure your father would have known.'

She held his strong hands.

'I'm quite sure he would have.'

He still kept his arms around her, the room had become very cold.

'I think it's time for bed,' Geoffrey said. 'Next time, you be careful.'

She got up from her old armchair and looked at his blond hair and blue eyes. He worked hard, he had his job, and he was faithful; he still played a good game of tennis and knew the rules of the countryside, how the weather came, how the brown trout rose and how the rivers ran. He was an engineer and built bridges for motor cars and people to cross. She drew him into her body. Geoffrey was helping to build Australia.

One month later in that dark winter, Geoffrey came home at six o'clock and walked down the hall to the kitchen. Marcia was there. She was ironing and there were clothes drying over the stove.

'Hullo,' she said, 'would you like a beer?'

'I'd love one.' He sat down at the table and looked at her.

'Okay then.' She smiled at him and went to the ice chest and got out a bottle of lager. Her hair was down around her shoulders and she looked beautiful. She prised the top off the bottle and poured out two glasses. They sat down in the kitchen and Geoffrey took his overcoat off and put it around the back of his chair. Marcia lit a cigarette and passed it to him, then she lit her own.

'How was your day?'

'I've been sacked. I finish up at the end of the week, they've had to cut down on trainee engineers and I've drawn the unlucky marble.'

She sat quite still. He drank his beer in the kitchen and looked at her.

'I'm going from door to door.'

'No,' she said, 'you can't do that. I can't make pot holders and I can't paint holy pictures.'

'That you cannot do.' He laughed. 'Maybe I should ask my mother.'

Marcia thought about asking him about the public service union and the rights of members. But what was the use? He wouldn't be interested. *You just get on and do things.* She said nothing and they drank their beer. Outside the house, it was threatening to rain and the southerly clouds were gathering. The factories were empty, the machines were silent and the starlings perched on the powerlines.

'Well,' Marcia said, 'it's come to us.'

'What?'

'The Depression.'

'I suppose it has, I'll do something, I think I'll go and see my father.'

'The pub will be closed.'

'That doesn't matter.' He smiled. 'I can get in the back door, he'll be drinking with Jack Hanrahan.'

'He's a good man.'

'Who?'

'Both. Go and see them.'

'Will tea wait?'

'Oh, for God's sake, Geoffrey, I haven't started it yet.'

'I love you,' he said.

'Yes, now go and see your father.'

'Okay then, I'll be home about nine.'

She didn't mind what time he would be home, she had

things to do. Geoffrey took his hat and coat and embraced her.

'I shan't be long.'

Marcia watched him go up the hall and heard the front door slam in the winter wind. She switched on the wireless for the news and listened, but it was too early and there was an American band playing:

> *Not much money,*
> *oh but honey*
> *Ain't we got fun?*

Marcia smiled and thought of their playing tennis and golf and dancing at the Menzies ballroom.

> *In the meantime,*
> *In between time,*
> *Ain't we got fun?*

The blinds were down in the Mountain View, the doors were securely locked and there were many men in the back bar. They were drinking after hours. Geoffrey Sawtell came in through the back door and saw his father talking to Jack Hanrahan at the bar. The place smelt of beer, cigarettes and old food, and the men looked shabby as they drank and talked over the small tables. Most of them were out of work and had nothing to do. Geoffrey looked at them: time was heavy on their hands, they had marched to the State Parliament, but the police had beaten them and the Premier had sent them away. He would not be like them; there was something he could do.

'Gooday, young Geoff,' Jack Hanrahan said from behind the bar, 'how would you be?'

'I'm okay. Hullo, Dad.'

'Ah, gooday.'

His father grinned and took him by the arm. Angus Sawtell smelt of whisky and he was drunk; Geoffrey

thought of his mother and put his hand around his father's
waist. He remembered the night they had walked home
under the gaslights when he had come home in 1919. He
turned to Jack Hanrahan and said:

'I'll have a whisky.'

Jack Hanrahan took down the bottle and filled the glass
nobbler. Geoffrey paid his shilling and turned toward his
father.

'I've been sacked.'

'Oh Jesus.' His father straightened up for an instant and
looked at the men drinking in the Mountain View.

'Have you been to the union?'

'Christ, Dad, I don't believe in all that.'

'Workers have their rights.' His father turned to Jack
Hanrahan and got another whisky. It seemed to Geoffrey
that the Mountain View was a bad place tonight. The
working men looked menacing and crowded around the
bars; they put their empty glasses on the counter.

'My son's lost his job,' Angus Sawtell said to Jack
Hanrahan. 'He's lost his bloody job and won't go to the
union.'

'You've got your rights,' Jack Hanrahan said and
coughed. 'Go to the union.'

Geoffrey knew it was no use talking to his father or Jack
Hanrahan, and said to the men at the bar:

'I've just lost my job, what do you reckon?'

'Aw, you could go rabbiting or digging for gold,' one
man said, 'there's a fortune out there for strong young
buggers like you.'

'They'll give you a free pick and shovel,' another man
said, 'there's a bit of competition, but there's money if you
work for it.'

'Have you tried?' Geoffrey said to the man.

'No, I never.'

'Well, I might try.'

'It's the British Lords,' Jack Hanrahan said. 'They're

screwing the arse out of the Australian worker. It's the high interest rates they're charging us, the English bastards are stripping us bare. They sent hundreds of our boys to their death in the War and they're doing it again in another way.'

'It's the Jewish bankers,' someone else said, 'and the Japs, they're flooding the country with cheap goods. Those little bastards will be here one day. They breed like flies and they want our space.'

Jesus Christ, Geoffrey thought, all this is no good to me, all I want is a job. He finished his whisky and bought another. What to do? The men crouched over the bar and argued and outside, in Bridge Road, the cold rain fell. There was one thing he knew: it was no good trying to find something in Melbourne. He had seen the long lines of men every morning outside the newspaper offices, waiting for the first edition, looking for jobs. Then he thought of Marcia, he'd give Melbourne a month.

'I remember the night you came home,' his father said, 'and we drank with Jack in the back room, do you remember that? Everything looked good then, now they've betrayed a generation.'

'Come on, Dad.'

'Don't you feel betrayed?' Angus Sawtell slid his empty glass over to Jack Hanrahan.

'Not particularly.' He was sick of hearing about the English lords, the Jewish bankers and the Japanese.

'There'll be another war,' his father said, 'that's the capitalists' solution.'

'Well, they can count me out, I've done my bit.' But he was back in the army again, the army of the unemployed. If he didn't get a job in town within a month, he'd go to the outback. He'd never been there. There was always something new to learn.

*   *   *

151

One Monday morning in that cold, wet winter, Geoffrey caught a tram from Richmond to Elizabeth Street and went to the Victorian State Savings Bank. He had pawned his suit and overcoat. The weather was bleak and the city trees hung down. Even at half past ten in the morning, the bank chamber was crowded with people. There were long queues at the counter and he had to wait some time. From what he could see, it looked as though they were all taking their money out. Some banks were still unsafe and people were nervous. They held their passbooks tight and nobody had cash in their hands. When it came to his turn, he said to the teller:

'I want to take all my money out and close the account.' He slid his dark blue passbook across the counter, beneath the grille. The teller said nothing, took the passbook and went to look at the ledger. He turned the pages, found the account and calculated the interest. Sawtell looked at the teller, who was an old and tired man. One of the lenses of his spectacles was broken, and his black jacket was shiny and threadbare. The teller looked at Sawtell in his old army greatcoat and gave him a handwritten note. There was £37.11.5d in the account. The teller opened the drawer, counted out the notes carefully and gave Geoffrey the coins. Then he cancelled the passbook. The bank was dark and cold. Sawtell left the queue, went to one side and counted the money. It was correct. He folded the notes and put them in his pocketbook. He put the coins in his trouser pocket, replaced the pocketbook inside his jacket and walked across the marble floor toward the doors. He noticed that everybody was counting their money and making it secure before they went outside into the street. Like the teller, they all looked old and their clothes were threadbare. The bank was very quiet, the clerks crouched over the ledgers and the people reminded him of the men at the front before they went up to the line.

Outside the bank, it was starting to rain and there was a

beggar in the street. Sawtell looked around for a tram, but there was none. The wind blew beneath his greatcoat and he could not avoid the beggar's gaze. He was a returned soldier, also wearing a greatcoat. He had a thin face like the trunk of a small tree. Sawtell walked down Elizabeth Street into the wind, but the soldier followed him, an old violin tucked under his arm. Sawtell had to stop for the traffic at Collins Street. He waited at the crossing as the motor cars and the horse-drawn drays went by. It seemed there were poor people everywhere, and he remembered the young girls running after him and throwing flowers as he had marched to the Town Hall. Then, the bands had been playing and the children had run under the green trees. The soldier stood beside him and said:

'Gooday, mate, you're a digger, aren't you?'

He shifted his violin under his other arm.

Sawtell looked up at the flagpoles and saw the Union Jack flying in the cold and bitter wind. The buildings were all covered with soot and smoke, the air smelt of exhaust and manure and the horse-drawn wagons clattered by. The draught horses were Clydesdales, big and strong, and breath streamed from their nostrils. Their iron shoes rang on the pavement. They were carrying beer barrels and the drivers were wearing cloth caps. Sawtell waited for the policeman to raise his hand so they could cross, but he did not. There were no beautiful women in long dresses and white blouses on the footpath today. The little children and urchins ran, and he heard the sound of the street musicians playing.

'Gooday, mate,' the soldier said, 'you're a digger, aren't you?'

At last, the policeman in his helmet and black raincoat raised his hand and the crowd crossed Bourke Street. On the other side, by the windows of a cheap tailor's emporium, there was a news stand and he stopped. *Weekend Riots in Germany, Nazis and Reds*. The Germans, he thought, the Austrian corporal, they had beaten them. The soldier stopped beside him. His hair was plastered down with the rain, and he had not shaved.

'What show were you in?'

'Passchendaele.'

'Cripes, so was I.' He coughed and shook. 'I haven't worked for two years. Can you spare half-a-crown?'

Sawtell looked at the soldier, his grey hair and the greatcoat. It could have been Smith or himself. He dug into his trouser pocket and said:

'Yes, here you are.'

He gave him the valuable coin, turned away and crossed the street to the Town Hall. He remembered the march and the pipers playing. The rain was hard now. From the other side, he watched the soldier and saw him talking to another man. Sawtell laughed as the cold wind and rain blew through the maple trees. Maybe he should beg off his old mates, but he knew he could not. He caught a Richmond tram and went home.

Marcia was sitting at the kitchen table. She was reading a book and turned her face toward him. He kissed her and picked up the book. It was called *Looking Backwards*.

'What's that about?' he said.

'Socialism.' She fiddled with her new glasses. 'Do you want a cup of tea?'

'That would be nice.'

He went into the front room. The fire had gone out. He cleaned the grate, laid the old newspapers and the kindling and lit the fire, watched it burn and tossed on a few lumps of coal. The house was cold. He went back to the kitchen. Marcia finished her page, then went to the stove and put the kettle on for tea. Geoffrey sat at the table and leafed through *Looking Backwards*. It looked boring and wasn't for him. He watched her at the bench as she made some bread and butter.

'I went to the bank,' he said.

'Did you? How much was there?'

'£37.11.5d. less the half-a-crown I gave to an old soldier.'

'An old soldier,' she laughed.

It was raining heavily and Marcia looked out of the kitchen window into the small backyard. The washing hung and she shivered. The kettle was boiling, she made the pot of tea.

'What are you going to do?'

'Well,' he said, 'there's nothing in Melbourne. There's thousands of men looking.'

'While the women wait at home.'

'Yes,' he said, 'while the women wait at home.'

Marcia poured the tea and Geoffrey drank. It tasted hot and good.

'What will you do?'

'I'll have to go away and try to find something in the country, gold-mining, rabbiting, there's got to be work out there.' She knew there would not, but said nothing.

'I don't know about *Looking Backwards*, it should be *Going Backwards*.'

'It's the finish of the system,' she said.

'If I don't get work, it's the finish of us.' He smiled. 'I leave the politics to you and my father, I'm a doer, not a thinker.'

'Where will you go?'

'North to Mildura, I'll give that a go.' He took her hand. 'I'm sorry.'

'Sorry? Why should you be sorry? It's not your fault. When will you go?'

'If a thing has to be done, it has to be done. I'll go tomorrow, I'll buy a motorbike, it'll cost about twenty-five quid. Can you manage?'

'Of course I can manage,' she said. 'You know that. You'll have to tell your mother.'

His mother, he hadn't seen her for ages.

155

'I'll tell her tonight.' He got up, still wearing his great-coat. 'God, it's cold. What are you going to do?'

'You know me, I'll survive, I'll work at the Unemployed Girls.'

'And march up and down the street.'

'And that too.' Marcia went to him and put her arms around his neck. 'Come on, Geoffrey Sawtell, go and buy your motorbike and try the country, you're sure to find something.'

'Okay, I can do anything, it'll only be for a month or two, then things must improve.'

Again, Marcia knew they would not.

'It's as well we haven't got any kids.' He'd always wanted a son of course.

'It's as well. Look, I'll be all right. Buy the motorbike and have a look. That's what you want to do.'

'I'm sure you'll be all right,' he said. 'You're a strong woman.'

'Yes, I'm a strong woman. Do you want some more tea?'

He remembered meeting her again on the cable tram. *I'll stand for an old soldier.*

'No, I'm okay.' He thought. 'I can get a good bike at Mr Costello's.'

'Go now,' she said. 'Give it a go.'

Geoffrey kissed her on the mouth and held her to him.

'Okay.' He grabbed his felt hat. 'I won't be long. Will you be here when I get back?'

'Yes,' Marcia said, 'I'll be here.'

She stood at the front door in the cold wind and rain and watched Geoffrey walk up the street until he disappeared around the corner. The street was empty and the wooden cottages crouched side by side, the fences down. The dank air was heavy with the smell of hops and malt from the Carlton Brewery, the garden shrubs were dead and the ragged blinds drawn. At the end of the street, she could see the familiar sign on the wall of Hall's shoe factory. *No vacancies.*

Marcia went inside and sat down in the kitchen. She picked up the paper. The Great Powers had legitimized the Japanese occupation of Manchuria and there were pictures of Jewish refugees arriving off the boat at Melbourne. What was going to happen? Maybe Geoffrey was right: you don't march and argue, you just get on and do it. But she knew that wasn't enough. She wondered what he would say to his mother. It didn't really matter: Geoffrey had left her when he got back in 1919. She picked up *Looking Backwards* from the table, then put it down again. What was it like to be a mother? She hadn't had any children purposely; she knew only one other woman who had done this. She wanted to contain herself and Geoffrey didn't seem to mind. He was a strange man: he didn't seem to care about anything. He cared about people, his father and Jack Hanrahan and, of course, her; but he seemed not to care about any ideas. Maybe that was the way to survive. She thought she would tidy up the house, then laughed. Nobody was coming: Geoffrey's mother had given up years ago. Angus sometimes called in and stayed for an hour or two. Marcia liked him even though he had a one-track socialist mind and was convinced that the capitalists were to blame for everything. They weren't of course. If Geoffrey couldn't get any work, they would have to sell the furniture and perhaps move. Marcia didn't mind that prospect; she could not tell Geoffrey, but she was looking forward to being by herself. Outside their small house, the rain fell and men looked for work all over Australia.

Geoffrey walked down Victoria Street. The trams, drays and motor cars rattled by. He remembered the Rugby Tourer; that had been a good car and they had often driven out to Doncaster for picnics. Those were the days: apple orchards, the long hot summers that never seemed to end, the sudden buzz of the cicadas in the afternoon, cold corned beef sandwiches, home-made pickles and the two of

157

them lying together in the long grass. Sometimes they had stayed until evening and looked heavenwards at the stars shining in the southern sky. There was a man standing outside the National Bank in Victoria Street. He was playing a mouth organ and his old felt hat lay upturned on the pavement. Sawtell walked by: there would be no more giving today. Uncollected horse droppings lay in the street and ragged children were pushing billy carts along the footpath. They were collecting firewood and bottles. All of them wore hand-me-down clothes and some of the younger ones had rickets and could scarcely walk. The women with them had hard, lined faces, and one was shouting and screaming. No one took any notice. Overhead, a steam train and carriages rattled by. Work on the tramlines had stopped, and the street looked like it was under siege. Sawtell needed a drink and went into Wrigley's Hotel. Inside, in the gloom, three men were standing silently, their glasses on the bar. None of them looked up as he came in. He bought a half whisky which warmed him up. The barman waited while he drank, and he thought about the other half but decided not. He would have one by himself somewhere, with no political talk, before he saw his mother. He was going to buy a motorbike.

'Gooday, Mr Costello,' Geoffrey said.

Mr Costello looked up from his work bench, littered with tools and old engine parts. The workshop was dirty and cold and Mr Costello looked tired. He was reading an old copy of *Popular Mechanics*.

'Gooday, Geoff, what can I do for you?'

'I've come to buy a motorbike.'

'Have you now?'

'What have you got for twenty-five quid?'

'Twenty-five quid?' Mr Costello wiped his hands and moved over to the row of machines. There were BSAs,

Imperials, Nortons and a Harley Davidson. Geoffrey wanted the Harley, it was a strong American machine, but he knew he couldn't afford it. He remembered the Indian Scout.

'Twenty-five quid will only get you a two-stroke,' Mr Costello said. He looked down the row of machines. 'I've got an Imperial here,' he said. 'Built to last, just done up, worth thirty quid but you can have it for twenty-five.'

Geoffrey knew that Mr Costello was an honest man. He was a friend of his father's. He looked at the bike carefully and it was in good condition.

'Okay,' he said.

'Are you going somewhere?' Mr Costello said. He hadn't sold a motorbike for three months.

'I'm going north to look for work.'

'Ah.' Mr Costello was embarrassed. 'I didn't know you'd lost your job.' He would not look at Geoffrey Sawtell and wiped his hands again with a piece of oily waste.

'I got sacked a month ago. I can't find anything in town so I thought I'd give the country a go.'

Mr Costello thought of the country; he had been born in western New South Wales. They had been Irish share farmers and the work from daylight to dusk had killed his father. He wiped his nose and looked at Geoffrey Sawtell in his old greatcoat.

'They say there's lots of work out there, digging for gold and trapping rabbits.'

'I'm young and strong,' Geoffrey said. He had played for Richmond Seniors and he had survived the War. 'I'll give it a go.'

'Good on you. What about the wife?'

'She'll have to stay here. She works at the Unemployed Girls.'

'Do you want to try the bike?'

'Thanks.'

Sawtell got on to the Imperial and kicked it over. The engine sounded good and tight. He put it into gear and rode out of the workshop and on to the street; he rode around the block past the small wooden cottages, deserted alleys and silent factories, and came back. He dismounted.

'Okay, Mr Costello, I'll take it.' He thought the Imperial would take him a long way and wouldn't use much petrol.

'You'll be needing some spares,' Mr Costello said. 'The roads up north are bad.'

'What do I need?'

Mr Costello looked at Geoffrey as he stood there by the Imperial.

'You'll be needing a spare tube, a repair kit and spark plugs.' He got them from beneath the counter. 'You can have the lot for five bob. It's no use going unprepared.' He liked Geoffrey Sawtell: he was a handsome, hard-working young man. Mr Costello took his twenty-five pounds, and his five shillings, gave him a receipt and the registration papers. Geoffrey thanked him and rode to Rotherwood Street.

His mother had grown old, and Geoffrey tried to remember her birth date but could not. The garden was unkept, the roses were dead, the forget-me-nots ran wild and seedy and rank weeds grew. The seat on the front verandah was broken and the Canadian maples were bare. His mother was sitting in the front room; it was cold and she had not lit the fire. He kissed her cheek and she did not respond. She was still using attar of roses.

'What brings you here?' She had been reading and her glasses lay on top of *Sorrell and Son*. He had given it to her last Christmas, Warwick Deeping was one of her favourite authors.

'I've come to see you, Mother.' He sat down opposite her by the piano. The lid of the upright was down and it had not been played for some time. The family photographs were still on the wall, but the vases were empty.

160

There were no flowers in this house and he knew he could not stay long. What could he say to her? He looked at the Ionian cross on the mantelpiece and the dusty bric-à-brac.

'Have you found anything?'

'No, Mother.'

'Have you been trying?'

'Yes, Mother, I have.' She knew about his drinking at the Mountain View.

'The Archbishop of Melbourne says we should all pay our way and wait for God's guidance, but that wouldn't interest you, would it?'

'Would you like the fire lit?' Geoffrey said.

'No, it makes too much mess. I hope you're not on the dole?'

'No, I'm not.'

'You've heard your father's in difficulties?'

'Yes, Mother, but I'm sure he'll be all right.'

'He's got his Irish friends to help him.' She touched her nose with an embroidered handkerchief and in the hall, the grandfather clock chimed. Geoffrey got up and stood by the piano.

'Would you like a cup of tea?'

'Yes,' she said, 'you know where things are.'

He left her with her book and went down the hall, past his room and into the kitchen. When he had filled the kettle and lit the gas stove, he looked in the cake tins for something to eat, but they were empty. While the kettle boiled, he went into his room and stood by his bed. Nothing had changed: there were still his few books, *Coral Island*, *Just So Stories* and his Sunday School prizes. He picked up his old BSA air rifle his father had given him for his fourteenth birthday and worked the action, then thought of taking with him the pile of *Boy's Own Papers* for old time's sake. But what was the point? Geoffrey turned on his heel, closed the bedroom door and went back to make the tea. His mother liked it very weak, he had not forgotten that.

161

She drank her tea and looked at him with her pale blue eyes.

'Well, what are you going to do?'

'I'm going north.'

'North where?'

'Up past Ararat and maybe to the Wimmera, there should be something there.'

'I don't suppose it's any use asking you to pray?'

He had not prayed since 1917, there had been no point.

'I might.'

'Well, if you decide to, take your prayerbook, it always helps. You've still got it?'

'Yes, I have.' His confirmation at St Stephen's and she sitting alone and proud. That seemed to please her and she gave him her willow-pattern cup.

'Do you want any more?'

'No.'

'Well,' Geoffrey said as he got up, 'I'll have to get home, I've got to pack.' He kissed her once more on the cheek.

'Don't forget your prayerbook.'

'I won't, and I'll write to you from wherever I am.' He knew he would not.

His mother didn't get up and he left the front room and walked down the hall on to the verandah. It was starting to rain and he was relieved to be out of the house. She hadn't asked after Marcia once. Why did he feel guilty? He couldn't understand it. The Imperial started at the third kick and he rode up Rotherwood Street in the rain, past the Mountain View and down Bridge Road. He rode home.

Geoffrey Sawtell rode north from Melbourne on the road to Ballarat, and was soon in the country. The market gardens were deserted. Acres of cabbages had not been harvested and their ugly stems grew thick and tall; the potatoes had been ploughed in and he saw people digging for scraps in the fields. Jersey cows bellowed by empty cowsheds, they were full of milk but there was no one to look after them. The Lister diesels were silent and the battered cream-cans lay at the side of the road, uncollected. The wind was cold as he rode the Imperial and the clouds flew high. Mr Costello had sold him a good machine and he was happy. He had his army blankets, some tins of food, his Winchester shotgun, and the country sped by. Here, at least, no returned soldiers were begging on the street and no children with rickets; if there were, he could not see them.

He stopped at Melton, went into the pub and bought a quart of muscat; in the evening that would keep him happy. He had one beer at the bar and went outside and surveyed the landscape. It was now a long, rolling hinterland of paddocks, stone barns, weather-beaten gumtrees, mills made of bluestone and fallen stockyards. Boulders grew from the earth and he remembered that day in the spring of 1925 with Marcia. That had been a good time; she had twice beaten him at golf. He rode north to Ballarat and the northern ranges; there, he thought, would be work. Now it seemed there were many on the road. Some were riding bicycles and horses and many were on foot. They all had packs on their backs and looked like defeated soldiers. The weather was cold and dry and there was no winter feed. Most of the shops in the townships were boarded up, the fences were down and the main streets deserted. He saw camps of men and their women and children along the roadside. They were living in huts made of cardboard, hessian and flattened kerosene tins. The camps looked a bit like the trenches and he remembered the smell of the Woodbines and the charcoal braziers glowing. Once when he stopped, he found himself listening for the thunder of the field guns and howitzers. But he was by himself and the Australian landscape was empty.

It seemed that the Imperial flew. Some of the men were

working on the roads, digging ditches, and others were cutting blackberries. The women and children were dressed in rags and he did not stop in case they tried to beg from him. There were people sitting before fires on the open ground, and it seemed to him that the whole of Australia had come to a standstill. Something had gone wrong, just like the Great War. At midday, he got to Ballarat and the unemployed were marching down the main street. There were policemen everywhere and men were shouting. It looked very bad to Geoffrey and he took a side route to avoid the procession; the last thing he wanted to do was get mixed up in street violence. He got lost once in a small suburb of corrugated-iron miners' houses, then found the main road and rode north.

At about six o'clock in the evening, he got to a town called Deep Lead. It was a mining town in the foothills of the ranges, and from the road he could see the vast wheatfields and dry plains of the Wimmera stretching northwards for ever. He could see the wheat silos, the farm houses, the rows of pines and the tree lines. The country went north and there was no end to it. Somewhere beyond was the Murray River, and north of that, the heart of Australia, a place where only a few steadfast men had been. One day, he thought, he might go there. Deep Lead was an old gold mining town. It had been big in the 1860s, with fifteen pubs, brick cottages, small suburban streets, a town hall, a Masonic temple and churches of four denominations. But now it had become reduced, pigeons fluttered in the eaves of vacant buildings, the poppet heads of the mines stood silent, and twisted wire and steel hawsers grew from the earth. The ground was barren, scoured and worked to death, and only the she-oaks and stunted gumtrees grew. There were no English oaks and Canadian maples here. Sawtell dismounted and looked upon the town. There were mullock heaps and ruined steel towers, immobile windmills and staggering outsheds, traction engines and discarded equipment. Kerosene lamps gleamed from several cottages, but there was nobody about. Then in the centre of the main street, he saw the town war memorial. *To Our Glorious Dead.*

In the bush outside the town, Geoffrey could see the glow of campfires, he watched the smoke and wondered what to do. He had to sleep somewhere, he wanted company and a drink perhaps. There must be somebody to share the muscat with; he thought of his father and did not want to drink by himself. He chose a pillar of smoke and rode the Imperial down a narrow, rutted road that he thought would never end. Then he saw a stalled Tin Lizzie, an abandoned Chevrolet truck and a burnt-out caravan. And through the trees he saw a big fire on the ground. Many people were sitting there, and when they heard the sound of his motorbike, some of them got up and watched him coming. He saw them all: old women and young women, old men and young men, children and dogs. The big fire burned, the evening dust rose and the sun was going down over the plains. Sawtell stopped the Imperial by a water tank and got off. Two big men came up to greet him; they looked strong and wore cloth caps and boots. He got off the Imperial very carefully with his Winchester shotgun and stood his ground. The collie dogs growled and sniffed at his boots.

'Gooday,' one of the big men said. 'What do you want here?'

'Gooday,' Geoffrey said, 'I've come a long way and I saw the fire and I'd like some company.'

'You'll get no company here,' the big man said. 'We're by ourselves.'

Sawtell pushed his riding goggles further up his head and put the Winchester down. He felt cold and tired. He could take on one of them, but two was a different matter.

'I think I've got a right to stay where I like, this is a free country.'

165

'What are you doing here?' the other man said.

'I'm looking for work, just like the rest of you.' They looked at Sawtell's greatcoat.

'You're a returned man, aren't you?'

'Me and a hundred thousand others.'

The big man looked into his face and saw a soldier.

'We're some of the others. What gear have you got apart from the shotgun?'

'A bit of food and blankets.'

'Well, bring it down then.'

Sawtell chained the Imperial to a tree, closed the Yale padlock, put the Winchester on his shoulder, swung his pack on his back and walked towards the camp.

There must have been fifty people sitting around the fire, with their belongings in old suitcases and sugar sacks. He saw two trucks parked through the trees: one was an old Diamond T, and the other a Ford. The two men introduced themselves; the big one was George and the smaller one was Charlie.

'We're all from Ballarat,' Charlie said. 'We travel around in them two trucks looking for work, but it's pretty bloody hopeless, and at the rate we're going we're going to be out of money for petrol by the end of the week. Then it's Shanks's pony.'

'Can't you sell the trucks?'

'You must be joking, no bastard can afford to buy them. Where've you come from?'

'Melbourne,' Sawtell said. 'There's nothing down there.'

'You've got to watch out in the country,' Charlie said. 'The local people and the bloody coppers move you on. What show were you in?'

Sawtell told them. It was a bit like being a Freemason.

'Charlie and me were at Pozières,' George said. 'We've been mates ever since.'

Sawtell thought of this comradeship, it was a good thing, they all had to stick together. The three of them sat by the fire and rolled their cigarettes. He reached in his kit and produced the quart of muscat.

'Do you want some?'

They grinned. 'Too right.'

Sawtell uncorked the bottle and passed it over. The three men drank and the wine tasted good. The fire burned as the darkness closed in. Sawtell thought of Marcia and wondered what she was doing. He hoped she was being careful at those demonstrations. From what he could see, the government was trying, but the problem was just too big for them. The communists weren't doing any good, just causing trouble. It was getting cold, and the evening star was climbing into the clear, dark sky. Soon they would see the Southern Cross and Sawtell remembered the lads cheering when they first saw it sailing home on the *Ballarat*. He pulled his greatcoat around him. This wasn't too bad, he would open a tin of beans in a moment and heat them on the edge of the fire. It had been a long time since he had slept out, not since the War. It was his turn at the muscat and he drank it down; the dogs and the children ran through the bush and the southern stars shone.

'Jesus, look at this,' George said suddenly. 'This is bloody terrible, we're living like Abos, those kids should be in bed, not running around in the bush.' He took the bottle from Sawtell.

'This is bloody terrible.'

Geoffrey looked across the fire at the women and children. His mother had always come into his room and tucked him in at night until he was fifteen, when he had asked her not to. She never came to his room at night again. He didn't know what to do about his mother; she still loved him but he did not love her. He hadn't loved her since he got back from the War. Something had changed that day in church in Richmond, and his mother hated Marcia because she was a free thinker and wouldn't have children because she wanted to work and do things. That

167

was okay by him, but not by his mother. Geoffrey realized he didn't know much about women: there was only Marcia and his mother. He got up from the fire, opened the tin of beans and put it into some hot embers at the side of the fire. Then he got out his spoon and waited for the bubbles to appear in the beans. It was his turn again for the muscat, and while he drank, Charlie got up and dragged another branch of gumtree and put it on the fire. Sawtell made sure of his beans, but Charlie was careful and they were okay. But now the Southern Cross was shining bright and all the stars were in their heavens. There would be a frost tomorrow and they would have to damp down the fire to keep it going. The women were trying to put their children to bed and some of them were crying. The babies were hungry and their mothers put them in blankets in the backs of the trucks. Poor little buggers, Geoffrey thought, it was hard for them. They had drunk a lot of muscat and he took his beans off the fire and started to eat them before he got too drunk. Maybe he could borrow a billy off one of the men and make a cup of tea. Then George got up, big before the fire with the bottle of muscat, waved it around and said:

'This is all bloody terrible, look at those kids, we're all living like Abos, what's the government doing, what's the King and Queen doing?'

'Steady on, George,' Charlie said, 'you'll drop that bloody bottle, then we'll all be up the creek.'

George sat down and passed the bottle. Sawtell saw that the big man's face was lined and caved in; it looked like shell-shock and his big bony body was shaking beneath his dirty overcoat. Several people around the fire were looking at him, then turned away. They were embarrassed. The muscat ran down George's chin and he started to sob.

'Steady on, George,' Charlie said, 'it's not that bad, have another drink, something will turn up.'

But Geoffrey Sawtell looked at George and knew it would not.

168

'He used to be so cheerful,' Charlie said, 'fair dinkum, a joke a minute.'

'I've got five kids at home,' George said, 'they'll all starve if I don't get a job.'

Charlie dug into his overcoat pocket and produced a harmonica.

'Come on,' he said, 'I'll play us a song.'

Sawtell threw the empty tin on the fire and wiped his mouth. He had another muscat and rolled a cigarette.

'Yes, come on, play us a song.'

Charlie played his harmonica and they sang:

> *Carolina moon keep shining,*
> *Shining on the one who waits for me*
> *Carolina moon I'm pining,*
> *Pining for the place I want to be.*

The fire burned and the stars shone, the women rocked their babies and the men sang and their voices lifted toward the trees and it seemed to Geoffrey that they could be heard all over the country. They drained the muscat and George went to sleep on the ground in front of the fire, his legs and boots sticking out from his overcoat. Sawtell wondered how long the Depression would last. He remembered his father saying that after a depression, there came another war. He shivered and thought that was impossible, got up with his haversack and blankets and found a hollow under the trees. He covered himself as best he could, but there was no one to love him and he wished he was at home by the fire with Marcia.

For the next two months, Geoffrey Sawtell's diet was bread, golden syrup, mutton and potatoes. There was nothing for him in the mining country around Deep Lead and he travelled north to the dusty plains of the Wimmera. He went up to Horsham, Dimboola and Warracknabeal and on to Hopetoun, but there was no work. Three times, the coppers ran him out of town and he slept under bridges and once in an overturned water tank. He wrote to Marcia once a week, giving her the name of the next town, but she did not reply. It was a cold dry winter, and as he got nearer the Big Desert, there were dust storms and the nights were bitter when he slept out in the open under his army blankets. The country was flat and there was no shelter; the north wind blew and it was hard to find a place to doss down. Sometimes he played football with other un-employed men, but mainly he kept to himself.

Finally, his money ran out and he sold the Imperial for £5. He kept going north and at last his luck changed: he got a job labouring in one of the quarries at the Zinc Corporation Mine at Broken Hill. The work was hard: they worked from 7.30 in the morning to 5.30 at night and he lived in a camp with fifty other men. At last Marcia wrote saying she was fine, she sent her love but didn't ask him when he was coming back. Geoffrey got friendly with a jackaroo who taught him to ride. Sometimes they went shooting and camped out in saltbush country. He worked there nine months. It was a hard life and it was tough country. Like the War, it stayed in his mind.

· IX ·

Wilcannia

SERGIUS DONALDSON woke at six and lay fully clothed in his blankets. It was always cold and hard, sleeping on the ground. His bones were old. He looked up at the ghost-gums, the bark splitting and peeling; he turned and gazed upon the leached and arid country. It was over-grazed and badly eroded, it was a dull and menacing land, the grass was dry, the trees spindly and dead. He had seen foxes, emu, kangaroo and wild sheep and cattle. The silence as he woke was appalling; there were no robins and chaffinches here. There was no health in this land. *Let your light so shine before men that they may see your good works*. The road was unsafe and they had kept to the river, but because of the trees, they could see nothing, except the river. The sky was dun-coloured and reminded Sergius Donaldson of Belgium. His lips were sore and dry and he licked them with his tongue. Then he saw a kangaroo, in a meadow, poised and waiting. He heard the inevitable sound of the crows and the parakeets. The crows were evil birds, they stole one's food and fed upon the eyes of lambs and other innocent creatures. They reminded him of the kites in India. Sergius Donaldson knew by now in this country, there were no meadows: only barren earth, red dust and stone. He licked his lower lip again. The meadows and parklands were potters' fields of fallen trees, broken timber, wormwood and gall. He lay in his army blankets and looked at the grey country and confusing, muddy river. This place was dark, undistinguished and unknown. God had created it, but why?

A sudden, small breeze blew. The leaves of the box gums moved for a moment, then all was still. Sergius Donaldson had noticed that as they had walked and ridden down the Darling, the smaller birds did not fly away as the men approached. This was stunted, confusing country. The river was like some old artery which had ceased to pump and cleanse the land. The ground was pitted with ankle-breaking rabbit holes and broken timber; this was the seventh day from Bourke and progress was slow. They had foraged at three stations on the river; two had been burned out and the other was ransacked and deserted. At the last homestead, a dog had been left to starve and die on its chain, but Kevin O'Donohue had shot and slaughtered two young ewes. That night, they dined off liver and kidneys, but the Australians would not eat the offal and preferred the mutton. The small town of Louth had provided nothing, and they had passed on, to sleep in the bush. There had been no rain. In one station, there was an old Bechstein upright piano, but someone had taken an axe to it and they slept in the woolshed as the house was overrun with rats. Most homesteads had pianos, and Sergius Donaldson found this strange.

Dead trees rose from the water and the spear grass: there were overflows and cul-de-sacs; the river did not move as the rivers of his childhood did. He remembered the canal at Hungerford, the willows and the clear water streaming through the lock gates. When he was a small boy, his father had turned up the threadbare carpets from aisles of eleventh-century churches in Berkshire and shown him the brasses and the strange masonic tiles beneath the altar rail. Here, there were no mysterious rings of stone, no familiar signposts, no visible signs of history. The artifacts here were beer bottles.

172

O God, thou has cast us out,
and scattered us abroad:
thou hast also been displeased:
O turn thee unto us again.
Thou hast shewed thy people heavy things:
thou hast given us a drink of deadly wine.

The leaves of the gum trees hung down. He listened for a sound and lit a cigarette; he looked and thought he saw a fox running through the saltbush. He thought of English foxes and the hounds. The other men were still asleep: Sawtell was lying on his back, his army slouch hat over his face, the Hollis shotgun always at hand. Counihan, St John Jackson and young O'Donohue lay like corpses on the barren ground as the parakeets screeched and flew from the ancient, brittle branches. The river still did not seem to flow.

Sergius Donaldson smoked his cigarette and opened his prayerbook again, this time at the Calendar. *September Hath Thirty Days.* They had been riding seven days since Bourke, and he had seen no cultivation and no crops. He put on his glasses and read. The date had to be between the eighth and thirteenth of September in the year of our Lord 1943, and he saw that those days called for Ezekiel. He turned the pages of his Bible, found the chapter and verse and read:

> *As silver is melted in the midst of the furnace, so shall ye be melted in the midst thereof; and ye shall know that I the Lord have poured out my fury upon you.*

He had marked the days off in the Calendar. They must be close to Wilcannia. He had heard it was another river port and that there were interesting Victorian buildings and churches in the town. Sergius Donaldson had not conducted Morning Prayer for some time. The blackfellows at Bourke had been beyond help and the Australians seemed to be most obdurate men, but God would forgive him for

173

not taking the services; it was better to strike at the enemy than to remain idle. God had chosen him to administer to the needs of soldiers; he had done that all his life, and with soldiers he would always be. Before this trip was through, they would need him, they would draw near to him in faith and take the Holy Sacrament. They had been four days without whisky and he hoped young O'Donohue would find something soon. The big grey kangaroo still waited; it was as though some strange God was watching him.

Then Sergius Donaldson saw Kevin O'Donohue stretch, put on his slouch hat and rise quickly from the blankets. The young man pulled on his boots, rolled a cigarette from his tin, lit it, coughed and strode through the fallen branches towards the packhorses at the picket line. He came close, wearing his braces, his shirt sleeves rolled above his elbows; he looked young and strong and tall.

'Good morning, Padre,' O'Donohue said. 'Another nice day?'

Sergius surveyed the menacing gloom and the graveyard of dead trees in the river. 'It is indeed.' It seemed that God had turned His back on this country. 'Do you want help with the horses?'

O'Donohue grinned. 'No, it's all right, Padre, I'll just take them to the river for a drink.'

The boy walked away quickly towards the meadow and Sergius Donaldson watched him move around the horses. As always O'Donohue examined their feet in turn, cleaning some with a hoofpick. He checked their shoes, undid the tethers, led them through the saltbush and disappeared. The sound of the horse bells drifted thinly through the trees. Then Donaldson saw Sawtell, Counihan and St John Jackson rising, stiff and cold, from their blankets. The Major, as usual, kicked at the ashes of last night's fire, threw on a few twigs, poured some water into his quart pot and set it to heat for shaving. The Padre took out his cut-throat, soap and brush from his haversack and went to join

174

his colleague. He walked through the sticks and stones to perform his toilet and have breakfast with his comrades-in-arms and suddenly remembered his Tennyson: *Yet all things must die; The stream will cease to flow; The wind will cease to blow.* A small breeze scattered the gum leaves.

Frank Counihan sat on a log in front of the fire, gnawed at his chop bones and watched his billy boil. He threw the bones into the saltbush, picked his teeth, spat, rose slowly and watched the Englishman shaving. He threw a handful of tea into the billy, rolled a cigarette and put his hat on.

'I wonder how long they'll go on doing that.'

'Doing what?' Sawtell said as he stirred the tea with a stick.

'Shaving.'

Sawtell looked at the Major and the Padre wiping their faces with their scarves.

'It helps them maintain their *esprit de corps*.'

'What?'

'They'll have to stop when we leave the river, they've got about ten days left.'

'Stupid bastards.'

Sawtell poured the tea into the pannikins and gave one to Counihan.

'Come on, Frank, old habits die hard and cleanliness is next to godliness.'

Counihan swallowed his tea and said nothing; then he got up, went to his haversack, fished out his lavatory paper and strode off through the trees. Counihan, Sawtell thought, would have to look out for those Englishmen. He would have to tell him shortly. He drank his tea and picked up another mutton chop. The meat was tough and woody because of poor feed and the drought. He looked at O'Donohue feeding the horses. The boy was giving the animals little as this was still reasonable grazing country. They would have to get more feed for the horses at Wilcannia and Menindee. He knew that the country south

175

of the lakes was dry and inhospitable with little to go on, and it was possible that the Japanese were at both river towns. He seemed to recall from his schooldays that the explorers Burke and Wills had stopped at Menindee, at a hotel, before striking north. Burke and Wills, he recalled, had been courageous men, but luck had run against them. That was in Victorian times, many years ago.

Major St John Jackson and Padre Donaldson came up to join him for breakfast and sat down before the fire.

'Good morning, Mr Sawtell.'

'Good morning, gentlemen. Would you care for some tea?'

The same routine, Sawtell thought, the same civilized routine. How long would this last? He passed the Englishmen the tin plate of cold chops. There was the sound of thunder and a few spots of rain fell.

'It looks like rain, Mr Sawtell,' St John Jackson said.

'If we get a downpour, we're coopered.'

'Coopered?'

'Stuck, but there won't be any.'

Sawtell saw O'Donohue fitting the pack saddles on the horses. The boy worked hard, tightening the girths, he was a good find. Sergius Donaldson, neat and clean-shaven, sat eating his cold mutton and he, too, threw his bones into the saltbush. St John Jackson stirred sugar into his tea and regarded the sky. For a man of his age, Donaldson looked lean and tough, but Sawtell wondered once again why he had asked the clergyman to come on this trip. Five men were better than four, and Donaldson was undoubtedly a soldier. It was the old chaplain from New South Wales, the young vicar at St Stephen's and his mother weeping in the garden. He might well have need of him. Once a Christian always a Christian? He laughed to himself and saw Frank Counihan coming back through the trees.

Frank Counihan, tall, dark-bearded and big-boned, walked up to join them. St John Jackson looked at the sinewy Australian, the black beard, the belt and braces and the Colt in the holster. This was a violent man, but undoubtedly capable. What would Sawtell do with him? They were all, indeed, strange bedfellows and he hadn't counted on what the bush would do to them: it was menacing and turned them in, each upon the other.

'Good morning, Mr Counihan,' Major St John Jackson said.

'Gooday, Major, you've shaved again, I see.'

'Indeed, clean faces are our custom, it seems to help the day.'

Frank Counihan sat down. 'And beards are ours.'

'And beards are yours.'

There was a silence, more spots of rain fell, and the three men sat before the fire. There was thunder in the flat hills, west of the river. Counihan looked over the river for smoke from the strange campfire, but there was none. A duck swam on the muddy water.

'We could do with some water fowl, Mr Sawtell, to vary the diet.'

'We could indeed, Padre, you could use your shotgun.'

'I shall, we shall have duck for supper. Alas, I never learned how to pluck them.'

Sawtell smiled and thought of the servants. 'Don't worry, Padre, we can look after that.'

Counihan crouched on his haunches in front of the fire. Every day that passed, he looked more like Ned Kelly and Sawtell wondered if they should make him some armour.

Counihan rolled two cigarettes, put one behind his ear and lit the other.

'It's Wilcannia today,' he said. 'Let's hope the Nips aren't there, we'll have to stock up, O'Donohue says we need shoes and fodder for the horses and by the time we get there, I'll be needing a big drink.'

St John Jackson looked at the bush.

'You're looking like Ned Kelly,' Sawtell said.

'The criminal?' Sergius Donaldson said.

Counihan nodded toward the Padre. 'He was a bushranger, an Australian who didn't like the authorities, a hero, you might say. He said we shouldn't obey the laws of England, that's the one thing I remember from school, they hung him in Melbourne gaol.'

Counihan was smiling as he crouched between the two Englishmen.

'Do you know what Ned said on the gallows before he was hung?' Counihan squatted and waited, his St Christopher medal hanging down his chest.

'I'm afraid not,' Sergius Donaldson said.

'He said: "Such is life".'

Sawtell listened to the conversation and thought of the enemy behind his back. Donaldson was silent and Counihan, his blue eyes gleaming, leaned forward and said:

'You don't like this country, Padre, do you?'

'It's not quite what I'm used to, Mr Counihan.'

He waved away the flies from his mutton chop. Sawtell listened and carved a notch in his date-stick with his sheath knife. They had been seven days out.

'Well,' Frank Counihan said as he reached into his tunic pocket, 'here's some wild mint to eat with your mutton. Mint grows in England, doesn't it? It grows here too down by the old river.' He stood up and ground his cigarette butt beneath his boot.

'Such is life, anyhow Wilcannia's quite civilized providing the Nips haven't got there first.'

'What is your plan of action, Mr Sawtell?' St John Jackson said as he drank his tea.

Sawtell tossed the dregs of his pannikin on the ground, got up and strolled over to his pack. He took out his father's watch: it was six o'clock. Then he found the ordnance map, came back and spread it on the earth in front of St John Jackson. Sawtell put his finger on the map and said:

'I reckon we're here, about two or three miles from Wilcannia.'

'What is there?' St John Jackson said.

'It's a run-down version of Bourke. In 1939, they had ten pubs, some churches, shops and hundreds of Abos. It makes Bourke look like London, but there's a big general store where we can stock up, if it's not been ransacked.'

Sawtell looked up at the sky through the branches. There was a big eagle flying high, but no smoke. It was hard to see this country. There was no sound and Sawtell folded up the map. They saw O'Donohue coming back from the horses, the chaff bag slung over his shoulder. He was carrying the fat-tin and had just greased his saddle and bridle.

'Gooday, Kevin,' Counihan said. He passed the plate. 'Have a chop and some tea. How are the nags?'

O'Donohue stirred the sugar into his tea and drank. 'They're okay. My pack saddle needs fixing or we'll lose the bloody lot.'

'Will it last the day?'

'Should do.'

O'Donohue finished off the chops and wiped his mouth with the back of his hand. He belched, stood up, looked at Sawtell and said:

'What's the plan?'

'How about you climb the tallest tree you can find and have a look?'

'Okay.'

O'Donohue went down toward the river, took off his boots and climbed a big river gum. He went up very fast, and Sawtell watched him and wished he was young again. He thought of the trees of his boyhood and the paddock by his house in Richmond, of the stream and the bridge and Marcia jumping the fence. O'Donohue climbed to the top of the river gum and the crows called and flew from the branches. The tree was very old and parts of it were dead. In a few years it would be so much firewood. The whole country was firewood. St John Jackson lit a Capstan and counted the cigarettes left in the packet. They would need tobacco at Wilcannia. Frank Counihan released the magazine from the butt of the Luger, checked the rounds, then pushed it back. Kevin O'Donohue came down from the river gum, walked back, stood in his socks and said:

'There's fires about three mile away.'

He pulled his boots back on and went back to the horses. St John Jackson smoked his cigarette carefully and said:

'We should reconnoitre, Mr Sawtell. If the bridge is down, it could be difficult.'

'It could.'

Sawtell saw Sergius Donaldson going down the river. His baptism. Counihan stood up and said:

'I'll go and have a look. Give me three hours. What time is it?'

Sawtell pulled out his watch. 'A quarter to seven.'

'Okay,' Counihan said, 'I'll be back by ten.'

'You look after yourself, Frank,' Sawtell said.

'No worries.'

Sawtell and St John Jackson watched Frank Counihan disappear through the trees.

Frank Counihan kept brushing away the flies as he walked through the bush very carefully. It was another grey morning and sometimes he saw the road when the river curved toward it. But he avoided the road and kept to the river. He was on the east bank and that made it easy. There was no way he could miss Wilcannia. He knew there was a bridge which crossed the Darling into the town. He hoped the bridge was still standing and that for once the VDC had not done their work. Getting the show across the river would be difficult. For the last three nights there had been no campfires down on the west bank, and now he and Sawtell weren't sure if they were being followed or not.

Now and then, the river curved back on itself into

anabranches, swamps of cane grass and billabongs and hundreds of dead box wood trees stood in the water. Sometimes there were clear, grassy meadows where big, grey kangaroos stood silently under the trees, watching him as he passed. Many old trees had fallen into the river, and upon the earth, and the ground was strewn with timber. Many emu ran in the meadows and there was a mist upon the water. They were ugly bastards. He'd heard you could eat the meat from their legs; hoped it wouldn't come to that. The morning had become sultry and the sky was covered by a thin haze. Dew was still on the dead grass as he walked, and the parakeets called and flew from the big trees. On one billabong, Counihan saw a pelican. He stopped and watched it fishing. Its head and big orange beak disappeared beneath the muddy water. It was hard to believe there were fish in that river. It was a very old river, and the water barely moved. He watched the pelican and went down through the spear grass to the edge. Some leaves drifted by very slowly. The river was flowing. The pelican did not see him, but suddenly it took flight, water streaming from its body. It took a long time to get airborne, but finally made it and disappeared through the dead trees to the north. Counihan had always liked pelicans and had never shot one. He thought they were big, ugly birds who worked hard for their tucker. He had heard they were bad eating anyway. He watched the seagulls flying south to the sea, a thousand miles away. He had not seen the sea since the fall of Newcastle.

Counihan crouched on his haunches by the river and picked at the cold sore on his lip. This was one of the few places where the bank was not steep: a small, muddy beach where the grey earth had been churned up by the wild stock which had come down to drink. He saw some watercress, washed it in the river and ate it. The cress tasted fresh and good. Counihan took out his watch; he had been walking a little under half an hour and he should

181

not stay here too long. But many birds flew in the trees; cockatoos, crows and kookaburras. There were egret, herons and black swan. It was a good place. There was a deep hole of water under a big old gum and Counihan wished he had some cuttyhunk line and a piece of mutton. There were sure to be freshwater crayfish in that hole. He remembered that he and Sawtell had caught a lot of crays in the rivers in eastern New South Wales when they had come down from Newcastle. After the defeat, that had been a good trip except for Wellington and Dubbo; they hadn't seen a Jap for five weeks. It was as though they hadn't landed at all, but they were there: they had fought them at Newcastle and the old bloke had seen the Zeros. He wondered if the Japs were at Ballarat. Maybe they had taken over the Town Hall and the shire buildings. What were his brothers and sisters doing? Thank God his father was dead, it was like the Chinese taking over the goldfields in his grandfather's day. If his mother had any sense, she would have gone to Mildura. Australia was a big place, the little bastards couldn't be everywhere. He looked at the muddy water. Then he remembered the big English oaks in the park in Ballarat, the military bands in the rotunda and the spring flowers, his younger sisters and brothers laughing and playing under the trees as they walked home from Mass on Sundays. *Who made you? God made me.* That hadn't been a bad time, looking back. His father would have fought the bastards, he was sure of that. Frank Counihan got up and stood in the mud and looked at the billabong and looked through the trees. He listened: there was no one around, nothing was moving. This was tricky country. He left the river and walked parallel, keeping the water in sight. The birds had stopped calling and there was no sound; bones of cattle and sheep lay everywhere.

After half an hour, Counihan saw the bridge over the river. It was still standing. The bridge was Victorian, painted green, made of iron and well built. It was a lift-up

182

for the masts of the River Darling paddle steamers. Somewhere a rooster was crowing. He crouched and crawled up through the stones and red earth and looked around. He took the Luger from the holster and released the safety, but there was no one. He considered the bridge and decided to wait ten minutes to see if there was any traffic. He could hear the sounds of people shouting beyond the trees on the other side of the bridge. They were Abos, he could tell. He saw the smoke rising and he smelled the meat roasting. If he went back to the river, he could rest and still hear what was on the bridge. Still holding the Luger, he got up and ran down the slope.

When he got back to the river, Counihan heard the sound of young voices and saw some young Abo children squatting on the far bank. They were fishing with hand lines and were laughing and talking. One of them was rolling down the muddy bank and climbing up again. He could now see the buildings of Wilcannia through the trees on the other side of the river. He could see the top of the big water tank on latticed iron work, the tin roof of a pub and the spire of a church. There were tin sheds, fallen fences, over-grown back gardens, smoke rising and the Abo children playing by the river. Counihan watched them. After ten minutes, he took out his watch from his waistcoat, listened for the sound of vehicles, went back to the hollow, crawled up to the road and looked at the bridge. There was no traffic. Then Counihan took the Luger from the holster, flipped off the safety catch again and ran across the bridge, his muddy boots drumming on the timbers. Nobody saw him, and from the hollow on the other side, he could see the main street of Wilcannia. He moved into a back garden by some out-houses, sat down by a peppermint tree and considered. Someone had worked very hard in the garden, but now all the vegetables and plants were withered and dead. A sunflower was still standing and grass grew through the piles of rubble on the old wharf. A pelican swam.

The blackfellows were sitting around open fires in the main street. Counihan saw big, fat black women in filthy dresses eating meat by the fires. The black children were playing in the dirt and some young men were carrying timber from ruined buildings and throwing it on the fires. Broken glass, bottles and corrugated iron lay all around. Some of the children were playing in old motor-car tyres, and from what Counihan could see from behind the peppermint tree, the shops in the main street were gutted and smashed up. The windows were black and gaping, dogs ran, the fires burned and some of the blackfellows were riding tired, bony horses. Counihan knew there was no good stock to be had here, but feed maybe? They had to have feed for the horses after they left the river at Menindee. Counihan knew they would miss the river. There was no good stock, but he looked for the Catholic Church and the Presbytery for they were worth inspection. The smoke drifted from the fires and he could not make out the buildings he knew so well. Country priests lived comfortably, they drank fine wines and good whisky, Frank Counihan knew that. They had come to his father's house in Ballarat at Christmas when he was a small boy, bearing port, whisky and claret, and had drunk with his father. He had sat with his mother and his brothers and sisters behind the kitchen door and watched his father drink with the priests.

There was a sudden movement in the trees, the wind blew, the dogs in the street barked and ran, the black children screamed and played in the dirt, the lubras sat by the fires and the men rode their tired horses. Counihan sat by the peppermint tree for half an hour and watched them. The north wind blew and it looked like a bad town, but it was free. The Japs weren't there, that was for sure. He rose, ran down the dusty garden, across the iron bridge, scrambled down the slope by the river and started the walk back to camp.

Sawtell was lying on his blankets and got up when he

saw Frank Counihan walking in. Counihan seemed fresh and happy, looked around the camp and said: 'It's okay, there's no Japs, the Abos are sitting around in the main street, cooking meat and burning stuff up. We can easily handle them.'

'Right,' St John Jackson said, mounting his chestnut mare, 'off we go.'

He adjusted his topee, kicked with his boots and rode off through the trees with his packhorse. Sergius Donaldson mounted and followed, then O'Donohue with his pack- horse and the spare. Sawtell threw his gear over his horse and slid the Lee Enfield into the scabbard.

'I could do with a drink,' he said. 'What are the chances?'

Counihan took up his saddle, swung it up and tightened the girth straps.

'There's a Catholic Presbytery there.' He picked up the Luger submachine gun. 'I didn't spot it, but there has to be one. The Abos can't have got it all.'

'Well,' Sawtell said as he mounted, 'back to church we go.' Frank Counihan swung up and they rode through the saltbush. He thought that Sawtell looked tired, but he was a big, strong man and knew what he was doing.

'They'll hear us coming over the bridge,' Sawtell said.

'They probably know we're here.'

'Yeah,' Frank Counihan said, 'they creep up, they know we're here, we haven't got the numbers, but we've got the guns.' As he rode, Sawtell thought of Counihan smashing the trestles of the water tank at Bourke, but said nothing.

It was easy. The five of them crossed the iron bridge with their guns on their shoulders and their packhorses on short lead ropes. The horses' hooves drummed upon the timbers of the bridge, and the five of them rode in. Major St John Jackson had his Purdey shotgun at the ready, Kevin O'Donohue flourished the Winchester, Counihan took out the Luger and the blackfellows got up from their fires as the white men came in.

Sergius Donaldson, his Hollis shotgun raised, saw that Wilcannia was a forbidding outback town. He saw the fires on the street, the black children running, the Queen's Head Hotel, the lines of ancient pepper trees, the tin shacks and the two-storeyed public sandstone buildings. There were cast and wrought-iron balconies, a spire and water tanks, pubs and tiny suburban streets, and the old river flowed. Padre Donaldson gave O'Donohue the lead rope of his packhorse and galloped up the main street, past the Knox & Downs General Store, the Athenaeum and the Shire Offices. And there beyond, were the fires, the shacks made of corrugated iron and flattened kerosene tins, the dirty washing drying on bushes and the diseased livestock and children running. Sergius Donaldson looked at all this, turned his horse and rode back to the Post Office and the Queen's Head. He was wanting a drink and knew this was a bad town. *Thou hast shewed thy people heavy things.* The flies buzzed around his head, and to the west he saw the dust storms rolling over the country where he hoped he would never have to go.

St John Jackson rode around very quickly in the dust and dirt; he smelled the town and saw the tin cottages, the pubs and the town war memorial; he turned left at the Post Office, glanced at the big water tanks on iron stilts and came back down the main street; but Sawtell, Counihan and O'Donohue had already gone through the blackfellows' fires with their big horses. The piccaninnies cried, the children ran and the women lumbered in fright from their fires and the young black men raced off on their bony horses through the trees. Then Sawtell took out the Lee Enfield from the scabbard, turned left and rode down to the Volunteer Hotel and the Court House. It was a tall, elegant, sandstone building gutted by fire and dead animals lay rotting on the small boulevard. He saw the war memorial, unkept hedges, rows of pepper trees and English oaks. Sawtell pulled his horse up at the war memorial and the monumental gates and considered the small, ornamental park. *Our Glorious Dead*. The smoke rose from the blackfellows' camps, where they were living on the ground. Sawtell looked at the memorial, the gates and the hedges and the steel hawsers around the marble plinth, kicked at his horse and rode back towards the river and over the bridge. When he got back, St John Jackson was questioning a blackfellow in the main street. The blackfellow was an old grey man with a beard and he was trembling before the Major and his horse.

'Who is here?' St John Jackson said. He waved his riding crop. 'Are there any white men or yellow men?'

The blackfellow crouched on the main street and could not reply and St John Jackson flourished his riding crop.

The blackfellow went down and said:

'There no white man here, boss.'

'And no yellow men?'

'No, boss.'

Sawtell swung up next to Counihan, who had come up from the river. Counihan had the Luger submachine gun out and the blackfellow crouched.

'Jesus Christ, Major,' Sawtell said, 'there's no point, the old man knows nothing, we've been through the town and it's ours, the Japs have never been here. There may be something of value, let's forage and get what we can.'

'You're quite right, Mr Sawtell, this old native knows nothing.'

Then Sergius Donaldson rode up, dismounted and said:

'I've found the St James' Church of England Vicarage, there could be some provisions there.'

'Good on you, Padre,' Frank Counihan said as he sat on his big horse. 'But I've found the Catholic Presbytery and that's what we want.'

'Right,' Sawtell said. 'Kevin, take the packhorses down to the courthouse, we'll doss down there. Do you want any help?'

187

'She's okay.'

O'Donohue led the horses away past the pepper trees.

Sawtell, St John Jackson, Counihan and Donaldson rode past the Post Office and the Queen's Head Hotel toward the Catholic Presbytery. They trotted past the Plaza Cinema, the small gardens and the picket fences; and the blackfellows, standing beneath the trees, watched the soldiers go. They saw the Catholic Presbytery standing among the gum trees with its balustrades, ornamental porches and boarded-up windows. There was a row of cypresses, tall, yellow and dying; the water tanks had been overturned and sunflowers and thistles grew in the priests' forgotten garden. The presbytery was firmly buttressed, built of sandstone and looked formidable. They trotted down the long, curving gravel drive to the carved oak front door where two oak trees were dying. The pedestals had been smashed and weeds grew between the flagstones of the steps, but it was a strong building and the Ionian crosses stood high. They rode up the weedy gravel path, their horses snorted and the pigeons warbled and flew from the broken eaves. Sergius Donaldson looked at the magnificent windows, boarded up with corrugated iron. God had abandoned this place. Sawtell rode around the back of the building, and there was a grove of orange trees. He dismounted, ran toward a tree and picked the fruit; he put it to his mouth, but the skin was tough and the flesh dry and woody. He looked west at the dust storms, threw the orange down, then led his horse around to the front door.

The men stood before the Presbytery; Counihan had run up the front steps. He was standing on the porch in front of the big oak doors.

'The priests used to live here,' he said. 'There's drink somewhere in the building.'

Sawtell left his horse, ran up the steps and looked at the lock. It was a massive bolted Yale hasp and staple and

188

would take some getting off. He saw Counihan taking the Luger from the holster.

'Come on, Frank, put that thing away, you'll kill us all. This is a crowbar job.'

Sergius Donaldson watched and waited on his horse and wondered if the Presbytery contained any whisky. They would have to search carefully. He dismounted and walked through the strange, dead garden. Across the earth, beneath an oak tree, he saw a calvary and walked towards it. He turned and saw Counihan riding back down the gravel path; Sawtell and St John Jackson were sitting on the steps of the Presbytery. Donaldson went toward the calvary and stood before it. It was cheap, made of plaster and had been desecrated by vandals, the Virgin's body had been smashed and the remains daubed with paint. Sadly, Sergius Donaldson returned to the steps and waited for Counihan to return. St John Jackson sat, said nothing and gazed toward the country in the west. The sand storms rolled, and they heard the crack of thunder. A few spots of rain fell. Sawtell's horse shied and he went down the steps to comfort it. He stroked its head and nose and spoke to it, then across the earth saw the calvary and went toward it.

'It's no use, Mr Sawtell,' Sergius Donaldson said, 'it's been destroyed.'

Sawtell stopped, he bowed at the clergyman, smiled and sat down on the step.

'Well, Padre, I think we could do with a big drink.'

He scratched his beard and looked upon the town and the trees at the river. The hot wind blew. He thought of the muddy water; there were redfin, cod and yellowbelly in the Darling. He would get out the cuttyhunk lines and go fishing in the morning. He should have brought his trout rod; he thought of the dark stream and the bridge and the brown trout lying in the water by the stones. His trout rod. He thought of Marcia. He laughed and waited for Counihan to come back with the crowbar. They all needed that drink.

189

St John Jackson looked up at the sandstone walls of the Presbytery and wondered who had built it. There must have been stonemasons working in this town; the Roman Catholics must have planned for expansion and increasing flocks, but their plans had come to nothing. He thought of his army life in India; most plans come to nothing. The disgrace at Meerut; he had not planned for that and after all his gallantry at the Somme, God had turned His back upon him. The starlings sat on the powerlines and the pigeons warbled; St John Jackson was reminded of the pigeons in his father's church and the swallows at dusk. Then he saw Counihan returning with the crowbar; up the gravel drive, he rode, straight-backed and military. He mounted the steps and Sawtell joined him. Again, it was easy; they levered and wrenched the old doors open and the four of them stepped inside.

All was dark and the building smelled of kerosene and candle-grease. Counihan strode across the varnished, wooden floors and tore down the corrugated iron from the windows; the sunlight flooded in; there were great shafts of light from the western sun and Sawtell remembered his mother's kitchen. They walked down the hall through the dining room and into the priests' rooms; their boots thundered and echoed on the wooden floors. Every room was bare and spiders' webs trailed delicately from the high, pressed-tin ceiling; they walked about and searched the dark interior, every room, but there was nothing of value. The priests had left and taken everything. There was nothing in this dark, vacant building – not even, it seemed, a page from a missal, a child's catechism or a discarded crucifix. There was no comfort here. Counihan ran up the broad staircase, his hands gripping the carved balustrades, and disappeared. They could hear his boots sounding on the timbers overhead, and the dust drifted down upon their heads. The sunlight streamed through the windows and Geoffrey Sawtell sat on the floor, his hands resting upon his knees. They had no right to be here: even though they had gone, this building belonged to the priests of Wilcannia. This presbytery, he thought, was a fine and silent place. It felt like a church in Belgium.

Frank Counihan came down the stairs as they creaked beneath his boots. He ran his hands through his dark, wiry hair.

'The bastards have left nothing,' he said, 'they've left nothing.'

The bastards? Sergius Donaldson thought, were his priests bastards?

'There's the kitchen and the cellar,' Counihan said. 'The cellar, that's where they keep it.'

'Right,' Sawtell said as he got to his feet, 'let's find the cellar.'

He went to the back of the building with Counihan, and the two Englishmen followed. It was fruitless: the priests had taken everything away.

The four of them sat on their horses outside the presbytery and Sergius Donaldson looked at the broken calvary.

'Jesus Christ,' Counihan said, 'there's got to be booze somewhere in this miserable dump.'

Then O'Donohue appeared from the top of the street.

'Gooday,' he said, 'there's some stables behind the court-house. I've put the horses and the gear in there, it's all safe and the Abos won't come near it. What's up?'

'We're trying to find liquor, O'Donohue,' St John Jackson said, 'to make this place a little more bearable.'

'Okay, we could split up, there's got to be some sooner or later.'

They divided; Sawtell, O'Donohue and St John Jackson went for the shops, pubs and the bondstore and Sergius Donaldson found himself with Frank Counihan.

Counihan rode quickly down the street toward the corrugated-iron cottages, wooden shacks and blackfellows' humpies. Sergius Donaldson followed him through the fires and the dying trees. They rode through the settlement, and the black women and children and dogs ran as they approached. Counihan searched the small deserted houses, sheds and shabby plywood caravans. From a distance, the blackfellows watched the two horsemen, but no liquor was to be found. Sergius Donaldson saw the sun going down below the purple, flat hills to the west. Still Counihan searched through the miserable camps and there was nothing. It was starting to rain and the Padre said:

'I think we should join the others, Mr Counihan.'

'Yeah, this place is as dry as a chip, I wonder what the buggers drink.' Counihan sat on his horse and surveyed the dismal landscape. 'What do the Japs drink?'

'Sake.'

'What?'

'Sake.'

Then Counihan wheeled his horse around and rode towards a shack beneath some pepper trees. The Padre followed. Smoke was rising from the tin chimney and kerosene tins and beer bottles were piled up in the weeds and timber. A starving dog was chained up and it jumped and snarled on the bare, pitted earth. Counihan dismounted and pushed open the door; Sergius Donaldson dismounted too and went inside. An old aboriginal woman was sitting at the table before a bottle of wine. She was blind and frightened and grabbed the bottle. The flies clung to her face and throat and the dog snarled outside. Counihan went up and took the bottle from the lubra's hands. He wiped the neck and proffered it to Sergius Donaldson.

'Here's your drink, Padre.'

'I think not, Mr Counihan.' *Thou shalt not tempt the Lord thy God.*

Counihan grinned and held up the cheap tokay. 'You're right, this stuff's deadly.'

He put the bottle back on the table, they went outside,

Counihan released the dog and kicked it as it went for him. They rode back into town.

The main street was deserted, the fires burned low and the blackfellows had gone. Counihan and Donaldson found the horses tethered outside the Volunteer Hotel, a light gleamed from the windows and they heard their comrades-in-arms moving around inside. The sun had gone down and the warm wind blew. Counihan and Padre Donaldson went inside as the moon rose over the dry countryside.

'Ah, gooday,' Sawtell said. He was standing at the bar with St John Jackson and O'Donohue. A kerosene lamp shone and the Major had taken off his topee and placed it on the counter. Sawtell watched his friend and the Padre come up. This place was like Wrigley's during the Depression. It was a bad pub, but they had to forage. St John Jackson looked tired and said:

'Did you have any luck?'

'No,' Counihan said, 'none at all.' He laughed. 'I suppose the best place to find booze is a pub.'

'That's right, Frank,' Sawtell said and looked out of the bar-room windows. 'The sun's gone down and it's time for a drink.' He moved round behind the bar and stood before the shelves of smashed bottles. Above his head, there was a notice board with scrawled obscenities and obscure country messages.

'Would you gentlemen care for a drink? Ice-cold lagers, perhaps?' He looked at St John Jackson. 'And for you, sir, a gin and tonic, a Singapore Sling?'

The Major laughed and said: 'Mr Sawtell, I think we should forage, this place seems to be our last chance.'

'Right you are, sir.'

Sawtell left the bar and went into the kitchen of the Volunteer Hotel. The blackfellows, he thought, can't have taken everything.

Cheap pots and pans lay on the floor with broken

193

crockery and rotting sacks of potatoes. It all seemed unpromising and they moved around empty beer barrels, broken spigots and the country rubbish of ten generations. It seemed to St John Jackson that nothing had been thrown away, that this town had always been preparing for a siege. Then he heard Counihan's voice from the back yard.

'Hey, I've found a ring bolt, I reckon it's a cellar.'

They went out the back and found Counihan crouching on the back path, and there it was: a trapdoor and a ring bolt. The weeds and dandelions grew.

'Kevin, get the crowbar,' Sawtell said, 'it's out the front.' They worked by the light of the kerosene lamp and, at last, they raised the trapdoor. There was a ladder and Counihan climbed down carefully into the dark. They heard him searching, then he heaved a crate up to Sawtell and said:

'That's booze, Christ knows what it is, but it's booze.' He climbed back up the ladder. 'There's nothing else down there, but at least we've got this.'

They stood around the crate and Sawtell prised the lid off with his sheath knife. He found twelve Imperial quart bottles with yellow labels. He knew the familiar smell. He took one bottle from the crate, held it aloft in the light of the lamp and said:

'Gentlemen, it's rum, twelve Imperial quarts of Bundaberg rum.' He withdrew the cork from the first bottle and passed it to St John Jackson.

'Well, Major, I've not drunk this stuff since 1917, but here's health to us all.'

St John Jackson drank from the bottle, felt the familiar warmth in his stomach and passed it to Sergius Donaldson, Frank Counihan, Kevin O'Donohue and Geoffrey Sawtell. Sawtell looked around the back yard, wiped his lips and beard and said:

'Let's drink in a civilized fashion, let's drink outside in God's pure air under the stars.'

194

Counihan carried the crate through the kitchen and the bar, out on to the street, and they sat in the gutter and watched the camp fires of Wilcannia. The rain had gone; it was a clear dark night, the west wind blew, the stars shone and the soldiers drank their rum.

'At least this stuff's better than the shit they gave us in the trenches,' Sawtell said. 'Whisky for the officers and rum for the men.' St John Jackson and the Padre said nothing and thought of the men they had lost. Sawtell wiped his lips.

'And rum for the men. This town used to be called the Queen of the West, but look at it now, it's not worth defending.' He opened another bottle and kept it to himself. 'Anyway, here's to Loos, Arras and the Somme.'

'To Passchendaele,' St John Jackson said.

'To Passchendaele.'

Frank Counihan listened to them talking. He wished he'd fought in that war, it gave a man stature. He got up, walked over and pissed in the street. Nobody was around, maybe all the Abos had gone bush. Then he went back and sat next to Sergius Donaldson, who was having his turn at the bottle.

'I didn't know Protestant priests drank,' Counihan said. 'I thought it was only our lot.'

'Our lot, Mr Counihan, do their fair share, and the absence of women is a contributing factor.'

'And things you want to forget.'

The Padre looked up and put down the bottle. 'And things you want to forget.'

'I'm going back to the stables,' O'Donohue said. 'There's lots of valuable gear in there, and anything goes in this town.'

'Good on you, Kevin,' Sawtell said. 'Do you want a drink before you go?'

'She's okay. I'll see you later.'

'Well, Mr Sawtell,' St John Jackson said, 'where are we at?'

'We're at Wilcannia, Major, and we're drinking rum in the main street, that's where we're at.'

'As enjoyable as it is, could you be a little more precise?' Oh Jesus, Sawtell thought, here comes a military lecture from a man born to rule. He raised the bottle, passed it to Counihan and rolled a cigarette.

'We need feed for the horses and O'Donohue's pack saddle wants fixing, then we should be off to Menindee. There's nothing to keep us here. The Queen of the West has not come up with the goods.' He tapped the bottle. 'Except this here.' Sawtell was getting drunk now, got to his feet and walked into the road for a piss. He came back, picked up the Lee Enfield and put it between his knees.

'One for the road. Come on, Frank, give us a song, give us *Bold Jack O'Donohoe*, something for our British friends.'

Counihan fiddled with his Luger as the southern stars shone.

'Give us a minute, Geoff, I want to oil my throat.'

Then as the rum-bottle was passed, they saw Kevin O'Donohue coming up the street. He was carrying his Winchester and another man was with him.

The man with O'Donohue was a young blackfellow and Kevin pushed him into the light of the kerosene lamp with his rifle. They all got to their feet, Counihan with the Luger and Sawtell with his Lee Enfield.

'I caught this bugger going through our gear,' O'Donohue said. Oh God, Padre Donaldson thought, when will these poor people ever learn?

'What was he going for?' Sawtell said.

'The binoculars, the compass and the ammo, what he could get.' The blackfellow stood before them and Sawtell went up close. He was about nineteen, tall and stringy and unafraid, unlike the rest; and Sawtell was reminded of the two black men back at Bourke.

196

'What's your name?'

There was no reply, and the black boy stood there in his moleskins and old riding boots. Sawtell turned to St John Jackson and said:

'The country's under martial law, whatever that means, and you're the commander of the Military Area of Bourke.'

'Mr Sawtell, you're in command of this expedition, the outcome is up to you.'

'It's only another bloody Abo,' Counihan said. 'We shoot him.' Sawtell stood there, irresolute.

'What do you think, Padre?'

'I have no advice to offer.' Blessed are the merciful.

Jesus, Sawtell thought, another Pontius Pilate. He stepped back and the empty rum-bottle rolled at his feet. There was no point in questioning the young black any further, this was a new kind of war.

'There's Madigan's orders,' Counihan said. 'Anybody collaborating with the enemy is shot.'

'There's no evidence of that, Frank, he's just another pilfering black.'

He thought of being run out of town by the cops in the Depression and hostile farmers with shotguns. Summary justice, no more discussion. Sawtell swung the butt of the Lee Enfield and broke the blackfellow's jaw.

'Okay, Frank, dump him on the war memorial.'

'Where?'

'The war memorial, it's down the street, it says *To Our Glorious Dead*.'

The next day, they foraged at Knox & Downs Bond Store. The pickings were slim, but they got three bags of oats, a few tins of vegetables and O'Donohue found some nails and pipe tobacco. They rode over the iron bridge at nine o'clock and followed the river. As they rode that day, the country improved and there were ducks, geese and cormorants on

197

the water. That afternoon Sawtell caught three excellent bream and Sergius Donaldson shot a duck. O'Donohue caught a freshwater crayfish and they lived off the fat of the land. But when Counihan went out for his evening stroll, he saw the campfire again. And early in the following afternoon, two Zeros flew over quite low, towards Bourke. That night, in his blankets, Sawtell thought about the young blackfellow lying on the war memorial in the main street. When they rode by in the morning, someone had taken him away.

· X ·

1934

GEOFFREY, HIS FATHER AND JACK HANRAHAN sat in
the vast amphitheatre of the Melbourne Cricket Ground.
Their football team, Richmond, had won its way into the
Grand Final. For the three of them, it was a great day. The
spring sun shone upon the crowd as they poured into the
world's biggest stadium and drank beer on this magnificent, early afternoon. The groundsmen had done their job
well: the pitch was perfect, and the brass and pipe bands
marched up and down in all their military splendour as the
people waited for the teams to appear. The trumpets,
drums and tubas played, and as the teams ran up the race
and on to the ground, a massive cheer went up which
seemed to echo down all the streets of Melbourne. In every
brick cottage, every ornate mansion and in every timber-
framed boarding house, they waited for the game to start.
All over the city and all over the country, people sat by
their wireless receivers and listened to the sounds of the
bands and the spectators cheering. This was their day. The
teams, Richmond and South Melbourne, faced each other,
shook hands and then stood to attention as 75,000 people
rose to their feet to sing the National Anthem.

This Grand Final was special: Richmond had won the
Premiership only once since 1921, and this was Melbourne's
Centenary Year. The Grand Opera season had started at
the Apollo Theatre with *Aida* and *Madame Butterfly* and,

at His Majesty's, there was a continuous presentation of Gilbert and Sullivan. The city streets and boulevards were decorated with all the flags of the Empire, bunting and triumphal arches for the arrival of the King's son and his wife, the Duke and Duchess of Gloucester. There were race meetings, public celebrations, dances and parties. Commemorative stamps were issued and King George had composed a special message to all the citizens of Melbourne; he was sending his son to take part in the celebrations. There had been an exciting air-race from London, and one of Britain's finest battleships, HMS *Sussex*, lay alongside Spencer Street Quay. On St Kilda Road, on a man-made hill, the Shrine of Remembrance to all those who had fallen in the Great War was ready to be dedicated on Armistice Day.

Geoffrey had been to every Grand Final with his father since the War, except 1921 when he had played and when he had been working at Broken Hill. They had a dozen bottles of Richmond Lager between the three of them, and Geoffrey opened the first bottle as the bell sounded for the start of the game. The noise was tumultuous, for this was a tribal battle and Angus Sawtell sat on the edge of his seat and said:

'This game's going to be a bobby-dazzler, a real bobby-dazzler.'

The umpire bounced the ball and the big men flew. His father was right: the game started with long drop-kicks, high marks and brilliant snap goals, with Richmond playing hard but fair. Both teams were full of their best endeavour; and at every goal the crowd got to their feet, roared and threw their caps into the air. By half-time, Richmond was twenty-eight points ahead and Angus Sawtell and Jack Hanrahan could smell the scent of victory. The street labourers, the factory workers and street urchins screamed and shouted; Angus Sawtell drank his whisky, bottles were passed and they drank more beer as the brass bands played.

'What do you reckon, Geoff?' Jack Hanrahan said as he rolled a cigarette. 'We've got it won, haven't we?'

'I don't know.' Geoffrey Sawtell remembered his past, bitter disappointments: battles won and then lost when, it appeared, God had given His blessing. 'It's too early, Jack, they could get up and we could be defeated.' He thought of the trenches. 'It could become a game of defence, they could creep up on us.'

'You're wrong, son,' his father said, 'we'll go through them like a dose of salts.'

'We'll see.'

'Christ, you're a bloody Jonah,' his father said. 'You don't believe we can win anything.'

Geoffrey looked at his father and Jack Hanrahan and the crowd, the flags, the brass bands and the bunting. He drank his beer and said:

'At half-time, Dad, anybody can get up and win.'

But Geoffrey was wrong: Richmond played brilliantly in the second half and won by seven goals. Richmond, the working-class city of factories and battlers, was triumphant; 40,000 fans cheered themselves hoarse, threw their caps into the air and, after the cup had been presented by the State Governor, made for the nearest pub to celebrate their victory.

The Mountain View was packed to the rafters and Geoffrey helped Jack Hanrahan behind the bar. He pulled the pumps and served the beer, the whisky, the rum and the port. The Depression still gripped Australia and most of the men in the pub were unemployed, but Geoffrey had got his job back with the Country Roads Board.

'Well, Geoff?' his father said.

'Well, Dad?'

'A great day?'

'It sure is.' He grinned; his father loved his football and, at last, his team had won the Grand Final again.

'But not quite as good as 1921,' his father said.

201

'Not quite.' That was the year Geoffrey had played, scored two goals and they had won by four points. Then, he had been the hero of Richmond and they had celebrated for two days.

When the pub closed at a quarter past six, Geoffrey considered drinking out at the back with Jack Hanrahan, his father and the other men, but decided to go home to Marcia instead. She had been alone all day. He left the Mountain View in the cold, showery evening, stopped and bought the evening paper and looked at the headline. *Military Dictatorship Planned in Japan?* He turned to the back and read the racing news while he waited for the tram.

When he got home, he went into the living room and lit the fire. All Marcia's books lay around, but she wasn't there and he went into the kitchen to make a cup of tea. He put the kettle on the gas stove and went back to the fire. The house was cold and silent, and there was nothing to do. Maybe they would play golf tomorrow. He sat close to the fire, turned the wireless on and read the sports news again. At half past six there would be a summary of the Grand Final: it had been a good day. Outside, it was starting to rain. When the kettle boiled, he made the tea and cut some cold mutton for a sandwich. He waited by the fire. Marcia didn't arrive home until half past seven.

'Hullo,' she said, as she dumped her old valise on the table. 'Who won?'

'We did.'

'Yippee, Richmond strikes back.' She kissed him. 'We won the Grand Final: you must be pleased.'

'Where have you been?'

'If I tell you, you'll scream.'

'Try me.'

'The Congress Against War and Fascism.'

'Aw, Jesus.'

'I said you'd scream.'

'It's a load of bullshit.'

'It's not, you know. Who got the goals?'

'Titus got six, he was brilliant, and O'Halloran and Harris got three.'

'Good old Titus. Your father must be out of his mind.'

'I'll say. I left him getting on the grog with Jack Hanrahan.'

'Your poor mother.'

'She doesn't follow football.'

'That's not the point: they should let women in pubs.'

'They do.'

'Not the lousy cat bar, the main bar. You know, in all the years I've known you, I've never set foot in the Mountain View.'

'Let's not get on to that again,' Geoffrey said.

'It's true. Why can't I drink with you in the main bar of the Mountain View?' Marcia stood beside him and warmed her backside by the fire. 'What do you talk about in there?'

'Me?'

'All of you.'

'Well, today it was the Grand Final. We talked about the game.'

'Not today, other days.'

'I've told you. This and that, sport, and Dad and Jack talk about politics until the cows come home.'

'What do other men talk about, women?'

'I don't know.'

'What do *you* talk about, then? Football, the War?'

'What war?'

'The Great War.'

'Jesus, Marcia.'

She kissed him again. 'I'm sorry. Is there any beer in the ice chest?'

'Yeah, I'll get some.'

She watched him go out to the kitchen, thought about

her day, and sat by the fire. Geoffrey came back with the bottle, poured her a glass and said:

'What's for tea?'

'I don't know, I'm a bit tired. What's there?'

'Chops and potatoes are all I can see.'

'That's it, then.'

'Do you want me to help you?' He shovelled some more coal on the fire and took her valise off the table.

'No, give me a moment. Did they have the bands and all the military regalia? Did they have the drums and the pipers?'

'Yes, and Lord and Lady Milne, and the State Governor.'

Marcia thought of her afternoon and said: 'Have you got a cigarette?'

He gave her one. 'You're smoking too much.'

'You ought to talk.'

'What happened at the meeting?'

'What meeting?'

'The anti-war thing you've just been to.'

'Oh, we discussed Mussolini, Abyssinia, Hitler and Spain.'

'Do you want a game of golf tomorrow?'

'You don't care what we talked about, do you?'

'Yes, I do, but there won't be another war. I've told you before, the Germans are too sensible for that. They lost the last one, they've learnt their lesson.'

'Look,' Marcia said, 'the whole world's preparing for war. Hitler, Mussolini, Franco, the Japanese. It's even happening here.'

'Here?' He laughed. 'What's happening here? All we've got is a couple of old destroyers, an army that couldn't pull the skin off a rice pudding and no air force.'

'It's not what we've got, it's the way we're going: military drills in schools, the preparation for the Shrine, the whole thing's a glorification of war.'

'If you're right about another war,' Geoffrey said, 'I

204

should have thought that military drill in schools was essential. And what's wrong with having a Shrine of Remembrance?'

'It's not the Shrine, it's the preparations, the thousands of school children practising for the Duke and Duchess of Gloucester, the drilling and the flag waving.'

'Aw, come on, Marcia. I don't give a damn about the King and Queen or the Duke of Gloucester, but the drill's okay. It keeps all the kids in good shape.'

'Have you seen those newsreels of the Nazi rallies at Nuremberg? It's almost the same thing.'

Geoffrey was beginning to wish he'd stayed at the Mountain View with his father and the other men. But he was hungry.

'I'm going to peel the spuds.' He still loved her, but why couldn't she be like other women?

'I won't be a moment,' Marcia said. 'I just want to finish my drink.' She sat by the fire and wondered about Geoffrey and her marriage. It was now their eighth year and she had never wanted children, but she was pregnant. The doctor had told her this afternoon. What should she do and when would she tell him? Should she just get on with it?

It was the beginning of November and the English flowers bloomed in his mother's garden. There were crocuses, violets and daffodils; it was her fifty-seventh birthday and Geoffrey had brought her a present. It was a book: *The History of Mr Polly* by H. G. Wells. Marcia had chosen it for him. He kissed his mother on the cheek and gave her the present, neatly wrapped in brown shopping paper.

'Happy birthday, Mother.'

Mary Sawtell put her knitting back into her bag and kissed him on the neck. She looked at her son and unwrapped the parcel.

'H. G. Wells?' she said. 'I haven't read him.'

'I understand he's popular, Mother,' Geoffrey said. 'I hope you'll like it.'

'I'm sure I shall.'

They sat in the garden and listened to the sound of the birds: the starlings on the power lines, the sparrows, the magpies and the crows. Geoffrey considered the row of pines over the other side of Rotherwood Street: they must be seventy years old by now. *Tempus fugit*. That was the one piece of Latin he hadn't forgotten from school. There was an eagle in the sky: it must have lost its way.

'Thank you, dear,' his mother said. 'How's Marcia?'

'She's okay, very busy.'

'Busy at what?' His mother picked up her knitting once more.

'Meetings, political stuff.'

'Not very suitable for a woman, don't you think?'

Geoffrey didn't think so, either. He was getting tired of Marcia's activities, but they had no children, so what else could she do? She was only working part-time at the Library.

'Things are changing, Mother.'

'They certainly are. She should be at home more, looking after you.'

Geoffrey laughed and picked up his mother's ball of wool.

'I don't need much looking after.'

'There's such things as children. You've been married eight years and not getting any younger. How old is Marcia now?'

'Thirty-two.'

'She hasn't got many years left.'

'She doesn't want children, you know that.'

'It's not normal.'

'It's what she wants.'

'Nonsense, everybody has children. Where do you stand in all this?'

206

'I don't mind. Look, Mother, I don't want us to have a row on your birthday, but I love her even if you don't.'

'You know, Geoffrey, that I've never approved of her and I very much doubt if she approves of me. We've only met a dozen or so times in the last eight years and they've not been what you might call a success.'

'You wish I'd married someone else, don't you?' He looked at the garden and at the paddock over the road. The eagle had gone. They'd had this conversation before. Why couldn't she just accept Marcia? But he knew the answer.

'Of course I do, you know that. She's a most unnatural girl.'

'Unnatural?'

'Yes, unnatural. You should have had at least two children now, like everyone else.' His mother looked him in the face. 'There's nothing wrong with either of you, is there?'

'Wrong? No.'

'Her not going to church is one thing, and you don't go any more anyway, but those bolshevik politics she's involved in. I can't understand it.'

'Dad's involved in what you call bolshevik politics.'

'And he's none the better for that, but he's a man and as far as I know, he's not involved in the anti-war thing. A woman should be at home with her children.'

Geoffrey was silent.

'Don't you want children?'

'Yes, I do.'

'Well, tell her then, insist upon it.'

'You can't insist upon it, Mother.'

'Where there's a will, there's a way. It might bring this family together. And tell her to give up all this ridiculous anti-war business.'

Geoffrey got up and stretched his legs. Maybe his mother was right, not about going to church, but about the anti-war stuff. It was a bloody waste of time.

'What did Dad give you?' he said.

'The usual, *Evening in Paris*, I'm sure it's the only perfume your father knows.'

'Where's he now?'

'At work, I hope. Thank God you got your job back, it must have been humiliating.'

'Yes, it was.'

'Well, take my advice and have children while you can. The country needs them, and so do you.' Mary Sawtell rose and gathered up her wide straw hat and knitting. She was going grey, but was still tall and very beautiful. 'Do you want a cup of tea?'

Geoffrey looked at his watch: it was almost half past four. Saturday afternoons were a bit empty now the football season was over.

'No, thanks, Mother. I must be going. Give my regards to Dad.'

'If you go to the hotel, you'll see him before I do.'

'Happy birthday, Mother.' He kissed her again, put on his hat and went down the path. He got into the Essex Tourer and drove up the hill to Bridge Road.

It was a spectacular spring afternoon and Marcia and Geoffrey walked along St Kilda Beach. The tide was racing across the Bay, the seagulls wheeled and flew in from the south; gaff-rigged yachts sailed in the gentle southerly and there was a tramp steamer in the channel, the smoke from its tall funnel drifting. It was going to some foreign port; the tugs had wound in their hawsers and were going home. The mullet flashed and broke the blue water and Geoffrey remembered the *Ballarat*, and the beautiful young women waiting for the returned soldiers on the pier. Marcia walked ahead of him, bare-footed and strong, her frock trailing. Geoffrey watched the clouds bunching and bundling, he heard the gulls screaming and looked back at the tall buildings of Melbourne and the factory chimneys smoking. Other couples were strolling, hand in hand, on the beach. It was a brilliant, blue Australian afternoon, and far from the south, he could see a dark weather change coming in from the ocean. They stopped and sat by the bathing boxes. Marcia's hair was down and she left him and paddled in the cold, clear water. He watched her, her dress hitched above her knees, her legs glistening. At last, she came up from the water and sat down beside him in the early November afternoon. Marcia was beautiful. He thought of the trees in the Fitzroy Gardens, the Bourke Street cable tram and the urchins dropping off without paying their fares. *Heavens, no, I'll stand for an old soldier.* She pushed her toes into the sand, stroked her legs and said:

'I'm pregnant.'

Geoffrey was delighted and said: 'That's marvellous.' He couldn't believe it. It had been a long time and he thought of his mother in the garden. They would have a child. He looked directly at Marcia. 'Is it marvellous, or not?'

'I'm not sure,' she said. 'I'm not sure what to think.'

Geoffrey waited and watched the tide running. The young couples strolled past, their arms around each other. There was a small boat in trouble, far out across the Bay.

'I've thought of having an abortion,' Marcia said.

'You aren't going to? Jesus Christ I hope not.'

'No, of course not. I'm taking your advice and just getting on with it. You've always wanted children, haven't you?'

'Yes, most men do, but you've got to have it, not me. All I can do is help.'

Marcia looked at her husband; he was still very strong and handsome. She went to say something to him, but didn't. He would make a good father and was obviously hoping it would be a son.

If a war did come in the next few years, it would be too

209

young to fight and, unlike Europe, Australia would be a safe place.

'When did you see the doctor?' Geoffrey said.

'Yesterday.'

'So you weren't at the meeting?'

'I saw him first.'

'What did he say?'

'He said I was six weeks pregnant, that I was strong and in good health.'

'No worries, then?'

'No.'

'You don't seem very pleased. I am.'

'I'm not sure what to think, I've got a horror of being trapped, house-bound. Most women live solely as shadows of their men.'

'I've never made demands on you.'

'No, you haven't, but you're still very conservative.'

'Not so much conservative, as self-reliant. I believe in myself.'

'That's what attracted me to you. You can take what comes, can't you? Football, getting a job, your work, all physical things. You're a very strong man. When do you go away again?'

'In the middle of the month, we're putting a bridge in at Woodend.'

'Your mother will be pleased.'

'At my going away?'

'No, at my being pregnant.'

'Yes, she will, and so will my Dad.' He smiled. 'The Sawtell line lives and flourishes. My Dad's very fond of you.'

'Yes, he is, but your mother?'

'She still refuses to accept you, your beliefs, your activities.'

'A woman's place is in the home. Do you believe that?'

'Not necessarily, I just want you to be happy. I'm a simple-minded fellow, I don't want a great deal.'

'Just getting things done?'

'If you like.'

'Getting things done for what?'

'For us, for Australia. It's the best place in the world.'

'But you haven't been anywhere.'

'Yes, I have, to France, London and Belgium. It's the best. I'm a patriot.'

'My country, right or wrong?'

'No. You decide what's best and get on and do it as best you can. Keep your knives sharp and your guns well oiled.'

'You always talk of killing.'

'Just an expression. Whatever you do, do your best, no fancy theories. You see that steamer out there? It's an old coal-driven tub built forty years ago on Merseyside, going to Singapore or some place; but if the men make no mistakes, they'll get her there. No theories, just skills and hard work.'

'The men,' she said. 'And I'll have to work hard at being a mother?'

'Yes, just as you work hard at your tennis and golf.'

'And my politics?'

'I don't know about that.'

'If there's a civil war in Spain, which side will you fight on?' Marcia asked.

'This is this Franco bugger?'

'Yes.'

'On the other side. I don't like generals, and having chosen the side, I'd fight the best I could down to the last cartridge, using all my military skills.'

'Just like football?'

'I suppose so. You choose your side and you fight.'

Marcia took his hand. 'It's not as simple as that.'

'Isn't it? I told you, love, I'm a simple-minded man.'

'Are you going to the dedication of the Shrine?'

'Of course.'

'Why?'

'All those men killed, they should be remembered. We gave our best.'

'But it was an immoral war, it could have been avoided if people had thought and acted in some other way. It's what I was saying to you, we've got to stop that happening again.' Geoffrey remembered his father and Jack Hanrahan talking about the War in the back room of the Mountain View.

'The War may have been immoral, I suppose all wars are, but the War was the War for both the Huns and us. It was a thing in itself.' He tried to explain. 'It became a world we all accepted, that's why I'm going to the Shrine.'

'I can't understand,' Marcia said.

'No, you can't, you thought you could when we first met, but I put you right on that.'

'I'm going to the Shrine, too.'

'You are?'

'To demonstrate.'

'To what?'

'To demonstrate.'

'Against what?'

'War.'

'You're bloody mad.' He got up from the sand and stood over her. 'You're bloody mad.'

'Why? It's what I believe in.'

'You're pregnant, and some old soldier might push you in the gut. Jesus Christ, what are you on about? The Shrine's all we've got and you're going to try bugger it up. I can't understand you.'

'Look, Geoffrey, we're trying to stop war, the celebration of war.'

'What are you going to do? Raise your skirts and dance on the pavement?'

'We're going to hand out pamphlets.'

'Oh, Jesus,' Geoffrey laughed, 'pamphlets. If you're not careful, somebody will stick a Lee Enfield up your bum.'

212

'What's a Lee Enfield?'

'You know what it is. It's the standard army service rifle.'

'Are you forbidding me to go to the Shrine?' Marcia said. 'You can't, you know.'

Geoffrey Sawtell looked at his wife whom he loved and who was now carrying his child. He thought of their honeymoon at Queenscliff, the Indian Scout, the stream, the tennis, the dancing at the Menzies ballroom and the quiet nights at home during the cold Melbourne winters.

'I know that. I think you and your radical friends are insane and wrong, but I suppose you've got the right. Just don't let me see you, that's all.'

'And if you did, would you disown me?'

'No, love, I would not. Just don't let me see you, and for God's sake be careful.'

'I shall, I plan to fight another day.'

He sat down and they took each other's hands. The steamer was out at the entrance now, its plume of smoke spiralling against the western sun, and the yachts were coming in across the southern water.

'What's that saying about disagreeing, but defending the right?' Geoffrey said.

'Voltaire: I disagree with what you say, but I will defend to the death your right to say it.'

They stood up and walked down the beach to the car. It was getting cold and they would have to light another fire tonight.

'May I tell my mother and father?' he said.

'Of course.'

'No baptism?'

'It's a long way off, but no baptism, no mumbo-jumbo.'

'My poor mother.'

'Yes,' Marcia said. 'Your poor mother.'

They left the beach and drove home silently. Geoffrey thought of the child: he hoped nothing would go wrong.

213

He wanted a son; he could take him to the football, and teach him fishing and shooting.

It was Armistice Day, the eleventh day of November, 1934 and 350,000 people packed the Botanic Gardens, St Kilda Road and the adjoining boulevards of Melbourne. The Shrine of Remembrance was a massive structure, built of granite, freestone, bronze and marble, with terraces and grecian columns, topped by a pyramidal dome eighty-eight feet high. Like the Acropolis of Athens, it was sited on a small hill, built by the unemployed and overlooking Queen's Domain and the ornamental gardens. The monument dominated the City of Melbourne and was visible from all points of the compass; it was a beacon to all ships coming up the Bay. On each of its walls was a buttress group of lions rampant and a chariot, dedicated to Patriotism, Sacrifice, Justice, and Peace and Goodwill. In the Inner Shrine lay the Rock of Remembrance, sunk below the polished marble floor where no man could touch it. On it was the inscription: *Greater Love Hath No Man*, while in the King's Book was the special message: *Let their names be forever held in proud remembrance.* The walls of the Shrine were decorated with life-sized friezes showing all the armed forces of Australia in battle: the Navy afloat, the Australian Flying Corps, the Engineers and Tunnellers, the Army Medical Coprs, the Camel Corps, Transport, the Light Horse and Infantry. It was a commanding, sombre temple to all those who had served the Empire in the Great War, 1914–1918. The weather was cool and cloudy, with patches of sunshine.

> Let all men know that this is holy ground,
> This Shrine, established in the hearts of men
> As in the solid earth, commemorates a people's
>   fortitude and sacrifice.
> Ye that therefore come after, give remembrance.

All the public areas were filled by 9 a.m. and the returned soldiers and sailors formed up in their old units and marched sixty abreast up each side of the central avenue lined with oaks, elms and cypresses. Thirty thousand returned soldiers marched in silence toward the Shrine. There was no music, not a single drum beat and the vast crowd murmured like the surf upon the ocean. Even little children were silent and held their flags still as the grim-faced men marched by. Geoffrey William Sawtell, Corporal in the First Divisional Engineers, his medals on his chest, his hat set square, his arms swinging, marched with the men in perfect time up the hill and towards the terraces and the steps where the armed guard stood and the flags flew in the gentle breeze. No one spoke, they looked neither right nor left and their boots rang on the pavement. The fine thoroughbreds of the Australian Light Horse trotted and danced on the bluestone. As the men proceeded, there came the muffled peal of bells from St Paul's Cathedral. The crowds and the dignitaries waited. When the men had at last assembled, there was a pause, and then the massed bands played Handel's *Largo*, followed by *Lead, Kindly Light* and *Nearer My God to Thee*. A choir of 3500 voices sang these old, sad tunes and many men and women wept openly. As he sang with the men in his rich baritone, Geoffrey looked across the terraces for Marcia, but could not see her. Somewhere his mother, too, was in the crowd.

Seconds before 11 a.m., the bells stopped and a gun sounded the hour. Suddenly, the sun shone through the clouds in a shaft of light on to the Rock of Remembrance in the Inner Shrine, and the Duke of Gloucester's hand trembled as he laid the wreath of poppies on behalf of his father the King. Outside, the multitude stood, bare-headed and silent for two minutes, and the War medals tinkled; then another gun sounded and the trumpeters played the *Last Post* and the *Reveille*. The wreath-laying party retur-

215

ned and the massed choirs led the singing of the *Old Hundredth*. After the Archbishop had dedicated the stone, a massive cheer went up and 10,000 pigeons rose and flew to the homing points with the news that the Shrine had been handed over to the people of Victoria. All that day, men, women and children filed into the Inner Shrine to look upon the Rock of Remembrance. There had been no such occasion in Melbourne before.

As Geoffrey walked down St Kilda Road through the crowds, the returned men, the women and the children, he saw Marcia handing out pamphlets at a tram stop. There were many people waiting, the afternoon was getting cold and the children were crying. It had been a big day, and Marcia handed out the pamphlets as a tram rattled down the tracks

'Piss off, miss,' a returned soldier said. He was a big man with a red face and carrying a gladstone bag. 'We don't want bolsheviks here.'

The crowded tram went past without stopping and the people gathered around Marcia as it started to rain. Geoffrey started towards her, then he saw a man and two women wearing red badges come up. There was an argument and the soldier knocked the pamphlets from Marcia's hand.

'Piss off, you bolshies,' the soldier said. 'Go and live in Russia.'

Geoffrey watched Marcia walk away with the man and two women; the man with a beard had his hand on her shoulder. He wasn't sure what to do. Should he go and take her home? That would be too embarrassing. He stood at the tram stop.

'Jesus, did you see that?' the soldier said to him. 'They should lock those people up. Bloody traitors.' He ground the pamphlets into the gutter. Geoffrey said nothing.

216

'Bloody pacifists,' the soldier said. 'What did they ever do? And as for the women, Christ, if they belonged to me. What show were you in?'

'Passchendaele.'

'Jesus, you know what it was all about, and so do I. I was at Gallipoli. They should pass a law and put that lot behind bars.' It was getting cold and at last, another tram came. The red-faced soldier picked up his gladstone bag and the bottles rattled. Geoffrey stepped aboard and went home. He needed a drink.

'I saw that little affair,' Geoffrey said as Marcia came through the front door.

'What little affair?' She threw her hat and coat on the sofa.

'The affair at the tram stop.'

'Oh, that.'

'Yes, oh, that.'

'What about it?'

'First of all, as I told you, you're bloody mad provoking returned men, and secondly, he could have hit you. You've been hit before, remember?'

'Where were you?'

'About ten yards away.'

'I didn't see you.'

'Obviously.'

'Why didn't you come up?'

'I thought discretion was the better part of valour. And anyway, you had your friends with you. Who was that man?'

'What man?'

'The bloke with his hand on your shoulder, the fellow with a beard who came up with those two women and extricated you.'

'Oh, him, just a member of the Congress.'

'Well, you can thank your lucky stars he turned up.'

'What if he hadn't? What would you have done?'

217

'God knows.'

'Look, Geoffrey, you told me that you choose your side and fight. Well, I've chosen my side, if you can call handing out pamphlets fighting.'

'It's the wrong bloody side.'

'Why?'

'Because you won't win.' He took up the poker and stabbed at the ashes of last night's fire.

'So you always choose the winning side?'

'You try to.'

'It looks as though we're on opposing sides.'

'Why?'

'You like war, I don't.'

'*Like* war? I don't like war.' He drank his whisky. 'I don't like war. I've fought.'

'So you keep telling me.'

'I've seen men holding their guts in their hands, I've seen men coughing their lungs out with mustard gas, I've seen strong men crying, I've seen men mutilated: legs, arms, noses, private parts; they're still hidden away now in repatriation hospitals. Don't tell me I *like* war. What you and your friends fail to understand is that the Shrine is all we survivors have got, it holds us all together, we've been where you lot haven't, you've got no bloody idea, and all you can do is try to bugger it up. You don't hand a soldier an anti-war pamphlet; you respect him, or at least, leave him alone.'

'Respect him?'

'Yes, respect him, he's fought and you haven't.' Sawtell got up and put his glass down. 'I can't stand any more of your bullshit, your farting around with pamphlets and trying to bugger up ordinary, decent, patriotic people. I'm going out and I'll see you later.'

Marcia watched Geoffrey pick up his hat and overcoat, the door slammed and he was gone. She heard the sound of the car being started outside in the dark, sat down and

218

drank the last of his whisky. The house was cold and there was no familiar fire burning. Why should he not tell her about the War? But she knew why: it was his business. She knew there would be another war and she couldn't sit back and accept it. Marcia went out to the woodshed, brought in the kindling, the logs and the coal, lit a large fire and drank another whisky. Geoffrey would be with his father and Jack Hanrahan at the Mountain View. Bugger Geoffrey, she thought, bugger him. She would go on. What she was doing was right. Why had she married Geoffrey? She had married him because he was steadfast and a soldier.

In the following January, Marcia had a miscarriage after a street demonstration against war and fascism. It was touch and go, but when it was over she could no longer have children.

· XI ·

To Broken Hill

THEY HAD SETTLED into a daily routine that made life
monotonous, but the going was steady. As St John Jackson
and Sergius Donaldson had realized, each man had to care
for his own mount and packhorse. Each looked after his
own gear; if something was lost or broken, it was the
owner's responsibility. Every morning and evening, you
fed and watered your horse and tended your pack animal.
This was the way the Australians worked. Kevin O'Donohue, however, kept a general eye on all the horses at the
picket line. Every morning, he carefully inspected their feet,
shoes and fetlocks. They rode seven hours a day and
walked the last hour. Counihan did the heavy work and
O'Donohue cooked. The weather was cloudy and humid,
there was often thunder and lightning late in the afternoon,
but no rain fell. It was now late September and O'Donohue, who knew this country, recognized the signs of an
early, hot summer. Once they left the river and the lakes at
Menindee, the going would be tough, the feed would be
bad and they would have to depend on water from the
tanks and wells in the desert country south of Broken Hill.
Sawtell knew this too, for he had camped out there eleven
years ago. But now on the river, the hunting was good. In
the cool, balmy evenings Sergius Donaldson shot ducks
with his shotgun, and St John Jackson took down
waterfowl with his Purdey. Sometimes, O'Donohue came

back from the river with freshwater mussels, birds' eggs and watercress. Some nights, Sawtell went fishing and caught freshwater bream. But mostly the Australians preferred to eat mutton, day after day, and St John Jackson and Sergius Donaldson could not understand this. Counihan said mutton was easy to throw on the fire. By the creeks and watercourses, wild mint, dandelions and forget-me-nots grew; and Donaldson thought this was some twilight Arcadia. There were kangaroos, eagles and geese, and the parakeets swooped and called among the trees by the river. Big flocks of emu raced away across the dry parklands with their chicks, and giant lizards lay in the branches of the box trees. They rode six days; every evening, Sawtell chose the campsite and they settled down under the river gums. Few words were spoken, and now, because they were close to the road to Menindee, they kept three-hour watches through the night. Each man took his turn, but there was no sign of the enemy and the bush was silent. When it was his turn to watch, Frank Counihan looked for the glow of the campfire west of the river. He fiddled with his Luger submachine gun, but for the last two nights there had been no sign.

On the afternoon of the seventh day, they heard the sound of a motor on the road. They stopped, dismounted and waited in the trees and the saltbush. The horses and the men smelt of sweat and they waited. The vehicle passed and the dust drifted through the bush as the rabbits ran.

'Okay, Kevin,' Sawtell said, 'you're the fastest, run up to the road and have a look.'

The boy took off like a hare and disappeared through the scrub. The four men waited by their horses, and the seagulls swam on the river. O'Donohue made it to the road and lay in the ditch. He saw an armoured personnel carrier in the distance and plumes of dust flew. It went out of sight up the road to Wilcannia. O'Donohue ran back, found them standing and waiting and said:

221

'It was a tank.'

'What?' St John Jackson said.

'A tank.'

'How big was it?'

'Small.'

'It was probably an armoured personnel carrier.' St John Jackson turned and said: 'Gentlemen, our first brush with the enemy.'

'It's unlikely they're at Menindee,' Sawtell said. 'I reckon they're on reconnaissance from Broken Hill.'

'I think you're correct, Mr Sawtell. Shall we press on?'

'There's not much else we can do. If they're there in strength, we can by-pass south.'

'We'd better try to pick up some tucker for the horses while we can,' Frank Counihan said. 'There's three homesteads on the river before Menindee.'

'And I suggest,' St John Jackson said, 'that this evening we strip and clean the Brens.' He coughed. 'We may have need to use them.'

They mounted and moved south through the box woods.

At five o'clock, they reached Riverside Station, and they saw the homestead. A two-storeyed, wooden nineteenth-century building with gothic windows stood tall by the river. Cypresses grew in the weedy front garden and no lights shone from the house.

'I'll stay here with the horses,' Sawtell said. 'Go and have a look.'

'If you don't mind, Mr Sawtell,' Sergius Donaldson said, 'I'll keep you company.'

'Okay.'

Sawtell settled down, rolled two cigarettes, gave one to the Padre, and watched Counihan, St John Jackson and O'Donohue walk towards the home paddock and the building.

'Pianos,' Sergius Donaldson said.

'Pianos? What about them?'

'All the homesteads we've been to have pianos.'

'The people who owned these places were often very wealthy, their children went to the best schools in Melbourne and Adelaide. It's the frontier, Padre, but it's not as uncivilized as it appears.'

'I'm beginning to see that.'

'They were mainly Scots, and Scots believe in education and husbandry.'

'Husbandry?'

'Looking after things, making the country work, clearing it of pests whether they be roos, rabbits or blacks. There's probably a grand piano in the front room of that house, and with luck, the Major can play us some Gilbert and Sullivan.'

'You like Gilbert and Sullivan?' the Padre said.

'Yes, Padre, I do.'

'And what is your favourite?'

'*HMS Pinafore.*'

Sergius Donaldson laughed. 'That, too, is the Major's.'

'I know.' Sawtell looked north-east up the river and then at the home paddock. The three of them disappeared around the back of the house.

'It looks as though there's nobody,' Sergius Donaldson said.

'Probably.' Sawtell ground the butt of his cigarette under his boot, 'but we have to be careful.'

'What's it like to have your country occupied?'

'It's not occupied, it's empty.'

'The Japanese.'

'What about them?'

'They've taken your family.'

'I don't have any family.' Sawtell saw Counihan moving through the back garden past the water tanks, and Sergius Donaldson looked at the river. 'My back's sore,' Sawtell said, 'I'm too old for this caper, I should be at home drinking whisky by the fire.'

Donaldson realized that none of them had any family. There was no one to return to. There were no home fires burning.

'How old are you?'

'Forty-six.'

'I can give you ten years.'

'Good on you, Padre, but you've got God to help you.'

'And you?'

'They're coming back,' Sawtell said, 'maybe we can have Gilbert and Sullivan tonight.'

'You can sing?'

'We can all sing, Padre, and I sang moderately well a long time ago. My mother taught me to play.' He waited for the men to come back through the long grass. *The Honeysuckle and the Bee.*

'Do you have a favourite tune, Padre?'

'Yes, I do.' He hummed a few bars. It was *And Sheep May Safely Graze.*

The others stood before them, Counihan with his Luger, St John Jackson with his Webley and O'Donohue with his Winchester.

'There's no bugger around,' Frank Counihan said. 'It's a big house, they were rich bastards.'

'Did you see a piano?'

'What?'

'Never mind.'

Sawtell gathered up the lead ropes of the packhorses and got up with the Padre; the moon shone and they moved in.

The house was magnificent, Sergius Donaldson thought, magnificent. There were high porticoes, a broad front porch, parquet floors and ornate, pressed-tin ceilings. He went over to the huge sandstone fireplace, where half-burnt red gum logs lay, then he opened the ruined folding doors to the next room. There was the Chappell grand piano, its lid down. Sergius Donaldson went to the keyboard and tried a chord on the dusty, yellow keys.

224

There was no sound and he lifted the lid to find every string and hammer had been broken. He closed the lid and looked out of the vacant windows at the bush. There was the river and the lakes, and to the west he saw a campfire glowing. *And Sheep May Safely Graze.* The north wind blew through the window and the corrugated iron creaked and flapped. The strange birds called in the trees, and in the darkness was the sound of nocturnal animals. Sergius Donaldson left the piano and joined the men in the other room.

Major St John Jackson was stripping a Bren and the pieces lay on the parquet floor by the light of the hurricane lamp. Kevin O'Donohue was watching him.

'Have you ever stripped a Bren, O'Donohue?'

'Nah.'

'Right then, there's a drill, I'll instruct you.'

Sergius Donaldson turned away and drifted through the house. He found Sawtell and Counihan in the kitchen; they were sitting on the stone floor, drinking rum.

'Gentlemen, may I join you?'

Sawtell looked up and smiled at the clergyman.

'Gooday, Father, have a drink.' He passed the bottle. 'Did you find the piano?'

'I did.'

'But there's no Gilbert and Sullivan tonight.'

'There is not.'

'Well then,' Sawtell said, 'all we have left is Kevin O'Donohue and his harmonica.' He drank from the bottle. 'I'm sure he can play Bach or Handel or a hymn composed by John Wesley.'

'We want a fire for our tea,' Frank Counihan said.

'There's no fire tonight, Frank, it's cold tucker, the light of the hurricane lamp's enough to attract any bastard.'

Sawtell raised himself slowly to his feet, felt his joints cracking and looked at the clergyman. 'My back's bad, it's cold food, oiling the Brens and rifles and into bed. The Japs

225

could well be at Menindee.' He coughed and stubbed out his cigarette on the stone floor. 'The Major's preparing us for battle lines.'

After tea, St John Jackson continued instructing O'Donohue on the use of the Bren and the others cleaned and oiled their weapons. Counihan and Sawtell lugged the kerosene cases of explosives inside, stripped and cleaned the Thompsons and put the Mills bombs in their saddlebags. O'Donohue learnt to strip and re-assemble the Brens very quickly: he was a practical country boy. St John Jackson was pleased. The young Australian was far removed from the spavined men from the Manchester slums he had instructed twenty-eight years ago.

'Good, O'Donohue,' he said as they crouched in the spacious dining room. 'Very good.' He looked at the open face and wished he were a young man again.

Next morning on the track, Frank Counihan came back and reported that Menindee was deserted. There was nobody, he said, not even blacks.

'Did you check out the railway station?' Sawtell said.

'Yeah.'

'And the pubs?'

'Yeah, there's only two, Maiden's and another. I didn't go inside, but there was no bugger about.' Counihan rolled a cigarette. 'There's just cats and dogs.'

They had started cold and they stood by their horses wearing their greatcoats. But Sawtell didn't like the sound of this: it might be a stake-out and they could be ambushed. He opened the holster of the Webley and put the lanyard around his shoulder.

'We may as well go in. What do you think, Major?'

'I don't see why not, the town might have something to offer. How big is it?'

'About half the size of Wilcannia. Maiden's Hotel is well known, Burke and Wills stayed there.'

'Burke and Wills?'

226

'The explorers.'

'Ah.'

Sawtell swung upon his horse. The others followed and they moved off through the bush.

It was a place of lakes and lagoons and wildlife abounded. Butcher-birds and brilliantly plumed cockatoos swarmed in the thick stands of box woods, black oaks and native pine. Pamamaroo Lake stretched north-west, and beyond that, the sullen, low ranges of the interior. Counihan rode out, returned and said there was no traffic on the road or the bridge. Sawtell wanted a mug of tea, but it was too risky to boil the billy. They proceeded slowly and the harnesses creaked. Emu and big, dark kangaroos bounded off through the meadows as they approached. They came to the road and stopped once more. The bridge across the river was another lift-up and on the other side, a small sunken paddle steamer and two derelict barges lay in the water. The buildings of the small town were visible through the trees. Sawtell considered.

'Let's go over one at a time, there's no point in all of us getting caught if someone's there.' He tossed the lead ropes of his packhorse to O'Donohue and rode up on to the road. They cocked their rifles and watched Sawtell ride over the bridge. The hooves of his horse sounded on the timbers and the crows screeched. Sawtell waved from the far bank and, with guns raised, they went across.

The main street was dusty, wide and exposed and they could see the low-slung, sandstone hotel about 500 yards away. The breeze was fresh, the dust flew and a windmill turned.

'This situation doesn't appeal to me, Mr Sawtell,' St John Jackson said. 'We've got no cover and if that personnel carrier should return . . .'

'I was thinking the same thing, let's get the outfit down there behind those buildings and trees.'

They found a spot among corrugated-iron outbuildings

and lean-tos where big river gums grew. O'Donohue strung up the picket line and put the explosives in the out-house.

'This is okay,' he said. 'They can't see us from here.'

'I think I'll stay here and put my feet up,' the Padre said.

'Right, you do that.' Sawtell noticed that Sergius Donaldson had a cold sore on his lower lip and looked tired. 'We'll go up to the pub.'

'I'll stay, too,' O'Donohue said, 'I've got some repairing to do.'

'Okay.' Sawtell looked at the boy. He knew what he was saying: if something happened, the Padre couldn't be relied upon to move fast enough. He didn't like the feeling of this place on the road to Broken Hill; they wouldn't stay here very long.

Maiden's Hotel had nothing to offer. They fossicked in the overgrown garden and wandered through the small bedrooms. Every window and bottle had been smashed and the splintered glass crunched beneath their boots. There was no drink and, this time, no cellar in the back garden. Counihan and O'Donohue went through all the outbuildings and back sheds without success. Sawtell rummaged in the bar, but all he found were some cheap football trophies and a framed photograph of six young men in military uniform. They were wearing slouch hats and puttees. Sergius Donaldson came up and joined them and they walked up the main street to the railway station. They stopped at a garage and found the remains of a Hupmobile. Sawtell looked at the big American car and thought of the years after the War, of picnics, of Marcia and playing tennis on country grass courts.

When they got to the station, Counihan jumped down off the platform and walked up the double set of tracks toward the points. He found they had been destroyed and then repaired. He crouched and put his ear to the lines. No sound. Counihan gazed north-west to Broken Hill; this line went south to Parkes and eventually to Sydney and was of great military value. He walked back along the sleepers.

'Well, Mr Counihan?' St John Jackson said from the platform. Counihan looked at the Major standing there with his topee and Webley. Jesus, he thought, this bastard's getting up my nose. He looked around for Sawtell and the Padre, but they had gone.

'Where's the others?'

'At the station master's house. Well, what did you see?'

Counihan hoisted himself up on to the platform and faced St John Jackson.

'Someone's been here. The points have been repaired.'

'Where does the line go?'

'Down to Parkes and on to Sydney.'

'It should be blown again then.'

'We'll see.'

Counihan turned on his heel and left the Major on the platform as he was getting out his binoculars. The stupid old bastard, somebody would have taken it out further down, they weren't the only outfit in the bloody country. He met Sawtell and the Padre at the station gates.

'Some bugger's done a repair job on the points.'

'That settles it,' Sawtell said, 'we're getting out.'

St John Jackson came up, binoculars in hand. 'We should destroy the line, Mr Sawtell, it's of strategic importance.'

'No way, Major, it's the mine we're after and it's the mine we'll get.'

The sun was hot now and the flies were about. Counihan spat between his feet and scratched his beard. St John Jackson surveyed the wretched settlement and the arid country south of the lake. This place, he thought, was hardly worth defending, nor were the people in it. Darwin, Bourke, Wilcannia and now Menindee; what lay ahead beyond and where they would end up, only God knew.

They packed and mounted within the hour, and after

229

three hours' ride left the river south-west to Cawndilla Lake. That night, they camped on a beach on the west side; they watered and swam the horses and O'Donohue shot two ducks which they cooked in the ashes. The last of the rum was drunk and after they had dossed down, Sergius Donaldson took the first watch. He sat on the beach and looked over the dark, moonlit water and wondered what God had in store for him. At midnight young O'Donohue relieved him and said:

'I hope you had a good look, Padre, that's the last water you're going to see for a long time.'

The vast, flat, grey plain stretched before them. The hot sun shone and they rode over the red earth through the saltbush.

With the river gone, the trees were small and fragile and their black branches crumbled at a touch. The sky was blue and cloudless; there was no shade and they missed the dark, mysterious recesses of the river. Sergius Donaldson now realized how that ancient stream had sustained them. The silence was profound and all that was heard was the creak of the harness and the sound of the horses' hooves on the earth. Every ten miles or so, was a tree-line, a creek which promised water. But this was not to be: the watercourses were dry, their beds littered with stones and the branches of gum trees washed down by some long-forgotten flood.

They rose at five in the dark, were on the track by six to avoid the heat of the day; then at 10.30, they stopped in a creek bed and boiled the billy. The food was hard tack now: bully beef, the eternal cold mutton and rabbit. O'Donohue said they would have soon to go on to roo as the mutton wouldn't keep in this weather. The flies were bad and each man covered his face with his scarf as they sat silently around the small fire. The eagles wheeled and soared in the limitless sky, and Sergius Donaldson thought of the seagulls and waterfowl, their wings cracking and water streaming from their feathers as they took off from the still waters of Cawndilla lake. He crouched on the stones and drank his tea: there were no birds' eggs and watercress here.

Sawtell left the fire and walked to the top of a sand rise where he took a bearing on a windmill. He looked west for the Barrier Range, but there was no sign and he went back for a cigarette and a second mug of tea. He looked at the clean-shaven Englishmen and smiled. From now on, standards would have to be lowered.

'There's a station north-west called Leonora Downs,' Sawtell said, 'and there's a tank on the way in. We should make it by the end of the day.'

Frank Counihan walked around the creek bed, kicked at the stones and timber. He pissed in the saltbush and came back.

'It's an early summer,' he said, 'the whole place is as dry as a chip.'

'When do you think it last rained, Mr Counihan?' Sergius Donaldson said.

Counihan looked at the old clergyman, grinned and said: 'Hard to tell, five years maybe, but this ain't too bad unless the tanks are dry.' He grinned once more at the Padre and the Major. Scare the bastards.

St John Jackson got up, ground his cigarette under his boot and said: 'Well, let's get on with it then.'

He strode to his chestnut mare, checked the load on his packhorse, mounted easily and waited. O'Donohue smothered the fire, hung the billy on the packframe hook and they all swung up to move away through the bush. As they rode, Sawtell again thought of the British officers on the bullring. They were born to lead, he thought, born to lead.

* * *

231

At half past three, they came to a small lake shining in the sandhills and an eagle was perched on a fence post on the beach. They were now in the heat of the day and there was no cover. St John Jackson was in the lead and rode down to the water as it lay gleaming in the sun. He let go the lead rope of his packhorse and it wandered back a few steps towards the scrub. This was indeed, a welcome sight. The Major got to the beach and stopped: it was salt. He sat upright on his horse as the others came down the slope in the shimmering heat. St John Jackson, disappointed, turned his horse and it went down through the salt crust to its fetlocks. The chestnut mare snorted, reared, plunged deeper, forward then back, and sank quickly to its hocks. Oh God, Sawtell thought, the stupid old bugger. The man was mad, like the generals in the War. The mare was their best horse. The eagle took off from the post. St John Jackson used the reins and his boots and tried to ride out, but the horse snorted, plunged forward again and fell back.

'Jesus bloody Christ,' Kevin O'Donohue shouted as he dismounted and ran down the bank, 'ride the bastard out, Major, ride the bastard out. Don't let it roll, keep it moving.' Counihan, the Padre and Sawtell swung down from their horses and ran down to the edge of the salt lake. The chestnut mare reared and bucked back and forward for two or three minutes, sinking further into the lake. The salt splintered like ice, cracked and the mud beneath was as black as coal. The Major's horse went forward and his topee fell.

'Turn the horse, Major,' O'Donohue shouted as he waved his hat. 'Turn it, get it around. Walk it.' He stood, powerless.

'We're going to lose this nag,' Counihan said to Sawtell, 'unless he can ride it out.' He, too, stood on the beach and shouted:

'Turn the bugger, turn it, Jesus, get it around.'

St John Jackson felt the mare shaking, again used his

boots and reins; the horse screamed, plunging and kicking. He knew now he couldn't ride it out. O'Donohue kept shouting and banging his hat on his knees; Counihan swore; Sergius Donaldson cursed and prayed and walked up and down the beach; but Sawtell reckoned the horse had gone, barring a miracle, and he didn't believe in them.

'Mr Sawtell?' The Padre said, his face steaming with sweat and dirt. 'Is it lost?'

'Padre, you know horses better than I do, your father rode them. It's gone.'

'Holy Mother of God,' O'Donohue said and grabbed a rope from his packframe, but they all knew the Major's horse was probably finished. They sweated, stood, shouted and smelled the black salt. The mare plunged forward and backward again, started to roll, and St John Jackson kicked his feet from the stirrups and bailed out. He dropped into the mud, sank above his knees, untied the girths and threw off the saddle and blanket. O'Donohue was still shouting:

'Get it out, get it out, it's our best horse.' He threw the rope to the Major. 'Get this around its neck.'

But he knew their chances were slipping away. It was very hot now and the sweat ran down all their backs. St John Jackson stood back in the mud and the chestnut rolled, snorting and shaking and panting hard, its flanks heaving and sweat foaming from its body. O'Donohue struggled through the salt toward the horse.

'Get up, you bastard,' he shouted. 'Christ Jesus, get up.' St John Jackson made one last effort, pulled at the rope, looked at the horse struggling and knew it was hopeless. The mare's ears lay flat, its tongue protruded and its flanks were covered with salt and foam.

'Maybe we can get another rope around its neck,' Counihan said as he stood in the mud. 'Maybe we can manhandle the bugger out.'

'It's our best horse,' O'Donohue said. 'We can't afford to lose it. We can't.'

233

But as St John Jackson struggled out through the salt, his uniform covered in filth and reeking of salt and carrying his saddle, they all knew the mare had gone.

'Well, Major,' Sawtell said, 'I think you've lost your horse.' He regarded the Englishman as he stood there, covered with salt and mud and holding his topee. St John Jackson wiped his hands with his scarf, then brushed the flies away.

'Mr Sawtell, I believe you're right. Please accept my apologies.' Nothing was said and they all looked at the chestnut mare. Sawtell took out the hunter: it was now almost four o'clock. They had to make Leonora Downs by nightfall; the Major would have to ride the spare, and with luck they would pick another up at the station.

The afternoon sun shone from the west as St John Jackson picked up the BSA. He cocked the rifle, went back through the mud, raised the gun and shot the chestnut between the eyes. The blood and mucus spurted, its head went down and St John Jackson removed the crupper, the bit and bridle. He clambered back, took up his saddle and blanket, threw them on the spare and stood by his pack-horse.

'Are we ready, gentlemen?'

Jesus, Sawtell thought as he looked at the Major, his topee set square on his head, his filthy uniform; there was the stiff upper lip. St John Jackson had liked that horse. Frank Counihan swung up and gazed at the Englishman. He squinted at the western sun and pulled his hat down. The others mounted and they rode away slowly through the bush. Sergius Donaldson looked back at the salt lake and saw the eagles and the crows flying in. Francis, he thought, was indeed a most courageous man. But as he rode, Sawtell knew that the country had tricked them for the first time: it was the enemy behind their back. And St John Jackson had made his first mistake.

* * *

234

There was water in the tank outside Leonora Downs and they gave the horses a drink at the trough. Kevin O'Donohue shot some rabbits with his Winchester; he hung them on his packsaddle and they rode into the station. It was dark and the buildings loomed in the night. The house had been gutted by fire, and only three stone chimneys stood. The night came down cold and clear and starry and they camped in the shearers' quarters; the building was made of stone and Frank Counihan found three bags of oats for the horses. O'Donohue gutted and skinned the rabbits and cooked them in the ashes of the fire. Counihan poked around the burnt timbers of the homestead while the Englishmen went down to the bore to wash themselves. Sawtell put on his greatcoat and sat by the fire with O'Donohue; he thought about the chestnut mare in the salt lake. There were no horses at Leonora Downs and they couldn't afford to lose another. The frogs croaked in the mud by the tank. The boy said:

'We shouldn't have lost that horse, it was a good one.'

'They don't know the country,' Sawtell said. 'It's new to them.'

'It doesn't get any better where we're going. You'd better tell them.'

Sawtell rolled a cigarette and looked at O'Donohue.

'All I want is that mine, then they can wash themselves six times a day and lose all the horses they like.'

'Are you going to ditch them?'

'Not necessarily, but they treat this place as though it's some part of Africa, to them it's all red on the map.'

'The clergyman's not a bad old bloke.'

'Yeah,' Sawtell said, 'he can ride that big waler and dispense the Holy Sacraments, and he can use that shotgun, he might come in useful.'

Kevin O'Donohue didn't understand Sawtell, and said nothing. They saw Frank Counihan coming back from the ruins of the homestead; he was empty-handed and stood by the fire. There was soot and ash on his face and in his beard.

'There's nothing around, not a bloody thing; that was a good horse, a strong bugger.'

'Yeah,' Sawtell said, 'it was a strong bugger, this country's tricky. I camped out here ten years ago.' He sat by the fire, he was tired and his body ached, he was covered with salt and mud and wanted to wash, but the Englishmen were at the bore.

'A salt lake's no place for a baptism; have you got your harmonica, Kevin?'

The boy reached in his coat pocket, and the cold stars shone.

'Yeah.'

'Okay, play us something.'

'What do you want?'

'*Bold Jack O'Donohoe*.'

The southern stars shone, and Sawtell sang as Frank Counihan tossed more wood on the fire, and O'Donohue played.

It was there for the sake of five hundred pounds
I was sent across the main,
For seven long years, in New South Wales,
To wear a convict's chain.
Then come, my hearties, we'll roam the mountains high.
Together we will plunder, together we will die.

Sergius Donaldson and St John Jackson came up through the scrub and heard the singing. They saw the Australians sitting by the fire and O'Donohue playing his harmonica. Sawtell's voice drifted into the night and they sat by the fire and listened to the big man singing.

Then come, my hearties, we'll roam the mountains high.
Together we will plunder, together we will die.

Sawtell stopped and said: 'You shouldn't have lost that horse, Major, it was a strong animal.'

Kevin O'Donohue put the harmonica back in his pocket and listened. Frank Counihan stood up in the black night as the gentle north wind blew.

'It was my horse, Mr Sawtell.'

'It was *our* horse.' Sawtell poked at the fire. 'From now on, keep off the beaches; this isn't Brighton where retired colonels sit on the pier.'

St John Jackson remembered Sawtell and Counihan coming in out of the night and drinking his whisky. Sawtell had invaded his premises, he had inspected his guns and photographs.

'If you are agreeable, gentlemen, I shall retire.'

He rose and went inside the stone building to his bedroll. Sergius Donaldson went to speak, but changed his mind. Sawtell got up, walked down to the picket line and looked at the horses. He inspected the gear, the explosives and the weapons, the Brens and the Lewis. He hoped that within three or four days, they would see the Barrier Range and Broken Hill. He walked through the scrub towards the bore to wash and thought of his mother's piano and singing. *The Honeysuckle and the Bee.* Losing that horse was bad. It was a cold, clear night.

St John Jackson lay in his blankets. He thought of Sawtell, the BSA and the chestnut mare's head going down.

If we confess our sins, He is faithful and just to forgive our sins, and to cleanse us from all unrighteousness.

The night was long, he could not sleep and was thankful when it was his turn to keep watch at midnight. He was awake when Counihan shook his shoulder. The tall bearded Australian stood by his bedrool, Luger submachine gun in hand. Nothing was said and St John Jackson pulled on his greatcoat, took up his BSA and went outside. The night was cold and silent as he walked around the country buildings and the windmill tower climbed high. The Southern Cross shone. The Major walked down the track to the

237

trough and looked east toward the salt lake where he had lost his horse. He saw a campfire glowing.

The dew was on the ground and they kept riding west. There was still no sign of the Barrier Range and they felt the sun on their backs. Soon, with the heat of the day, the flies would come. Sergius Donaldson and St John Jackson rode together at the back of the line as the dust rose into the clear morning air. The morning sky was infinite, blue and cloudless.

'Sergius,' St John Jackson said, 'what do you think of our man Sawtell now?'

The Padre looked at his comrade. They were sweating and their bodies reeked.

'You're referring to the horse?'

'The horse was a bad show.' He coughed in the dust.

'And Sawtell's rebuke?'

'Also a bad show, I am the senior officer.'

'You placed him in command.'

'One does not do these things publicly.'

Sergius Donaldson picked at his lip and ran his hand over his chin. He had not shaved this morning. And already his back ached.

'Francis, I venture to suggest that we are hardly in the officers' mess at Meerut now.'

'A damned pity we're not, the man's uncouth, they're all uncouth. My God, what are we coming to? Singapore, Darwin and now this god-forsaken place; Counihan's a barbarian, and God knows what's happening at home.'

'Home?'

St John Jackson looked at the Padre. 'England.'

'Ah.' Sergius Donaldson suddenly realized that he had not thought of the Downs for some time now. He considered the bush and thought of Counihan proffering the bottle at Wilcannia.

'Sawtell's a strange man, God knows what goes on in his mind, that prayer book, his singing, he's an enigma, but Counihan is straightforward.'

'A killer.'

'I fear so, but war makes strange bedfellows of us all. War is about killing.'

'And after this show at Broken Hill?'

'God will decide.'

They descended into a creek bed where big gums grew, and already O'Donohue had a fire going for the billy tea. The packhorses were unloaded and tethered: the inevitable routine. Sergius Donaldson walked up the bank and on to the crest of a sandhill. Kites, eagles and plovers flew and the plain went south for ever. Suddenly his heart lifted, God was with them and this country was at last becoming beautiful. He thought he was beginning to understand. But he was not.

Frank Counihan sat on a log, drank his tea and chewed his cold mutton. 'This stuff's going off,' he said. 'We'd better kill a roo.'

He looked over at Sergius Donaldson. 'That's a bad lip you've got there, Padre, have one of these.' Counihan reached into his saddlebag and tossed over a wild lemon. 'They're a bit tough, but they keep the sores away.'

The clergyman took out his pocket knife, cut the woody skin and sucked the bitter juice. 'Thank you, Mr Counihan.'

'Do you want any, Major?'

'No, thank you.'

'Suit yourself.' Counihan took out his tobacco tin and rolled a cigarette. 'How are we doing, Geoff?'

Sawtell looked at the Englishmen. Except for the horse, so far so good; they didn't look too bad. St John Jackson was still like a ramrod and the Padre was a tough old bugger. He wished he'd met him in the trenches when he'd needed help.

'We should be at Willeila Station this afternoon, then it's Eaglehawk and the road to Broken Hill. Four more days and we'll see some action.'

'We're still being followed,' St John Jackson said, 'I saw a campfire to the east last night.'

'We could be, Major, who knows? Maybe it's soldiers like us, maybe it's riffraff, but I'm not prepared to find out. It's not the Japs, that's for sure. They won't camp out in this country, there's no sake and no rice.' He laughed and sat on the river stones. He thought about the campfires behind them. St John Jackson drank his tea and wondered again what had happened at Stalingrad. If it had fallen, he supposed there were groups like this all over Russia, and both places were equally uncivilized. Both people were tribesmen. Counihan got up, tossed his cigarette on to the fire and kicked sand into the flames.

'Okay then. Do you want to ride out, Kevin? We'll get ourselves a roo.'

'Yeah.' O'Donohue looked at Sawtell. 'Can I have a lend of your rifle?'

Sawtell tossed the Lee Enfield over to the boy.

'You've got eight rounds, don't use them all. We'll take your packhorses.'

'No worries.'

Sergius Donaldson stood and watched Counihan and O'Donohue ride up from the creek bed and disappear into the scrub. Uncouth, these Australians might be, but they were indeed resourceful men. And resourcefulness had built an Empire. Sawtell was loading his packhorse. He turned and said:

'Major, do you want to lead? The track's quite clear.'

'No, Mr Sawtell, I shall leave that to you.'

In the middle of the afternoon, they reached Willeila Station, rested for an hour and gave the horses a drink. Somebody had smashed the pump on the windmill and they had to use the tank. The level was low and the water

240

was muddy. Wild sheep and cattle had fouled the tank, and the rabbits ran. Sawtell and St John Jackson went through the homestead, but it was stripped bare, verminous and overrun with rats. In every room, everything had been torn to pieces. They looked for evidence of the Japanese: tracks of army vehicles, cigarette butts, food and cartridge cases, but there was none. It was a hot and desolate place, and Sawtell knew the drought was on. There were only three bores from here to the road. They looked at the stock-yards: there were no animals of any kind. Soon, he thought, they must see the Barrier Range; he wanted to get off the plain, and they needed a spare horse. The sky was high and empty. Where were the aircraft? He stood with the Major in the heat of the bare and dusty yard. Who was following them? Then they heard the sound of horses and St John Jackson reached for his Webley. Counihan and O'Donohue rode up out of the small spindly trees. There was a butchered carcass beneath a blanket over the withers of O'Donohue's big black horse.

'Ah, gooday,' Kevin O'Donohue said, wiping his beard, 'we've got our roo.' He swung down. 'Here's your rifle, Mr Sawtell, there's seven rounds left.'

Sawtell smiled and looked at the strong, dark-haired country boy. 'Good on you, Kevin, you'll get the best steak tonight.' Frank Counihan wiped his face with his scarf and brushed away the flies.

'What's in the house?'

'Nothing but rats, thousands of the bastards.'

'Aw, Jesus, no grog?'

'Not a drop.'

Counihan sat on his big grey gelding and looked at the homestead.

'Right,' Sawtell said as he walked back to his horse, 'let's get on to the next well, it's about ten miles away, we should make it by nightfall.'

Well, Sergius Donaldson thought, as he strode back

241

across the yard, perhaps this Australian was born to lead. He now preferred the sun and the open plain to the dark and confusing river. *Let your light so shine before men.*

That evening, they made the tank to the north. It was a quarter full, very muddy and they spent some time getting all the horses down the bank to drink and up again. They could not drink the water and it had to be boiled. O'Donohue had trouble finding strong trees for the picket line and they had to camp out in the open. There was no creek with river gums to shelter them; the wind blew and the night was uncomfortable. This was a bleak place. But the kangaroo steaks tasted good, the tea was hot, and as they ate, the southern stars shone upon the plain. O'Donohue hung the kangaroo meat in the old muslin bags from the branches of the tallest trees he could find, and they turned in as best they could. They were all very tired. Sawtell kept the last watch from three to six in the morning. He saw the sun come up and thought of the fire ten years ago at Deep Lead. He watched the men sleeping in the early dawn, gathered the small sticks and leaves, threw them on the ashes and made yet another fire. He watched the smoke drift into the sky and made himself some breakfast tea, but as he sat alone by the small fire, no birds called in the broken branches.

At noon on the fifth day, the low, ragged peaks of the Barrier Range appeared from the plain at last. Sawtell estimated that the hills were sixty miles away, but he inwardly rejoiced: they were twelve hours' good ride from the Silver City Highway, and the mining town of Broken Hill lay to the north. They stopped and looked at the tops of the purple hills; it was very hot and they drank from their water bottles. Sawtell wiped his face and said:

'We've done it. If all goes well, we can cross the road sometime after midnight.' He turned and looked at St John Jackson. 'What's the reading on the thermometer?'

The Major took the instrument from his saddlebag, dismounted and crouched in the shade of a small she-oak.

'Ninety-seven degrees.'

'There's no point in stopping here, there's no shade,' Counihan said. 'We can make Eaglehawk by six.'

They rode five hours and walked the last; the sun shone hammerlike on the men and animals and O'Donohue didn't like the look of two of the horses. The Major's spare had its head down, and Counihan's packhorse had a sore back. It was a long, hard day. Thank Christ, O'Donohue thought, for Eaglehawk.

They found the tank a little after six, stood at the top and looked down the red clay banks at the water. The water was very low and two carcasses of cattle lay rotting in the slime.

'Jesus Christ,' Frank Counihan said. He ran down the bank, stumbling in the hoof marks and Sawtell followed. Crows sat on the carcasses and the smell was bad.

'What do you think?' Counihan said.

'It's hard to say, they could have got caught in there and died.'

'Or dumped.'

'Whatever's happened, the tank's useless. There's got to be another close by on a place this size, let's try that.'

Sawtell went back to the top and said:

'That tank's foul, go on into the homestead, there should be drinking water there. Frank and I'll look for another tank.' They soon found one, by its smell. Two more rotting beasts lay in the putrid water. Counihan and Sawtell sat down on the red earth.

'All right,' Sawtell said, 'it's deliberate, it's some of Madigan's men.'

'Just like us.'

'Just like us. Think of all the wells we've poisoned, Madigan's orders. Christ, *we're* Madigan's men. It makes sense, we're close to Broken Hill.'

'I wonder where the bastards are?' Counihan said.

'Christ knows. Those bodies are over a month old.'

243

'What about those buggers following us?'

'If we are being followed, God knows, they're not the VDC, they'd have made contact by now.'

'We haven't made contact with them.'

'Okay, go back and find them.'

'No way, maybe there's another tank.'

They rode through the bush; there was another, and it, too, was poisoned, this time with dead sheep.

'This is bloody mad,' Counihan said, 'we're all poisoning each other.'

'It looks like that, but you know Madigan's orders: harass, deny and destroy, leave nothing to the enemy. We aren't the only outfit doing it, there must be lots like us out there. Let's get to the homestead, there might be something.' But they both knew there would not be.

It was inevitable: the house had been pillaged, every corrugated-iron water tank had been punctured with .303 ammunition and the trestles smashed. The station was waterless and they stood out in the bare and unrewarding yard. Two of the packhorses now had their heads down and O'Donohue said:

'Let's unload the poor buggers.'

They worked in the dark, they stacked the boxes, the weapons, the petrol drums and the gear; they removed the packframes and saddles and sat down in the yard. Sawtell struck a match and looked at the gold hunter: it was half past eight. He went over to his gelding and stroked its head. It felt okay, it was a good, strong horse and he wouldn't lose it. He lit a cigarette, blew the smoke from his lungs and wound his watch.

'The VDC have been through. How's your horse, Major?' St John Jackson looked at Sawtell, then around the yard and the upturned tanks. After a hard day's ride, he missed the company of his fellow officers, the drink and the chat about the day's activities. There were no villagers or the smell of curry on the evening breeze.

'It's not exactly a thoroughbred.'

'And yours, Padre?'

'It seems that big Australian walers never give up.'

'Do you have any advice?'

'Where is the next water?'

'About six hours away.'

Sergius Donaldson laughed in the dark. 'I've always been what is known as a muscular Christian. I believe that God helps those who help themselves.'

'Right,' Sawtell said, 'let's get on with it. We'll give the horses all the water we've got and we'll go without. We'll stop in three hours.' Fortune, he thought, favours the brave. They packed up, left Eaglehawk Station and rode west into the night.

The night was clear and cold, they put their greatcoats on and followed the track in the moonlight. The earth was soft and the going was easy, but they could travel only as fast as the slowest horse. They knew they had to cross the road that night and be well to the north-west before daybreak. At half past eleven, they stopped, poured all the water they had into the bucket and gave each animal a drink. O'Donohue went round the pack-horses.

'They're not too bad,' he said, 'but we've got to get water sometime tomorrow.' He looked up at the starry sky. 'And it's going to be bloody hot.'

St John Jackson came up. 'What's the next station, Mr Sawtell?'

'A place called Pine Point. There's a tank a couple of miles before you get to the homestead.'

'That's probably buggered,' Counihan said.

'We'll see, they might have got tired; dragging dead cattle into tanks is hard work. The other problem is that the homestead seems to be less than a mile from the road, a convenient place for troops to bivouac.' Sawtell turned to the Major. 'We should make Pine Point in three hours, then it's action stations.'

'I agree, it's likely the place is occupied.'

Luck was against them: the tank had been fouled and lights shone in the homestead. They lay in the scrub and watched the house. There were two army trucks in the yard and a soldier walked about, the bayonet of his rifle fixed.

'Well, Kevin,' Sawtell said, 'there's your first Jap.'

'What are they like close up?'

'Haven't you ever seen one?' Counihan said.

'Nah, there were no Japs in Gundagai.'

'What about a Chinese fruit shop?'

'Yeah, there's always one of them.'

'They're like the Chinese, but tougher.'

'Christ, and they've come to Australia. I wonder what things are like up in Sydney.'

'Rather ghastly, I imagine,' St John Jackson said. 'They're particularly bestial to women.'

'Go on?'

'This conversation's not helping the war effort,' Sawtell said. 'Let's get back to the Padre and the horses, we'll cross the highway further down.' There were a number of wells and tanks on the other side, and he hoped the VDC hadn't got them all.

They crossed the highway half a mile south of Pine Point, struck north into the scrub and settled down for the remainder of the night. As they unpacked the horses, they could see the Barrier Range and the broken country to the north in the bright light of the moon. Sawtell took the date-stick from his saddlebag and carved another notch. They were thirty-one days out of Bourke. Sergius Donaldson looked at the hills. Besieged by a millennium of winds, the Range sprawled toward the interior, low-topped, black and mysterious. The hills were rich in silver, lead and zinc, but he had been told they supported no life of any kind.

246

They were like nothing he had ever seen before. He thought of Christ in the wilderness and licked his sore lips. He was very thirsty.

At dawn, they saw Broken Hill rising from the plain, the spires of the churches, the poppet heads of the mines and the huge mullock heaps standing against clear sky. The sun glittered on the tin roofs and latticed towers and smoke drifted from tall chimneys. It was Eldorado and the Zinc Corporation Mine was working.

· XII ·

1939

MARCIA WATCHED GEOFFREY playing on the sand with the strange children. They were building a big sandcastle, with moats, walls and turrets. The castle walls were decorated with seashells, and slender sticks of driftwood stood proudly on the turrets as flagpoles. Geoffrey helped them build the walls and showed the children how to make the ramparts and defensive buttresses. The little boys and girls ran down to the sea, filled their buckets, ran back and tipped the water into the moat. Their bodies were healthy and brown, and they laughed and ran in the sun. The tide was coming in and Geoffrey helped them dig a channel toward the water to fill the moat. The children made roads and bridges around the castle and it looked very grand. Now and then, a wall crumbled or a bridge collapsed and the children laughed and cried and shouted.

Marcia sat on the sand and looked at Geoffrey and the children. Ford V8s, Chryslers and Rugby Tourers were parked by tents and caravans under the gum trees; there was the smell of steaks cooking in the noonday heat and couples sat on deck chairs in the shade of the Norfolk Pines. The cicadas sang and a gentle wind blew. It was the New Year and, it seemed, the whole of Australia was on holiday. Far off and beyond the bay, smoke from bushfires rose from the flat, yellow hills. Marcia waited for Geoffrey and hitched her sun-dress above her knees, her toes wriggling in the sand as the distant fires burned and the smoke billowed and drifted to the south-east and over the Pacific Ocean. The fires were far away, and Marcia ate a peach from the picnic hamper, the juice running down her chin. She got her handkerchief from her shopping bag and wiped her face. It had not rained for three months and the whole continent lay baking in the sun. Many tanks, wells and dams were dry. In the north there were dust storms, farmers were shooting stock, burying the carcasses and leaving their properties. It was the hottest summer since 1914 and for six days the temperature had been over 100 degrees. Not far away, in the shade of a Norfolk Pine, there were some foreign people, a family from Europe, their skins white and their accents strange. The boys were wearing skull caps and they sat quietly watching Geoffrey and the Australian children building the sandcastle. Marcia waited for her husband and looked at the Jewish children as they sat in the shade of the pines.

At last, Geoffrey left the children, ran up and sat down beside her. His body was brown and there was sand in his blond hair.

'Ah, gooday,' he said, 'those are good kids, the tide's coming in.'

Marcia did not reply and watched the Jewish family under the tree and the Australian children digging on the beach and building the castle. The gulls wheeled and flew and couples splashed and swam in the warm, blue water. Geoffrey stretched out on his beach towel and looked at Marcia sitting very still on the sand. He brushed his strong hands through his hair, swatted a bushfly and said:

'God, it's hot. I'm going in for a swim, do you want to come?'

Again, Marcia did not answer and looked at the white-faced Jewish children and the distant fires burning. Then she said:

'I have a lover.'

'You sure do. Let's have a swim.'

'It's not you, it's someone else.'

'Someone else?' The flies buzzed around his brown legs and he brushed them away. 'You must be joking, people only have lovers in books.'

'They don't, you know. I met him while you were away.'

'Away? You're joking.'

'When you were at Broken Hill.'

He remembered the returned soldiers, the fire, the women and children at Deep Lead, his labouring in the quarry at the Zinc Corporation Mine seven years ago. He sat up, looked her in the face, then at the sea and the children digging and playing.

'It's been seven years since I worked at Broken Hill.'

'It's been seven years since I've known this man.'

Sawtell felt cold and said: 'So, for a long time you've been carrying on behind my back? Is that what you're telling me?' Marcia pulled her dress down below her knees, felt the hot wind on her body and said: 'Yes, Geoffrey, I've been carrying on behind your back.'

He sat quite still. 'Who's the man?'

'A friend.'

The Jewish family were leaving now; they were folding their deck chairs and packing their baskets. One of the little girls was crying and her mother picked her up. The weather was too hot for them. They had fled from Germany and could go no further.

'A friend?' He kept looking at her. There was a fly on her face, but she didn't brush it away. 'I'm sure he's a friend, what does he do?'

Marcia ran her hands through her long, black hair and thought about the question. What does he *do*?

'He teaches at the university.'

'An anti-war man, a radical?' He thought of her father.

'If you like.'

The Jews were packing their cheap car, and the parents

250

looked very hot and tired; they were in a strange and hostile country.

'Jesus,' Geoffrey said, 'I can't believe this, after all we've been through.'

'What have we been through?'

'Thirteen years of marriage, the Depression, the War.'

'The War? I didn't go through the War, you've never told me about it.'

Sawtell shivered and put on his shirt. He looked around the beach and the camping ground at the families eating their lunch. They were laughing and talking and the men were sitting on the running boards of their cars, rolling cigarettes and drinking beer. The smoke from the fires was drifting west now, and he wanted a drink.

'You don't *talk* about War. It wasn't like last Saturday's football match, it wasn't some bloody political meeting.'

'Yes, you do, you talk about the War, you talk about all wars, you talk about the Depression, you talk about the next war.'

'And your friend does?'

'Yes, he does.'

'Did this bloke go to the War?'

'No.'

'I bet he didn't. The War was the War, it can't be talked about.'

He remembered coming home and his father and Jack Hanrahan asking him questions in the Mountain View. The awful, secret memories. 'I've told you before, I don't believe in talking.'

'What do you believe in then?'

'I believe in doing. I got a job in 1932, it took me six months, but I got one. I didn't sit around on my arse talking about causes and solutions, and I didn't carry on with women behind *your* back.' He laughed. 'A fat chance I had of doing that. Look at my father, he's talked all his bloody life about politics and now he's on the pension,

251

bankrupt, kept by my mother. You don't talk, you just get on with it.'

'That's not my way.'

'No, it's not, but while you're talking, as you put it, with your friend, while you're at some bloody meeting, a Hun or a Jap will put a bullet in your back. If it's your friend's, so much the better.'

Geoffrey looked at the children playing, the brambly foreshore and the shadows in the pines. There was a man cranking an old Essex while his family sat inside and there was no one to help them.

'I'm going to leave you,' Marcia said. 'I'm sorry.'

'You're what?'

'I'm going to leave you.'

'For this man?'

'Not just for him, for myself.'

Geoffrey looked at her as she dug her feet into the sand.

'You've gone mad. Thank God we never had any children.'

'You know I never wanted children, I didn't want them to end up like that family in the car.'

'What family?'

'Those Jews, they're from Europe, they've got no place to go.'

'What have the Jews got to do with us?' He watched the man cranking the Essex while his family waited.

'Hitler's driving them out, there's a war coming.'

Sawtell thought of the War and the dying men on stretchers being carried into the medical tents, the mutilations and the ambulance dogs. He thought of the drum head services, the French .75s and the limbless men being taken away to the repatriation hospitals. The next war couldn't be like that. Cinders fell on the sand and the children laughed and splashed and played.

'I can't believe this,' he said. 'We've been married thirteen years, you've been carrying on behind my back for

252

the last seven and now you're going to leave me.' Once again, things were being done to him, the enemy was at his back. She could leave him, he would manage alone. 'I'm going for a walk, I can't just sit here.' He got up and saw the Essex jerking away through the pine trees. It was Sunday and the hotels were closed. He should have known, you could count on nobody.

Together they walked along the sprawling beach where the waves broke and the children ran. The west wind blew through the tea trees and the pines, the clouds flew and the summer was endless. The wooden hotel stood above the road, its turrets high against the southern sea, its spacious dining rooms, its stained glass and shady, creaking verandahs. Geoffrey walked ahead of Marcia, looked back and saw her summer dress billowing from her strong, brown body. She ran a step or two and caught up with him as he walked. There were some rocks where fishermen stood with their rods and lines facing the sea. The gulls and the thick kelp streamed. This was a dangerous coast and many Victorian sailing ships had foundered here. They stopped and faced each other.

'I told you once,' she said, 'that I believed marriage wasn't for ever.'

'You did.' He remembered the barren stream and the high lonesome road, the hard games of tennis and the Indian Scout.

'You also said you loved me.'

'I did.'

'But now you don't?'

'I'm not sure what love means, it can't mean staying with someone for ever.'

'I'm sure: it means standing by people through thick and thin, it means not letting them down. I've never let you down, I've always looked after you, I've always earned money, a lot of men haven't done that.'

'I don't want to be looked after, I want to be myself.'

253

'Bloody rubbish, you want your fancy man, you want to sit on your bum talking about politics.' He took her by the shoulders and turned her around on the sand. 'You see that hotel there? It was built by men: timber workers and carpenters, it's on a difficult site by the sea, but they didn't sit around talking about the problem, they went ahead and built it. Those fires burning over on the Peninsula, the men aren't sitting around discussing what caused them, the poor devils are fighting them.'

'And the women?' She shook herself free of his hands.

'They help, the good ones look after the men. When do you see this bloke?'

'When you're at work, when you're in the country.'

'Has he got a wife and kids?'

'Yes, but he lives by himself.'

'You mean he's left them, buggered off.'

'If you like.'

'Jesus, what a mess.' He faced her in the wind. 'What a bloody mess you've got into. You're carrying on with some bastard who's ditched his wife and kids, who probably doesn't know one end of a shovel from the other. When you're in bed, what do you talk about?'

'Hitler, what's happening in Europe, Munich, the Jews.'

'You're obsessed by the Jews. I don't care what's happening to the Jews, they can look after themselves, they've all got money. What if something happened to us?' Sawtell waved his arm toward the hotel and the camping ground. 'What if someone like the Japs came here and rounded up all those people. Would the Jews help? Would anybody in England or Europe help? No way. We've got to look after ourselves and we won't do that by marching up and down the street, or going to meetings or rolling round in bed with some bloody teacher who's deserted his wife and kids.'

Marcia stood on the beach before him. 'Have you ever slept with another woman?'

'No, I have not.'

'Have you ever thought of it?'

'Now and then, you know what men are like, but I've never done it. I believe in trust, or I used to, I don't like people who betray me. I learnt that in the War.'

'The War,' Marcia said. 'Why is it always the War?'

'Because the War made me, it made me what I am.'

'What has it made you?' But she knew the answer, she had always known.

'It's made me self-reliant and tough; you know what I can do: practical things, build bridges, catch fish, ride a horse, shoot game, play tennis, survive. Why do you ask me? You've known long enough.'

'I used to admire all those things, I still do, but now it's not enough.'

'I'm not bright enough for you, am I?' Sawtell said. 'I've left all the reading and thinking to you, but I tell you what, if there's a war, it'll be me who'll survive, not your teacher friend.'

'You're still a soldier, aren't you?'

'Yes,' he said, 'I suppose I am.'

'It was a mistake.'

'What was?'

'Our getting married.'

'Not for me, it wasn't. I've enjoyed it, despite the fact that we never had kids. I loved you enough to let you have your way. I've never had any close friends, except a few blokes at the Football Club and the RSL, but that didn't seem to matter. They all had kids and we didn't. But there was you at home, tennis and picnics, fishing and walks in the country, I liked being at home working around the house, you had your friends, they weren't my style, but that didn't seem to matter. Thank Christ that child never came, at least you got that right.' He kicked at the sand and started down the beach.

Sawtell walked away from her and looked at the fishermen standing on the rocks and the big sea rolling in over the reef. The wind was in the right quarter and the light was fading. He wished he was by himself on the rock with his rod and line. There would be salmon in the dark blue trough beyond the reef. Marcia watched him as he looked at the men fishing and the ocean. She had done a dreadful thing, but it had to be done, and he would never understand. She remembered him once saying to her, after he had been to Church with his mother, as he had reached for the whisky: *there is no health in us*. She watched him coming back from the rocks.

'You know,' Sawtell said, 'being with you in the country was the best thing that ever happened to me. When I showed you that stream where I used to fish, I thought you understood.'

'But,' Marcia said, 'you've never said anything about how you feel. You've never told me.'

He shrugged and shoved his hands into his trouser pockets.

'As you said, I'm still a soldier, I'm certainly not a poet. Look, I'm getting tired of this and I need a drink. If you want to go, you go. When we get home, take what you want and leave. Go to this man, or live by yourself, it's got nothing to do with me.'

Marcia watched Geoffrey as he strode away down the beach, his big body and his shirt tail flapping. She now knew that, after all this time, neither understood what the other was about. Marcia followed him slowly along the sand, dragging her toes through the water. It was getting dark, the gulls flew inland and the fires burned.

The drive back to town seemed endless and neither spoke. Geoffrey thought. Who was the father when Marcia miscarried in January, 1935? That was one question he would never ask.

* * *

256

Sawtell got off the tram at Union Street and walked down Bridge Road towards the Mountain View. The hot north wind blew, and dust and smoke obscured the sun. The heatwave continued, the tar ran down the street in rivulets, some tram tracks buckled and many suburban rail services had ceased. Few people were about and the blinds of the small shops and brick cottages were drawn against the heat. Yesterday, there had been a dust storm in the city and it had been pitch black at noon. Birds fell from the sky and the English oaks in Melbourne's grand parks and ornamental gardens stood bare. He stopped at a newsagent, bought the *Herald* and a packet of cigarettes. The news was bad: nineteen people had died, overcome by the heat, and a visiting English writer, H. G. Wells, had called Hitler a certifiable lunatic. Marcia had been gone two days and his house was silent and empty. He would have to tell his mother and face her moral judgement, but first he would see his father and buy him a drink. He sweated and walked into the north wind for his cold beer and whisky.

The bar of the Mountain View was dark, the blinds were down and the lights were on. Sawtell looked for his father, but he was not there. He put his hat on the counter.

'Gooday, Geoff,' Jack Hanrahan said. 'Haven't seen you for a bit.'

'Gooday, Jack, I've been busy. I'll have a beer to wash the dust away.'

'Right you are. How's the wife?'

'She's fine. Have you seen my dad?' Sawtell drank the cold bitter brew and lit a cigarette. He looked around the bar and saluted the regulars. He had been coming here for twenty years and the place had never changed. There were still photos of the racehorses and the last season's football calendar on the varnished wall. The saloon bar reeked of ale, honest sweat and a million cigarettes. It was a good pub and Sawtell put his foot on the bar rail and talked to Jack Hanrahan.

'Your dad?' He shouldn't be long, a quarter of an hour, I'd say.' Jack Hanrahan coughed and rolled a cigarette: his skin was translucent and his body skeletal, but the tuberculosis hadn't killed him yet.

'Why don't you go round home? That's where he'll be.'

'I thought I'd buy him a drink.'

'Do you know, Geoff, it's almost twenty years to the day since you first came in here? Jesus, time flies.'

'It sure does, Jack. How's the health?'

'Aw, not bad.' He waved the cigarette. 'I should give up these buggers.'

'Maybe, but life's short.'

'That's right.' He looked at Sawtell's waistcoat, the gold watch and chain. 'You've still got your father's timepiece, that'll be ticking away long after we've all gone. Do you want another?'

'Yeah, and give me a whisky to go with it.'

'Good on you. I always remember you said that the officers had whisky and the men had rum.'

'That's right.'

'There's going to be another, you know.'

'What?'

'War.'

'Yeah, I suppose.' He thought of the Jews in the old car and Marcia facing him on the beach.

'That old bastard Chamberlain let us down at Munich, typical bloody Tory.'

'I haven't followed it closely.'

'You should have, those bastards will let us down.' Jack Hanrahan leant across the counter. 'But you know the biggest threat?'

'What's that?' Sawtell knocked the whisky back and slid the nobbler across the bar.

'The Japs.'

'You could be right.'

'Too right I'm right. Those little yellow buggers want

258

this place, bushfires and all. Christ, there's that many of the little bastards, if they all pissed on the fires, they'd put them out.' He saw two men sitting at the bar. 'Just a tick, I'll be back.'

Oh God, Sawtell thought, old Jack Hanrahan with his politics and messages of doom. He'd heard them a long time now from Jack, his father and Marcia. He wondered what she was doing. She had a lover; Jesus Christ, he would find out and kill the bastard. The Jews, the Spanish Civil War and Fascism, street processions and no bloody action. He had fought, he had got a job in the Depression, he had worked his guts out while those buggers sat and talked. He had helped build this country while they had not. If she came back, he'd knock her bloody head off.

'It's the Nips,' Jack Hanrahan said, leaning over the counter.

'They breed like rabbits, thank God for Singapore, at least the Brits got that right.'

'Yeah,' Sawtell said, 'thank God for Singapore.'

Then he saw his father at the door of the Mountain View. Like Jack Hanrahan, he had grown old, his hair was grey but, when he saw his son, there was spring in his step.

'Gooday, Geoffrey,' his father said as they embraced and went back to the bar.

'Gooday, Angus,' Jack Hanrahan said, 'I was just saying we haven't seen Geoff for ages.'

Sawtell was pleased to see his father and to be with Jack Hanrahan and the other men in the Mountain View.

'What'll you have, Dad? It's my shout.'

'Well, Geoffrey,' his father said, 'seeing I haven't seen you for some time, I think I'll have a very good Scotch.'

'Okay then, you name it.' He put his hand on his father's shoulder.

'A Johnnie Walker Black Label?'

'Done. Make that two, Jack.'

259

'Well,' his father said, 'the heat's bad, lots of fires. How's Marcia?'

'She's fine. I thought I might drop in for tea.'

His father looked at him. 'Did you now? Your mother's in bed, nothing serious, just a summer cold. We can rattle something up, she'd love to see you.'

Sawtell saw Jack Hanrahan coming back and said:

'Let's sit down, Dad, it's more comfortable.'

They sat down at the corner table, father and son, in the Mountain View. The working men talked quietly and the hot wind blew under the door.

'How *are* you?' Sawtell said.

'I never was much of a business man, you know that. I spent too much time in here, and other things.'

'Money?'

'It's not too bad, we scrape along. I've got the pension and sometimes your mother does some sewing. The house is paid off, we scrape along.' He raised his glass. 'I don't often get to drink Black Label.'

Sawtell thought of his father and mother locked in for ever at Rotherwood Street. If any marriage was a mistake, that one was, but he couldn't ask his father why he had stayed. Maybe he couldn't do without his mother, maybe if it weren't for her, he would be one of those old men who shuffled endlessly up and down Bridge Road.

'Marcia's left me.'

Angus Sawtell sat up. 'Not for some other bloke?'

'No, she says she wants to be on her own.'

'She always was an independent girl, no kids, politics, out and about. How long's she been gone?'

'Two days.'

'That's not long, she'll be back, it's a passing phase. Can you lend me ten bob?' Sawtell gave his father the money. 'Are you going to tell your mother?'

'Yes, I'll have to.'

'Why?'

'I wouldn't want her to hear from someone else.'

'I won't tell her.'

'That's not the point, I think she should know.'

'All right. She'll say, I told you so, she never did like Marcia, you'll have to put up with that.'

Once again, Sawtell felt guilty about his mother, not his father. Why was that? Angus stood up and patted his son on the back.

'Come on, Geoffrey, she'll come back, let's have another.' He felt the good whisky in his gut and smiled.

'Okay, same again.'

He watched his father, talking to Jack Hanrahan at the bar. He was still the neat, little man, drinking and puzzling over the affairs of the world; a veteran, he remembered. While the drinks were being poured, his father chatted with some other men at the table. They were big-boned and Irish and burst into laughter. Then his father came back with the drinks on a tray.

'Do you know where she is?'

'No. With a friend.'

'Not another bloke?'

'No.'

'Well then, don't tell your mother, she'll be back, we all need a break now and again.' He looked at Geoffrey. 'I suppose that's why I spend a bit of time here.'

They sat silently and drank their beer and whisky. The bar was filling up, it was five o'clock and the rush was starting.

'How's work?' his father said.

'Not bad, we're putting in a bridge at Rubicon.'

'You'd better look out for the fires.'

'They aren't up that way yet, I can look after myself.'

'What will you do if there's a war?'

'I haven't thought about it. Join up, I suppose.'

'Aren't you too old?'

'Probably, but there must be something I could do.'

261

'You said once that you'd done your bit.'

'That was twenty years ago and if Marcia doesn't come back, there'll be nothing better to do. I don't think there'll be any trenches this time.'

'Why?'

'Tanks, aircraft, armoured divisions.'

'Do you think Hitler will invade Poland?'

'Probably, the man's mad. He should have been put away years ago.'

'What about the Japs?'

'God knows. There's Singapore, that should stop them.'

'For someone who's not interested in politics, you've been following things.'

'Christ, Dad, you can't avoid them. Anyway, these are military matters.'

Angus Sawtell drank his whisky and filled his pipe from his buckskin pouch.

'Why have you never had children?'

'Marcia didn't want any, and then couldn't.'

'Nothing to do with you?'

Sawtell looked at his father and lit a cigarette.

'No.'

'It's upset your mother.'

'Lots of things have upset my mother.'

'Yes,' his father said as he looked around the bar of the Mountain View. 'They have.'

'You don't seem that surprised about Marcia,' Sawtell said.

'She's an extraordinary girl, I knew her father a bit, a strange man, radical politics.' His father laughed. 'He wasn't exactly your style, was he?'

'You're wrong, Dad. I liked George Smith, he was an independent man, he knew how to look after himself, he was a tough bugger. An intellectual if you like, but he gave me a run for my money at tennis and golf.'

He remembered the cold, wet winter mornings at the

Yarra Bend course, the three of them playing intently. Sawtell always out-drove her father, but his chipping on to the greens was deadly accurate. George Smith had won many games around the bunkers where the shots really counted. He remembered her father's long, delicate putts and his raising his club triumphantly at the eighteenth. He also remembered Marcia's grief when her father died, the secular funeral and his bohemian friends and the scattering of the ashes in the strange, unkept bush-garden; the baroque music and the sad, cheerful drinking at the wake. He had liked George Smith and he wished he were alive. Sawtell watched his father drink his whisky down. He loved him.

'Like father like daughter, eh?' His father coughed. 'And like son-in-law?' Sawtell thought of the dark stream and the windy plateau and did not answer.

'You were always an independent boy,' his father said. 'You never had many friends, did you? You relied upon yourself, fishing, shooting, football, you never really cared for the team. Where did you play?'

'Centre-half forward.'

'Ah,' Angus Sawtell said as the beer ran down his chin, 'you were a star.'

'I played in the Finals once,' Sawtell said, 'then if you remember, I was put in the Reserves.' He lacked endeavour and had become indifferent, the coach had said.

'You were great,' his father said as he drank his bitter. 'How tall are you? I've forgotten.'

'You know, Dad. Six-foot-four.'

'Christ knows where your height comes from, it certainly doesn't come from me.' His father coughed again and inhaled the pipe-smoke. 'You were always good at sport, at physical things. When you won that Final, I got drunk for a week.'

'I remember that, Dad.'

They both laughed, and Sawtell took his father's arm,

they both shook hands. It was a very hot evening, but the whisky tasted good and the beer was cold.

'I'm going for a piss,' Angus Sawtell said. 'What about another?'

He watched his father go to the lavatory and went to the bar.

'Gooday, Geoff,' Jack Hanrahan said. 'Same again?'

'Why not?' He took his hat from the counter and put it on. He saw himself in the mirror, the waistcoat, the watch and chain; he was still a big, strong man. He could survive.

'How's your Dad?' Jack Hanrahan said. 'How do you find him?'

'He's fine, there's life in the old bugger yet.'

Sawtell threw a shilling on the bar. 'How about one for yourself?'

'We'll have one after closing time. Okay?'

'You'd better have it now, Jack. Dad and I are going home tonight.'

He thought of his mother in bed with her summer cold and of Marcia. He would tell his mother and face her judgement as she lay in bed this hot, summer night as the bushfires burned.

His father came back and sat down at the table.

'The Tories are going to recognize Franco.'

'Who?'

'Franco, the Spanish Fascist.'

'Look, Dad, I don't give a bugger what's happening in Spain, it's what happens in Australia that counts.'

He thought of the families under the pine trees, the Ford V8s and the children on the beach. He looked at the men drinking in the Mountain View and thought of the dark stream where the brown trout swam and the ducks rising from the sedgelands and estuaries of the south coast. He thought of the hard, dry country south of Broken Hill where he had worked and camped out in 1932. He remembered the vast, dry plains north of Deep Lead where he had slept in overturned water tanks, and the quarry at the Zinc Corporation Mine. It was his country, and he was proud of it.

'Look, Dad, let's go and see Mum. She's alone and in bed.'

'She is indeed,' his father said. 'How about one for the road?'

'I think not,' Geoffrey said as he rose to his feet. 'I'll buy some bottles and we can have them at home.'

'You know as well as I do, that your mother won't have drink in the house. We'll have to use the back shed.'

Geoffrey stood there and said: 'I'm forty-one years old, I'll drink in the house where I grew up.'

He left his father and went back to the bar and bought half-a-dozen bottles of Richmond Lager. Then he came back and said:

'Have you got any Scotch at home?'

'Yes, well over half.'

'That'll do. Let's go and see Mother.'

The sky was dark with dust and Sawtell could not see the garden clearly; but he knew the English trees and flowers were dead. Only Australian native trees could survive this heat. He looked across the street: the pines had been felled and their massive trunks lay askew in the long, dry grass.

'What's happened here?' he said to his father.

'They were cut down before Christmas, someone's building a bungalow.'

Sawtell, holding the beer, considered the fallen pines, then mounted the front steps and sat down in the smoke. What was happening? Was the whole State going up? There would be no brown trout rising in the rivers. His father opened the front door and said:

'I'll tell Mother you're here.'

Geoffrey followed his father inside, went down the hall

to the kitchen and put the beer on the table. Nothing had changed: still the fine bone china, the Coronation mugs and religious knick-knacks. The door to his room was closed.

His mother was in bed, propped up on the pillows, and he kissed her on the cheek. She had been reading *How Green Was My Valley* by Richard Llewellyn; it was from the Public Library and he remembered she always put three dots on page one hundred to make sure she had read the book and wouldn't take it out again.

'How are you, Mother?' Geoffrey said.

'I'm all right, just a summer cold, nothing to make a fuss about.'

He sat down on a chair by the bed and looked at her. She was still a good-looking woman, her blonde hair now mostly silver, the English complexion and the pale blue eyes.

'Welcome, stranger.'

Geoffrey shifted on the chair and looked around the bedroom, the dressing-table with its dusty bottles of perfume and lavender water, most of them Christmas presents he and his father had given her over the years. There, on the bookshelf were her prayer book and her favourite authors: A. J. Cronin, Warwick Deeping and H. V. Morton. He heard his father moving about in the kitchen; he was opening a bottle no doubt. He hadn't slept in this room for years.

'It's strange to have a cold in all this heat.'

'Just a bug I picked up. You smell of drink, have you been with your father?'

'We had one or two, it's hot and I wanted to see you.'

'What for?'

'To see how you were.'

'Oh. How's Marcia?'

'She's fine.' He thought. 'She's gone away for a bit.'

'Gone away?'

266

'She needed a break, she's been working hard.'

'Where is she?'

'With a friend.'

'With a friend?'

'Just someone she knows.'

'Not another man, I hope?'

'No, Mother, nothing like that.'

'She's left you, hasn't she?'

'No, Mother, she's just gone away for a bit.'

'Well, I won't say I told you so.' She placed her book mark in *How Green Was My Valley* and put it on the bedside table. 'I shall say a prayer for you both. It had to happen.'

'Would you like a cup of tea, Mother?'

'No.'

'Anything to eat?'

'No.'

'Are you quite sure?' He had to leave the bedroom.

'A cup of tea, then.'

'I won't be a moment.' Thankfully, he left.

His father was not in the kitchen. Geoffrey lit the gas, put the kettle on and measured one teaspoon of tea into the aluminium pot. He went outside and found his father in the back shed. There were all his books, papers and files, minutes from countless meetings and firm resolutions.

'Have you told her?' his father asked.

'I suppose so, I said she was with a friend.'

'And what did your mother say?'

'She said she would say a prayer for us.'

'Did she?' His father laughed. 'That calls for a drink.'

'Maybe, but I'm not drinking out here. I'll see you in the kitchen.'

Sawtell went back to the house through the dark and dusty garden. He would drink in the house where he was born, he would sleep in his own bed. But as he made the tea for his mother, he knew that was the last thing he would do.

His mother was reading as he brought in the tea. She laid down her book and said:

'What are you and your father going to eat? He can't cook, can you?'

'A bit, we'll rattle something up.' Sawtell poured her tea. 'Is there anything you want?'

'No. Do you think Marcia will come back?'

'I'm sure she will, she just wants a break.'

'Thank God you never had any children, they always suffer in times like this. What are you going to do?'

'Nothing. She'll be back in a day or two.'

'You're always welcome here, you know that.' She wiped her mouth with her handkerchief. But Sawtell knew he was not, and took the cup and saucer. 'Your father can't cope,' she said, 'you know that?'

'Look, Mother, you want something to eat?'

'No.'

'In that case, I'll go and help Dad.'

Jesus Christ, Sawtell thought. He went outside on to the front verandah and smelt the fires, and the red moon shone dimly through the smoke. He had to get away, to the bush, maybe. Tomorrow, he would see the boss and get a job with an outfit in the country. There, nobody would ask him questions, he could go fishing and hunt game. In the meantime a drink was required.

His father was rummaging in the cupboards.

'There must be something we can have.' He had put a packet of custard and a tin of pears on the table. 'I can't make custard.'

'What do you usually have?'

'She usually leaves me something in the oven, a roast or a pie.'

'Where's the beer?'

'In the ice-chest.'

Sawtell got out the bottle, opened it and poured out two glasses.

'Can't you find a tin of meat? There must be some stuff we can put on the stove.' He lit a cigarette. 'I don't care what we have.'

'This'll do,' his father said and put a tin of braised steak and onions on the bench.

'Okay, let's have a drink.'

Sawtell took his jacket off and sat down in his shirt and braces. His father filled his pipe and took up his glass.

'One thing, your mother's a good cook.'

'Yeah.' Sawtell thought of all the silent meals and the endless cups of weak tea. He had preferred Marcia's mess and laughter.

'I wonder what the temperature is?' his father said.

'In the nineties, I imagine,' Sawtell said as he poured himself another beer. This was a bad summer in all respects. 'I'm getting out.'

'Getting out? Where?'

'Out of Melbourne. I can probably get a job with an outfit in the country.'

'I thought you said Marcia would be back.'

'You said that, I didn't. I think I prefer the company of men.'

'They're certainly less trouble. Look at Jack Hanrahan, I've known him for over thirty years, never any trouble, we're the best of mates. You haven't got a mate like that, have you?'

'No.'

'You always were a loner, you can't beat old friends.'

Sawtell was about to say that he was married to one, but remained silent. Then he said:

'I've always preferred my own company.'

'Heaven help a man who can't stand his own company, but you've got to have mates. I better put the tea on. Is your mother all right?'

'She said she didn't want anything.'

'That settles that.' His father opened the tin, spooned the meat into a saucepan and lit the gas. 'I must say it's good to see you.'

'And you, Dad.' Sawtell smiled and raised his glass. 'Here's to you.'

They both drank in the darkened kitchen.

'There's nothing like a cold beer on a hot day,' his father said. 'But these are bad times, the fires, another war, it could almost turn me into a believer.'

Sawtell laughed. 'Not you, Dad.'

'Do you reckon Australia could be invaded?'

'The yellow peril? It's most unlikely, but God help us if we were. They'd have a field day.'

'And if there's a war, you'll join up?'

'Yeah, in a strange way I like the army, not the War, the army.' *You're still a soldier, aren't you?*

'The Russians won't stand by,' his father said. 'They won't give in to Hitler.'

'Or do a deal.'

'That's impossible.'

'You've got a higher view of human nature than I have.'

'Karl Marx had principles.'

'I haven't read him, but Lloyd George didn't.'

'That old bastard. We shouldn't fight other people's wars, it'll be the death of us.'

'On that, Dad,' Sawtell said, 'we can agree. What's that meat doing?'

Angus Sawtell got up, went to the gas stove, tipped out the food on to the plates and got out the knives and forks.

'What about another beer, Dad? It's one way to beat the heat.' They ate their tea, and the hot wind blew down the streets and through the gardens of Melbourne.

'If you'd have asked me,' his mother said, 'I'd have cooked you something better than that.'

270

She stood at the kitchen door in her lilac dressing-gown and looked at the bottles.

'You needn't have got up, Mary,' Angus Sawtell said. 'We're managing.'

'I take it that you two intend drinking all night?'

Sawtell pushed his plate away, stood up and said:

'Yes, Mother, we intend to drink all night, the whole country's on fire, there's a war coming and we intend to drink all night. Do you want to join us?'

'You've forgotten one thing, Geoffrey, another excuse, if you need one.'

'What?'

'Your wife has left you.'

'And my wife has left me.'

His mother stood there for a moment, then closed the door.

'Mothers and sons, husbands and wives,' Sawtell said, 'I can't work it out.' He reached for the bottle. 'I should have thought the situation was worth a few drinks.' He thought of going to his mother and telling her what he was about, what had made him. Then he remembered the conversation in the garden when he had come home from the War. There was no point. He turned to his father and said:

'Dad, I'll tell you a story.' He told his father about cleaning up after the bombardment, about Smith singing in the crater, and about the Padre from New South Wales. His father listened, stayed silent and understood. 'Do you know what I'm going to do now?' Sawtell said when he had finished.

'No.'

'I'm going into the front room and I'm going to play the piano. Please join me, I'd welcome your company.'

Sawtell took a bottle of beer from the ice chest and went down the hall.

There were the family photographs: his brother Henry, himself after the christening at St Stephen's, the Under-

Nineteens' Football team, and his mother and father on their wedding day. There was one of his mother and father by the river at Walton on Thames. She had long blonde hair and was very beautiful; his grandfather had a big, black moustache and was tall and handsome. He lifted the lid of the piano stool and leafed through the sheet music. There was Bach, Stephen Foster, Handel, Edward Elgar, and Gilbert and Sullivan. He found the score for *Floradora*, opened the lid of the piano and wiped the dusty keys with his shirt sleeve. The keyboard rang in the silent house. Sawtell lit a cigarette and poured himself a drink; he hoped his father would join him. He played a few bars of *I Want to Be a Military Man*, he laughed and drank in the empty room. I want to be a military man. He got up and opened the window, there were no crickets singing in the grass tonight and the hot wind blew through the casements and into the house. The cinders floated on to the keyboard as he played *And Sheep May Safely Graze*, *Carolina Moon* and a variety of Stephen Foster melodies. The piano echoed and his father joined him. He sat down by his son and opened the bottle of whisky. Geoffrey hummed and played and waved to his father and drank his beer and then the whisky. Then he found *The Honeysuckle and the Bee*, and sang:

You are my honey, honeysuckle, I am the bee,
I'd like to sip the honey sweet from those red lips, you see;
I love you dearly, dearly, and I want you to love me,
You are my honey, honeysuckle, I am the bee.

'Well,' his father said, 'that brings back old memories.'
'Yes, it does.'
'Play us another.'
'I don't think so, Dad. I think there's been enough singing and drinking for one night.'
'Maybe you're right.' Angus Sawtell was slumped in his chair and the house was silent once more.

'I'm off now,' Geoffrey said, 'I'm going home. Thanks for the tea.'

'Thanks for the ten bob, I'll pay you back.'

His father got to his feet and saw his son out. They shook hands on the verandah. Sawtell put his hat on, thought, and said:

'Can you lend me that bottle of whisky?'

'Sure.'

Angus disappeared and came back with the bottle in a paper bag.

'Thanks, Dad.'

Sawtell embraced his father and walked into Rotherwood Street, past the Mountain View and up to Bridge Road. When the tram came, he was the only passenger and he sat quietly watching the lights of the factories and brick cottages gleaming in the smoke.

Sawtell did not get to Rubicon to help put in the bridge. The next day, Friday, the whole State of Victoria burned. A terrifying wind blew, giant fire-balls exploded, townships disappeared, people crouched for shelter in rivers and creeks and some, seeking shelter, were boiled alive in water-tanks. Seventy-one men, women and children died and thousands of square miles of country were devastated. For three days, a horizon of fire burned on the edge of the earth and the temperature in the city reached 117 degrees. The fires sucked the oxygen from the air, and people and animals dropped in their tracks. The water in bores, dams and wells evaporated and many Victorian homesteads were destroyed. The smell of roasted flesh infected the dark and smoke-filled air. Again, in Melbourne, darkness fell at noon and the City Morgue stayed open twenty-four hours a day to receive the bodies. Over 2000 homes were reduced to ash, and dazed, terrified people clustered together on race-courses, picnic grounds and any open space they could find. A thousand fires burned out of control for three days and nights; millions of acres of fertile top-soil were

273

incinerated and only rocks were left standing on the earth. It was a holocaust.

When the fires had abated on the fourth day, Sawtell was sent, with fifty other men, into the fire zone. It was a battlefield where refugees trudged across the blackened earth, and through the skeletal remains of once great forests, for aid and comfort at makeshift clearing stations. Ants ran wildly in the ashes, bottles were melted, cars and trucks were gutted and the roasted bodies of prime sheep and cattle lay piled high in the yards. Horses were found, still harnessed in their stalls, dead, their limbs contorted. Already, the sound of rifles and shotguns echoed as professional hunters slaughtered the blinded and maimed livestock. The carcasses were being collected and dumped into huge pits where the earth still smouldered. The army and the volunteer militiamen had moved in, the church services for the dead were being held in marquees.

Sawtell and the men worked, clearing the roads of fallen logs and debris. It was still very hot, and sweat poured down their blackened bodies. Some of the local men were still too shocked to help, and stood silently, tears running down their lean and bony faces. Children were crying and searching for their household pets and toys. Sawtell and the men worked with tractors, hauling away timber, bricks and roofing iron. They worked all day without a break and Sawtell remembered a newsreel he had seen of the Rape of Nanking. It was like a bombing raid, but there had been no aircraft, just the fires and the Australian bush. Then as they tossed the rubble, the charred furniture, the fence posts, the twisted household items on to the trucks, Sawtell saw a young woman standing by the chimney of her house. She was carrying a baby on her hip and looking at her small, ravaged rural holding. She was young and beautiful, but there was soot and ash in her blonde hair, her dress was stained with sweat and he watched her as she moved around the smouldering graveyard. He went up to her and said:

274

'There's a place down the road you can go, we'll take you there.'

'I've lost my husband,' she said.

'He'll turn up, go and wait at the clearing station, he'll be there.'

'No, he won't, he was down in the paddock when the fire came. He was trying to save the animals.'

'I'll take the baby,' Sawtell said.

She gave him the sleeping child. It was a boy and Sawtell held it to his chest. He took her hand and said:

'Come on, we'll take you down to the clearing station, there's a priest there, he'll help you.'

The young woman was sobbing, and Geoffrey carried her baby as they walked to the truck. He looked at the endless, blackened ridges and helped her as she moved through the debris of her tiny homestead. He held the sleeping baby. There was nothing more he could do for her. They said it would take thirty years for the land to recover.

On March 16, Australia decided to raise a standing army and all able-bodied men between the ages of eighteen and forty-five were required to register for military service. Veterans of the Great War were called in to form a war reserve and Sawtell became an instructor in the Volunteer Defence Corps. No uniforms were provided and they trained in the bush at weekends. Sawtell was issued with a Mark 3 Lee Enfield rifle and a 1914 Webley Service revolver. Neither had been fired for twenty years. On September 1, Germany invaded Poland; and on September 3, Britain and France declared war on Germany. Later that day, Australia was at war. The Japanese congratulated Hitler on the success of his drive to the East.

· XIII ·

Broken Hill

THE TANKS WERE FOULED at the next three stations, and neither man nor horse had water to drink. That night, they had three hours' sleep and at dawn struck west toward the hills; this was their twelfth hour without water and Sergius Donaldson wondered how long they could go on. He picked at the cold sore on his lip and the blood ran down his chin and on to his scarf as the flies swarmed around the horses. After two hours, Sawtell dismounted and foraged around in the scrub; he looked at the horses as they stood still on the earth. He got the map from his saddlebag, took out the hand compass and walked over to the sand rise, where he took a bearing. They all dismounted and Frank Counihan yawned and scratched at his beard. High in the sky, the birds were flying south. Sawtell came back, looked at the horses again and said:

'We've got two choices: a station to the south or a tank to the north.'

'The station could be occupied,' St John Jackson said.

'You're right, Major, we go north to Edgar's Tank.' He looked at the Padre. 'I hope to Christ the VDC's not there.'

O'Donohue went round the horses as they stood and said nothing.

'How are they, Kevin?' Counihan said.

'They'll do.'

St John Jackson removed his topee and hit it on his trousers; he ran his hand over the stubble on his chin and said:

'It's north to the tank.'

'Okay,' Sawtell said, 'we'll have to ride and walk one hour. At this rate we'll get there in three hours.'

As he walked through the saltbush, St John Jackson thought they had to make the tank. He rubbed his chin again as the dust rose from his boots and the horses' feet. To fail now would be unthinkable.

At half past ten, they saw some sheep in the scrub and then some kangaroos. They stopped and looked, but it was impossible to see which way they were going. It was a confusing landscape and the only thing constant was the Barrier Range where no help lay.

'There's sheep and roos,' Counihan said. 'There's water somewhere.'

Sawtell did not reply and walked with his horses. He hoped the bearing was right.

'Say the tank's been fouled?' Counihan said.

'Aw, shit, Frank, we'll find good water somewhere.'

An hour later, they saw the windmill turning above the trees. O'Donohue threw the lead ropes of his horses to Counihan and ran through the scrub. They walked and watched the boy go as the crows called. They stopped and waited; Sawtell rolled a cigarette, but couldn't lick the paper and put the tobacco back in his tin. They waited for fifteen minutes; the horses were too tired to browse and the feed was unpromising; St John Jackson looked at the sky and pulled his helmet down over his face. His horse, he judged, would not last another two hours and the afternoon heat was still to come. Then Kevin O'Donohue appeared and said:

'The tank's a bit shitty, but it's okay.'

They struck camp. Edgar's Tank was muddy and low, the horses could drink but, for the men, the water had to be boiled. The earth was littered with broken timber and fouled with sheep droppings. All of them kept their scarves around their faces because of the bushflies. The earth was red and the ants ran wildly, carrying tiny grains of sand. There were eagles in the sky and bony sheep wandered in the bush. The fences were down and the stockyards were ruined and deserted. O'Donohue and Counihan foraged a short way to the north-east toward the Pinnacles Station. They kept clear of the homestead in case it was occupied and came back with two young ewes which Counihan slaughtered and cut into chops. They considered the risk of lighting a fire to boil the water and cook the meat. Finally, one was lit in a nearby creek bed and they chewed the half-cooked mutton and drank the warm black tea. They were six miles from Broken Hill, and when they stood on high ground, they could see the spires of the churches and the poppet heads of the mines. Now and again, the sound of military traffic rumbled on the stony surface of the Silver City Highway. Dust rose and billowed in the sunlight and the smell of petrol and exhaust was on the air. They set up the Lewis and the Brens and kept their rifles and shotguns close by. Counihan cradled the Luger submachine gun.

'Right,' Sawtell said, as they crouched in the scrub, 'for better or worse, I'm the only man who's worked in a mine.' The sun shone upon them and they sweated in the heat. 'Shaft mines are all basically the same. There's a winding tower and the shaft beneath. In the shaft, there's a cage which takes the miners and dump trucks up and down to the galleries beneath. The cage is raised and lowered by two steel wire cables by means of two big pulleys at the top of the tower. The cables are driven and stored on two large drums in the winding house. The winding drums are usually powered by a diesel motor with a clutch and brake mechanism. It's simple engineering.' He drew a diagram with his pencil on the yellow paper, showing the tower and the winding house, the cables and the machinery. Sawtell passed the drawing around. 'There are two jobs we have to do: one is to disable the winding tower by blowing the castings and bearings of the pulleys on the top. If we do that, they can't raise and lower the cage. The second is to disable the diesel that turns the winding drums. We've only got enough dynamite to blow the pulleys on the tower, so we'll have to set fire to the winding house and the diesel with petrol. It's probably a Lister with a generator and electrics. There'll also be a switchboard.'

Sawtell looked at Frank Counihan. 'I can handle the tower, Frank, if you and the Major can look after the winding house.' He got up from his haunches and rolled a cigarette.

'Okay.'

'How high is the tower, Mr Sawtell?' St John Jackson said as he looked at the drawing.

'Sixty feet, I imagine.'

'And you have to climb it?'

'That's right, to the top. There are usually three platforms, and I go up the safety ladder with the dynamite and the reel of fuse.'

'How long will it take to place the explosives?' St John Jackson said.

'If all goes well, about an hour.'

'And preparing the winding house?'

'About the same time, if the job's done thoroughly.'

'What happens in the winding house?'

'As I told you, there'll be a big Lister diesel, two drums and the cables, the generator and the electrics.'

'And?'

'When you've soaked the oily waste in petrol, you stuff it in the inspection plate of the Lister, on the bearings of the winding drums, in the electric gear and in any drums of lubricating oil you find around. Go for the Lister and the generator and scratch channels in the dirt and sand. Pour

279

petrol in the channels and light it when I've fixed the tower. We blow them both at the same time.'

St John Jackson said: 'It all sounds quite feasible to me.'

'Right,' Sawtell said, 'here's the split-up: Kevin can help me with the tower, and Frank and you, Major, can take the winding house. I'm sorry, Padre, I'm asking you to stay in the camp and look after the horses and the gear.'

'Please don't apologize, Mr Sawtell, they also serve who only stand and wait.'

'What time have you got in mind?' St John Jackson said.

'In the early hours of the morning, say, around two o'clock.'

'0200 hours.'

'If you wish.'

'The mine is no doubt guarded.'

'Probably, who knows? I shouldn't think they'd expect a job like this.'

'And if it is?'

'We have, as they say in boys' stories, to overpower them.'

'Quietly.'

'Yes.'

'The night'll be cold and clear,' Kevin O'Donohue said, 'and there's a full moon.'

'A mixed blessing,' St John Jackson said. 'We can see and they can too.'

'I'll have to take a lamp up the tower,' Sawtell said. 'I've got to see to fix the fuses.'

'That'll be tricky,' Counihan said. 'For Christ's sake don't drop the bloody lamp.'

'That'll be the last thing I'll do. I can carry the dynamite and fuse in a saddlebag on my back.'

'There'll be a fence around the mine,' Counihan said.

'We can't climb it,' Sawtell said, 'we've got ten gallons of petrol, the dynamite and our weapons. We'll have to cut through. How long will it take?'

'I'd say five minutes with the bolt cutters. It won't be electrified or anything, will it?'

'It's highly unlikely, they wouldn't count on sabotage this far out.'

'Say the fence is patrolled?'

'Christ, Frank, we'll deal with that when we come to it. If a Jap's there, stick that sheath knife of yours in his back.'

'Okay,' Counihan said. 'Just asking.'

Sawtell knew he could do it.

'Gentlemen,' Sergius Donaldson said, 'what will we do if they're operating the mine around the clock? What will we do if the mine's working and there are men in the galleries?'

'Jesus,' Frank Counihan said, 'I hadn't thought of that.'

'If the mine's working, if there are men in the winding house and men beneath, the job's off,' Sawtell said. 'I only hope to God they're not working night shifts.'

'It's quite possible with forced labour,' the Padre said.

'It is. We'll have to take a look tonight.'

'Maybe we should go for the power station,' Counihan said.

'I want that mine, Frank. Anyway, the power station will be heavily guarded, that's always number one on Madigan's list. If we were to blow the power station, they could always raise and lower the cage with a truck.'

'It seems to me, Mr Sawtell,' St John Jackson said, 'that you've done your homework. Quite admirable.'

Sawtell got up, stretched his legs and looked toward the towers of Broken Hill.

'If I hadn't done my homework, Major, I wouldn't have come all this way. I'd have spent the last two months foraging the outback stations and country pubs.'

'One last thing,' Sawtell said. 'If something goes wrong, if one of us gets hit, the others go on. Okay?' They all agreed.

'Where do we go after we've blown the mine?' O'Donohue said.

281

'Silverton, an old mining town west of here. It's about two hours' ride, maybe three. There's a pub there.' Sawtell laughed. 'Maybe we *can* forage. I can't remember when I last had a beer. I don't think the Japs will be there.'

'And after that?' St John Jackson said.

'North, to a station called Sturt's Meadows. We can hole out there for a week or two.'

'And then?'

'It depends how far they come after us, it depends on what happens. There's a one-horse town called Tibooburra near the State border.'

'And then?'

'We'll have to see. Maybe we can get through to Alice Springs.'

'That's a long way, Mr Sawtell, another five hundred miles.'

'It is, Major, but it's that or going south to surrender.'

'I've surrendered twice before,' St John Jackson said, 'and I don't intend to surrender a third time.'

'Then we all ride north to fight another day,' Sawtell said. He looked at the Barrier Range and the dark, flat hills of flint and stone. Then he took out the hunter: it was almost midday and he guessed the temperature was in the nineties. All they could do now was to wait the day out and reconnoitre the mine tonight. 'If you'll excuse me,' he said, 'I'm going to catch some sleep.' He found what shade he could and stretched out on the earth, his head on his saddle. His back ached and he hoped he could climb the tower.

Counihan and O'Donohue got up and went over to the picket line to look at the horses. The traffic on the highway had ceased and all was still.

'They're not too bad,' Counihan said.

'My packhorse has got a sore back,' O'Donohue said, 'and the Padre's has cast a shoe.' He picked at his black fingernails and stared about. What if there were patrols?

Would they be discovered? He thought of the Japs at Pine Point Station.

'Not the waler?'

'Nah, his packhorse.'

'Maybe we can rig something up at Silverton. We're out of spare shoes.'

'There might be some horses there.'

'Maybe.' Counihan blew his nose and spat. 'Christ, this is an arsehole of a place.' He swatted the flies with his hat and rolled a cigarette. 'I like being on the move. What if some Japs come barging through the scrub? We're sitting ducks.'

'How long will the war go on?'

'The war? It's a bloody queer one. I don't know, somebody's got to come and bail us out. No one knows what's happening. The Yanks might come back, that bugger MacArthur's sitting on his bum in New Zealand. He's got a whole division there. All this bullshit about "I shall return", this could go on for years with us living in the bush like bloody savages. Christ, I'd like a beer and a day at the races.'

'We'll need some feed for the horses at Silverton,' O'Donohue said. 'This saltbush is no good.'

'All right, son, we'll find you some feed. Maybe there's a nice, friendly pub there and we can all get pissed.'

'Do you reckon Mr Sawtell can do the tower?'

'No worries, he's a strong bugger and knows all about that kind of thing. He'll knock it off. Let's poke around a bit, it's something to do.'

Rifles in hand, they wandered off through the scrub. The crows called from the branches of the small trees, and fires burned in the hills to the north. Once more the traffic echoed from the highway.

'Well, Sergius?' St John Jackson said.

They sat in the shallow creek bed amid the debris of long-forgotten floods.

'I would like a glass of cool German white wine, something from the Rhine Valley. It must rain here sometimes, look at the timber caught in the branches. What a strange place.'

'What do you think of Sawtell's plans?'

'Eminently practical, the nature of the man, I'm sure he can do it. I'm sure you all can, it's our best way to strike a blow against the enemy. We *are* soldiers, and we cut the cloth according to its measure. These Australians are resourceful men, and disciplined, thank God. They're not all rabble. I sometimes wonder if our countrymen would be any better in the same circumstances.'

St John Jackson thought of some of his men in France. 'Probably not.'

'Well then. God has cast us together on this strange mission and time will tell.'

'God.'

'Yes, God. I think that, basically, our Mr Sawtell is a believer.'

'You think so?'

'There are all the signs: the prayerbook, the crucifix.'

'The crucifix?'

'He has a crucifix, I've seen him looking at it.'

'How odd.'

'Not necessarily, one finds the most unpromising believers.'

'I'm sure we shall destroy the mine,' St John Jackson said, 'but after that, God knows.'

'As the Americans say, In God We Trust.'

'The Americans, they've let us down. General Douglas MacArthur has feet of clay.'

'That may be, but I must confess to you that this expedition excites me for all the discomfort.'

'Excites you? Why is that? I don't find the flies, the food and our friend, Counihan, particularly exciting.'

'Let us say, Francis, it's a lot more bearable than the

Somme or Loos. We can ride and it's an adventure of sorts. Remember Robert Falcon Scott, Livingstone and T. E. Lawrence, the marvellous dash to Akabar. There's some similarity.'

'The similarity escapes me. And after the mine?' He threw a pebble into the creek bed.

'Francis, I'm fifty-six, you're fifty-three, we each have no family and it seems to me that all that's left for us is to do our best.' Sergius Donaldson thought about the Great War, his prep school and his days at Oxford. He had once won the 5000 metres final. That had been his best day. 'Francis, we do our best: we fight, we ride and we take it day by day.'

'And Counihan?'

'A difficult fellow, but a Catholic, and they always return to God.'

'Well,' St John Jackson said, 'I think I should inspect the weapons. If something should go wrong at the mine, you may be on your own.'

'Indeed, Francis.'

They left the creek bed and St John Jackson and Sergius Donaldson started stripping and cleaning the Brens, the Lewis and the Thompson guns. Sawtell was awake and helped them. They worked all the afternoon.

It was dark by eight and Sawtell, Counihan and St John Jackson moved carefully through the scrub toward Broken Hill. It was already cold and they wore their greatcoats. The moon was full and they walked parallel to the Silver City Highway. The track was soft and dry and they made the Pinnacles Station in an hour. Counihan carried his Luger submachine gun, and Sawtell and the Major had their Webleys. They saw the station homestead through the trees. There were no lights on, but they kept clear of the building. Stray cattle and sheep moved through the parched vegetation and the shadows and soft noises were menacing and unnerving. Then they saw the poppet head of a mine against the night sky and stopped. There were no lights and no activity, and they crouched by the broken fence. Something moved in the scrub and Counihan disengaged the safety on the Luger. Sawtell and the Major stood motionless.

'That's not what we want,' Sawtell said. 'I think it's the Pinnacles Silver Lead Mine. The Zinc is much bigger. We've got another three miles to go.' They moved on up the track in the darkness, their boots breaking the soft crust of dry earth.

After another hour, the going became difficult and the ground treacherous. There were craters, heaps of spoil and rubble, discarded dump trucks, hawsers and oil drums. The track broke up and disappeared into a ghostly, confusing wilderness.

'Jesus,' Counihan said, 'this is a bloody No Man's Land.'

Sawtell crawled up to the top of the mullock heap and in the distance saw lights gleaming. They looked like sodium lamps, but it was hard to tell. He slithered down the heap and said:

'I think we're close. I've seen some lights.'

They picked their way through the forbidding wasteland. The earth was leached and nothing grew. At last they came to a fence and St John Jackson looked at his luminous watch. It was a little after half past eleven.

'It's taken us three hours,' he said, 'if indeed this is the mine.'

'I think it is,' Sawtell said. 'If you two stay here, I'll go down the fence.'

He disappeared into the night. Counihan and the Major sat in the darkness and said nothing. They listened for the sound of machinery, but there was none.

After half an hour, Sawtell reappeared, sat down on the earth and said: 'It's the Zinc Corporation Mine, and there are men working.'

286

'How do you know it's the Zinc Mine?' St John Jackson said, 'I've heard there are more than one.'

'There are three. The others are Broken Hill North and the South. They're too hard to get at and they're beyond our resources. I know the Zinc, you'll remember I worked there.'

'What about the men working?' Counihan said.

'We'll have to wait and see what time they close down.'

'Was there any sign of the enemy?' St John Jackson said.

'Not by the fence, but there are four shafts.'

'Four?'

'Four, we can only take out one.'

'This makes our journey rather futile. Have you always known there were four?'

'No, I've always reckoned two: the main, and one abandoned.'

'How do you know there are four?'

'There are four winding towers, I counted them. Look, Major, God knows how many railway engines there are in France, but that doesn't stop the Resistance from blowing one up. If we take the main shaft out, it'll slow them up a bit.' The Major fell silent and Sawtell said: 'As we both know, there are rarely any clear-cut victories. I suggest we wait by the wire to see what happens to the night work.' Please God, let there be no work around the clock. They had come a long way. The three of them set off down the fence and nothing more was said. In the dark, the crickets sang.

Through the sheds and the piles of spoil they could see the four towers, the lights were on and now they heard the sound of machinery. They could see the headlights of trucks moving along the dirt roads of the mine. It was impossible to see either soldiers or men. They settled down in the scrub and waited. The great heap of rubble from the mine stood against the moonlit sky. They waited in their greatcoats, cold and unseen. At one o'clock, the lights went

287

out and the mine fell silent, then they saw the trucks' headlights disappearing and all was silent.

'That's it,' Counihan said, 'the bastards stop at one.'

'It looks like it,' Sawtell said. 'Let's wait another half an hour in case something happens.'

There was no more activity and they knew the job was on.

The three-hour march in the dark was difficult and the Major, Counihan and O'Donohue took it in turns to carry the petrol cans. Sawtell had the explosives, the fuse and the bolt cutters in his saddlebags. When they got to the fence, Sawtell and St John Jackson sat in the scrub with the gear while Counihan and O'Donohue went down to have a look at the main winding tower. They came back in half an hour and Counihan said:

'It's the same as last night, they're working and the fence is patrolled.'

'It wasn't last night,' Sawtell said.

'Well, it is tonight, they must have some crazy system. There was a soldier walking along the inside of the fence where we planned to go in.'

'Inside the fence?' St John Jackson said. 'How do we get at the devil?'

'I climb the fence, go down the line and get him,' Counihan said.

'Say there's more than one?' O'Donohue said.

'I get them both.'

'You're sure you can do that, Frank?' Sawtell said.

'I'll have a bloody good try.'

Sawtell was about to ask him if he'd killed anybody before this, but decided not. Counihan gave O'Donohue the Luger submachine gun and said:

'I won't be needing that.'

He scaled the fence, dropped down on the other side and

disappeared. Sawtell picked up the saddlebags and they moved off down the track. When they reached the spot, they found Counihan standing inside the fence. The lights shone from the mine buildings and the winding tower and there was now a gentle breeze from the west.

'As easy as pie,' Counihan said. 'Got me first Jap right between the shoulder blades.'

His shirt was streaked with blood; he fingered the bone handle of his sheath knife and grinned.

'Never thought it would be that easy. Like slaughtering a sheep.' He ran his hand across his throat. 'They're not like us, are they?' His body reeked with sweat despite the cold.

'No,' Sawtell said, 'they're not.' It was Counihan's first kill, he knew that.

'Don't think much of their weapons,' Counihan said, holding a Meiji rifle with a fixed bayonet. 'Shoddy stuff.'

'It might come in handy,' Sawtell said. 'Is there anyone else around?' He checked his watch; it was almost half past twelve. The mining machinery rumbled and the headlights gleamed. There was no point in starting on the fence until one o'clock in case another patrol came along. 'We're going to sit in the scrub until the shift's over. Can you make yourself scarce?'

'Okay,' Counihan said. 'I'll look out for any more of the bastards.'

'Where did you put the first one?'

'Dumped him in a pit. See you later.'

Sawtell went back to the others and sat down. He was ready for a cigarette, but couldn't risk it.

'Was there a patrol?' St John Jackson said.

'Yeah. Counihan fixed it.' Sawtell ran his hands down his beard. The Major thought and said nothing.

The work stopped at one o'clock and, shortly after, the lights went out. O'Donohue went to get up, but Sawtell held on to him and said: 'Hold your horses, Kevin. We don't want to rush it.' They waited another fifteen minutes with their greatcoats wrapped around them, then Sawtell went back to the fence with the bolt cutters. Counihan was there.

'No sign of anything?' Sawtell said.

'Quiet as the grave.'

St John Jackson and O'Donohue came up with the gear and Sawtell started on the wire. It was easy and they were inside in five minutes. They stood uncertainly in the dead trees, then Sawtell slung the packsaddles and rifle on his back and half-cocked the Webley.

'We might as well go,' he said, and they made for the main tower. The ground was tricky and it took them some time to get to the tower and the winding house. They crouched behind the piles of pit-props and studied the scene. The winding tower loomed high into the night and dump trucks and trolleys sat on the railway. A guard was standing outside the winding house. He was wearing a forage cap and carrying a rifle and fixed bayonet.

'Jesus,' Counihan said, 'what do we do now? We can't shoot the bastard, we'll wake the neighbours up.'

'You got the last man, Mr Counihan,' St John Jackson said.

'And I'll get this bastard.' He took out his knife. 'I'll dodge round the back of the shed.'

Counihan crept away through the dump trucks while the others watched and waited. My God, Sawtell thought, if Frank buggers this one up. Kevin O'Donohue crouched and stared at the guard. Moths fluttered around the light on the winding shed. Counihan reappeared from behind the shed and came up on the guard. Sawtell thought he must be seen, but the soldier went down and Counihan, holding the knife, stood over the body.

'Right,' Sawtell said, 'let's get on with it.' He released the safety catch on Counihan's machine gun and gave it to O'Donohue.

'If anyone comes, use this. But for Christ's sake be careful, the bloody thing is lethal.'

He struck a match, lit the hurricane lamp and opened the saddlebags. There were twenty-four sticks of dynamite tied in bundles of six with fishing line, a reel of fuse and oily waste.

Counihan picked up the waste and bolt cutters and went to start on the locked door of the winding house. Sawtell looked up at the tower, slung the saddlebags over his shoulder and took up the lamp.

'Give me half an hour and when you see the fuse burning, light the petrol. I'll see you later.'

'Okay,' Counihan said. 'You be careful.'

'I'll try.'

Sawtell started to climb the narrow ladder. It was an awkward ascent and the hurricane lamp kept banging loudly against the steelwork. He climbed carefully, made the first platform and looked down. O'Donohue was standing under the light of the winding house with the Luger at the ready. Jesus, Sawtell thought, why doesn't he stand in the shadows? He was about to call out, but decided against it. Counihan and the Major had disappeared: they must be in the shed. Sawtell's heart pumped, his joints were stiff and he started the climb for the second platform. The work was harder than he expected and he had to stop twice and cling to the ladder. When he got to the second platform, he felt giddy and had to sit down. He had never had a head for heights. His body was shaking and he looked down over the mine. The lights gleamed at the other winding towers and the stars shone. The moon was bright and he could see the buildings of Broken Hill. He felt dizzy and gripped the cold rails as the lights swung through his vision. No sound came from the winding house. Sawtell stood up, breathed heavily and started for the top. The climb was taking him much longer than it should and his arms and legs ached. The ladder was

291

slippery with dew, he missed a rung, almost fell and clung, his head reeling with vertigo. He stopped three more times before he got to the top of the tower. He shivered in the cold breeze, rested for a time, then tied the hurricane lamp to the rails near the pulleys and started work. Thank God, it was straightforward; he had laid charges before, but in tunnels, not on towers. He tied the dynamite to the bearing castings of the pulleys with fishing line, one pack each side, inserted the fuses, joined them and double tied them to the main fuse. It took him about twenty minutes and he fixed the explosives very carefully. Once, he thought he heard the sound of a motor, stopped and listened. He hoped Counihan and the Major hadn't struck trouble in the winding house. Frank would know what to do and would improvise something. All his years on the railways and knocking about. He thought of Counihan and the two Japanese guards. *They're not like us, are they?* If they did this job, it would call for a drink, but then he remembered they didn't have any. Jesus. When everything had been checked, Sawtell blew out the lamp and started the climb down, running the main fuse out from the reel. The fuse tangled twice and he had to stop and free it; he had to make sure it didn't break or all his work would be for nothing. He rested at the second platform and saw Counihan and St John Jackson coming out of the winding house; they were pouring petrol in channels scratched in the dirt. There was no sign of O'Donohue and no sound. Sawtell felt better now and his body had stopped shaking: it was going to work and Colonel Madigan would be proud of them. At last, he felt the concrete platform under his boots. He rubbed his sore hands against his trousers; he could never do this sort of thing again.

When he left the ladder, Sawtell found O'Donohue waiting for him and said, 'Is everything okay?' He was glad to be down from the tower.

'Yeah, they've done the winding house.'

Sawtell cut the fuse with his pocket knife: 'Here, hold this, you can have the pleasure of lighting it.'

He looked at his watch: it was half past two. They had been here too long and their luck had to run out: it was the law of averages. He ran down to Counihan and the Major.

'How's it going? I've fixed the tower and the fuses are ready.'

'Good,' Counihan said, as he finished pouring out the petrol, 'there was lots of flammable junk lying around in the shed, drums of sump oil and stuff. We're ready.'

'Let's light up and get out,' Sawtell said. 'Our luck won't hold much longer.'

'I agree, Mr Sawtell,' St John Jackson said. 'It's time we retired. Fortune doesn't always favour the brave.'

'Right, we'll light the fuse.'

Sawtell ran back to O'Donohue, grabbed the weapons and saddlebags and said: 'Okay, Kevin, light up.'

The boy struck the match, but it went out. His hands shook and he dropped the box.

'Bloody hell, Kevin,' Sawtell said, 'don't let go the fuse.' He searched on the ground for the matches and saw the petrol flaring in the dark toward the winding house. Sawtell groped for the matches on his hands and knees, finally found them and lit the fuse. They stood and watched it burning up the tower.

'Sorry, Mr Sawtell.'

Sawtell said nothing. Then he heard the sound of a truck and saw the headlights.

'Jesus,' Sawtell said, 'come on, Kevin.'

They ran into the dark, Sawtell tripped and fell heavily, got up and followed O'Donohue toward the fence. Somewhere he heard men shouting as the winding house burst into flames; then the tower went up, the explosion echoing across the country. The sky was lit and the top of the tower glowed and burned. Then they saw St John Jackson and Counihan running up in the dark.

'We'll have to move quickly, Mr Sawtell.'

An alarm sounded as they made it for the fence. Sawtell fell again, and Counihan grabbed him and helped him up; they got to the fence, but couldn't find the hole in the wire. Christ Almighty, Sawtell thought, I can't take much more of this. Counihan and O'Donohue cursed and ran up and down the fence line in the darkness, and lights shone in the scrub as the sky glowed. They doubled back and disappeared. Sawtell braced himself and said to the Major:

'We'll have to go over the top.'

'Right you are.'

St John Jackson seemed to climb easily in his greatcoat, his rifle across his back. He reached the top and dropped on to the track. A second alarm sounded and Sawtell climbed slowly, his boots jamming in the steel mesh, the saddlebags twisted around his body as the Major crouched and waited. More lights gleamed, the sirens moaned and strange voices echoed in the night as men ran through the saltbush. St John Jackson unshouldered his BSA and cocked it as Sawtell clambered. A soldier appeared, the Major rested the rifle on the mesh, sighted carefully and fired. The man dropped but they heard the sound of vehicles coming up as the tower burned in the sky, lighting up the buildings and the fence. Come on, man, St John Jackson thought, come on. He considered tossing a Mills bomb, but decided not. At last Sawtell got to the top, jumped, picked himself up and ran into the scrub toward the Pinnacles Silver Mine.

When he heard the explosion, Sergius Donaldson went down to the picket line and started to saddle the horses. Sawtell had done it and the Padre was pleased: it had given a purpose to the long ride. When he had finished the mounts, he started on the packhorses, but did not load the packframes. He worked by the light of the lamp with his loaded shotgun close by and now and then stopped and listened for sounds in the bush. After the explosion, all was quiet. He stacked all the gear neatly, the Brens, water bags, ammunition cases, the food, and smothered the fire. He left the Lewis on its tripod, loaded and ready. Everything was ready to break camp quickly when the men returned.

As Sergius Donaldson got out his communion case, he saw a glow in the sky and he guessed it was the fire in the winding house. He opened the case and took out the small chalice and paten: he wondered how long it would be before he would take the Holy Eucharist again. It had been a long time now. There was a noise in the scrub and Sergius Donaldson picked up the Hollis shotgun and cocked it. He stood quite still by the embers of the fire and waited in the dark. The night was cold and he shivered in his greatcoat; then he saw the shape of a sheep moving through the small trees. *And Sheep May Safely Graze*. He kicked more earth on the fire, sat down and waited. If all had gone well at the mine, they would be back in three hours. He hoped there had been no casualties and thought of turning out the first-aid kit, but he knew where it was and did not want to tempt Providence. He smoked and wondered why they had seen no blackfellows since Wilcannia; they were indeed a strange race. Where did they go? Was this not their part of the country? Had he been a younger man, this was one place where he would not have been a missionary: it would have been a fruitless task. He remembered the blackfellows at Bourke and Wilcannia. Like the Hindus, they were obviously impossible to convert. It seemed the Devil had made them an abject and amoral people. The Muslims and Hindus were hardly any better: a native was a native wherever one went. He coughed and thought of his life as an army chaplain; it had been discipline, good soldiering and faith. Those were the qualities that would see them through the north to Alice Springs. We all ride north, Sawtell had said, to fight another day. What was there? He

295

had heard it was wilderness, a place without towns, settlements and rivers. It was the world's last frontier and he had been chosen to go there. Sergius Donaldson threw his cigarette butt into the ashes and waited in the dark. The horses snorted, the saddles creaked and the stars shone. There was no glow in the sky now, but he knew there was a fire at the mine and that they had succeeded. He hoped there might be some whisky at Silverton. He lit another cigarette and walked around the camp: he must not go to sleep. An aircraft flew through the night, and on the highway the enemy traffic rumbled.

Shortly after four, Sergius Donaldson heard voices and noises in the bush. He picked up the shotgun, cocked it, then saw the light of a lamp and men in greatcoats.

'Good morning, Padre,' Sawtell said, looking at the shotgun and the Lewis on its tripod, 'you were expecting visitors?' He laughed. 'We got the mine.'

They shook hands and St John Jackson said: 'It was an efficient piece of sabotage.' But he remembered Counihan with the knife and the guard falling. He looked at the saddled horses and the neat stacks of gear. 'You've not been wasting your time?'

'Indeed not, we can be away in half an hour.'

'Thank Christ,' Frank Counihan said, as he started to load his packhorse.

'Are we being followed?' Sergius Donaldson said.

'Probably.' Sawtell put his rifle into the scabbard on his horse.

'They'll be after us.'

'And you saw them?'

'Yeah,' Counihan said. 'We saw them.'

'Then it's off to Silverton?'

'Yeah, it's off to Silverton.'

The Padre was right: they worked hard loading the gear, and were ready in half an hour. The horses drank at the tank, they filled the water bottles and canvas bags and rode

296

west before the dawn. As they rode, they kept looking back, but they couldn't be sure. Sometimes Sawtell thought he heard the sound of motors; it was like being back on the road to Bourke. The enemy was at their backs. Kevin O'Donohue rode in front on his big, black horse and the dust billowed in the darkness. The moon went down, and at dawn, they saw another winding tower above the gum trees. It was Silverton.

· XIV ·

1941

THE ARMY CAMP was on a dusty plateau, and the
Northern Divide rose from the high plain where the rocks
grew from the earth and small, barren streams flowed.
There were tree lines on the plain, and the soldiers drove
old army trucks along the meandering roads toward
inhospitable bivouacs and stony creek beds, where they
trained with Lewis and Bren guns among the logs and
branches of fallen gum trees. Much of the country was
burnt out, the fence posts blackened, and the crows sat on
the telephone poles. It was the start of another Australian
summer, and they drilled on the bull ring as the officers
sat upon their groomed, thoroughbred horses. The flies
swarmed in the heat of the day. Sleeping out in tents was
cold and difficult; the bright moon shone upon the plain,
and in the mornings the bull ants ran through their
uniforms and over their food. The war news was bad.
General Rommel's forces had surrounded Tobruk, Leningrad was besieged and the Nazis were only 140 miles from
Moscow. In Japan, Lieutenant-General Tojo had been
commanded by Emperor Hirohito to form a new government. In the Atlantic, HMS *Hood* had been sunk by the
Bismarck. The soldiers had been given plywood identification discs which they wore round their necks. His read
Sawtell, G. W. 61523 and he had been made a Sergeant.
They were now in uniform, but the equipment was run-

down and obsolete. The battalion had a fleet of old Bedford trucks which continually broke down, four Bren Gun Carriers, three anti-tank guns, a collection of tired cavalry horses, Lewis and Vickers machine guns and two-inch mortars. Ammunition was in short supply and the anti-tank guns had not yet been fired. The shells had not yet arrived. Sawtell had bought his own horse, a big grey waler, which he rode in the evenings, and he had also acquired a Hollis double- hammer shotgun. He had stripped and restored the Lee Enfield and the Webley and now both worked perfectly. Many of the men were veterans from the Great War, and there was much to talk about at the end of the day. Despite the heat, the cold and the bad equipment, Sawtell was happy. There was much to be done. They had leave at the weekends; Sawtell drank with his father at the Mountain View and slept at the YMCA. Sometimes he visited his mother. He had not seen Marcia since January 1939; his mother had been right. Some nights, they went out kangaroo shooting. It was against orders, but the Brigadier turned a blind eye. It varied the tucker and kept the men together as they drilled and worked at the anti-invasion exercise. The American talks with Japan were continuing, and last night at the camp cinema, they had seen *Buck Privates*.

Sawtell lay on his bed reading the *Sporting Globe* as the new men arrived. They had been at the range all day, learning to use the Thompson submachine gun. He didn't care for the Thompson even though it was an efficient weapon. Sawtell had seen Al Capone's men use it in gangster movies, and it was impressive when used in the field. But he preferred the Lee Enfield and the Mauser: one good shot could kill a man like Smith in the sap, and to win a battle in this war in the bush, one good man was all you might need. Sawtell lay on his bed as the new men moved in.

'Gooday,' the strange soldier said, as he threw his kit on

the next bed. Sawtell put the paper down and looked up at the new-comer. He was tall, dark and very strong with blue eyes. There was stubble on his chin, and he had a cigarette stuck behind his ear. Sawtell knew he was an Irish Catholic; he had seen many such men in the Mountain View.

'Gooday,' the soldier said. 'My name's Frank Counihan.'

'Geoff Sawtell.'

They shook hands and Frank Counihan sat on the bed and lit his cigarette. He looked around the hut and said:

'What's this outfit like?'

'Aw, bit of a shambles, not bad, the best we can do.'

'What's the drill?' Counihan looked at the stripes on Sawtell's tunic. 'What's the drill, Sergeant?'

'Anti-invasion exercises.'

'No kidding?'

'It makes sense,' Sawtell said. 'It's possible.'

Men came into the hut; they were laughing and chatting and throwing their kits on the floor. Some were opening bottles of beer and Sawtell was reminded of a football crowd on a Saturday afternoon.

'Who's it going to be?' Frank Counihan said. 'It can't be the Huns, they're too far away.'

'The Nips.'

'You could be right, they're close.'

Sawtell remembered his father and Jack Hanrahan and the beer and whisky at the Mountain View, and said:

'There's Singapore.'

'Aw, shit,' Frank Counihan said, 'I've heard the guns all point the wrong way.'

'Well,' Sawtell said as he looked at the new men and the bottles of beer, 'I suppose that calls for a drink.'

Counihan grinned and delved into his kitbag. He produced a bottle of Australian whisky, pulled the cork out and passed it over. Sawtell looked at Counihan and drank it down. It tasted raw, but good. It wasn't Johnnie Walker Black Label.

'Where are you from?'

'Ballarat.'

Sawtell remembered the fire in the quarry, the Ford trucks and the babies crying; the bottle of muscat and the big men weeping.

'Well,' he said as he got up from his bed, 'I'd better get these men to order.'

'Yeah,' Frank Counihan said as he drank the cheap whisky, 'you do that. Is this bed going?'

Sawtell looked at Counihan and considered. He usually liked a bit of space. 'You can have it.'

'Thanks, I'll get in the rest of me gear.' Counihan watched the snowy-headed Sergeant go down the hut. He was a big bugger: he would have to be careful.

The new men were a varied lot, a mixture of boys and veterans. They were from town and country, and God knows what could be made of them. Some looked fit enough to be in the AIF and others too old and tired to do anything. He wondered how the selection was made and what was happening at the recruiting centres. He thought of the broken-down trucks and the out-of-date weaponry and looked at the men as they came in with their gear and stood around the hut. If this was the way the war was being managed, they were never going to win. In Melbourne, the first trial blackout had been a farce with lights left on everywhere. Few people had heard the practice air- raid sirens. There were very few bomb shelters, and in case of an enemy attack, citizens had been told not to panic and to stand in doorways. Somebody only had to drop a few incendiaries in the bush and the whole damned place would go up. Sawtell got the new men into some kind of order, allocated them beds and said, 'Have you blokes eaten?'

They shook their heads. One man looked old enough to be his father.

'Go down the mess; you'll find some tucker there. And put away those bottles or some bastard will do you in.'

They straggled off into the evening. Sawtell watched them go and heard them laughing and talking outside. Jesus Christ, he thought, if something bad happened, what use would they be?

Frank Counihan was lying on his bed, his gear neatly stacked at the foot. The whisky had been put away, and he lay stretched out, staring. He was long and lean and his face was darkly lined. Sawtell thought he could be a miner or quarry man.

'Do you want anything to eat?' Sawtell said. 'There's grub down at the mess.'

'I'm okay, I've eaten.'

Counihan took out his tobacco tin from his tunic pocket and rolled a cigarette. Then Sawtell saw the submachine gun propped up against the wall. It was a Luger Parabellum, clean and oiled and in very good condition.

'Where did you get the Luger?'

'Me brother.'

'Where did he get it from?'

'Some dead Hun on the Somme.'

'Have you fired it?'

'Too right, in quarries and the bush. It takes 9 millimetre, the ammo's easy to get.'

Sawtell picked up the weapon and cradled it in his arms. He removed the snail magazine.

'It's years since I saw one of these, they're awkward buggers.'

'They'd scare the shits out of any bastard and they're better than Tommies.'

'You didn't fight?' Sawtell said.

'Fight?'

'At the War.'

'Nup, I was too young. Me brother did. I missed out.'

This man had missed out, Sawtell thought.

302

'Where's your brother now?'

'Dead of TB. He gave the Luger to me when he knew his time was up.'

Counihan looked at the big man with the submachine gun. 'Did you go?'

'Yeah.'

'That's why you've got them stripes?'

'Yeah.'

'Well, you survived. The gas got me brother. What time do we get up?'

'Six.'

'That's late for me, then what?'

'Physical jerks, breakfast, drill, manoeuvres, farting around in the bush. Can you drive a truck?'

'Yeah.'

'Ride a horse and use a rifle as well as the Luger?'

'Yeah.'

'I think you'll do.' Sawtell gave the submachine gun back to Counihan, laughed and said: 'That's not quite army issue.'

'Australia's short of weapons, isn't it? It might come in handy. Where are you from?'

'Richmond.'

'Ah, the mighty Tigers.' Counihan looked at Sawtell. 'Did you ever play for the Seniors?'

'A long time ago.'

'We got our last Grand Final in 1934, were you there?'

'Yes,' Sawtell said, 'I was there.'

'A great game, we pissed all over South Melbourne.'

'We did.'

'Where did you play?'

'Centre-half forward.'

'You look like it. Any Grand Finals?'

'One.'

'Which?'

'1921.'

'Against Carlton, that was a great game, we won by four points.'

'We did.' Sawtell remembered.

'Did you get any goals?'

'Two.'

'Sawtell,' Frank Counihan said, 'I remember you, the big centre-half forward. That was twenty years ago, I went with my father.'

Sawtell was pleased and said:

'Okay, Counihan, I'll take you over to the canteen and buy you a beer.'

The militiamen stood around in their threadbare, ill-fitting uniforms in the makeshift canteen. Like everything in the outfit, facilities were minimal: there was only bottled beer, a few tables and chairs, a dartboard and an old piano. Counihan seemed quite at home and drank his beer. A wireless was playing *The Bing Crosby Show*.

'Why aren't you in the AIF?' Sawtell said.

'Volunteered, but got turned down, shadow on the lung, a real bugger, would have liked to have had a go.'

'If you'd been in Crete, you'd be in a POW camp by now.'

'Yeah.' Counihan didn't seem to care. Sawtell knew he was a loner: it was in his face, it was the look of the men he had worked with at Broken Hill. Counihan put his empty glass down and said:

'I reckon the Japs do want Australia.'

'Why?'

'Space. There's millions of the bastards and they've nowhere to go. They've had their eyes on us for bloody ages.'

'Well, you might get your chance in the VDC,' Sawtell said, 'that's what we're supposed to be about, invasion, but no one takes us seriously, not least the Army. The gear they've given us to work with is shit.'

Counihan grinned. 'We'll just have to do what we can,

304

one foot after the other, that's what me Dad always said. One thing's for sure: we won't get any help from the Brits, they won't have a bar of us.'

'Then if something happens, we're on our own?'

'That's how I see it.' Counihan put half-a-crown on the bar.

'Do you want another?'

'Okay.'

Sawtell looked around at the men in the canteen; they weren't a bad lot, but at the drop of a hat, they'd all rush back to their wives and families. Counihan pulled a silver watch from his tunic pocket.

'What time does this show close?'

'Ten, we've got our own regulations.'

'That's one good thing.'

'Yes,' Sawtell said, 'it is.' He wondered if Marcia's friend had joined up, he thought not. He was probably a bloody pacifist.

'Have you got a wife and kids?' Counihan said.

'A wife, no kids. I see her at the weekends. You?'

'I've got nobody, except me mother in Ballarat, five sisters and one brother. They're all married with kids, all good Catholics. Who runs this outfit?'

'A man called Jamieson, Brigadier Jamieson, Melbourne Grammar.'

'Jesus Christ.'

'He's all right, he got the M.C. at Pozières.'

'Did you get anything?'

'No, I was just an ordinary sapper. They gave us all a silver medal when we got back.' He remembered the naked warrior on the charger and the skull and crossbones at its feet.

'I suppose that was the least they could do.'

'They didn't do much else, they gave us back-blocks farms nobody could do a thing with.'

'Did you do that?'

'Christ, no, I looked after myself, no bloody hand-outs, I'm a civil engineer, roads and bridges. What about you?'

'Railway fireman, last on the Broken Hill to Port Pirie run.'

'I've worked up there,' Sawtell said. 'That's tough country.'

'It makes a man out of you,' Counihan said.

Sawtell remembered the cold, starry nights and the immense heat of the day, the Barrier Range and the mysterious country to the north. 'Look,' he said, 'one for the road, and I'd better get back and see what those poor new buggers are doing.'

They drank their beer silently, each considering the other, and Sawtell said:

'Okay then, reveille's at six.'

'I'll be awake, you can count on that.' Counihan watched Sawtell go. A centre-half forward for Richmond Seniors, a man you could rely on.

For the next month, they trained on the plateau and in the bush. The Bren Gun Carriers never left the workshop, the anti-tank guns remained unfired; Sawtell taught the men how to use dynamite and safety fuses, one old soldier died of a heart attack and the weather suddenly turned cold with rain and snow sweeping the State. The Australians fought on in besieged Tobruk and the Nazis stepped up their onslaught on the Moscow front.

After his mother's phone call, Sawtell went to see Brigadier Jamieson, who gave him compassionate leave. The Brigadier also offered him his Ford Ten, and Sawtell took it and drove down to Melbourne. The weather had changed yet again and the evening was hot; the car had half its headlights blacked out and he drove carefully along the dirt road, down into the small gorge and up on to the highway. There was no traffic and the gum trees and hedges drifted by. A big, hard moon shone on the land. He had thought of ringing Marcia, but he didn't know where

306

to get hold of her. She had always liked his father. It took him two hours to get to the Freemasons' hospital and the streets of Melbourne were dark, silent and deserted. Now and again, he had to avoid piles of sandbags dumped in the roads in case of fires from air raids. Around the hospital, they had dug bomb shelters and built brick walls to break the blast. The sister at the desk told him his father was in ward seven and the lift was operated by an old Boer War veteran who was wearing his medals. The ward was half lit and smelled of carbolic. As he followed the nurse, Sawtell could hear the sound of men coughing. His father was in the end bed by the window that looked out on to the parks and ornate Victorian buildings. Few lights from the city were to be seen. Angus Sawtell raised himself from the pillows and they shook hands. Geoffrey noted the thin face, the skin in folds and the yellow, brittle fingernails. His father had to be over seventy-five; he had forgotten how old he was. The other men in the beds were lying still, but one coughed quietly. It was after visiting hours and there were some spring flowers on several of the small tables. Geoffrey sat down on the bed by his father and said:

'This is no good.'

'I'll say.'

'Where's Mother?'

'She was in earlier, but couldn't wait. She's not that good herself and it's a bugger in the blackout.'

'What happened?'

'Pains in the chest, couldn't breathe, then couldn't get up.'

'A heart attack?'

'Looks like it.' Angus looked at his son and smiled. 'You haven't got a drink on you?'

Sawtell laughed. 'No, Dad, I have not.'

'Just wondering.'

Sawtell thought of his father's fifty years of talking, drinking and arguing for causes. Keir Hardie, Karl Marx,

Sidney and Beatrice Webb, party pamphlets, Bertrand Russell, books he had picked up and glanced at, but never read. Theories, causes and books: they did not interest him; he was a practical man, but his father loved him and understood. For his father, those two goals in the Grand Final had been equal to all the books in his life. There was a puzzle about thinking and doing.

'What's next?' Sawtell said.

'I don't know, they don't say much, lots of rest.'

'How do you feel?'

'Weary. What's army life like?'

'Okay, nothing moves except the horses and they're half dead, old men and young boys; the way we are now, we couldn't play a decent game of football against the Girls' Friendly Society.'

'All our men are away,' his father said, 'I told you before we should have looked after ourselves.'

Sawtell thought of the Mountain View, Jack Hanrahan, the stones growing from the earth, the wheatfields and the distant river lines. There was much to be lost. He got up and looked out of the window at Melbourne; he saw the shapes of the old buildings and remembered arriving home when the fish flashed in the water and the crowd cheered. It was a beautiful, colonial city. He came back to his father, took his hand and said:

'No more drinking for a bit.'

'Will the Germans take Moscow?'

'I don't think so, but if they do, the Russians can always fall back; it's like Australia, they can scorch the earth and never give up. The Russians are like us: we've both got space.'

'What's it like out there?' Angus said.

'Where?'

'In the outback, where you were in 1932.'

Sawtell thought and said: 'I can't explain, I've never been to the centre.' He thought of the hills of stone lying to the north, the hinterland where brave men had died and eagles flew. 'I think God lives there.'

'I wish I'd been.'

'When the war's over, Dad, we'll go there, we'll buy a truck and go to the centre, we'll drink whisky, shoot game and live off the land.'

'And meet God?'

'Jesus, Dad, from an old rationalist.'

'I was baptized once. Do you believe in God?'

'Yeah,' Sawtell said, 'probably.'

'Have you heard from Marcia?'

'No.'

'That's a shame.'

'It is.'

'She left you for some other bloke, didn't she?'

'Yes.'

'I won't tell anybody.'

'I know you won't.'

It was a secret between them and Sawtell sat on the hospital bed with his father.

'What's going to happen?' his father said.

'To what?'

'The war.'

'God knows. It could last a long time, the Huns are an efficient, hard-working mob.'

'You should know that.'

'And the Japs are treacherous; they're all over the place, Borneo, Timor, the Dutch East Indies, they've probably looked us over.'

'Will they invade Australia?'

'They'll go where they can, they need the resources and this place is wide open; the Volunteer Defence Corps is a laugh. It's a wonder they haven't recruited that poor old bugger in the lift.'

'The Boer War man?'

'If somebody came here,' Sawtell said, 'we'd be like the

309

Boers, we'd be farmers at war: the raid in the night, the knife in the back, the enemy by day and us by night.'

Angus Sawtell was feeling tired and said:

'What are you going to do now?'

'I'm due back in camp at six in the morning, I suppose I should go and see Mother.'

'You should.'

'I've brought you a present, Dad,' Sawtell said.

'A present?'

Sawtell reached into his tunic pocket and gave his father his Great War medal. His father took the medal and looked at it in the half-light of the hospital room. *1914–1918, Cpl G. W. Sawtell, For Faithful Service.* His father coughed and said:

'Thank you.'

'I'm a soldier again, Dad.'

'Yes, I suppose you are.'

'I'd better go and see Mother.'

'Okay, you do that. I'll get some sleep.'

'You look after yourself, Dad.'

'I'll try.'

For the first time, Geoffrey Sawtell kissed his father as he lay in the bed; he rose and went down the ward past the sleeping men. In the lift, he saluted the Boer War veteran and walked out of the hospital past the bomb shelters and into the dark.

The lights were out, Bridge Road was in darkness and Sawtell turned down Rotherwood Street past the Mountain View. He parked the car and looked across the road at the bungalow. The pines had been felled and the new house stood proud in the night with its new lawns and small ornamental trees. He went up the path and knocked at the door. His mother came to the threshold and looked at him.

'Hullo, Mother,' he said, 'I've just seen Dad.'

She opened the fly-door and he went inside. In the hall,

he sensed the familiar objects and memories. He followed his mother down the hall and into the kitchen. All was spotless and undisturbed: the willow-pattern plates sat on the dresser and the cups were ready for tea. An unfamiliar cat sat on the window ledge. Sawtell sat down at the table and said:

'He doesn't look too bad to me.'

'It's drink. You should know.'

'It's also hard work and age.' Sawtell looked at his mother as she filled the kettle and got the milk from the ice-chest.

'I think he'll be okay. How have you been?'

'As well as can be expected.'

He saw she was quite grey now, but still proud and beautiful. She was wearing a white, handknit cardigan and had put her hat on the table. The house was silent and he thought of his father in bed with the War medal and the men coughing.

'Do you want a drink?' she said. 'Your father's bottle is in the cupboard.'

'No Mother.'

'Well, it had better be tea.' She got out the cups and saucers and they sat at the table. Sawtell didn't know what to say to her and she got up when the kettle boiled. Should he talk about his father, his drinking, their marriage, his marriage? Should he try to tell her what it was like coming home in 1919, the service at St Stephen's and his sermon about the nation being purified by war? He took out his watch: it was after ten, too late to knock up Jack Hanrahan.

'What time are you due back?' his mother said.

'At six in the morning.'

'How did you get here?'

'Someone lent me a car, the Brigadier, he fought at Pozières.'

'Petrol rationing is one problem I haven't got.'

'How are you off for money?'

'There's his pension.' She drank her tea silently.

'Army life's okay; some new men arrived today. They were pretty terrible: odds and sods.'

'Do you want some more tea?'

'Yes, thanks.'

'And something to eat?'

'It's all right, I'm not hungry.' Sawtell laughed. 'Army meals are quite solid.'

'What do they give you?'

'Sausages, spuds, chops, cabbage, it's okay.'

'Have you heard from Marcia?'

'No.'

'I thought not.'

Sawtell thought of having it out with her, the whole damned thing: the War, religion, his father, Marcia. But he looked at her. She was old now and his father mightn't come through. What had happened since 1919? Thirteen good years of marriage: he should be thankful for that. But it seemed that things were being done to him again and he didn't like it. He was losing control. He thought of asking her to sing for old time's sake while he played the piano. They could have some old songs: Victor Herbert, Richard Tauber, Noël Coward. He remembered that he and his father used to sing *The Bold Gendarmes*. When was Mothering Sunday? Was it May?

'You're quiet,' she said, 'what are you thinking about?'

'Dad. I hope he'll be all right.'

'We all do.'

He lit a cigarette and his mother got up and put an ashtray on the lace tablecloth.

'You're smoking too much.'

'Yes, Mother, I must give it up.' He wondered how many he'd smoked: it must have been millions. He'd started in the trenches; at least he didn't stick them behind his ear. He looked at his mother and the kitchen. There was nothing to be gained by staying. 'Well,' he said, 'I'd better

312

be getting back. I'll be down at the weekend, but you'll ring me if something happens?'

'I will.'

They walked down the hall, past the front room where they used to sing, and she stood at the door. Sawtell kissed his mother on the neck and said:

'I'm sure everything will be all right, there's loads of life in the old dog yet.'

'Yes,' she said. 'Goodnight.'

He went down the path, got into the Ford Ten and started the drive back to Lancefield, the Camp and the men.

One week later there was another telephone call. Sawtell was out on manoeuvres with the men in the bush, and when he got back late at night, there was a message: *Your father has passed away, please ring your mother.* He rang her and she seemed quite calm; she said that he had died in his sleep early that morning and that the funeral would be the day after tomorrow. Geoffrey asked if she was okay, and should he come down right away. She said that wouldn't be necessary, the neighbours and the parish priest were coming in to help, but to come down early on Wednesday morning. He thought about pointing out to her that his father had been a free thinker and that he wouldn't have wanted a church funeral, but he didn't do it. What could he arrange instead? Had Marcia been there, he could have done something. And where was she? He had phoned the Library once six months ago and been told that she had left. He was alone now and remembered his father's advice about good friends. Would Jack Hanrahan go to the funeral? He was a Catholic. There would be very few people there as most of his father's mates had been Holy Romans. It wasn't their fault they couldn't go, but maybe those who weren't and who remembered him when he had the bakery, would turn up. His father had been a popular and honest trader. Sawtell

313

stood by the telephone and listened to the sounds of the men laughing and talking in the evening.

'What's up?' Frank Counihan said. 'Do you want a beer?'

'My father just died.'

'Aw, Jesus, I thought he was doing okay.'

'He died this morning.'

'Jesus, that's no good.'

'The funeral's on Wednesday.' Sawtell didn't bother to tell Counihan about his father being a free thinker.

Counihan thought and said: 'Do you want me to come down?'

Sawtell was surprised: he'd only known Frank for six weeks.

'You're a Catholic.'

'That doesn't matter, I haven't been to Mass for years, I'll keep you company and we can have a few drinks afterwards. The way things are going, I don't think me turning up to a Prot funeral is going to cause a row.'

'Isn't it a mortal sin?'

'Aw, shit, Geoff, if you can get me the leave, I'll come. Let's have a beer.'

They went to the canteen and drank to his father.

Brigadier Jamieson, once again, gave Sawtell compassionate leave, and Counihan was allowed to go too. Jamieson also offered his car a second time, and at six on Wednesday morning, Sawtell and Counihan drove down to Melbourne. The Brigadier had said that returned men had an obligation to help each other out, and he would expect the same. As he drove back down the highway, Sawtell thought that having been to the War came in handy sometimes, and thank God for some public schoolboys. It was raining and they passed tank traps on the bridges and deserted petrol garages; the cows were waiting outside the sheds for milking and when they got to the outskirts of the city, the trams were running and people were going to work. Counihan slept for a bit and they got to Rotherwood Street

just after nine o'clock. When they passed the Mountain
View, Sawtell said:

'That's the pub where my Dad and I used to drink.'

'There's a pub on every corner in Richmond,' Counihan
said, 'we'll have a few when the funeral's over.'

Sawtell parked the car outside his mother's house, they
went up the path and Sawtell knocked at the door. After a
few moments, she appeared and he kissed her. She had been
crying and he kissed her again. Counihan stood on the
verandah with his slouch hat under his arm and Sawtell said:

'Mother, this is Frank Counihan, he's from camp and
came down with me.'

She looked at the tall, rough, Catholic soldier.

'How do you do, Mr Counihan.'

'Pleased to meet you.'

They went down the hall to the kitchen and his mother
said:

'It's good of you to have come, Mr Counihan.'

'Aw, it's no trouble.'

They sat down and put their hats on the table.

'You didn't know Geoffrey's father?'

'No, I've just come down with Geoff.'

His mother went to the bench and got down the tea
caddy, the cups and saucers.

'Would you like a cup of tea?'

'We would, Mother,' Sawtell said.

'You know where everything is, Geoffrey. I must go and
change, I've been making sandwiches. Make Mr Counihan
a cup of tea.'

She closed the kitchen door.

'Is it okay if I smoke?' Frank Counihan said.

'Yeah, I'll get an ashtray.' Sawtell, now he was home
once more, couldn't believe his father was dead. Maybe he
was out the back and would come through the door with
his pipe and his books. He opened a cupboard for the sugar
and there was the half-full bottle of whisky. He put the pot

315

of sugar on the table, filled the kettle and lit the gas. This was the table he had sat at in 1919, the same cupboard, the Dewars whisky, his father at the meetings of the Victorian Labor Party with his black notebook. Marcia. *She left you for another bloke, didn't she?* He got the bottle of milk from the ice-chest and sat down. He looked at Counihan.

'Would you like a drink, Frank?' He pointed at the Dewars.

'What about your mother? She'd go crook.'

Sawtell closed the cupboard door, the kettle boiled and he filled the pot.

'You'd have liked my father,' Sawtell said, 'most of his friends were Holy Romans; Irish nationalists, Sinn Fein, de Valera, Daniel O'Connell.'

'The Sinn Fein are mad bastards.' Counihan tidied his cigarette with a match. 'You know a bit about Catholics, don't you?'

'Yes, you'd better meet my Dad's mate, Jack Hanrahan, who runs the Mountain View.'

'Is he practising?'

'I don't know. Probably.'

'He won't be at the funeral then.'

'He might turn up.'

'Don't think so, it's only heathens like me. You look like your Mum. When's the missus coming?'

'Who?'

'Your missus.'

'She won't be, she's gone away and I can't get hold of her.'

'That's no good, you could do with your missus at a time like this. I expect there'll be lots at the church.'

'Maybe not,' Sawtell said. 'I told you: most of his friends were Catholics.'

'That's a bit of a problem.' Counihan smoked and drank his tea. 'One step at a time, Geoff, don't worry; we're all only human.'

'Is your father alive?'

'Not sure, he buggered off years ago. I expect he's around the place somewhere.'

'So your dad deserted your mother and the family?'

'Yeah, he's got a right. I remember him, he was a nice old bugger. Me brother dying didn't help and he got on the grog.' They drank the strong, sweet tea silently; the clock ticked and the strange cat came in and jumped up on the window ledge. Sawtell thought of his father and hoped nothing would go wrong in the church. He must ask his mother about the pall-bearers, and he hoped Jack Hanrahan would be there. They sat in the kitchen and waited for his mother. Sawtell gazed out of the window at the garden. Thank God, the rain had stopped. He looked at the stacks of sandwiches under the muslin, the tea cups and the spoons and cake-forks gleaming.

He entered St Stephen's Church, Richmond, with his mother and Frank Counihan. There were more people than he expected: his mother's friends and neighbours whom he hadn't seen for years; parishioners, and men from the Richmond Branch of the Labor Party. His father had been popular and been remembered. Sawtell looked around the church and at the flowers and the coffin; as far as he knew, his father had never set foot in the building. His mother had had the last word. Then he saw Jack Hanrahan sitting by himself on the other side of the church. The organ was playing hymn number 400, *Christ will gather in His own*, and Sawtell opened his prayerbook at the Burial of the Dead. The parish priest stood behind the coffin, lifted his hands and said:

'Let us pray.'

Sawtell knelt by his mother.

I am the resurrection and the life, saith the Lord: he that believeth in me, though he were dead, yet shall he

317

live: and whosoever liveth and believeth in me shall never die.

They prayed, sang the ninetieth Psalm, *Lord, thou hast been our refuge: from one generation to another*, and the slow service proceeded. The priest read the long lesson from Corinthians, and as he sat in the church, Sawtell heard the familiar words: *O death, where is thy sting? O grave, where is thy victory?* He looked at his mother; she was still and pale in her black dress, but not crying. Counihan sat beside him, his hands between his knees, staring straight ahead. Two more hymns were sung, the Lord's Prayer and the Collect said and, at last, the service ended. Sawtell rose, and with the other pall-bearers, carried the coffin down the aisle to the hearse outside.

As the organ played, they stood around in the church yard and his mother talked to the priest and her friends. The rain clouds had been blown away and it was a fine, clear morning. Jack Hanrahan was standing by the hearse, looking at the wreaths and flowers, and Sawtell went over to him. Tears were running down Jack Hanrahan's thin face and they shook hands.

'There goes one of the best mates I ever had, Geoff.'

'Thanks for coming, Jack.'

'God's one thing, but your Dad's another. I'm sorry I can't come to the cemetery, I've got to get back.'

'Thanks, Jack.' Sawtell still held his hand. 'We'll be down later.' He watched the old publican walk slowly past the oak trees into Church Street to wait for a tram.

'Who was that?' Counihan said.

'Dad's best mate, Jack Hanrahan.'

'He came then, good on him.'

Sawtell saw the undertaker talking to his mother and the priest as people were getting into their cars.

'Do you want to come out to the cemetery, Frank? It won't take long.'

318

'No worries.'

Sawtell went back to his mother, shook the priest's hand, he gave him some money for the poor-box and the small cortège finally moved away. As they drove slowly down Church Street, past the grand terrace houses and small shops, the passers-by stopped and removed their hats. At the graveside, the priest said the last rites, flowers were thrown, and Sawtell and his mother stood by the headstone. As they went back to the car, Sawtell said:

'I shall miss him, Mother, I shall miss him a lot.'

'We'd been married forty-five years, Geoffrey, and I shall miss him too.' She stopped on the gravel path by the cypresses.

'When we've had afternoon tea, I want you to thank Mr Hanrahan. I only hope when I pass away, a Holy Roman will do that for me.'

'When I saw Dad last time,' Sawtell said, 'I gave him my War medal.'

'I know you did, they put it with him. You've been a good boy, Geoffrey, even if you have stopped going to church, and I'm sorry about Marcia.'

He kissed her: they had made their peace. Maybe his father had been wrong about God.

Mr Costello was in the Mountain View, and when he saw Geoffrey, he came up and said:

'I'm sorry I couldn't come, Geoff.'

'That's all right, Mr Costello. I understand.'

'I'll buy you a drink then.'

They moved over to the bar and Frank Counihan was there, talking to Jack Hanrahan.

'What'll you have?'

'Put your money away,' Mr Costello said. 'It's my shout.'

'No, it's not,' Jack Hanrahan said, 'it's mine and no arguing.'

He took down the bottle of Dewars and banged it on the counter.

'Have a go at that for the sake of dear old Angus.'

My God, Sawtell thought, and turned away. Counihan watched him.

'We haven't met,' Mr Costello said.

'I'm Frank Counihan, a mate of Geoff's.'

'And I'm Dan Costello, a mate of his, too. Do you know, he got work in the Depression when most of the blokes sat on their arses?'

'It was the motorbike you sold me,' Sawtell said as he drank his whisky.

'It was your guts, just like your father, he had guts. Here's to Angus Sawtell.'

They all drank the whisky down and Geoffrey looked at them. Thank God for the Irish. What would the world be without them? Then Jack Hanrahan leaned over the bar and said:

'So you're back in uniform, Geoff. What's it like?'

'It's all right.'

Jack Hanrahan filled up the glasses from the bottle and turned to the others.

'He doesn't say much, he's never said much, but he's a doer and that's what's made Australia. If any bugger comes here, he's got Geoff Sawtell to contend with, the man who won the Grand Final in 1921.'

'Aw, come on, Jack.'

'It's true.' He went to get down another bottle.

'Hold your horses, Jack,' Frank Counihan said as he put a pound note on the bar, 'it's my turn.' These were his people and he knew there wasn't a penny in running this pub. 'We'll have Johnnie Walker Black Label.'

Mr Costello put a ten-shilling note on the counter.

'You can cut me in too.'

'No, Dan,' Counihan said, 'put that money away. Some other time when you're thinking of Geoff's father.'

They all looked at Frank Counihan as he stood at the bar. He was a tough bugger.

'What do you do, Frank?' Dan Costello said.

'I'm a soldier.' He looked at Sawtell. 'He's training me.'

Jack Hanrahan pulled the cork from the bottle.

'With you two bastards, they haven't got a chance.'

'We'll see,' Sawtell said. 'We'll see.' Maybe his father would come through the door; he would like Frank Counihan. He looked at the hunter: it was five o'clock. His Dad normally came in about this time. He must see his mother before he went back; the neighbours and priest had probably gone and she was alone.

'I'll have one for the road,' he said to Frank Counihan. 'I'd better see my mother.'

'Yeah,' Counihan said. 'You'd better do that, you've only got one. I'll see you back here.'

Sawtell had two more Black Labels, left the bar and went down Rotherwood Street. It was getting dark and the crickets sang in the small dusty gardens.

His mother was sitting in the front room by the piano. The afternoon tea dishes had been cleared away and the room was as it always had been; it seemed nothing had happened. Sawtell sat down on the sofa and looked at his mother. She was pale and calm.

'Did you thank Mr Hanrahan?'

'Yes.'

'There were more at the church than I thought.'

'He was a popular man.'

'He was. I didn't know how popular.'

She barely knew him, Sawtell thought, after forty-five years of marriage and domestic routine, after the loss of a child and the War. Had it been a waste? He didn't know.

'Mr Counihan's a friend?' she said.

'I've not known him long.'

'You're like your father, you go for Catholics.'

'It's coincidence.' He thought of Frank Counihan

321

stretched out on the bed with the German submachine gun; he was the best man in the outfit by far, strong and capable, a natural in the bush. Sometimes, Counihan unnerved him: he was tireless, an expert shot and horse rider, but there was a chip on his shoulder; something had happened to him, and he knew he would never find out.

'No word from Marcia?' his mother said.

'No.'

'That's a shame.'

'She had the right, I've learnt that.'

'You think people should leave each other?'

'I think so, if they're unhappy.'

'I think not. Marriage is a sacrament.'

A sacrament? He'd forgotten what that was. He got up and walked around the room, looking at the family photographs.

'What are you going to do?'

'What can I do? Stay here and pray we win the war.'

'We will,' Sawtell said, 'we always do. It's the biggest Empire in the world, it won't go down.'

'Will the Japanese come?'

'They can't, there's Singapore and the British Navy.' But he knew he was taking the training in the bush seriously.

'Would you like a cup of tea?'

'No, thanks, I'd better collect Frank Counihan and get back to camp.'

'I suppose you should.'

His mother got up and they walked down the hall to the front door. Sawtell opened it and looked out at the night.

'How will you manage the garden?'

'A boy will come and cut the lawns and I can do the rest.' She smiled. 'It was never Angus's strong point.'

They kissed each other and Sawtell said: 'You take care of yourself, Mother.'

'I shall, you know you're always welcome here. I hope Marcia comes back, there's always time.'

Sawtell wondered if he wanted that now, but said: 'If she does, I'll be the first to let you know.' He put on his slouch hat and went down the steps.

'I'll be down in a fortnight.'

'I'll make a fruitcake and we can sit in the garden.' She watched her son go down the path and closed the front door.

Sawtell and Counihan stood, drinking beer in the main bar of Young & Jackson's. The pub was crowded with soldiers on leave and civilians, and the races droned on the radio.

Sawtell took up his fresh glass, read the afternoon paper and said:

'The sinking of the *Sydney* is bad, it looks like 645 have gone down.' He looked down the casualty list edged in black, but didn't know anyone in the Navy.

'Yeah,' Counihan said. 'Poor buggers.' He looked around the bar at the young men, drinking and talking. 'They should conscript those young bastards. How was your Mum?'

'Not bad, coping well, she's stronger than I thought.'

'Never underestimate anybody, I don't.'

'What do you want to do this afternoon?' Sawtell said.

'I don't know, we could stay here and get pissed.' Counihan wondered why Sawtell didn't go and see his wife. 'It's a pity the football season's over.'

'Yeah. It says here the Japanese warships are moving south.'

'The bastards. We could go to the pictures.'

'It's too nice a day.'

'We'll stay here then. What's happening in Russia?'

'Nothing fresh.' Sawtell turned the pages; there were still the Social Notes. 'The Huns are still outside Moscow and Leningrad. They'll never beat the Ruskies, they can go back and back.'

'That's what my father used to say.'

'He was right. A pity I never met him.'

'Yeah, you'd have liked him.' Sawtell took out the hunter. His father would have been at the Mountain View now, arguing the toss with Jack Hanrahan and Dan Costello. He thought of his mother in the silent house in Rotherwood Street, the garden and the felled pines, bike riding and the Chinese market gardens. Something was happening to Australia and even the Empire. Counihan cleared his throat and rolled another cigarette; the young civilian men banged their coins down on the counter and the barman turned up the radio for the third race at Flemington. If something bad happened, Sawtell thought, all this could go. If there was an air-raid or an attack, what would these people do? They had three more beers and Sawtell said:

'What about some food?'

'Yeah, I could do with some steak and eggs.'

'Okay, let's get out, we can come back and wait for the train.' They left the bar of Young & Jackson's and went out into Spencer Street.

The trams were lined up, the crowds milled outside the railway station and the paperboys shouted. There were no young girls throwing roses, the clouds were flying high and there was a weather change coming. Pigeons were perched on the towers of the ornate, Victorian buildings and the smoke drifted from the tall factory chimneys. Sawtell and Counihan looked at the news boards. *Royal Navy On Way To Singapore.*

'The Brits have arrived,' Counihan said.

'It's about time.'

As they strolled up Swanston Street, Sawtell looked over at the Town Hall where the birds sat on the parapets and the flags flew. A Salvation Army band was playing on the corner, and he remembered the ceremonial march to the troopship in 1915 and the dedication of the Shrine; it seemed there wasn't quite the same enthusiasm this time. He wondered what the Japs would do: it looked like there was no way they could be kept out of the show now. The war was nearer home. They turned into Collins Street, stopped at a cinema and looked at the stills of *Goodbye Mr Chips* with Robert Donat.

'It doesn't look like my cup of tea,' Counihan said. Sawtell remembered Marcia's father, his cluttered house full of books, his strange school he'd been to once with her, and looked at Collins Street. Horses and wagons clattered by, and there were walls of sandbags outside the public buildings, the shops and the emporiums. There was the smell of charcoal on the air from the car gas-producers and the windows were taped against blast. Outside the underground public lavatories, there was a sign: *Emergency Air Raid Shelter*.

'There's a grill room around in Elizabeth Street,' Sawtell said and they walked into the fashionable Block Arcade, where the shopping was expensive and the merchandise rare. Then he saw Marcia, standing by herself, looking into a grocery-shop window: there were the salted herring in baskets and the exotic teas from India and Ceylon. Her hair was still pinned up and she was wearing a white cotton frock and cardigan, her shoulders were square and she was reaching into her shopping bag. Sawtell wished Frank Counihan was not with him. They were still married and he had done nothing about getting a divorce: he didn't know how to. It would have been public and killed his mother. Divorce was for film stars, not ordinary people. Anyway he still loved her. He went up behind her and said:

'Hullo, Marcia.'

She turned and looked at Geoffrey in uniform and the soldier beside him.

'Frank,' Sawtell said, 'this is my wife, Marcia. Marcia, this is Frank Counihan.'

'Pleased to meet you.' Counihan took her outstretched hand.

'How are you?' Sawtell said.

'All right, I've been away and just come back.' She stood in the doorway of the shop and looked at Geoffrey as the people strolled up the arcade, their footsteps echoing on the marble. Counihan knew something was up and said:

'Look, I've just remembered I've got to see a bloke. I'll see you at the train, Geoff. Nice to have met you, Mrs Sawtell.' They watched him go down the arcade and out into Collins Street. Marcia pushed at her glasses; Geoffrey hadn't changed.

'Do you want some coffee? There's a place here somewhere.'

'I know, we've been there. I know where it is.'

They walked together with the shoppers, neither touching the other.

'You're back in uniform,' she said.

'Yes, as you once said, it's what I do best. Where have you been?'

'In Sydney for six months.'

'With another friend?'

'Friends, women.'

'I've never been there, what's it like?'

'It's not like Melbourne, there's the bridge and the harbour.'

'More exciting, more ideas, more to talk about?'

'Not necessarily.'

'Melbourne does me.'

Marcia did not reply. They found the café, went inside and found a table by the window. Sawtell took his hat off and she noticed his fair hair streaked with grey.

'What part of the Army are you in?' Marcia said.

'Part of the Army?'

'Unit.'

'I'm in an outfit called the Volunteer Defence Corps,

326

an anti-invasion force full of cripples and old soldiers. It seems that I live with men and you live with women these days.'

'It seems like it.'

'How's your lover, the man with the ideas?'

'I haven't seen him for some time.'

'Didn't work out eh?' Marcia didn't reply, and Sawtell said:

'My father's dead.'

Marcia's face went like stone and she took him by the arm.

'My God, when?'

'Two weeks ago.' The waitress came up and Sawtell said, 'What do you want, tea or coffee?'

'Coffee.'

'Anything to eat?'

'No.'

He ordered and lit a cigarette.

'Geoffrey, I'm terribly sorry, I loved him.'

'Just like you loved me.'

'Yes. How's your mother?'

'Bearing up.'

'And the funeral?'

'No hitches, there were lots of people, including Jack Hanrahan.'

'He went?'

'Yes, he's now going to hell because of an old mate. That's friendship for you.'

'Geoffrey, I wish I'd been there.'

'Yeah, you were missed, several people asked after you, even my mother.' Their coffee came and they drank it. 'Why did you leave me?' Sawtell said. 'Why couldn't we have had kids and been like everybody else?'

'It wasn't in me, I tried, I don't want to be like everybody else.'

'Well, I do. In my book, there's nothing wrong with that.'

Marcia finished her coffee, took one of his cigarettes and lit it. 'In *my* book there is.'

'Why?'

'Because I want to be myself, and I can't be that with you.'

'What are you doing?'

'Reading and writing.'

'Writing what?'

'Poetry and fiction.'

'Jesus Christ, poetry, fiction and pamphlets, you should be in the bloody army, there's a war on. Writing won't win the war, guns and men will.'

'Look, Geoffrey,' she said, 'you were in the Great War.'

'Yes.'

'Have you ever read a book about it, a novel, a poem, somebody's diary?'

'No.'

'Have you ever read a novel called *All Quiet on the Western Front*?'

'No.'

'You should have, you would know more about yourself.'

'I don't want to know more about myself, I know what I'm doing.'

'You're fighting?'

'Preparing to.'

'And you're not prepared to think what it does to you?'

'What?'

'War.'

'I know there's a job to do. I've never forgiven you for buggering about at the Shrine.'

'Buggering about?'

'Handing out those pamphlets.'

'Those pamphlets were against war and killing.'

'You and your lot disturbed the ceremony, you had no place there, it was our show.'

'Whose show?'

'The soldiers, the men who'd come back and those who'd fallen.'

'What about the nurses?'

'They helped, good on them, but they didn't fight, they weren't there.'

'Where?'

'At the front where the lads were.'

'I've asked you to tell me about it, but you never have.'

'No, it was our show.'

'It's like Freemasonry.'

'What?'

'Freemasonry.'

'I hadn't thought of that. I suppose it is. Do you want any more coffee?'

'No.'

'I was going to tell you once, but you weren't there.'

'When?'

'By the stream, when I had the Indian Scout.'

She remembered the stream and Geoffrey crouching by the dark water, the boulders in the paddocks and the muddy, rutted road.

'When I went to tell you, you'd gone away, a chance missed, you might say.'

'We were married thirteen years,' Marcia said, 'there must have been plenty of other times.'

'No, there weren't.'

'There must have been, there were beaches and streams and walks in the country, there was us in bed.'

'No, there weren't, that was the only time.' Sawtell looked at his wife. 'The War's buggered me up.'

Marcia didn't know what to say and took his hand. The shoppers moved outside the café window and the waitress came with the bill. She couldn't understand the affairs of men: she wasn't allowed to. She watched him as he took out his father's watch and fiddled with the brass badge on his slouch hat. There were people waiting at the door for their table.

'I've got to go,' Sawtell said. 'The train leaves at five and Frank Counihan will be waiting.'

'He's your friend?' Marcia said.

'Yeah, he's a good mate, a good soldier.'

'What's going to happen?'

'To what?'

'To Australia.'

'It's uncertain, that's why we're training. Look, I'd better be off. Write me a letter at the VDC Lancefield.'

She watched him as he got up in his uniform and put half-a-crown on the table. He kissed her on the neck and said:

'I never was a reader and a writer, doing things is all I know. I still love you, but God knows why. If something happens, go to the West. Okay?'

He moved out, and the chair tumbled; Marcia saw him through the café window, in his uniform, striding through the civilians and he disappeared. Marcia sat at the café table. *He's a good mate, a good soldier.*

On the way to Spencer Street Station, Sawtell stopped at Young & Jackson's bottle shop and bought a bottle of Johnnie Walker. He drank it back at the camp with Frank Counihan. They both got drunk, but Sawtell didn't talk about Marcia and Frank didn't ask and they talked about the great days of football and cricket. The following Monday morning, they learnt that the Japanese had attacked Pearl Harbor, that Japanese naval units were headed for Thailand and the Gulf of Siam. The Japanese struck at the Americans in Guam and the Philippines, and at British bases in Malaya, Hong Kong, North Borneo, Nauru and Ocean Island. The Empire they had all believed in was going.

That night, Sawtell lay in bed and thought about

Marcia, the War and being a soldier again. She was right: he should know more about himself.

On 19 December 1941, Japanese troops entered the British colony of Hong Kong and shortly after, the invasion of Burma and Thailand began. The tough, little Asiatic men could not be stopped and on 15 February 1942, to everyone's horror, General Percival surrendered the impregnable British base at Singapore where thousands of newly arrived Australian troops were taken into captivity. By early March 1942, Batavia, capital of the Dutch East Indies was overrun and the invasion of New Guinea began. In May, the American naval forces attempted to halt the Japanese drive south at the Battle of the Coral Sea; but after a three-day engagement, in which they lost four capital ships and dozens of smaller craft, they were forced to retire.

The invasion of Australia began on 12 June 1942, with Japanese landings at Darwin, Cooktown and Cairns. The major assault was on the New South Wales coast at the industrial town of Newcastle with other landings at Tweed Heads, Coff's Harbour and the Hawkesbury River. Sydney came under naval bombardment and was dive-bombed by carrier-attack bombers from the aircraft carrier *Zuikaku*. The evacuation of Sydney was total, unorganized and chaotic and, in early July, the remnants of the US 41st Division and Commander-in-Chief, General Douglas MacArthur sailed from Port Melbourne for New Zealand. The Federal government fled from Canberra to Perth and by the end of that year, Colonel Jack Madigan and his untrained Volunteer Defence Corps did their best to implement his policy of Scorched Earth. Marcia Sawtell was one of tens of thousands of people who trekked to the West. The events of the outside world had come to Australia.

· XV ·
To Tibooburra

A STEAM ENGINE was standing on the Silverton railway with several rusty wagons and a battered guard's van. Sergius Donaldson inspected the brass plate on the locomotive: *Beyer & Peacock, Manchester, 1882.* British machinery travelled far. A canvas hose hung from the water tank and O'Donohue turned the cock, but the tank was empty. A piece of paper was blowing along the rail-tracks and St John Jackson picked it up. It was torn and badly printed and he read:

PARDON CERTIFICATE
Do not die for nothing. Your wives and children
have nothing to fear . . .

Counihan read over the Major's shoulder. 'Jesus,' he said, 'the bastards have been through.'

They all stood uncertainly on the gravel by the locomotive and the empty dump trucks and looked down the line towards the ghostly buildings of Silverton. No smoke drifted in the sky and nothing moved. Not even a bird flew and there were no cattle or sheep browsing here. Sergius Donaldson thought he saw a building with a cross on its roof, started to walk toward it, then turned back. St John Jackson took up his Purdey shotgun and considered scouting the wrecked battery and crushing plant in the gum trees, but decided not. Sawtell took the Lee Enfield from the scabbard and stood in the middle of the narrow dirt road to Broken Hill and waited, but there was no sound. It was like being on the road to Bourke. Then an emu bounded across the tracks, they all turned and watched the ungainly bird disappear. Counihan cursed and walked fifty yards up the track, he put his ear to the rails and listened, then went on to the road and looked towards Broken Hill. All was still, but now an eagle flew. He checked his pocket watch: it was a quarter to seven and he could feel the coming heat of the day on his back. To the north, lay the low range of dark hills; they would have to get there as soon as possible. He walked back and squatted down on the earth next to Sawtell and St John Jackson. The horses snorted and whinnied; the ground was open and exposed and Counihan thought there was no way they couldn't be seen. He waited for the rattle of rifle fire and machine guns. The morning sun beat down on the rocks, discarded rolling stock and abandoned mining machinery. A wild cat ran from the scrub. Counihan turned, cocked and raised the Luger. Where were the little yellow bastards? He thought of last night's killings. The buggers could be anywhere. He sweated and said:

'This place scares the shit out of me.'

The Major was surprised and looked at Frank Counihan.

'Me too,' Sawtell said, 'it's open ground and they can get us anywhere, but we've got to get into town and get what we can. We need feed, water and shoes and nails for the horses, and whatever else we can get. We've got a long ride ahead.'

'Will anybody be there?' Sergius Donaldson said.

'Christ knows, it's doubtful, the mine closed years ago. There could be an old-timer or two hanging around, there are some men who hate to leave a mine.' He thought of the Pardon Certificate. From what direction might the enemy come?

'We'd better go in, Major, and then get out as fast as we can.'

'In that case, Mr Sawtell, we should post a man on the road with a horse and a Bren.'

'Who?'

'O'Donohue, I think. He should be able to do it, he's been instructed.'

'And if they come, we lose him?'

'If the enemy come, we need covering fire.'

'He's only eighteen, Major.'

'Your age at Passchendaele, Mr Sawtell. He has the fastest horse and he's the best rider.'

'I'll do it,' Frank Counihan said to the Major. 'Riding out is my speciality.' You old bastard. He looked at O'Donohue working at his broken packsaddle.

'Right, Frank,' Sawtell said as he looked at his watch, 'give us an hour and we'll meet at the Court House. We'll go out on the Umberumberka road to Yanco Glen, it's the last pub before Tibooburra.'

Counihan got the Bren and tripod from his packhorse, swung up on his horse, saluted and said:

'I'll see you.'

He rode down the road to Broken Hill. He watched for the Japs, but all he saw was a lone dingo running.

'Okay,' Sawtell said to the Major and the Padre, 'we've got one hour. We want fodder, water, shoes, tinned food and boots if we can find them. There's got to be a general store, even in Silverton.'

'Boots?' Sergius Donaldson said.

'Boots, Padre. Where we're going, a pair won't last a month.'

'And if there are none?'

'We'll solve that problem when we come to it. Let's get in.' They mounted and Sawtell rode alongside O'Donohue on his big, black horse. It would be a pity to lose him. When the war was over, Australia would need boys like that.

334

Three churches stood upon the hill: the Roman Catholic, the Anglican and the Methodist; and below them, the Masonic Temple. All the places of worship were boarded up; a soft, southerly breeze blew and the broken glass, the smashed beer bottles and the quartz gleamed in the morning sun. As they rode in, guns cocked and raised, they were met by the remains of neat, laid-out streets and small city buildings made of stone. This was once a thriving silver town, planned and built by stalwart Cornish men, but the mine had been worked out and the desert had beaten them. In the main street, there were abandoned Ford trucks, drays, wagonettes, sulkies and farm machinery. The settlers had brought ploughs, harrows and seed sowers, but the land had yielded nothing and the rains were uncertain. The soil was unprofitable, and only kangaroos, emu and bush rats survived. They dismounted outside the Court House and walked over to the general store over the road, its windows blank with corrugated iron. It was now a fine, sunny day and nothing moved, not even a cat or a dog, and the parakeets swooped and flew from the gum trees down at the creek by the abandoned crushing plant. Sawtell got out a Thompson submachine gun and gave O'Donohue the crowbar.

'Kevin, you and the Major and the Padre do the general store, and I'll do the pub.'

'Right you are,' Sergius Donaldson said and went over to the verandah with his loaded shotgun. Sawtell helped them lever the front door open, and then walked through the dust to the Silverton Hotel. He mounted the wooden porch and the timbers creaked beneath his boots. The ornate leadlight windows had long been smashed and Sawtell knew the front bar would yield nothing; it was better to try the cellar in the kitchen at the back. He thought of the rum they had found at Wilcannia; even that would be welcome now. Then he remembered the young blackfellow Counihan had dumped on the war memorial. The back of the

335

pub was a ruin of tin sheds and stockyards; then he saw a horse standing at a trough and tank by the back fence. The horse puzzled him, it was quiet and well broken. He stood by the trough with the Thompson. Whose horse was it? Was somebody here, and watching them? The animal looked in reasonable condition; it was a brown gelding and only God knew how it came to be there. He was not surprised: they should be thankful for small mercies. They would take the horse and there was water. He went over to the trough: the water was fresh and the ball-cock and float were working. He tasted the water: it was hard and cloudy, from a bore, but would more than do. The ruined town was silent like the grave and he returned to the back of the hotel and fossicked around in the outbuildings. There was nothing they could use and he opened the door of the kitchen. It was hopeless: the cellar was empty and the cupboards bare. He looked at his watch: it was almost half past seven. There was half an hour to go. He went outside and stood in the shade of an old peppermint tree; he wondered about going up to the Catholic Church. Communion wine perhaps? He laughed: there had been no Mass for years. The pigeons warbled in the roof of the hotel; and the small, stone villas stood, gutted and vacant, on the street. There were no old-timers. He picked the stem of a wild hollyhock and thought of his mother. Men had tried here and had turned their backs on the desert and the black hills of the flint and country stone. This place had once been like a part of Richmond: there had been church services, smart ponies and traps, pretty Victorian women and handsome young, bowler-hatted miners watching them promenade on Sunday afternoons. Jesus, Sawtell thought, these people had worked; this was the strangest town he'd been in: all the planning and efforts of the city fathers, the men and women, had come to nothing. He lit a cigarette and started back to the general store. It was hot now and he hoped Frank Counihan was okay. As he walked, all he heard was the sound of the soft wind in the trees and the pigeons cooing in the carved, wooden eaves of the buildings. No children laughed and shouted in the barren school yard.

Kevin O'Donohue was carrying out a bag of oats.

'What did you find?' he said to Sawtell.

'No booze, but there's a good horse in the yard at the back of the pub. Do you want to go and get it? I'll help the Major and the Padre. What's in there?'

'Not much. Oats, a few shoes, a bag of flour.'

'Weevils?'

'Probably, it's all shitty stuff.'

Jesus, Sawtell thought, they would have to live off the land with a vengeance. There might be something at Yanco Glen; one step after another.

'Okay, get a halter on that horse, take ours up for a drink and fill the water bags. We've got twenty minutes.'

Sawtell looked up the main street beyond the Court House and the Shire Office. There was no movement. O'Donohue took the horses over to the hotel and Sawtell went inside the general store. The air in the building was rank and dusty.

'The pickings are slim, Mr Sawtell,' Sergius Donaldson said. The clergyman stood in the rubbish and the gloom. 'I fear the rats and the vandals have got it all.'

'Where's the Major?'

'Outside.'

'No boots?'

'None.'

'I've found a horse and a trough where there's fresh water, O'Donohue's up there now. Let's get out.' Then Sawtell saw the rats running over the fouled and verminous merchandise. Their fur shone and their eyes were bright.

'Let's get out.'

St John Jackson appeared, empty-handed, and said:

'Our black friends have been here.'

337

'How do you know?'

'Empty wine flagons.'

'All I've got is a horse, no liquor.' Sawtell looked at the Padre. 'It seems that God is not shining His light upon us.' They left the store for O'Donohue, the horses and the trough.

They had almost finished watering the horses and filling the bags when they heard the sound of hoof beats on the street. St John Jackson pulled out his Webley and the Padre raised his shotgun. The dust flew: it was Counihan on his big, grey station horse. He pulled up, dismounted and said:

'There are motors on the road. In this air, you can hear the bloody things for miles.'

'You're sure?' St John Jackson said.

'Too right I'm sure, there was dust and the sound of motors. The bastards are on their way.'

They listened and heard the sound. Was it thunder? They couldn't tell.

'Okay,' Sawtell said, 'we're off.'

They mounted and rode quickly down on to the Umber-umberka road, then turned north into the flat hills. The flies were bad, and they rode three hours without stopping. Now and then, they looked back toward Silverton. The thunder rumbled across the country, but they couldn't tell one sound from another.

At eleven, they were still in the foothills of the Barrier Range, and the going was harder than expected; they stopped, dismounted and sat on the ground. The trees were small and there was little cover from the sun. There was no wildlife and the ants ran.

'We'll stop for an hour,' Sawtell said. 'Let's unload the packhorses.'

'Is that wise, Mr Sawtell?'

'Yes, Major, it's wise, unless we want to bugger the

338

horses. The Padre's packhorse has cast a shoe, O'Donohue's has got a sore back and his packframe's falling to
pieces. We'll have to re-distribute the loads.'

'Where is the next water?'

'I'm not sure. Yanco Glen.'

'You're not sure?'

'Let's unload the horses, we've got an hour to rest.'
Sawtell got up, went to his packhorse and St John Jackson
followed him.

'You're not sure? I thought you knew this country.' The
others watched and listened.

Sawtell started to unload his horse, it seemed, for the
500th time. He put down the Lewis, the Brens and the
ammunition cases. His back ached, he faced St John
Jackson and said:

'I've not been north of Broken Hill.'

'We're going solely by the ordnance maps then?'

'We are. I take it you can read maps and navigate?'

'Of course I can.'

'Well, it's easy, we ride parallel with the road.'

'I'm not concerned with the damned road, any fool
could follow that. I'm concerned about water.'

'We all are. Look, Major, if I were you, I'd unload your
horse. Compared to where we're going, this country's a
Sunday stroll in Hyde Park. We can ride to Yanco Glen,
there'll be water and maybe a drink.'

'I doubt it.'

'It's possible. I know this country, we look out for tanks
and windmills. Unload your bloody horse, it's easy days
yet.'

'How can you know this country? You haven't been
here.'

'It's Australia,' Sawtell said. 'I know which way the birds
fly and the rivers run.'

'There are no rivers.'

'A figure of speech. You leave it to me, Major.' He took

339

the packframe off his horse. 'Kevin, can you start a fire? We'll have a cup of tea.'

Sawtell watched St John Jackson go to his horse. The Englishman hadn't shaved for a week now, and his beard was grey. We are being levelled, he thought. He took down the water bag and filled his pannikin for the tea.

They sat by the fire, the billy boiled and they drank their tea and ate the bully beef. Sergius Donaldson thought about St John Jackson and Sawtell. This was the second clash: first, the horse and now, this. Francis had placed Sawtell in command, and in command he was. He was surprised that Sawtell didn't know the country north of Broken Hill, but he couldn't recall his saying he did. In any case, who better to lead them? As Sawtell said, it was his country. He hoped the division between them and the Australians wouldn't deepen. If it did, what would he and Francis do? They couldn't go south and they couldn't survive in the north on their own. If it happened again, he would have to try to mediate. The Padre poured himself a second mug of tea. Then there was the sound of an aircraft; it was flying low and quickly appeared over the ridge. They were caught in the open and there was nothing they could do. They waited for the sound of machine-gun fire, but there was none. It was a light reconnaissance plane and they saw the orange insignia on its wings. Counihan thought about setting up the Bren, but there was no time. They watched the plane make two passes and then disappear to the south.

'So much for our cup of tea,' St John Jackson said.

'Thank Christ it wasn't a Zero,' Counihan said. 'They could've spotted us anywhere, we had to give the horses a spell.' My God, Sawtell thought, what to do now? It would take the spotter plane about half an hour to return to Broken Hill; they had about forty-five minutes before the Zero arrived. Would one come out? It was probable. There was no point in going on; they would have to find cover.

'I don't see any point in going on,' he said. 'They'll gun us down, we won't stand a chance on the move.' He turned to O'Donohue. 'If you have a go at finding somewhere, we'll pack.'

'Okay.' The boy hung his mug on the hook of his packframe and mounted his horse.

'And be quick, we've got about half an hour, just find the best place you can.'

They watched O'Donohue pick his way up the rocky slope and started to pack. As he worked, St John Jackson thought about Sawtell: the mine had been a success, but now they were paying the consequences. Maybe he should have stayed at Bourke, but he knew, of course, that he should be in Singapore with his men in Changi. There had been rumours that some of the prisoners had been taken to Burma to work on the railway. He wished he were with them: at least he would have the company of his fellow officers in a country he knew well.

When they had packed and smothered the fire, they waited in the heat for O'Donohue to return. They looked at the sky and listened as the flies clung to their faces and bodies. My God, Sergius Donaldson thought, this was inhospitable country.

Counihan was sitting on a rock. Nothing seemed to affect that man: he was like one of those trees that grew in the desert. Sawtell came striding up the slope, where he stopped, looked and waited for O'Donohue. The horses snorted and sweated in the heat. They listened for any sound and stood by their mounts, and at last the lad appeared and talked to Sawtell.

'I've found something.'

'What?'

'An old shed about fifteen minutes from here.'

'Right.' Sawtell ran down the slope. 'Lead the way.'

They mounted and followed O'Donohue over the broken, flinty ground. The quartz glistened in the sun and

341

the snakes lay curled in the rocks. Counihan looked up: a flock of parakeets was flying north-east. There must be water at Yanco Glen.

The shed was built of slab timber and stood in a gully; some she-oaks grew nearby and a line of small gum trees stood a short distance away by a dry creek.

'Good on you, Kevin,' Counihan said. 'Let's get the nags down to the trees, we can rig up a picket line there.'

The cover for the horses was sparse, but better than nothing. They split up, Counihan and O'Donohue going to the creek and the others to the shed. They sweated and waited for two hours, but no sound came. Then Sawtell stood at the door and said:

'In some ways I wish the plane had come, at least we'd have known where we were. The trip to Sturt's Meadows is going to require nerves of steel.'

St John Jackson went outside, gazed at the sky and kicked at the broken timber.

'It's Yanco Glen, then. How long will it take?'

'We've lost two hours already and O'Donohue had better shoe that horse. I'd say sometime late tonight.'

The Major said no more, and the three of them went down to the picket line. There were dark clouds away to the west, but Sawtell knew it wouldn't rain.

They got to Yanco Glen at half past eleven that night. When they had unpacked, Sawtell and Counihan walked up and down the stones, looking for water in the creek. The billabongs were dry. In the moonlight, Sawtell noted the big ghost gums: the creek must usually flow to support trees of that size. The dry season had started early this year.

'It's a bit dry,' Counihan said.

'Yeah, but we're okay for the moment. Was the windmill going?'

'I don't think so.'

'We'll look at it in the morning. Do you want second watch?'

'Okay, we'll let the Brits sleep.' He poked around in the creek. 'You got us here.'

Sawtell laughed and smoked his cigarette.

'As the Major says, any fool can follow the road.'

They sat down in the creek bed. The stars and moon shone.

'What are we going to do with them?' Counihan said.

'Who?'

'The Brits.'

'They can't survive without us, we'll have to educate them.'

'Educate?'

'Teach them our ways. No more bloody arguments.'

'You can say that again.'

'Let's doss down, I'm buggered.'

During his watch, Kevin O'Donohue borrowed Sawtell's shotgun and walked half a mile down the road by the light of the moon. As usual, the night was clear and cold. He stopped at the top of a rise on the highway and looked down at the broken country; it had changed a lot since Silverton. It was saw-toothed and shadowy in the moonlight. Then he thought he caught the gleam of a campfire away to the south-east, but he couldn't be sure. He looked, but couldn't be sure.

In the morning, St John Jackson, on the last watch, saw the Yanco Glen pub through the trees. He looked at the men sleeping under their blankets, threw some leaves and twigs on the fire and poured some water into the billy for the tea. He thought that Sergius was taking all this very well: the trip, the hard ride and the company, if you could call it that. Where would they end up? They could ride and scratch around in this damned country for ever. Sergius had his faith to sustain him; he wished he was as strong. One day at a time, Sergius had said. St John Jackson picked

343

up his shotgun, rubbed his chin and walked over to the
pub. When he went around the back, he found the building
had been half burnt down. It was unlikely the Japanese had
been here, so it must have been some local people or
blackfellows. Why did they destroy everything? Then he
remembered Madigan's orders. There was a windmill, a
tank and trough; but the trough was dry and the blades
were stationary. He heard someone coming up behind him
and turned with his shotgun. It was O'Donohue.

'There's no water, O'Donohue.'

'Doesn't look like it.' The boy picked his nose and
looked at the pump. 'The pump's okay, I could go up the
tower and have a look.'

'Would it be worthwhile?'

'Nah, probably not, when those things are buggered,
they're buggered.' They turned and walked back to the
camp through the broken branches. 'I thought I saw a fire
last night.'

The Major stopped. Could it be the same people? They
would have to find out. Would anyone follow them all this
way? It was inconceivable.

'Where did you see it?'

'I said, I thought. Away to the south-east, probably
Abos.'

'But we never see them.'

'Aw, they skulk around. Tricky bastards. You never
know where they are.'

The Major thought: Why was this place so lonely? Why
was nobody to be seen?

They sat around the fire, drank their tea and ate their
bully beef. St John Jackson scratched at the stubble on his
chin; they were starting to look a wretched lot. Most
unmilitary. Their uniforms were filthy and he noticed that
the tops of his boots were cracking. Counihan watched
him and said:

'Your boots are going, Major. Here, catch this.' He

tossed over the fat-tin and it landed at St John Jackson's feet.

'You've got to keep your boots oiled.' He yawned, got up and pissed in the scrub.

'There's no water here, Mr Sawtell,' Sergius Donaldson said.

'No, Padre.' Sawtell looked at the map. He hoped it was accurate, but doubted it. 'The next place is Smith's Well Creek. We should make it by late morning.'

'And if there is none?' St John Jackson said.

Sawtell rose and hung up his pannikin. 'Jesus Christ, Major, sometimes I think my faith's stronger than yours.'

He got out the bucket and waterbags and went to give his horses a drink. St John Jackson oiled his boots with the animal fat and said to the Padre:

'O'Donohue saw a fire again last night.'

'Did he?'

'He said, he thought he did. If it's there the next couple of nights, we should investigate.'

'I don't see how we can, they'd hear us coming for miles.'

'So we allow ourselves to be followed?'

'If we are being followed.'

They left the fire and walked to the picket line.

'How do you feel, Sergius?'

'Feel? Reasonably chipper.'

'We all have cold sores, have you noticed that?'

'Indeed, it's our diet. I would love a roast with a plate of vegetables and Yorkshire pudding.'

'Ah, those were the days. And a shave and a bath.'

'Not to mention a whisky.'

They packed, saddled up and left for Smith's Well Creek at half past six. Sawtell took them north-east into the ranges: the cover was better and there was more feed for the horses. There was enough water in the billabongs at Smith's Well Creek for them to fill the waterbags and clean

345

themselves up. The water was cloudy and low and they stood naked up to their haunches, their filthy underwear hanging on the branches of the box gums. They passed the tin buckets around and poured the water over their heads and shoulders while the horses drank and browsed on the salt bush. Refreshed, they continued to the north-east into the hills.

Late that afternoon they came to a small hidden valley, an escarpment of red rock where veins of marble shone. They stopped: this was an unexpected, restful place. Several grey kangaroos, the females with young in their pouches, bounded through the small, green parklands, and parakeets swarmed in the branches of the big, white river gums. The river stones were smooth and polished, and as they proceeded, they came upon deep pools where fresh water ran. On the walls of the escarpment, there were paintings of hands, and on the flat rocks there were carved drawings of animals and birds. They unpacked, watered the horses and strung up the picket line. There was an abundance of good, hard timber lying around and they stood in the shade of the trees. Green grass and wild flowers were growing by the creek. It was the nearest thing Sergius Donaldson had seen to a meadow in Australia.

'This is a break,' Frank Counihan said. 'I reckon the Abos used to live here.' He picked up his rifle. 'I'll get us a roo before dark.'

Sawtell walked up the creek where it wound between the red walls of the escarpment; there would be fish in the shady pools. He would get out his hooks and hand-lines and have a go. He dug at the rotten logs with his sheath knife and saw the familiar grubs. As he came back, he collected timber for the fire, they would have a big one as the night would be cold. Sergius Donaldson was gazing at the hand-paintings and the decorated rocks.

'The natives could draw and paint, Mr Sawtell.'

'Apparently, it looks like an old camp. There's good

346

cover, we might stay here tomorrow and jerk some meat. If we're lucky, we might catch a fish or two and vary the diet.'

Frank Counihan came up on his horse.

'Fresh tucker tonight, I'll get one of those big grey buggers and we can jerk the meat tomorrow.'

O'Donohue rode up and joined them.

'Not a bad spot eh? Maybe we're in luck.'

'Yeah,' Sawtell said. 'It makes a change.' He gave O'Donohue the Lee Enfield. 'See what you can get, the time's right.'

The two men grinned and saluted and rode off down the creek.

'A remarkable change, Mr Sawtell.' St John Jackson sat by the fire and considered the small valley. Hundreds of parakeets perched in the trees.

'It's remarkable country.' They heard rifle shots echoing in the rocks. 'They've got something.' Sawtell looked at the light of the sun on the red cliffs. 'This is not a place I'd like to be trapped in.'

'It's of some significance, I think,' Sergius Donaldson said. 'If you'll excuse me, I want to look at those engravings.' This was the first sign of an ancient civilization the Padre had seen.

'Watch out for the shooting,' Sawtell said, and they watched the Padre pick his way through the flat rocks. He went to his saddlebag and got out the maps. He looked at the Major.

'I'm not sure where we are, but we seem to be safe.'

'So it seems.'

'We could spend tomorrow here, resting up. Counihan can jerk some meat and we can repair O'Donohue's packframe.' Sawtell smiled. 'I might stay in bed tomorrow, just like the good old days.'

'Who's behind us?'

'God knows, if there's anybody, blackfellows, another outfit.'

347

'We could go back and see.'

'We'd have to circle them miles to the south in the dark, we'd wear ourselves out.'

'I suppose you're right.'

Sawtell lay back on his greatcoat and saw the evening star rising.

'You placed me in command of this expedition, Major.'

'I did, but I do have the right to question your decisions.'

'You do, any of you does, but in the end it's up to me.'

The Major did not reply and pulled on his cardigan. Then he said:

'I could do with a whisky, Mr Sawtell.'

'And so could I, we'll have to keep looking.' He studied the map. 'There's a station called Acacia Downs half a day's ride away to the north. We'll call in there. Something might turn up.'

'Like Mr Micawber.'

Sawtell lay on his greatcoat and thought of his school-days. It was odd: he and the Major must have read many of the same books. What story was Mr Micawber in? His father could have told him. What was Marcia doing? And what had happened in the cities? The Japs were a cruel mob, but he was sure Australians could take it. This couldn't last for ever, it was just a matter of time and patience. They would win, they had before. He hoped they hadn't caved in; those men at the Mountain View would show the Japanese a thing or two. The evening star was high now and the sun was going down behind the trees on the ridge. He saw the Padre coming back and thought of his father's funeral and St Stephen's Church. The Padre was a tough old bugger and Sawtell was glad they had asked him along.

'What did you see, Padre?'

'Quite amazing, primitive art. You should look.'

'I'll see it in the morning.'

348

Counihan and O'Donohue rode up, each with a young kangaroo over his horse. The boy was grinning.

'We got two, fresh steak for tea.'

'Right, I'll light the fire.'

'I'll do the slaughtering now,' Counihan said, 'while there's some light.'

'Would you save some liver for me?' Sergius Donaldson said.

'Liver?' Counihan looked at the Padre. 'Okay.'

O'Donohue and Counihan moved off into the trees, and the three older men sat and watched the fire as it crackled and burned in the dry timber. The smoke drifted and the moon was rising. Sawtell rose, walked around the camp, checked the horses and came back. This was the best place they had been and he thought of sleeping out in the bush, picnics, the smell of steaks on campfires, and himself and Marcia sitting in the dark. Those had been good times. He looked at his watch: it was half past five and the sun would be gone in half an hour. Sawtell sat down by the two Englishmen. The white parakeets were settling down for the night.

'What's India like?'

'India?' St John Jackson said. 'It's hot, dirty and dusty. And violent.'

'It sounds as though it's like Australia.'

'Not at all, there are lots of people, four hundred million of the beggars, all unable to help themselves. You have to imagine half a million villages like Wilcannia.'

Sawtell thought and said: 'There's a man there called Gandhi.'

'There is, indeed,' Sergius Donaldson said. 'A misguided troublemaker.' He turned to St John Jackson. 'Passive resistance.'

'A lot of tommy rot, they kept on letting the fellow out of gaol. The Indians couldn't do a damned thing without us.'

'The blackfellows here,' Sawtell said, 'haven't resisted at all.'

'From what I've seen, Mr Sawtell,' the Padre said, 'they don't have the spirit. Quaint rock carvings are one thing, resistance is another.'

'I wonder what's happening in the Western Desert,' Sawtell said. Many Australians were there.

'Rommel must be on the run by now, but the Huns are an efficient, hardworking lot,' St John Jackson said. 'We all know that.'

'And courageous.' Sawtell thought of the German sappers and the vast fortifications. 'And the Jews?'

'The Jews, what about them?'

'The Germans hate the Jews.'

'Most unfortunate,' the Major said, 'but I must say I've never cared for them myself.'

'And the Japs?'

'Dreadful little people, but fierce fighters, and they've taken your country.'

'Not really, Major, the three of us are sitting by this camp fire.'

'They have us on the run.'

'We'll see.' Sawtell was going to ask them both what happened at Singapore, but decided not. It was their affair; they had both fought and that was enough. The less people knew about each other, the better.

'What's on the agenda tomorrow?' Sergius Donaldson said.

'I thought a day of rest, and then a place called Acacia Downs. We could forage there, who knows? There might be some liquor.'

Sergius Donaldson thought of the pegs of whisky and the officers skylarking in the mess. 'We all could do with a drink. What day is this?'

'I've forgotten, Padre, maybe it's Sunday.'

'Sunday. Perhaps it is. No, we'll make tomorrow

350

Sunday.' They lay on their greatcoats and watched the moon and the stars rising.

The next day, Counihan and O'Donohue jerked the kangaroo meat: they cut it into strips, dipped it in boiling brine and hung it in the sun to dry. It would last for weeks and would make a change from bully beef. The Padre had his liver for breakfast, the broken gear was repaired and they lay around in the shade of the big trees. Sawtell fished in the deep pools and caught four freshwater bream which they had for lunch. It was like being on the Darling without the gloom of the river. In the afternoon, the Englishmen went for a walk, Counihan and O'Donohue played pontoon and Sawtell slept. Then, shortly after four, they heard an aircraft. This time it was a Zero flying low, due east. They waited, but it did not reappear.

'What do we do now?' Counihan said.

'Nothing,' Sawtell said. 'They didn't see us, and there's no point in blundering around this country at night.'

'And the fire?' Sergius Donaldson.

'We're having a fire, we've got fresh meat and I'm buggered if I'm going to be cold tonight. I trust you agree, Major.'

'I do.'

They ate and slept well that night and, refreshed, left at dawn for Acacia Downs.

After the valley and the hills, the country opened out into undulating prairie; it was dry with no feed or trees of any kind, the sky was infinite and they felt very exposed. It seemed certain they must be seen, but by whom? There was nowhere to bivouac or hide. Sawtell's horse picked up a three-cornered Jack and he spent ten minutes digging it out with a hoof-pick. They stood and waited on the plain. All was still and silent, there was no wind and the sun shone.

'This is some place to get caught,' Counihan said as Sawtell probed with the hoof-pick. 'You can see for forty miles.'

'Or be seen. If we're not picked up, I'll start believing in God. I can't get the bloody thing out, it's half under the shoe.' But he did, and they continued to ride across the vast landscape.

'Who would farm here?' Sergius Donaldson said, his hat pulled down and his scarf over his face.

'Brave men,' Sawtell said. 'The land's not worth a cracker, some of the stations cover a hundred square miles. One sheep to twenty acres. It's Australian optimism, good seasons, bad seasons, give it a go.'

'I can see why you're proud of it.'

'Yeah, it's ours, they can't have this lot. There should be a well at Acacia Downs.'

'And a piano?'

'Maybe.'

For three hours, they rode silently, their guns cocked and raised. There was no living thing, except the birds wheeling high in the sky. They hung, still, over the plains and lizards scuttled through the stones.

At Acacia Downs, a dog had died of starvation on its chain. Its bones were white and the wire netting around a chicken yard had collapsed and blown away. They inspected the well, but it was dry. The house was as empty as the church and there was nothing to be had. Sawtell stood in the yard and rolled a cigarette. He looked at the Barrier Range, fifty miles away. The sooner they got there, the better. All the trees in the orchard were dead and the implement sheds were empty. Living here would take courage, he thought. There was no piano. Counihan came up through the dirt and scraps of the farm yard.

'What do you think, Frank?' Sawtell threw his saddle on the brown gelding.

'There's bugger-all here, let's get on to Sturt's Meadows.'

'How long will it take?'

'Now I've changed horses, about three hours.'

352

'Let's get on with it.'

They mounted and left the yard, and as they rode away, St John Jackson looked back at the homestead. How could people live here? In India, there were villages, children and old men under trees, but here there was nothing.

The homestead at Sturt's Meadows stood on a rise overlooking the parched and yellow land. It was built of sandstone; it was nineteenth-century with five ornate chimneys and very grand. As they rode up, Sawtell guessed it must have been built in the 1870s. There was a garden, out-houses, sheds and an orange grove, and the owner had placed the big house upon the hill.

'It's a magnificent building, Mr Sawtell,' the Padre said. Sawtell looked at the verandahs, the garden and the ornate porticoes.

'It is.'

They stopped at the shearers' quarters. The building was low-slung, also made of stone; the doors and windows were vacant and old gum trees grew. The shearing shed was high and lofty, with morticed supports and beams, the walls had fallen and the mortar crumbled. An old donkey engine stood outside the shearing shed: it had powered the shearing equipment and many men had worked here in the season. They poked around the rubble.

'There's nothing here,' Sawtell said. 'Let's get up to the house.'

Sturt's Meadows was a big station and its owners were wealthy. This homestead had to yield something of value. They dismounted in the yard and started to scout through the buildings. St John Jackson stopped at the aviary and looked at the tiny skeletons and bones littering the earth, then he and Sawtell moved into the garden. The others walked down the hill to the implement sheds.

The verandahs were broad and shady and the garden extensive. At the front, there was the orange grove; they picked the fruit, but it was dry and woody. Sawtell

353

fossicked while the Major forced the front door and went inside. The lady of the house had worked hard: there were grapevines, standard roses, flower beds and fruit trees. It had been an oasis in this dry country, but now everything was withered and dead. He dug with his knife in the vegetable patch and found some potatoes. That was something: boiled spuds for tea. The leaves on the lemon trees were yellow and the fruit was turning brown. Sawtell picked a lemon, cut it in half and sucked the bitter juice. There were several dozen on the tree and Sawtell's heart lifted: they all needed vitamins. He then went over to the house water-tank and turned the cock; the cloudy water flowed and Sawtell drank and washed his face. Another blessing had been bestowed upon them, and he entered the house. Inside, all was dark and cool and he heard the Major's boots echoing on the timbers. The rooms were spacious and high-ceilinged with generous fireplaces and venetian blinds still hung at some of the tall windows. They would have a big log fire tonight. He looked at the lead-lined stained-glass doors, went down the long hall and joined the Major in the kitchen.

'An imposing house, Mr Sawtell.'

'It is. There are lemons and potatoes in the garden. Have you found the cellar?'

'Not yet.'

'All these places have one, they lived in style. It could be in one of the out-houses.'

They went past the shabby garden seats and an old kerosene refrigerator. In the laundry, they found the trapdoor, lifted it and saw a crate. Sawtell went down the ladder and prised the lid off. There were a dozen bottles of red wine and he looked at the labels. He passed a bottle up to St John Jackson.

'It's French wine.'

'French wine?' The Major studied the label. It was Chambertin 1937. 'It's excellent wine from one of the best

354

vineyards in France.' He couldn't remember whether 1937 was a good year or not.

'It's better than nothing,' Sawtell said.

'It certainly is.' St John Jackson smiled; Sergius would be pleased.

'We should see what the others have found,' Sawtell said. They put the crate of French wine on the garden seat and left the house.

They met O'Donohue coming up the slope; he looked excited.

'There's a truck.'

'A truck?' Sawtell said. 'What kind?'

'A Chevrolet two-tonner.'

'Will it go?'

'Frank's looking at it now. And there's petrol.'

Jesus Christ, Sawtell thought, it was either a feast or a famine. If they could get the truck going, things would change considerably. They followed O'Donohue towards the outbuildings. They passed tractors, split bales of wool and up-turned carts. Counihan and the Padre were standing in front of the truck, an old Chevrolet, a model made in the mid-thirties. The hood was raised and they looked at the motor. It was filthy and the radiator hoses were perished.

'What do you think, Frank?' Sawtell said.

'Buggered if I know. The tyres are no problem, there's a pump.'

'The motor?'

'I'll have a look. There's petrol. It's worth a go.'

'What about the hoses?'

Counihan waved his arm around the shed, the tractors and equipment.

'There's so much bloody stuff in here, we can rig up something.'

'If we get it started,' said Sergius Donaldson, 'what do we do with the horses?'

355

'A good question, Padre, but let's think about that when we get the truck going.'

'What's in the house?' Counihan said.

'A dozen bottles of French wine.'

'What?'

'French wine, the Major tells me it's very good.'

'No other booze?'

'We haven't done too badly, Frank. Compared with the others, this place is an Eldorado.'

'What kind of wine?' the Padre said.

'Chambertin '37.' St John Jackson waited for the reaction.

'Good Lord. Anything else?'

'Water, potatoes and lemons,' Sawtell said.

'Riches indeed. We shall dine well tonight.'

'What's the time?' Counihan said.

'Almost half past three.'

'Kevin and I may as well work on the truck while there's light.'

'Okay,' Sawtell said, 'we'll get organized in the house. At five o'clock, you can have a rare and expensive glass of wine.'

'I don't know about that.'

They left Counihan and O'Donohue and went back to the homestead. Sawtell built a big fire in the big front room and stood, watching the flames, the shadows and the sparks flying. He remembered the fires at home in Rotherwood Street before the Great War, his brother, jigsaw puzzles, Grimm's Fairy Tales and his father, cheerful in carpet slippers. After tea, on Sundays, his mother always played the piano, her fine soprano voice drifting through the house. He went to the window and looked out on the shadowy landscape. The dormer windows rattled gently now: there was a wind blowing. He wished there was a piano. The Major came in; he was carrying a bottle of the wine.

356

'A penny for your thoughts, Mr Sawtell.'

He turned and faced the Major.

'You might draw that cork, I've never drunk wine from France.'

'You didn't drink it in the War, in those small estaminets?'

'I had forgotten.'

St John Jackson drew the cork, passed Sawtell the bottle and said: 'A votre santé.'

Sawtell drank the fine red wine and passed the bottle back. It tasted good.

'Where are we going, Mr Sawtell?' St John Jackson drank the Chambertin and sat on the floor by the fire.

'North, we have no option now. South means defeat and captivity.'

'I'm aware of that.'

Sawtell looked at the fire and the elegant, colonial house.

'We can't stay here long.'

'That, too, I'm aware of.'

'Sooner or later, the enemy will arrive, we're in limbo.'

'You think so?'

'Yes, neither heaven nor hell, No Man's Land, we have to get out.'

'Where?'

'Alice Springs, the Gulf of Carpentaria, it's possible.'

'It will be a long ride.'

'It will.'

'And you will lead us there?'

'Yes.'

'You and Counihan?'

'Yes.'

'To ride and fight another day?'

'That's the idea.'

'What path do we take?'

'The best one, the one I choose.' Sawtell drank from the bottle.

357

'The one you choose? You don't know the country.'

'Yes, I do, Major. It's mine, and I know it.' Sawtell kicked the logs on the fire. 'In a strange way, it's like being in the War. We've got no option, ask the Padre.'

'Ask the Padre?'

'God will decide.'

Frank Counihan came in. He was covered with dirt and oil. They drank all the wine and that night slept soundly by the fire in the homestead.

Three days later, Counihan got the truck going, drove it round the yard, down to the shearing shed and then along the narrow station roads. The engine sounded rough, but he had done his best. There were no spares. There was now the problem with the horses. They stood in the sun by the animals.

'I must confess, Mr Sawtell,' Sergius Donaldson said, 'that I've become rather attached to my waler.'

'They're all good horses,' Sawtell said, 'they've served us well.' He looked at his big grey horse; it had taken him a long way. 'You've got the biggest problem, Kevin.'

The boy looked down. 'I've had that horse for three years.'

'You can't ride alone. This is the best place to put them out, there's feed and water.'

'If you don't mind, I'll go for one last ride.'

'I'll go with you,' Counihan said.

'It's all right, I want to be by meself.'

They watched O'Donohue saddle up his black horse and ride off over the dry paddocks.

'Poor young bugger,' Counihan said.

'I've had to shoot horses before this,' Sawtell said, 'and so have others.'

'How much petrol do we have?' St John Jackson said.

'About thirty gallons.'

358

'And how far is Tibooburra?'

'About 100 miles.'

'And the country?'

'I imagine it won't get any better.'

'What if the truck breaks down?' Sergius Donaldson said.

'We're in trouble, it's a calculated risk.'

'Gentlemen,' St John Jackson said, 'the whole expedition is a calculated risk. Let's get on with it.'

They started to pack and when they had finished, turned the horses out and drove to the highway. They stopped at the junction and looked south. The road was deserted and the land lay baking in the sun. The sky was empty and they turned north to Tibooburra. As the Chevrolet rattled on the rutted surface, Sergius Donaldson looked at the country, then at O'Donohue. Like the boy he preferred horses to machines; if the truck broke down, God help them.

The cabin of the Chevrolet could take three men only so they took it in turns to ride outside in the back with the food, weapons and saddles. The dust rose and billowed and they swathed themselves in their scarves and great-coats despite the heat. After three hours of bone-shaking travel, they stopped for half an hour to stretch their legs. Counihan inspected the petrol drums for fractures and they filled the tank. The engine sounded rough and it was only a matter of time before it packed up. Would they find horses at Tibooburra? No one dared ask the question. An hour later, they came to a large lake shining in the sun. They stopped again and took their canvas bags down to the water. The lake was salt. They stood on the shore, sweat running into their eyes and down their backs.

'Things are not what they seem, Mr Sawtell,' St John Jackson said. He thought of the chestnut mare.

'That's the first rule in this country,' Sawtell said. At last the Major was learning.

O'Donohue sat in the shade of the truck and wondered

about his big black horse. Then he got up and kicked the back tyres. This old bastard had better keep going; they wouldn't last twenty-four hours if it broke down. It was his turn inside and he sat next to the Major while Counihan cranked. At last the engine rattled into life and they drove slowly once more up the broad, winding dirt road to Tibooburra.

For once, luck was with them and the Chevrolet lasted the trip. Then the ancient hoses blew and the truck stopped about five hundred yards from the Tibooburra Post Office. The motor steamed and blew, and Counihan knew it was beyond repair. They saw the Australian flag flying in front of the small, wooden building. The telegraph line was down and the wireless mast lay against a tin shed at the back. An eagle perched, proud and tall, high on the branch of a pepper tree. It was quite still and reminded Sergius Donaldson of a gargoyle on a cathedral. A yellow dog crouched in the middle of the dirt street and watched them. Counihan took up the Luger submachine gun and got down from the cab. He stood squinting in the late-afternoon sun, but there was nobody. He saw the Tibooburra Hotel beyond the Post Office on the right-hand side of the street. There was a line of pepper trees, but no blackfellows and no fires burning on the ground. The Tibooburra Hotel was a wooden, two-storeyed building with shady verandahs, balconies, iron lace and a red tin roof. It looked dark and inviting and its bedrooms were, no doubt, empty. Counihan slung the Luger on his shoulder, strolled to the side of the road and pissed in the dust. There was a small, hot breeze and the yellow dog watched him. He considered shooting it, but his rifle was in the truck.

St John Jackson got down stiffly and said: 'I shall inspect the Post Office.'

'Right then,' Sawtell said, as he stood with his Lee Enfield, 'mind how you go.'

'I shall.'

The Major drew out his Webley and half-cocked it; they watched him as he walked, small and upright, toward the building, the dust rising from his boots. He reached the flagpole, opened the door and stepped inside. The blow-flies buzzed and the smell was intolerable. The body of a young woman in a cheap frock lay sprawled over the switchboard; she had been taken in the chest with a shotgun and the small office had been ransacked. St John Jackson knew it was not the Japanese: they did not use shotguns. This was a barbarous country; then he remembered Wilcannia and knew he was part of it. The drawers were open, the cupboards smashed, official posters ripped from the walls and the cheap safe door prised open. This was the work of common hooligans and murderers, this was the work of someone like Frank Counihan. St John Jackson held his breath, took out his scarf and wrapped it round his nose and mouth. He inspected the Post Office. The stamp books had been torn to pieces and the wireless transceiver destroyed: the delicate glass of the valves splintered beneath his boots. He looked once more at the young woman: she had been fair-haired, an English rose perhaps, in this remote town, a diamond engagement ring on her left hand where the blowflies crawled. He turned on his heel and left the building. Outside in the fresh hot air, St John Jackson replaced the Webley in the holster and saw Counihan approaching with his Colt revolver in his hand.

'You can put your revolver away, Mr Counihan, there's nothing of value in there.'

'Nothing?'

'A young woman killed with a shotgun.'

'Abos, they're everywhere.'

St John Jackson gazed at the empty landscape and the deserted town.

361

'Well, Mr Counihan, I don't see any.'

'They hit and run.'

The Major watched Frank Counihan turn and go back to the truck, and followed him. That man, he thought again, needs constant watching.

At the Chevrolet, Sawtell, Sergius Donaldson and Kevin O'Donohue were unloading the saddles and packframes, the weapons, the water bags and the food. They had to find horses. It was another hard afternoon, and to the east, the iron hills stood up from the plain. The crows called and the birds flew.

'How was the Post Office?' Sawtell said as St John Jackson came up.

'As I said to Mr Counihan, there's nothing of value. The place has been ransacked and a young woman shot.'

'Not the VDC?'

'Abos,' Counihan said.

'Who knows?' Sawtell said as he dumped a bag of flour on the road. 'C'est la guerre.' He wiped his beard with his hand. 'I take it the telephone exchange is out of action?'

'It is.'

'Good. Let's get this gear up to the pub, then we can have a go at the town.'

'We need horses, Mr Sawtell,' St John Jackson said.

'I know that, Major. Kevin, go up to the pub and have a look.' He grinned. 'Maybe there's cold beer on tap.'

'Okay.'

O'Donohue took his Winchester and started up the street.

'You look after yourself,' Sawtell said.

'No worries.'

They sat on the running board of the truck and watched O'Donohue step carefully on to the porch of the Tibooburra Hotel, open the bar door and go inside. Then they saw him appear on the verandah and wave his gun. It was all clear. Counihan picked up his saddle and packframe

362

and went up the main street toward the pepper trees and the broken buildings. Sawtell followed him and hoped that, this time, there would be no blacks and no war memorial. There was little more they could do today.

· XVI ·

To Four Mile Well

IT WAS A SMALL OUTBACK TOWN with two pubs, the
Tibooburra and the family, five shops, a petrol garage and
two public halls. There was no war memorial and there
were no churches. Nobody was to be seen. They camped in
the empty dining room of the Tibooburra Hotel. Watch
was kept from the upstairs verandah and in the morning
they started to search the town and outskirts for horses.
According to the map, there were two stations nearby, and
Sawtell said their chances were good: the VDC couldn't
have been this far north. If they couldn't get horses, they
were finished, but this was not discussed. The food situation was satisfactory: they had flour, tea, sugar, salt, rice,
bully beef, jerked meat and plenty of ammunition. But they
needed animals to carry the load if they were to get
through to the north. They split up, Sawtell and St John
Jackson going east to the racecourse and Mount Stewart
Station, and Counihan and O'Donohue going north to a
homestead called Mount Argyle. Sergius Donaldson stayed
to forage in the town. The stations were several miles away
and the search would take some time. Dun-coloured clouds
gathered in the eastern ranges and it was threatening to
rain.

The Padre walked up the main street past the boarded-
up shops and cottages. He thought of Wilcannia and the
presbytery. This was an unusual place: there were no

364

churches. Where did people get married, where did they take Holy Communion and where were they buried? He looked for a tower and a cross, but there were none. This was the most puzzling of all Australian outback towns. It was truly at the frontier. He was soon at the outskirts of the settlement and gazed northward at a flat, endless, horrifying plain and the low ranges to the east. There were no trees and no river lines; off the road, there was nothing to guide the traveller except the sun and the stars. Sergius Donaldson stood on a small rise and surveyed the scene. There was no wildlife he could see. If it couldn't support animals, how could it support men? How could they get to Alice Springs? He thought of mysteries. *And yonder all before us lie deserts of vast eternity.* It was starting to rain, spots of rain fell on the ground and, in the hills, the lightning flashed and the thunder rumbled. Did it rain in deserts? He felt the spots of rain on his face and didn't know what to think. They had searched both hotels and the shops and had found nothing to sustain them. The Chambertin at Sturt's Meadows had been a welcome surprise, but whisky or rum was essential for the trip ahead. Sergius Donaldson turned and thought: perhaps the trenches and the comradeship were better than this. He hoped there were horses at the stations. He was tired and felt a blackness descending upon him. His faith seemed not to sustain him.

Sawtell and St John Jackson walked steadily east toward Mount Stewart Station. The racecourse had yielded nothing; the small grandstand had been burnt to the ground and thistles grew on the track. Spots of rain fell as they marched, and St John Jackson looked at the ranges looming before them.

'This is unpleasant country, Mr Sawtell.'

'It is.' He hoped it wouldn't get any worse, and there had to be horses at the station. Sawtell marched down the track, the Lee Enfield on his shoulders, his boots cracking and worn, and his legs tired. 'We'll get horses, Major.'

'I trust we will.'

They walked three hours, the spots of rain fell and the lightning flashed in the hills. The small trees were dead and their branches crumbled at a touch. St John Jackson wondered why on earth people would choose to farm this country. Sawtell saw a small grey kangaroo, raised his rifle, but it had disappeared into the ghostly hinterland. He squinted at the rocky outcrops, and the thunder cracked: it was a minefield and he waited for the Spandau fire. No trout streams were flowing in this country. The Major walked alongside silently up the track, his topee down, his Purdey shotgun raised and ready. Sawtell walked with him step for step and knew he was a tireless military man. Then the shabby buildings of Mount Stewart Station appeared; the windmill was turning, the pump creaked and smoke was rising from the homestead chimney. They stopped and considered the farm buildings, the tanks and the stock-yards; they smelled the horses and saw the dust rising. Sawtell and St John Jackson crouched by the fence and wondered if anybody was in the house, despite the smoke.

'I think we've got our horses, Major,' Sawtell said.

'So it seems.'

'I'll inspect the house, Mr Sawtell, if you'll inspect the horses.'

Sawtell saluted and ran down behind the house to the stockyards, where the horses ran. It was a lonely station and the smoke drifted. The light rain fell on the dry land.

St John Jackson walked carefully up to the house and stood by the door. He smelt the fire and listened: there was the sound of music from a gramophone. It sounded like Harry Lauder; he remembered the music halls of London. He pushed open the door and said:

'Good morning.'

An old man swung round from the wood stove and reached for his shotgun, but the Major had his gun cocked and raised.

'Christ, mate, you might have knocked, you don't just barge in.' The man was in his seventies, grey-bearded, small and wearing a dirty waistcoat. His sharp eyes gleamed and St John Jackson thought he looked tough and tricky. He was of mean country stock, not a man to be trusted, and would be difficult to deal with. The Major stood in the doorway of the cluttered farm kitchen.

'Do you own this station?'

'Too right; lock, stock and barrel.' The old man looked at the Englishman, the topee, the uniform and the expensive shotgun.

'Who the hell are you?'

'I'm an officer of the Volunteer Defence Corps.'

'The Home Guard?'

'The Volunteer Defence Corps, the army.'

St John Jackson closed the door and stood by the gramophone. The recording of Harry Lauder had finished and the needle scratched. Two ginger cats were asleep in the corner of the room and fouled fly-papers hung from the ceiling.

'What do you want?'

'Do you have any horses?'

'Horses? Nah, not a one, they've all buggered off.'

The kettle boiled on the stove and the lid rattled.

'I think you do.' The Major lifted the needle from the record.

'If I have, what's it to you?'

'If you have, we must commandeer them.'

'We?'

'I have a colleague outside.'

'Where are you from?'

'Bourke.'

'Bourke? That's bloody hundreds of miles away.'

'Indeed. Your name, may I ask?'

'Hector Munro.'

'Well, Mr Munro, we need horses.'

'I suppose I could sell you a couple.'

'That, Mr Munro, is not possible.'

'Why?'

'Because we don't have any money, and if we did, what would you do with it?'

'I'd forgotten. We could trade.'

'We have nothing to trade.'

'There's the shotgun.'

'You already have one, Mr Munro.'

'You can't just come in here and pinch a joker's horses.'

St John Jackson was starting to lose patience with this crafty old man. He took up the farmer's shotgun and said:

'Come outside with me, Mr Munro.'

'What for?'

'Do as I say, sir.'

'Jesus Christ.'

'Mr Munro, there's a war on, your country's occupied.'

'I haven't seen the bastards, it's got nothing to do with me.' The Major motioned with his Purdey and they went outside and walked round the house to the back stockyard. There were the horses, a dozen maybe, and Sawtell was leaning on the rail appraising them. He turned and saw the Major and the old man. It was still raining.

'Mr Munro,' St John Jackson said, 'this is my fellow officer, Mr Sawtell.'

'Gooday.'

The farmer was apprehensive of the big, bearded soldier with his rifle and hat. He was a tough customer.

'I've explained our situation to Mr Munro,' the Major said. The old man stood by the stock rail and blew his nose into the dirt.

'You can't come in and pinch a joker's horses.'

'Look, Mr Munro,' Sawtell said, 'we're soldiers, we can take whatever we like.' He studied the horses. They were a mixed bag of bony hacks and brumbies, but would have to do.

'Have you seen the enemy?'

'The enemy?'

'The Japanese.'

'I've never seen a Jap in me life.'

This was the first local person they'd seen in two months and Sawtell tried to be reasonable.

'They're around,' he said. 'They're at Broken Hill.'

'Well, they're not up here, and if they do come, I'll shoot the bastards.'

'I'm sorry, Mr Munro, we need those horses. Which one do you ride?'

'I ride them all.'

Sawtell came up close. 'Which one do you usually ride?'

'That one.'

The farmer pointed to the big brown mare; it was the best animal in the bunch.

'We'll leave that one to you. We want halters and lead ropes.'

'I haven't got any.'

'Jesus Christ,' Sawtell said. 'Major, would you look after our friend while I look in the shed?'

'By all means.'

St John Jackson considered the horses and wondered how far they could go.

Sawtell searched the shed, soon found what he wanted, came back and threw the halters and lead ropes over the rail. Neither man appeared to have moved.

'Have you got any more guns, Mr Munro?'

'No.'

Like the Major, Sawtell didn't trust the man. A shot in the back as they left was more than possible.

'Where's the privy?'

'What?'

'The dunny, the shit-house.'

'Over there.'

'Right, come on.'

'I don't want to have a crap.'

'I know you don't. Come on.'

Sawtell pushed the old farmer with his rifle and they crossed the yard. He opened the door of the privy.

'Get inside, Mr Munro.'

'You can't do this.'

'Get inside.'

Sawtell pulled the door shut, found a piece of heavy timber and jammed it tightly beneath with his boot.

'You stay there, Mr Munro.'

There was silence and Sawtell joined the Major. They haltered the horses, but left the mare alone. There was a hack that Sawtell thought might do him, and they went round the animals. They were undernourished and neglected, but beggars couldn't be choosers. Two of the horses needed shoeing and one had a badly cut leg; the brumbies were in reasonable shape and would do as packhorses.

'Not good, not bad,' Sawtell said as they moved around the yard. 'They all need decent feed for a month, but we haven't got the time.'

'There are no dogs,' St John Jackson said. 'Isn't that odd?'

'Very. Unless they're out.'

'With someone else?'

'Correct.' Sawtell looked at the buildings and the land beyond.

'Christ, this is a miserable dump.'

They finished the horses and went back to the house.

The kettle was still steaming and Sawtell said, 'I could do with a cup of tea.' He rummaged on the shelf, found the tea, threw a handful in the pot and made a strong brew.

'There could be more weapons,' St John Jackson said. 'I'm going to search.'

He left the kitchen and Sawtell sat down at the table and looked around. They shouldn't stay here too long; he was sure someone else was about. A calendar for 1942 was pinned to the wall. Sawtell knew it was October, but what would the day be for 1943? It must be the fourteenth or fifteenth. Summer was close. He found a mug and drank the tea. What did the old bugger live on? Sawtell went through the cupboards and found flour and quantities of tinned meat. He thought of taking it, but what would Munro do? The Major appeared, carrying two rifles and boxes of cartridges.

'Where did you find those?' Sawtell poured another mug of tea.

'In the bedroom, if one could call it that.'

Sawtell thought that any man could live as he pleased. Munro was typical of the outback: tough, resilient and defending what he'd worked for. This was beyond St John Jackson. One gun was a BSA .22 and the other an old Remington-Lee. The Major unloaded them and tossed the cartridges into one of the boxes. He drank his tea.

'So much for the weapons. Are there any provisions?'

'Flour and tinned meat. We should leave it, taking his horses is enough.'

'I agree. Excuse me.'

St John Jackson took the two rifles, the shotgun and ammunition, crossed the front yard and hurled them into the scrub. That would give them time to get away. He went back to the house and found Sawtell having a cigarette and a second mug of tea.

The Harry Lauder record was playing on the gramophone. Sawtell was thinking of his father.

'We should leave, Mr Sawtell.'

Sawtell looked up. He was tired. What was the time? He took out the gold hunter. It was over two months now, and still this bloody formality. He put the mug down, left the familiar music and went outside. The rain had stopped and the earth was dry; it would take three months' downpour to make anything grow. The Major roped up the horses

371

and led them through the gate while Sawtell had a last look in the sheds. He found a bag of oats, and threw it on the back of one of the brumbies and tightened two ropes under its belly. The horses were a scrawny lot, but at least they were quiet.

'Okay, Major,' Sawtell said, 'I'll go and let the poor old bugger out.'

He went round the back to the privy and found the door open: the old man had gone. Oh Jesus, Sawtell thought as he looked around the sheds and across to the scrub, the bastard's gone to get help. He wondered how many beds were in the house, he'd forgotten to ask the Major. Sawtell glanced around again and went back to the stock yard.

'The old bloke's gone, how many beds were there?'

'There weren't beds, there were mattresses and blankets.'

'Well, somebody else does live here. I only hope to Christ they're a long way off.'

They couldn't ride, they had no bridles or saddles. It was going to be a long walk back.

About an hour from Tibooburra, they came on Munro and another man standing in the middle of the track. Two dogs were crouching in the dirt. The new man was carrying a shotgun, and as they got closer, Sawtell thought he looked like a younger brother. At about fifty yards, they stopped and faced each other.

'We want our horses back,' Munro said, 'or me brother will blow your bloody heads off.'

The man cocked and raised his shotgun. This is insane, Sawtell thought, our first run-in and it's our people. Then he remembered the boy on the road to Bourke. He would not lose patience this time. The flies settled and they all stared at each other.

'Look, you bloody old fool,' Sawtell said, 'we're soldiers, the country's at war, we've got the legal right.'

'I don't see no war,' the brother said. 'All I see is you've stolen our horses and we want them back.' He turned the shotgun at Sawtell. 'You should know what happens to horse stealers even if your Pommy mate doesn't.'

'We don't want bloodshed,' Sawtell said.

'It'll be your blood, not ours.'

The Munros stood their ground and one of the dogs yawned and scratched itself. It was a grey afternoon and more rain threatened. Damn these people, Sawtell thought.

'Leave this to me,' St John Jackson said. He stepped two paces forward. 'We are senior officers in His Majesty's Defence Forces. Your very action with the firearm amounts to treason, a crime punishable by death. I'm coming forward and I'm ordering you to put down that weapon. If you comply, no harm will come to you.'

'Like hell I will.'

The Major gave Sawtell his Purdey.

'Take this, Mr Sawtell. He dare not fire on an unarmed officer.' Sawtell stared at the Englishman and watched him walk forward briskly up to the man with the shotgun. St John Jackson took it, broke it open, removed the two cartridges and ground them into the earth with his boot.

'Thank you, Mr Munro,' the Major said. 'Take my advice and return home. It's about time you realized that my colleague and I are defending your country and we need your horses to do it.' He gave the shotgun back. 'Kindly step out of our way.' Sawtell led the horses along the track and they continued.

'There's only one way to deal with people like that,' St John Jackson said. 'Firmness. We are soldiers under the command of His Majesty and we should not forget it.'

Sawtell thought and said nothing.

Sawtell and the Major led the horses up the main street of Tibooburra and Sergius Donaldson ran down to meet them.

'Success, gentlemen.' He looked at the horses and counted: there were eleven.

'A modest success, Padre,' St John Jackson said. 'They'd hardly be chosen for the Derby, it was the best we could do.'

'We'll get O'Donohue to patch them up,' Sawtell said. He laughed. 'Their breeding line is somewhat uncertain.' He looked up the street. 'Where are Counihan and O'Donohue?'

'They haven't returned as yet,' the Padre said.

'They must have horses, too,' Sawtell said. 'We don't want to depend on this lot. What's in the town?'

'Nothing of any value that I could find.'

'No liquor?' St John Jackson said.

'I'm afraid not.'

'This is becoming a dry trip,' Sawtell said. 'We'll want something strong for the next few weeks.'

They took the horses round to a yard behind the hotel where there was a trough and Sawtell opened the bag of oats.

'Where did you get them?' Sergius Donaldson said.

'At Mount Stewart Station from a somewhat unco-operative old gentleman called Munro.'

'No killing?'

'No.' Sawtell smiled. 'I'm sure the Major will tell you. I'm going to meet Counihan and O'Donohue, so I'll see you later.' The Major and the Padre watched Sawtell walk slowly up the street.

'Sawtell looks tired, Francis.'

'Yes,' St John Jackson, 'he does.'

Sawtell walked to the edge of town. It was a dark and gloomy afternoon now. He thought of the Major. *He dare not fire on an unarmed officer.* Lieutenant Atkins leading the charge over the top and the Padre with one arm. It was courage and snobbery. Maybe those people were born to rule, but he doubted it. Frank Counihan would have killed

374

the Munros. St John Jackson had style, there was no doubt about that: he was a proud and brave soldier. He sat down by the road sign. *Warri Warri Gate 25 Miles*. Warri Warri Gate? He thought: it must be the fence between New South Wales and Queensland. It was a full day's ride, and they would have to camp by the fence. He wondered about the country to the north: it didn't look too promising. Would Counihan and O'Donohue have any horses? He hoped so. And booze? That was too much to ask for. Sawtell sat by the road sign and waited. The clouds rolled to the north-east and spots of rain fell. *There's only one way to deal with people like that. Firmness*. Those were his people. He thought and waited on the road side with his Lee Enfield.

Just after five, Sawtell saw Counihan and O'Donohue coming down the road. They were leading two animals, and as they got closer, Sawtell saw they weren't horses: they were donkeys or mules. God, he thought, it was turning into a circus. All they needed now was a camel. Some of the early explorers had used camels. Was it Burke and Wills? He couldn't remember. Sawtell got to his feet and walked up the road to meet them. O'Donohue was carrying a wooden box. Was it liquor?

'Gooday,' Counihan and O'Donohue said.

'Gooday. What have you got there?'

'Mules and booze.' They all grinned and shook hands.

'What kind?'

'You won't believe it, Johnnie Walker. Five bottles.'

'My God.'

'Yeah, my God.' Counihan sat down at the side of the road and rolled a cigarette.

'Where?'

'Argyle Station,' O'Donohue said.

'Any killing?' Sawtell thought of Sergius Donaldson's question.

'Nah, what you might call good foraging.'

'What did you get?' Counihan said.

'Eleven horses.'

'No kidding?'

'They wouldn't win the Melbourne Cup, but they'll carry us a mile or two.'

'Jesus,' Frank Counihan said, 'not a bad day. How's the Major? Is he still with us?'

'Yeah, he's still with us.'

'Any trouble?'

'Not really.'

'I reckon all this calls for a drink,' Sawtell said.

'It sure does.'

'Have you had one already?'

'Of course not. We're waiting for you.'

Sawtell put his arm around Counihan's shoulder and they walked back into the town.

'Where did you get the Scotch?'

'It took some finding,' Counihan said. 'It was well hidden, maybe the buggers were thinking of coming back. It was in a shed behind the house.'

'Why wouldn't they take it?'

'Christ knows. Who cares? We've got it.'

'And the mules?'

'In the yard,' O'Donohue said. 'They'll come in handy, they're strong buggers.'

'What was Argyle Station like?'

'Nothing there, apart from the booze and the mules, but that was enough. What about Mount Stewart?'

'A mean old bugger called Munro, but we fixed him.'

'How?'

Sawtell saw the Major and the Padre coming up.

'I'll tell you later.'

'Gooday gentlemen,' Frank Counihan said. 'You won't believe it, but we've got five bottles of Scotch.'

There was silence in the street.

'What brand, may I ask?' said Sergius Donaldson.

Frank Counihan paused for effect, the Luger submachine gun over his back and the two mules following. O'Donohue watched the proceedings.

'Johnnie Walker.'

'Good Lord.'

'Good Lord indeed, Padre,' Sawtell said. 'Horses, mules and whisky, I think we'll live to fight another day.'

'Indeed we will.' Sergius Donaldson smiled. 'We could have a small celebration at the hotel.' He looked at the mules.

'Those are sturdy, reliable animals.'

'Kevin,' Sawtell said, his spirits lifting, 'I want you to look at the horses first thing in the morning, they're a mixed lot.'

'Okay.' Kevin O'Donohue looked at Sawtell. He was sure they would get through to the north. It began to rain once more; they celebrated but drank carefully that night. They had all seen the country they were going to and they knew they would need the whisky. It had been a satisfactory day.

At dawn, O'Donohue inspected the horses. He took some time and said:

'They've not been looked after, have they? Bad feed, cuts and sores. They all need cleaning and two of them need shoes. How will we choose the mounts?'

Sawtell rolled a cigarette and thought. The rain clouds had gone and the morning was clear and bright; the sun was coming up behind the eastern ranges and the country was beautiful.

'We could draw straws, that's the democratic way.'

'Okay. I'll do me best, we'll have to cold shoe, there's no smithy.'

'I want to leave at eight,' Sawtell said. 'It's a full day's ride to the border.'

'That's okay,' O'Donohue said, 'if we all pitch in.'

'We will,' Sawtell said, and went back to the hotel.

They cleaned the horses' feet, did the shoeing and drew

the lots for the mounts. The Major drew the hack that Sawtell had his eye on. His was a lean and bony animal and Counihan's wasn't any better. Such was life. They packed carefully, using the brumbies as pack animals. They would use the mules in the hard country to the north. Sawtell and the Major crouched on the street and looked at the map.

'It's a day's ride to Warri Warri Gate, Major, then another to Four Mile Well. There are five tanks on the way, it seems.' He looked up: the sky was blue and clear, and the sun shone. The weather looked fixed, and it was going to be hot.

'Warri Warri Gate, Mr Sawtell, what does that mean?'

'A gate's a gate. There's a fence on the border, but there could be a station there.'

'Why is there a fence on the border?'

'To keep the dingoes out of New South Wales. It's a vermin-proof fence.' Sawtell had heard about it once.

'How odd.'

Sawtell looked at the horses, the pack animals and the deserted main street. The yellow dog had appeared again and slunk around the hotel verandah posts.

'Look Major, as you know, I'm not sure, but as you said last time, let's get on with it.'

St John Jackson smiled at Sawtell, adjusted his topee and rose to his feet.

'Mr Sawtell, I agree.'

They left Tibooburra on time and rode north. At a distance, the yellow dog followed them.

It was unnerving country and Sergius Donaldson felt it was waiting to pounce on them when they made their first mistake. He remembered their trip down the Darling. That had been Arcadia. Few trees grew and there was little wildlife: only the emu ran over the silent, stony land. There was a muffled, insistent wind, the bright morning had gone and clouds were banking from the east. He searched for tree lines, but he knew there would be none. He wished

378

they had saved one bottle of Chambertin; it would have been good with dinner. Sergius Donaldson rode slowly on his strange horse and felt the soft rain falling on his shoulders. This country depressed him, it was unpredictable and menacing. They would have to be careful and avoid mishaps. Sawtell and Counihan rode together.

'Will it get worse than this?' Counihan said.

'Probably. It's going to be tough. We should be okay for water: there's five tanks from here to the border.'

The condition of the horses worried them all, and after an hour a badly fitting packframe slipped on one of the brumbies. It was carrying the Lewis and the ammunition. O'Donohue started to unload the gear.

'We've carted that bloody thing over 500 miles,' Counihan said, 'and it's not fired a shot.'

'Let's ditch it,' Sawtell said. 'There are hardly massed battalions where we're going. What do you think, Major?'

St John Jackson considered; he did not like to jettison equipment. It reminded him of an army in defeat, but they still had the Brens and there seemed no point in carrying the Lewis this far north. He shrugged and agreed. Counihan smashed the breach and Sawtell threw the heavy belts of ammunition into the scrub. This was the first valuable item they had discarded, but it was more important now not to lose a horse. Then Counihan saw the yellow dog slinking in the saltbush.

'Jesus, that bloody animal,' he said, 'I should have shot the bastard back in town.' He raised the Luger Parabellum.

'If there's one thing I can't stand it's bloody mangy hounds.' The dog cocked its leg, pissed and started to run, but Counihan was too fast, fired ten rounds with the Luger and blew the animal apart. The gunfire echoed forever towards the ranges.

'Grub for the crows,' Counihan said and wiped his nose with his sleeve.

'Steady on Frank,' Sawtell said.

'Aw, Jesus.'

St John Jackson and Sergius Donaldson stared straight ahead. The animal was like pi-dog, but what of Counihan?

No sooner had they got under way than Sawtell's mount cast a shoe. They were down to four spare shoes and, as he worked, Sawtell cursed Munro. Why couldn't people look after their animals? They'd only been going three hours and the horse looked tired already. A wind sprang up and light rain started to drift in from the hills; Sawtell threw the hammer and the clinchers back into his saddlebag and they continued up the narrow road. The weather had become strange and depressing and the thunder rumbled. It was a silent, monotonous ride, each man keeping to himself; they stopped at noon for tea and bully beef, watered the horses at South Warri Tank and, at half past five, the fence appeared in the gloom.

The fence was twenty feet high and strongly built of steel mesh. It ran east and west as far as they could see. Counihan dismounted in the strong wind and inspected the gate. It was locked with a chain and big Yale padlock.

'It's locked,' Counihan shouted. 'Some bastard's locked the gate.' The wind was driving now and the sand and rain flew. They all dismounted and stood around the gate in their ragged greatcoats.

'How long is the fence?' St John Jackson said. He didn't like the look of this: the ground was completely open and windswept, and there was no cover of any sort.

'Hundreds of miles,' Sawtell said. 'We've got to get the gate open.'

Sergius Donaldson peered through the gate at the country beyond.

'That's Queensland,' O'Donohue said.

'Thank you for the information.' A twenty-foot fence in the middle of the desert: this place baffled him.

Sawtell glanced at the weather. It was packing up and it looked as though there was a sandstorm looming. He thought of using a Bren against the lock, but the risk was too great; they would have to break the chain with the crowbar. This took them half an hour and at last the chain snapped and parted. The big gate swung free in the wind and they crossed the border. As he mounted, St John Jackson took out his watch: it was almost six, darkness would soon be upon them and the country was most unpromising. The sand flew; he rubbed his sore eyes and covered his face with his scarf. This was, by far, their worst day and there was nowhere to bivouac. Counihan was riding out in circles in the scrub, his hat pulled well down, trying to find shelter. It was hard to see now, and Counihan looked like some ghostly rider as he moved through the dusty half light. They rode aimlessly for some time and darkness covered the land. There was no shelter for the night. Sawtell and Counihan met and compared notes.

'This is an arsehole of a place,' Counihan said. 'There's nowhere.'

'We'll have to doss down right here,' Sawtell said. 'There's nothing else we can do. It's going to be uncomfortable: we can't light a fire and we can't rig up a picket line. We'll have to hobble the horses, and that means losing some.'

They had no alternative: they unpacked, hobbled the horses, each had one whisky and bully beef for tea and lay on the ground beneath their blankets. The wind blew all night and Sergius Donaldson thought that where they'd been seemed now positively civilized. He thought of Robert Falcon Scott. They had come to the loneliest place in the world.

The morning dawned bright and calm, the wind had gone and O'Donohue counted the horses. Three had disappeared, including Sawtell's. He looked around the scrub, but there was no sign. Sawtell was awake and lay there in his blankets, staring at the sky.

'Your horse has gone,' O'Donohue said.

'Oh Jesus. Light a fire and we'll have a cup of tea.' He saw St John Jackson sit up and rub his chin and eyes. 'An unpleasant night, Major.'

'It was.'

'And three of the horses have gone.'

'We shall find them.'

The Major rose, folded his blankets and walked away while Sawtell filled the billy from his waterbag and made the tea. Counihan had soaked some jerked meat overnight; he threw it in a pot with some rice and made a stew. He looked at Sawtell rubbing at his eyes as he sat on the ground and drank his tea.

'I'll go and look for the horses with Kevin.'

'No, I'll go, it's my bloody horse.' Sawtell got up and smiled. 'Save me some stew.'

O'Donohue went one way, and Sawtell the other. As he walked, Sawtell wondered about the trip and considered their chances. They had to be good, they were all still fit and even country like this was feasible, providing they could get water. The big problem was the new horses, but with care, they should hold out; if the going got worse, they could ride two hours and walk two. What if something disastrous happened? A broken leg, some kind of accident or illness? They each had the option of going back south, but that meant rotting away in Tibooburra and waiting for captivity. In a day or two, they would not have even this option; they would be beyond the point of no return. How would the Englishmen go, and who would be the first to falter? He thought of his father asking him about the centre and the plans they had to live off the land. Then, thank God, he found his horse, unhobbled it and started to walk in a wide circle back to the camp. After ten minutes, Sawtell realized he had lost direction; the country was featureless and there was nothing to guide him. He stopped, listened for a sound and sat down. All was still. There was only the sound of the breeze. He found he was

382

not afraid, just confused; something would happen, and he rolled a cigarette. Then he thought of the ignominy of being found by a search party and he continued to walk, hoping the direction was right. The sun was up and he started to sweat; then he saw O'Donohue moving through the scrub with two horses.

'Gooday, you got it.'

Sawtell stood by his horse as the boy came up.

'Yes, I did.'

'The buggers wander a long way, don't they?'

'They do.' He put his hand on O'Donohue's shoulder. 'Let's get back and have breakfast.'

They walked and rode two hours all day and, shortly before five, got to Four Mile Well. The windmill was turning, the pump was working and the trough was full. The country had improved, but the feed was poor. The trees were big enough for a picket line and they set up camp in a creek bed. A fire was lit and while there was light and water, the Padre and the Major shaved and the three bearded Australians washed in the trough. The evening star rose and the night was going to be cold and clear. Sawtell knew the signs: hot weather was ahead for three or four days. Their daily tasks and duties done, they sat by the fire and Sawtell got out the maps.

'What about a whisky?' Frank Counihan said.

'A capital idea,' the Padre said. 'Life is looking up.'

'All spick and span, eh, Major?' Counihan poured the Johnnie Walker into the mugs.

'Yes, Mr Counihan, all spick and span.'

'A good close shave lifts the spirits, eh, Padre?'

'Indeed it does.'

Sawtell looked at St John Jackson.

'You're having trouble with your eyes, Major?'

'A little.'

383

'Sandy blight.'

'What is that?'

'Ophthalmia, dust behind the eyeballs. It's common in the desert.'

'Can it be serious?' St John Jackson drank his whisky and looked at the fire and Counihan's stew. It was dreadful tack, worse than any camp he'd been in.

Sawtell was about to say that sandy blight could result in temporary blindness, but decided against it.

'No, just be careful.'

'And how do I be careful?'

'Wash your eyes whenever you can. Horses are very prone to it.'

Sawtell spread the grimy map on the ground before the fire.

'Tomorrow, we strike west for a place called Inna-mincka.'

'A settlement?'

'A station, I think. It's by Cooper's Creek, I seem to remember Burke and Wills camped there.'

'Burke and Wills,' the Padre said. 'That's the third time you've mentioned them.'

'They were famous Australians,' O'Donohue said. 'We learnt all about them at school.'

'National heroes, like Ned Kelly?'

'Ned was a bushranger,' Counihan said. 'Burke and Wills were explorers.'

'The same rough courage?' Sergius Donaldson said.

'If you like,' Sawtell said. 'They were both Irish: Edward Kelly and Robert O'Hara Burke.'

'With Irish obstinacy?'

'Courage.' Sawtell remembered Jack Hanrahan and the working men at the Mountain View. 'Do you want another whisky, Major?' He tipped some into his mug and passed the bottle over. He wished his father was alive and with them at this camp.

384

'We have our heroes,' Sergius Donaldson said, 'Robert Falcon Scott, Livingstone and Burton.'

'Who was Burton?' Sawtell said.

'A Victorian explorer who travelled in the Arabian desert.'

'He was like Burke and Wills then,' O'Donohue said.

'Not quite, O'Donohue.'

'What the Padre is saying,' Sawtell said, 'is that this man Burton had a better education than Burke. Burke was rough Irish, a common policeman. Burton was probably a public schoolboy. I've no doubt he kept a diary and gave many lectures when he got home. Burke and Wills kept a diary of sorts, but both died. That's obstinacy.'

He rose, rolled a cigarette and considered the landscape. He watched the blades of the windmill turning slowly in the evening breeze and listened to the sound of the pump grinding. The crows had settled on the struts of the latticed tower. They had seen no wildlife all day; he hoped there would be kangaroos on the way to Innamincka. Counihan served out the stew and they ate from their battered mess tins. The moon rose, the fire burned and the crows on the windmill went to sleep. The moon was big and the night cold. They put their greatcoats on and O'Donohue put the billy on the fire for a cup of tea. Sawtell looked at the map.

'We go west against the lie of the land.'

'Against the lie of the land?' St John Jackson said as he threw the scraps of his meal in the embers.

'It looks as though there are numerous sand ridges.' Sawtell studied the map; large areas of the country were uncharted, but there was a station called Epsilon. They could forage there; they would have to, for feed and water and whatever they could get. When had they last seen fresh water flowing? He thought of the old man working in the greenery of the Fitzroy Gardens, the greenhouse and Marcia on the Bourke Street cable tram. *I'll stand for an old soldier.* He was on his second pair of boots and they were worn and splitting. What was the eternal diet of kangaroo meat and bully beef doing to them?

'Epsilon's a day's ride away,' he said. 'Then to Innamincka and Cooper's Creek. We'll get fish there, mussels and watercress, we'll live off the fat of the land.' He thought of the stream, the mysterious pool and the ruined country bridge. Sawtell stood up and looked at the barren country in the light of the moon. He drank from his mug, went to his blankets, laid his head on his saddle and dossed down. The fire burned and the hard stars glittered.

That night during his midnight watch, Sergius Donaldson thought he heard someone or something moving around in the scrub by the camp. He cocked his shotgun, watched and waited, but his ears must have been deceiving him.

· XVII ·

To Innamincka

THE MORNING WAS COLD and clear, and there was no cloud cover. They left Four Mile Well at seven on a rough track due west, the sun on their backs and the dust rising from the horses' feet. Within an hour, the country changed. Sawtell's map was correct: endless sandhills rose with gullies between, and when they topped a rise all they saw was the same. There were no distinguishing features and nothing to guide them if they left the path, except the sun. The track became hard and stony, and the ground was hard on the horses' feet. Feed was sparse and the animals browsed on desert bushes and she-oaks, and on some of the sand-hills, strange flowers grew. By mid-morning, the heat was intense, the flies clustered on the horses' backs and suddenly one animal went down. It was an old, spare hack and it dropped to its knees. Counihan dismounted and Sawtell looked at the horse. It was by far the worst of the bunch; there was no point in trying to rest or revive it. He gave Counihan his Lee Enfield.

'Shoot the bugger and we'll get on our way.'

Sawtell and the others watched Counihan walk over to the animal. It was due for the knacker's yard, Sawtell thought. God damn Munro. Counihan shot the horse, point blank, between the eyes and they left it on the track. As they rode on, the crows moved in. If they lost horses at this rate, St John Jackson thought, they'd never get there. He rode up.

387

'Was that wise, Mr Sawtell? We could have rested the animal.'

'Of course it was wise. Do you think we could wait around here in this heat, waiting for the damned thing to recover? I know horses.'

'And, sir, I know them too.'

Sawtell sweated and brushed away the flies.

'Not Australian horses, Polo ponies. You had grooms all your life until you came here. That horse was knocked up. We're wasting time, we must make Epsilon.'

Sawtell cursed to himself and rode up the track; the ground was flinty, they would have to walk and ride. He looked back and saw the crows perched on the dead animal. The sandhills rose, running north and south: they were travelling against the order of things. He hoped the homestead was standing at Epsilon.

At ten o'clock, they stopped in a gully for a rest and a cup of tea. St John Jackson looked at the thermometer: it was 98 degrees. He took his Purdey out of the gun case; it was filthy and there was no point in cleaning it. Furthermore, there was no wildlife, there was nothing to kill: only ants and lizards ran. The Major stood motionless in the heat and saw Sergius Donaldson rubbing his eyes. He thought of his days in Central India, the immense dun landscape, and his regiment at the end of the day. Where was the flaming scarlet, a gold mohur tree? Where was the laughter of the men? Here, there was only silence and loneliness.

'Do you want to unpack?' O'Donohue said.

Sawtell stood in the dust and flies, and thought. They would probably be here for three-quarters of an hour. If they kept on unloading and loading in this heat, they would wear themselves out.

'We won't be here long. Can you get some water on for tea? Use as little as you can, one pannikin each, no more.'

O'Donohue looked at the horses: they were nervous and already thirsty.

'Nothing for the horses,' Sawtell said. 'We'll give them a drink this afternoon.' He got the map from his saddlebag and walked to the top of the sandrise. Sergius Donaldson joined him.

'Well, Mr Sawtell?'

'Well, what, Padre?'

'You and the Major.'

'What about it?' Sawtell studied the map and looked at the landscape.

'There's some dissent.'

'There's dissent, as you put it, Padre, because he has the habit of continually querying every decision I make. I was placed in command, if you remember.'

'Continually?'

'Look, Padre,' Sawtell faced the clergyman and noticed his sore, red eyes, 'the Major and I are from different schools. He has his way, I have mine. And it's mine at the moment.' He looked at the claypans, shining in the sun. According to the map, Epsilon was west of a vermin-proof fence. But where was the bloody fence? Somehow, they had missed two bores called Ashby and Cook's. He was starting to make mistakes. They would have to go west for the fence, unless the map was wrong. He couldn't tell; this country defied all logic.

'You've got sandy blight, Padre.'

'I have?'

'You have. Cover your eyes with your scarf and wash them whenever you can.' Sawtell gazed west for the fence. 'Let's have some tea.'

They drank silently: there was nothing to say. The sun shone, the flies crawled over the men and the horses and they were now running short of essentials: water, tea, meat and tobacco. There were three bottles of whisky left, and that was for the end of the day. Counihan rolled a cigarette and used the last paper. For his next smoke, he would have to go back to Geoff's prayerbook. They smothered the fire, mounted and moved west over the sandhills. Sergius Donaldson realized that now there were no familiar tree lines; they had been sign posts and had sustained them. They rode and walked for three hours. Sawtell kept looking at the fence; they topped sandrise after sandrise. Did God live here? He doubted it.

They stopped, the horses' heads were down and two were lame.

'The map's wrong,' Sawtell said. 'Epsilon must be east of the fence.'

Where was the fence? He waited for St John Jackson to argue, but he did not. Sawtell looked at the gold hunter: it was half past three. He turned east and they covered their tracks through the sand hills and salt pans. As they rode, another spare horse went down. They watched it, on its knees. St John Jackson took out the thermometer: it was 120 degrees. The heat was beating through his head like a hammer and he pushed at his filthy topee. He missed his men, the afternoon rugger matches; this was a bloody awful place.

'That's your horse, Major,' Sawtell called. 'If you want to get it up, we'll come back and get you.' He rode on and watched St John Jackson. They had to find Epsilon before dark. Thunder cracked and echoed, but there were no clouds. The land was still, and the birds flew. The Major took out his BSA and shot the horse. The crows swooped and perched on the branches of the dead trees.

Shortly after half past five, they came on the buildings of Epsilon Station. Counihan looked for a windmill, but there was none. He rode out and looked for the station tank; the homestead had been burnt to the ground and only the stone chimneys stood. Counihan cursed and rode over the sandy ground, looking for the tank. At last, he found it and the muddy water shone in the western light. He rode back to Sawtell and O'Donohue, they unpacked and led the horses down the pitted sides of the tank. Sawtell watched the horses drinking. The big, bright moon was rising; it would be hard to sleep tonight.

'This, Major,' Sawtell said, 'is Epsilon Station.'

'How many horses do we have left, Mr Sawtell?'

'You should know, Major. Two have been shot, we have nine, and the two mules.' There were no Munro brothers here, there was no one to stand aside as they marched through.

'Mr Sawtell,' St John Jackson said, 'today, you misled us. Perhaps it would be better if you left the map reading to me.' Sawtell wiped his face.

'I navigate, or to put it bluntly: I lead, you follow.' He turned his tired horse round. 'I'm going to have a Scotch.'

It was the last of the jerked kangaroo meat and Counihan opened another tin of bully beef and threw it in with the meat and the rice.

'We've got to get a roo tomorrow,' Frank Counihan said. He opened his tobacco tin. 'I'm out of papers.'

Sergius Donaldson tossed his packet over. 'Use mine.'

'Thanks, Padre.' Counihan grinned in the firelight. 'That's generous of you, I thought we were back to the prayerbook.'

'Not quite yet, Mr Counihan.'

'I could do with a Scotch while the stew's cooking,' Sawtell said. 'Where's the booze?'

O'Donohue got up and took the bottle from a canvas bag on the packframe. He pulled the cork and handed Sawtell the Johnnie Walker. Sawtell poured out a measure into his mug and passed the bottle on. He raised his drink and said:

'Cheers, gentlemen.'

They drank by the fire and the ruins of the Epsilon homestead. The outbuildings were empty. Not one word was spoken and they looked upon the land where they had travelled. The night was becoming cold and they put on their greatcoats. The fire glowed and the stew steamed.

This station had yielded nothing except the muddy water at the tank. The horses stood at the line and the moon shone.

'How many days to Innamincka?' O'Donohue said.

'Three days,' Sawtell said. 'It depends on the country and the horses.'

'And to Alice Springs?'

'A month.'

'It's quite a trip.'

'If Burke and Wills could walk to the Gulf of Carpentaria, we can get to Alice.'

Sawtell drained his mug. He got up and stretched his legs by the fire and the ghostly ruins, the three chimneys and the collapsing outbuildings.

'My father,' he said, 'used to drink Johnnie Walker at a pub called the Mountain View.'

'He did,' Frank Counihan said. He remembered Jack Hanrahan and Dan Costello and the pound notes on the bar after the funeral. He recalled Jack Hanrahan saying, God help the Japs if they came, and Geoff scoring those two goals in the 1921 Grand Final. Those were the days, and he passed the bottle back to his mate. Where was his mother now? He'd almost forgotten her. He poked at the stew with a stick.

'Where were you born, Padre?'

'Born?' The cold night was closing in and the birds had gone to sleep. 'A place called Hungerford. My father was the Vicar of the church there.' He thought of the River Kennet, the barges, the Evensong and hay-making in the fields, his confirmation at the hands of his father. He had laid his hands upon him, and afterwards the young curate had come and taken tea and eaten fruitcake with his mother and father in the garden.

'The stew's ready,' Counihan said. They got out their mess tins and ate. The Southern Cross was high in the heavens, the night was black and a shooting star fell. St

392

John Jackson drank his whisky: he would have a look at Sawtell's map tomorrow. They went to bed and Frank Counihan knew there would be no roos in the morning.

Kevin O'Donohue woke at six, pulled his boots on and went over to the picket line. He went round the horses: two of them needed shoeing and, without good feed, none of them would last very long. He opened the large bag of oats, watched them feed and led them to the tank. It was another fine, clear morning; there were no clouds, and when the horses had finished, he took them back to the line. He picked at the cold sore on his lips, looked at the men sleeping and lit the fire. The Padre came down from the sandhill, his shotgun in hand.

'Good morning, Kevin.'

'Gooday.'

'How are the horses?'

'Not too good. I've used the last of the oats, we're on the country now.'

Sergius Donaldson looked at the sandhills and salt pans; there was no succour here. They lit yet another fire and carefully tipped the water into their pannikins for their morning cup of tea.

They left Epsilon at seven and moved slowly west, Sawtell reading the tattered map and the crows following them. The dust was in everything: their guns and the food, their boots were worn, half the waterbags were empty and remote explosions sounded across the land. They worked their way over the sandhills, from creek to creek, but there was no water, no kangaroos, nothing to kill and eat. There was nothing to say, and they crawled like insects across the land. The only birds they could see were the crows and emus. After three hours, they could see flat, ancient ridges in the west. They were now walking on old, brown country stone. Some cloud hung in the sky, but no sign of rain. Sawtell looked at the map; it appeared that the next water was at a place called Dulingari Waterhole. He tried to

393

estimate the distance, but could not. It was in South Australia, and he wondered if the border would be marked. Would there be another fence? He hoped so; it would be something to guide them. By agreement, they all carried their own water now and it was up to each man to conserve it. The sand ridges became higher, fiery red and almost insurmountable. Both men and animals struggled up the ridges, down into the gullies and up the next ridge, only to see the same scene before them. The temperature rose and the horses became irritable. As he walked, Sawtell realized the logic of this country: the next camp you struck was worse than the one before. They could expect nothing to improve on this leg of the trip, but the country had to improve north of Cooper's Creek. The early explorers had covered this country, and so could they. There was a noise: somewhere in the iron hinterland, red rocks were splitting and breaking in the heat. The prehistoric land, like the men, was exhausted and it seemed that nothing grew and nothing could live.

Toward midday, another horse went down, its pack-frame slipping and its lead rope tangled. It was carrying the food: bully beef, flour and rice. O'Donohue ran back to the horse, threw off the food and the packframe and looked at the animal. It was partly blind and shaking as it sat on its knees in the sand. The flies settled and two eagles circled. Frank Counihan looked at the horse; it was bony but would feed them. He stood in the heat and wiped his face. There was no cover and a hot wind blew.

'We can't save the bastard, but I could butcher it.'

Sawtell turned to St John Jackson. His topee was filthy and stained with sweat.

'Have you ever eaten horse, Major?'

'No, Mr Sawtell, I have not, but I'm prepared to.'

'Good. Neither have I, but now's our chance.' Jerking the meat would take at least six hours, and they couldn't wait that long.

'Shoot and butcher it, Frank. We haven't the time to jerk the meat, we'll carry it fresh. The meat should last until evening.'

'Okay,' Counihan said. 'I'll get what I can, I wouldn't mind a fresh steak for tea, even if it's horse.'

Counihan shot the horse and he, Sawtell and O'Donohue dragged the animal into the scrub. The butchering began and Sawtell found some filthy muslin bags for the meat. Counihan got the axe and knife, cut steaks from the rump, threw them into bags and heaved the bones and offal into the bush. He was black with flies and blood. After half an hour, he had finished and Sawtell said:

'Do you want a wash, Frank?'

'Yeah, I do.'

Sawtell tossed Counihan his canvas bag as the eagles flew in.

'You can't ride like that.'

Counihan washed his face and hands with the water, O'Donohue put the packframe on one of the mules, loaded it, and they rode on.

In the afternoon, they came to a vast, shallow depression. There were no trees and no creek beds: it was a huge amphitheatre of sand, rock and iron. Sergius Donaldson found he could not see and hoped his horse would lead him. An insistent wind blew and the sand pitted their skin. This was the worst country they had yet traversed; it was waiting to pounce on them and grind them to death if they made the simplest error of judgement. They walked and rode slowly, being careful to keep the sun in their faces. St John Jackson stopped to adjust the frame on his packhorse and found his fingernails had become as brittle as glass. He kept on hearing the sound of thunder, but no rain fell. He looked at the thermometer: it was 129 degrees. It was worse than the Warri Warri Gate, and when the cold night came, there would be nowhere to camp.

By five o'clock, they were too exhausted to go on and

they struck camp in the dunes. The horses drank the last
of the water and were hobbled. O'Donohue looked at
them shaking; at least they were too tired to wander far in
the night. After they had unpacked, they sat by the fire
and a terrible silence fell upon them. This was their third
night out from Four Mile Well; the country showed no
sign of changing and tomorrow they had to find Dulingari
Waterhole. God help them if it was dry. St John Jackson
got out his shotgun and the ramrods; it was his routine,
something to do. The stillness was death-like and the
moon rose. Sergius Donaldson remembered how it had
sustained them when they had travelled along the Darling
and in the country south of Broken Hill; now it was
menacing and so bright they could not sleep. He tipped a
little water into his pannikin and washed his eyes and
hoped he wouldn't lose his vision again tomorrow.
Counihan grilled the horse meat, but it was tough and full
of gristle and sinew and they had to wash it down with
water and a little whisky. Sawtell filled his water bottle
from the canvas bag and knew they would have to find
water tomorrow. He was confident they would: defeat
was inconceivable. He knotted his broken bootlaces and
wondered about the campfire behind them; there had
been no sign since Yanco Glen and that seemed a long
time ago. There seemed no point in keeping watch any
more after they had stopped after Four Mile Well. They
went to bed silently, their greatcoats thrown over their
threadbare blankets. Sergius Donaldson lay on his back
and stared at the moon. For the first time, after all his
years in the army, he felt a terrible apprehension; it was
worse than anything in the trenches. He turned on his side
on the hard ground and remembered a childhood prayer
he had not said for a very long time.

Jesus, tender shepherd, hear me.
Bless thy little lamb tonight,

Through the darkness, be thou near me.
Keep me safe till morning light.

In the morning, they found that the four brumbies had gone. Jesus bloody Christ, Kevin O'Donohue thought, as he climbed a sandrise. He surveyed the country and there was no sign of them. The brumbies were the strongest animals and if they couldn't find them, they were down to five hacks and the mules. He looked at the hacks. There was no water for them this morning, all were in bad condition and three had sandy blight. Sawtell and Counihan trudged up the rise and joined O'Donohue.

'Nothing?' Counihan said.

'Nup.'

Sawtell took out his watch. It was a quarter past six. They had twelve hours to make the waterhole.

'We've got two hours to find them. They can't be far.'

'They're brumbies,' O'Donohue said, 'bred for this country and can throw off hobbles. They could be bloody miles away.'

'We'll see,' Sawtell said. He remembered getting lost at Warri Warri Gate. 'Light the fire and chuck some bags on it. We don't want to lose the camp.'

The Major and the Padre walked down the track. Their eyes, thank God had improved.

'What are our chances, Francis?'

'Of finding the horses or getting through?'

'Of getting through.'

'I have no idea. It depends on the country, Sawtell's map reading, our fortitude and God; and we all know that He moves in a mysterious way. Despite it all, we're not in bad shape. How do you feel?'

'Apart from a headache, reasonable.'

'I must say for a man of your age you're quite remarkable.'

'And you too.' Sergius Donaldson laughed. 'I suppose

we've both led reasonably clean lives. And Alice Springs?'

'That's too far ahead to contemplate. As you've often said to me, sufficient unto the day.'

'And Sawtell?'

'There's a gulf between us. I can't get through to the man.'

'Or Counihan?'

'Counihan.' The Major laughed. 'That man's one of the original convicts. Unfortunately every army has men like Counihan.' He thought of the Irish rabble in the men's barracks in India.

'We've got two hours to find these damned animals. Look after yourself, my friend, and keep your eye on the smoke.'

They parted and moved through the thin scrub. The five men searched for two hours, but they could not find the brumbies.

Sawtell stood by the gear and whacked at the flies with his hat.

'We're down to the mules and that means chucking stuff away. We'll have to travel light, there's no option.'

'It looks, Mr Sawtell,' the Major said, 'as if our options are closing.'

'Not necessarily. I've always believed that most things can be worked out. This requires skill and strength, and I think we've all got both. It's been done before by men less prepared than us, so we can do it.'

If nothing else, St John Jackson admired the Australian's conviction.

'The Brens, Thompsons and ammunition have to go,' he said.

'They must.' Sawtell smiled. 'They haven't exactly been over-used.'

The breeches of the Brens and Thompsons were smashed and the ammunition scattered. The mules were loaded and each of the men went through his personal gear. St John

Jackson found that his soap and candles had melted; he considered throwing out a ruined pair of boots, but decided not. For old time's sake, he stuffed the sheet music for *HMS Pinafore* into his saddlebag. Sergius Donaldson took out his communion case and found that the heat had sprung the delicate morticed joints and brass screws. Silence descended upon them as they worked in the heat. Then they heard the sound of an aircraft; it was flying high and could not be identified. It disappeared to the south.

'What's that bugger doing out here?' Counihan said.

There was no reply, and leading their horses, they left the camp shortly after eight.

By eleven, the country was an inferno and not even a crow or eagle flew. They struggled across the blinding land and looked for water in the rocks, but there was none. Flies crawled in their eyes, mouth and ears and St John Jackson started to dream in the fiery heat. This vast, flat landscape was like India, but where were the banyan trees and the forts standing on the plain? He listened for the sound of a brass band playing in the village and looked for the dust rising from the cows. He would be in Simla when his tour of duty was done; the air would be moist and he would ride through the woods and dance a step or two with the women in the evening. Was that the sound of a copper-smith bird hammering in the trees? He must keep fit or he would catch some dreadful disease; many of his fellow officers had died inexplicably. Tennis and squash was the answer, tennis and squash. Tonight he would have a peg of whisky. They stopped. There was a tree line shimmering ahead in the heat. It was the first familiar sign for three days. The creek was no doubt dry, Sawtell thought, but it was something to aim at. Beyond that would be another tree line, but anything was better than the sandrises. He thought of having a rest and some tea, but there was no shade and they marched on.

As they approached, the trees grew bigger on the horizon: it was obviously a creek of some size. Sandy tributaries and wash-aways meandered into the main creek and the exhausted men and animals stumbled over stones so hot they burned through their boots. The creek was dry, but there was shade under the coolibah trees. On one branch there was a flock of parakeets which shrieked and flew. It was half past four and they sat motionless on the tumbled, fallen logs.

'Birds mean water, don't they?' Counihan asked.

'They're supposed to,' Sawtell said. 'Have you got any tobacco, Frank?' The tin was tossed over and he rolled a cigarette. He was confident of finding the waterhole and looked at the parakeets; the bush manuals said, follow the birds, but that was a joke. They'd keep going west toward those hills. They all peered at the map. It was falling to pieces. 'Strezlecki Creek,' Sawtell said. 'I wonder if this is it?' He was very tired and his head ached.

Sergius Donaldson looked at the rocks, trees, tributaries and channels. This was no creek, it seemed not to run anywhere. Sawtell's horse suddenly went down on the rocks; it was trembling and sweating, its ears were laid back and its eyes cloudy. O'Donohue went over and pulled at the reins.

'It's had it.'

'Such is life,' Sawtell said. 'So much for Mr Munro's bloodstock.' He took up his rifle. 'Seeing it's mine, I have to shoot it.' He did so, took off the saddle, the bags and the blanket. 'I don't want to lose these; some day I may ride again. Who can carry them?'

'I can,' O'Donohue said and put the gear on his horse's neck.

'Right,' Sawtell said, 'we've got two hours to find the waterhole.'

They got off the creek and left the parakeets. There was no time to butcher Sawtell's horse. O'Donohue's horse carried Sawtell's gear and they trudged west into the sun as it sank below the hills. Huge, forbidding tablelands rose from the plain. The country was now broken and there were splitting outcrops of iron stone. No quartz gleamed: this was red country rock, the stuff Australia was made of. Then, late in the afternoon, in the twilight, they saw some big trees and birds circling. Sergius Donaldson could see none of this and clutched the lead rope. O'Donohue thought he saw a kangaroo in the trees against the brilliant sky. A brumby ran through the scrub and the birds called and chattered: it was the Dulingari Waterhole.

The sun rose, but Sergius Donaldson could not see it: he felt the heat on his blankets. In the dawn, Counihan went to the waterhole, filled the bucket with muddy water and put it on the fire to boil. He worked the breech of his Luger submachine gun, put it down on the rocks and opened a tin of bully beef. The water boiled in the billy and he drained it off for the tea, then rolled a cigarette. The tea and tobacco were almost gone; there must be some at Innamincka. He thought: hope springs eternal, and walked out through the trees and up a rise. A plume of smoke was spiralling into the sky about five miles away. It was a campfire. Counihan watched the smoke and went back to the fire where he made the tea. He saw the Padre struggling to get up from his blankets and knew he was blind.

'Do you want a hand, Padre?' He took the clergyman's hand and hauled him upright.

'Thank you, Mr Counihan. I seem to have lost my vision.'

'It'll come back in a few days, Padre. Do you want a cup of tea?'

'I would, indeed.'

Counihan gave him the pannikin and Sergius Donaldson drank the tea down.

'We got here, Mr Counihan.'

'Yeah. Do you want some bully beef?'

'No, thank you, but some more tea, if that's possible.'

Counihan gave it to him while the other men slept.

'How long will the blindness last?' Sergius Donaldson said.

'Not long, a day or two, we'll rest up at Innamincka. You'll be okay.'

'Tell me, Mr Counihan, do you go to church?'

'No, not any more, never have the time.'

'But do you believe in God?'

Counihan thought and looked at the Padre as he stood, unseeing, by the fire.

'Yeah, I suppose so. God helps those who help themselves.'

'Indeed.'

'Geoff Sawtell believes in God.'

'Does he?'

'Yeah, he told me.' Counihan helped Sergius Donaldson down.

'You sit there, Padre, and when the time comes, we'll give you the best horse. We'll do it easy.'

'Thank you, Mr Counihan.'

St John Jackson got up. He had heard the conversation and thought about Frank Counihan. The trees around the waterhole were the oldest he had ever seen. They were made of stone and the birds flew and screeched; it was their domain and the men were not welcome here.

'How do you feel, Sergius?'

'Fine, I'm having a little trouble seeing. This tea is welcome.' St John Jackson looked at Counihan, took up the bucket and went to the waterhole. He intended to shave and wash.

'Good morning, Major,' Frank Counihan said.

'Good morning, Mr Counihan.'

'We made it.'

'We have still to get to Innamincka and beyond.'

'We will, no worries.'

'And the Padre's blindness?'

'It'll go. We'll rest at Innamincka. How's yours?'

'My what?'

'Sight.'

'Perfect.'

'Good.' Counihan grinned at the Major and went over to the horses. One of the hacks was still in reasonable shape and the Padre could have that. The other three were exhausted, but would probably make it to Innamincka, and the mules were standing up well. He hoped they could stay at the waterhole and rest up until tomorrow. The campfire puzzled him and he gazed back to the east. The smoke had gone.

Later in the morning, O'Donohue shot a small grey wallaby and they had fresh meat. Water was boiled in the bucket and the billies and the bags were filled. The temperature rose to 128 degrees and they lay around in the heat amid the endless shriek of parakeets and swarms of mosquitoes. Despite the water, it was a most uncomfortable and depressing place. After he had eaten, Sergius Donaldson tried to sleep beneath the trees, his scarf over his eyes. His sight was not returning. All of them had developed painful boils and sores because of the lack of fresh vegetables. Sawtell poked around the waterhole and thought of unleashing his shotgun at the parakeets; but what was the use? They would return. They dozed; Counihan and O'Donohue played a desultory game of pontoon and they whiled the day away until evening. Lethargy descended upon them and it took them all their time to get the evening meal of wallaby. All the meat they could cut was cooked and put into food bags to have cold next day. It was hung from the trees, they each had a whisky and turned in. At last, the birds fell silent and the inevitable, cold darkness covered the land.

Early next day, they moved north off the waterhole up a

small creek, keeping the sun on their right and the table-lands on their left. Sergius Donaldson rode the hack and the others walked. The country soon broke up into rocky outcrops and confusing tracks, and it was impossible to know whether they had been made by men or by animals. At ten, they stopped under a tree, built a small fire and had tea and cold meat. There was no conversation and, after they had smothered the fire, they got under way. By noon, it was obvious that this was going to be the hottest day yet. Counihan's horse was the next to go: it buckled, staggered and went down. The shot from the Lee Enfield echoed in the hot, still air. He removed the bridle, reins and bags, but had to leave the saddle where it lay. The monotony became unbearable and for the first time, Sawtell found himself cursing the land. It was one foot after another across the stony ground; there was no sound but for the horses' feet and the creaking of leather; sometimes one of them fell, got up and trudged on; it was now a time of silence, fear, flies and dust. Sergius Donaldson's horse stumbled and he started to pray. It seemed the land had seized them by the throat.

At two o'clock, Sawtell stopped and the Major walked into his back. He, too, could not see.

'Well, Mr Sawtell, I think it's possible we may have bitten off more than we can chew.' But St John Jackson still stood firmly by his horse, his topee square on his head.

'I don't think so, Major. While there's life, there's hope.'

'Never say die, eh?'

'That's right, sir.'

St John Jackson heard the familiar Australian accent and found himself rallying.

'How's the Padre?'

'All right, he'll make it.' Sawtell looked at the Major and thought of the English explorers, the tales of courage and heroism at school. 'Okay, Major, we have little in common, but one thing we do have: we're both veterans.

I'm going to have a look around, and when I come back, you will take my arm.'

'I'm much obliged, Mr Sawtell.'

Sawtell got out his compass and struggled up an outcrop. He looked at the land he had cursed: the endless vistas of stone, the glittering claypans and the dark tablelands. It was horrifying and beautiful: something strange was happening, he was glad he had come here, even if he should die. He thought of Lancefield, the dead sheep in the wire and Marcia. She would understand this country. Then to the north, he saw a tree line. He looked through the haze and prayed it was Cooper's Creek. That meant Innamincka.

They walked, the Major on Sawtell's arm, and the tree line got bigger. It looked like a forest, but that was impossible. Then they saw game: emus, dingoes and birds. They marched, the Padre on the hack, the Major's hand on Sawtell's shoulder and O'Donohue with the mules. Counihan, the strongest of them all, was at the front, the Luger submachine gun over his back and dust rising from his boots. Another hour passed and they saw a windmill, two tall chimneys and a stone building with a tin roof. Then there was the creek, sprawling and winding away to the north and south, a thousand trees, a windmill turning; and to the north-east, an immense, stony desert which stretched to the horizon. There were monuments of stone and iron and, as they approached Innamincka, they heard the sound of a million parakeets, saw some emus, and the horses and mules smelt the water in the billabongs. O'Donohue walked by Sergius Donaldson's horse.

'It's Innamincka, Father.'

'Thank God.'

'It's Innamincka and Cooper's Creek, Major,' Sawtell said.

St John Jackson stopped and stood. He put out his hand.

'Allow me to congratulate you, Mr Sawtell.'

They went down the hill toward the creek. The building with the two chimneys was made of concrete with big platforms, surrounded with dead oak trees and a fence. Frank Counihan ran across the stones to the low-slung building with the shabby red tin roof and the windmill turning. No living thing was seen as he approached. It was a pub: the Innamincka Hotel.

· XVIII ·

Cooper's Creek

THE MEN AND THE ANIMALS DRANK at the trough as the hot wind blew and the pump creaked. They collapsed under the verandah of the hotel. Sawtell rejoiced at the thickly wooded river line: it was Cooper's Creek.

'Can you see at all, Padre?' Sawtell said.

'Very little.'

'And you, Major?'

'The same, I'm afraid.'

'The blindness is temporary.' Sawtell pulled at his beard and looked around. 'There are two buildings here: the pub and an odd-looking place opposite. We'll get you both inside the pub. Stay there and keep your eyes covered, and we'll investigate.' He got up with Frank Counihan. 'There's also a station to the north; we'll get something.'

O'Donohue took the horses and mules into the yard at the back of the hotel and tethered them to the rail. He doubted if the horses would go anywhere for some time; two of them were blind and all three could barely stand. Feed was essential and he started to scout around in the outbuildings. He considered Innamincka: of all the places he'd seen this was the worst. What was the strange building out the front? He was dog-tired and walked slowly over to the sheds. As he went, he looked at the plain to the north. There was no end to it, but if anyone could get them through, it was Geoff Sawtell. That thought comforted him. His boots were done: he had to find some way of repairing them. And they had no shoes for the horses; from now on it could be Shanks's pony.

The Innamincka Hotel appeared to have been cleaned out; the shelves and cupboards behind the bar were empty, but in the tiny dining room Sawtell saw the cheap upright piano. He raised the dusty lid, played a chord and the thin sound rang through the stone building. The Padre would be pleased. He also found a few old books and went through the dirty, tattered collection. There was one he knew: *How Green Was My Valley* by Richard Llewellyn, but there were no dots on page one hundred. He followed Counihan into the kitchen and they went through the storage cupboards.

'Shit,' Frank Counihan said, 'this is some dump, and the Abos have got it all.'

They continued searching the kitchen and the outside buildings. In the end they found a flagon of port, some tea, a case of bully beef and a sack of rice. There was no feed for the horses. Sawtell, Counihan and O'Donohue stood at the bar.

'It's not too bad,' Sawtell said, 'it could have been worse. If you get the gear inside and set things up, I'll go and look at that building. Keep your guns by you; this place gives me the creeps.' He looked at his watch, wound it and went over to the building; it would be dark in an hour. The sun was going down behind the trees at the creek and he could hear the sound of the parakeets. To the north lay Innamincka Station: it looked like a full day's walk across the iron stone plain. He would do the trip in a day or two with Frank. Away from the creek, the country dismayed him: he thought it would have been better than that. His expectations had been too high and he could have made a mistake. A pelican flew over low towards the water and he considered going down to the trees to look at the wildlife. They had plenty of time now and would do that tomorrow.

The concrete building was a bush hospital and nursing home: the Australian Inland Mission, 1929. Sawtell thought of the Catholic presbytery at Wilcannia, religious hopes, plans and preparations: an evangelical mission in Central Australia. He opened the door and went inside. Every window had been smashed, the place was gutted, the wind blew through the columns of crumbling masonry and the bush rats ran: the land had won. There were eight rooms on two floors of ferro-concrete and he climbed the stairs. The place was built like a fort and would have taken a howitzer to demolish it. Through the windows, Sawtell could see the hotel; the gear had been taken inside and a fire burned out at the front. Counihan was sitting on the verandah cleaning his Luger; it was just like home. It was getting dark now and Sawtell searched the Mission but nothing was to be found. He went outside, sat on the concrete steps and fiddled with his father's watch and chain. The Mission chimneys stood tall in the dusk and he suddenly thought of Cloth Hall at Ypres and the Sunday service at St Stephen's in 1919. *At the going down of the sun and in the morning, we shall remember them.* The piles of country stone looked like the forts at Messines and St Julien and he shivered as the cold came down. A whisky was required and they would make plans in the morning.

The five men sat on the pub verandah by the fire and listened to the frogs croaking down at the creek. The moon hung in the sky and they crouched in their greatcoats as the stew steamed. O'Donohue came up with more wood and threw it on the heap; they would try to keep the fire going as long as possible while, in this remote place, it comforted them.

'Can you see the fire, Padre?' Sawtell said.

'I can.' The clergyman wiped and passed the bottle.

'Good. You might be okay in the morning.'

'And you, Major?'

'I'm much improved. There's game here, I take it? We might go hunting tomorrow.'

'There's pelicans,' Counihan said. He remembered the birds on the Darling.

'A wonderful bird is the pelican,' Sergius Donaldson said. The whisky tasted good and warmed his stomach.

'We want feed for the horses.' O'Donohue warmed his hands by the fire and looked up at the stars. There was no cloud cover and it would be hot again tomorrow.

'There's a piano inside,' Sawtell said to the Padre.

'Indeed? In working order?'

Sawtell laughed and poked at the fire. 'It makes sounds, but it's not up to Albert Hall standards.'

'Maybe you can play us a tune tomorrow, Mr Sawtell.'

Play the piano and sing, Sawtell thought, old tunes his father had enjoyed. He'd not played for a long time. When was it, 1939? O'Donohue dished the stew into the mess tins and they ate silently. When they had finished, Counihan got up, took the Luger and walked out in the moonlight past the Mission and down towards the creek.

'What's the building opposite?' Sergius Donaldson said. 'I meant to ask.'

'A mission.'

'Good Lord. What denomination?'

'Protestant. It's a bush hospital.'

'Even out here?' the Major said.

'Even in the outback,' Sawtell said, 'I suppose people have their physical and spiritual needs.'

The Padre looked at Sawtell as he crouched by the fire, this silent, laconic man with whom he'd ridden for over 700 miles. What was he thinking about, and would he get them through? The presence of the Mission reassured him; he would see it tomorrow, God willing, if his sight fully returned. He had the feeling that they had come to the end of their journey, but he was very tired and would feel refreshed after a good night's sleep.

'Can one bathe in Cooper's Creek?' St John Jackson said.

'I haven't seen it yet,' Sawtell said, 'but according to the map it goes for 200 miles. There must be billabongs, fish and waterfowl, we can wash up tomorrow.'

'And make plans.'

'Yes, Major, and make plans. I'm going up to Inna-mincka Station in a day or two.'

'How far away is that?'

'I'm not sure, a good day's walk. We can't use the horses, they'd never make it as they are.'

'What *are* our chances?'

'Good. As I've said before, other men have done it, and so can we.' Sawtell's back and limbs ached and he found himself shaking.

'If you'll excuse me, I'm going to bed.'

The three of them dossed down on the floor as the fire burned in the cold night, and O'Donohue picked up his Winchester and went to find Frank Counihan.

They met outside the Mission and walked round the stone hotel in the light of the moon.

'What did you see, Frank?'

'The creek, it's bloody big, with lagoons; we can go for a swim tomorrow, and there'll be fish and mussels.'

'Nobody around?'

'No, but you can't be sure, the Abos keep themselves hidden.'

'Do you reckon they're here?'

'For sure, it's their kind of country. They can live off the smell of an oily rag.'

'The Japs?'

'Nah, they'd never make it, they like the jungle, they're the least of our worries.'

'Will we make Alice?'

Counihan put his hand on O'Donohue's shoulder. 'No worries, we've made it this far, we'll pick fresh nags up.'

'What about the Padre and the Major?'

'I'm starting to change me mind. They're tough old bastards. I never thought they'd make it this far, but they have. Come on, let's doss down, I'm done like a dinner.'

They all slept heavily that night and all was silent in the vast land.

The billabong on the Cooper at Innamincka was over a quarter of a mile long, the water a muddy green, and huge river gums and coolibah trees hung down, their roots exposed by floods and perpetual winds from the north. Thousands of parakeets, galahs and cockatoos screeched and swooped from the branches. Wildlife abounded: ducks, seagulls, herons, pelicans and rats. The air was still with endless swarms of mosquitoes and flies. Plovers, eagles and crows flew and centipedes and lizards crawled over the rocks. They all stripped, hung their filthy, ragged clothes on the trees and waded into the warm, cloudy water. They washed and swam and floated in the pool, then they washed their uniforms and put them on the rocks to dry. This place, Sergius Donaldson thought, was a blessed relief, despite the insects. He and the Major boiled some water and tried to shave without soap and with their blunt cut-throats. It seemed that beards were inevitable. Their sight had fully returned and their spirits lifted.

When they had finished washing in the billabong, St John Jackson and Sergius Donaldson decided to go shooting in the lagoons, south, down the creek. The Major carried his Purdey. It was beautiful country and they returned with six plump, brown ducks. Sawtell went fishing and caught a dozen black bream and Counihan took some freshwater crayfish. They cleaned and gutted the game at the trough: this was a feast indeed. The fire was built up with dense river timber and they waited for the charcoal and ashes. The day was hot and they worked,

412

stripped to the waist, in their trousers and braces. After midday, O'Donohue returned with the horses and mules from the creek. The waterfowl and fish were placed on the embers and they stood around in the heat. As the food cooked, Sawtell carved another notch on his date-stick: they were sixty-two days out of Bourke. He got out the ramrods, the pull-throughs and the gun oil and cleaned the Lee Enfield, the Hollis and the Webley. The Major watched and broke open his own shotgun.

'A necessary routine, Mr Sawtell.'

The flies crawled over the food on the embers and Sawtell stopped cleaning his guns and waved them away with his hat.

'You never know when you might have to use a gun, Major.'

St John Jackson surveyed Innamincka, the Mission and the cluttered tree line. 'I must say it seems unlikely here.'

'Major,' Sawtell said, 'I'm wondering if we could break the mess rules and have a port *before* dinner.'

St John Jackson thought, smiled and said: 'Rules are made to be broken.'

Counihan got up, went into the pub and came back with the flagon. St John Jackson put out his hand and said: 'May I, Mr Counihan?' The flagon was passed over and they waited.

'Not a brand I'm aware of, but needs must.'

He pulled the cork from the dusty flagon and poured measures into their pannikins.

'Not Portuguese,' the Padre said.

'But okay.'

'Yes, Mr Counihan, okay.'

Sawtell looked at O'Donohue standing in the dust in his worn-out boots and torn moleskin trousers. He was a good lad and had come far; he knew little about him except he was from Gundagai and excellent with horses. He thought about the boy's last ride on the big black gelding at Sturt's Meadows.

'When's your birthday, Kevin?'

'I'm not sure.'

'Well,' Sawtell said, as he passed the boy a mug of port, 'today, by my reckoning, is the eighth of November, 1943. That's your birthday.'

Kevin O'Donohue grinned, drank the port, crouched on his haunches and watched the fish and the game roasting in the ashes.

The smoke rose from the fire and at last, the food was done. They sat on the verandah of the hotel and ate the fresh fish, carved the breasts of the ducks with their sheath knives and tossed the bones into the fire. It was the best meal since Cawndilla Lake and the Darling. Sawtell looked at his watch: it was half past three, they had come to Cooper's Creek, rested, washed and eaten well. It was time for another drink. He took up the flagon.

'Now, Major, I'm suggesting a port *after* dinner.'

St John Jackson looked toward the west.

'The sun's getting towards the yard-arm, Mr Sawtell.'

The flagon was passed round and they all drank and lay around on the stone verandah in the heat. Sergius Donaldson thought of the piano in the dining room.

'What can you play, Mr Sawtell?'

'Play?'

'On the piano.'

'Ah.' He thought of Marcia, his mother and father, and the men, women and their babies around the fire at Deep Lead. The old repertoire. 'I can play *I Want to Be a Military Man*, *The Honeysuckle and the Bee*, *Carolina Moon*,' he drank his port down and reached for the flagon, 'Stephen Foster melodies and selections from *Naughty Marietta*.'

'Gilbert and Sullivan?' the Major said.

'And Gilbert and Sullivan.'

Sergius Donaldson stood up in the heat and wiped his hands on his scarf. He had fed well and thought of a whisky in the evening. Beyond the hotel the parakeets called and shrieked by the creek and the eagles hovered above the plain to the north.

'Gentlemen,' he said, 'I'm requesting Mr Sawtell to play the piano.'

'Right,' Sawtell said as he got to his feet, 'I'll give it a go.'

Frank Counihan rose, took up the flagon, picked up Sawtell's Webley and they went inside to the dining room. Counihan put Sawtell's Webley on top of the piano. The port was poured, they all drank and a box was found for Sawtell. He struck a chord on the old upright.

'Seeing it's your birthday, Kevin, the first one's on you.'

It was *Bold Jack O'Donohoe*, the boy took out his harmonica and they played.

It was there for the sake of five hundred pounds
I was sent across the main,
For seven long years, in New South Wales,
To wear a convict's chain.
Then come, my hearties, we'll roam the mountains high.
Together we will plunder, together we will die.

Some of the songs Sawtell played were unfamiliar and they could not join him, but the old discordant piano echoed and he sang in his soft baritone. The flagon was passed in the dining room of the Innamincka Hotel and then St John Jackson went to his saddlebag and got out the sheet music for *HMS Pinafore*.

'Some Gilbert and Sullivan, Mr Sawtell?'

'Right you are, Major, but here's one song we should all know.'

He drank his port and played. It was *The Bold Gendarmes*.

415

We're public guardians bold but wary,
And of ourselves we take good care,
To risk our precious lives we're chary,
When danger looms we're never there.

But when we meet a helpless woman,
Or little boys who do no harm,
We run them in, we run them in,
We show them we're the bold gendarmes

We run them in, we run them in,
We run them in, we run them in,
We show them we're the bold gendarmes.

They all knew the old military song and sang. St John Jackson applauded and handed Sawtell the port. They stopped for a drink and the flagon was passed around. It was a good day, and they drank to their good fortune.

Then they heard the sharp sound of a safety catch being released and a young blackfellow was standing at the door of the dining room. He wore an old Akubra hat, a dirty striped shirt without a collar and was holding Counihan's Luger submachine gun.

'You whitefellows sure rode a long way.'

They looked at the stranger. He was lean and dark, his face was lined and bearded and the submachine gun was raised. Cockatoo feathers decorated his hat and he brushed the flies away.

'Jesus Christ,' Frank Counihan said. He stood still. 'That's my gun.' This proved all his theories about Abos.

'You don't say?' the black man said. 'Some fancy weapon. Foreign, ain't it?'

'It's tricky and deadly,' Sawtell said as he sat on the box, his back to the keyboard and his drink between his knees. Now he knew: the campfires behind them.

'You'd better put it down.'

'Yeah?'

O'Donohue's heart thudded and the sweat down his

back turned cold. Sergius Donaldson didn't like the look of this and tried to play for time.

'Who are you?' he said.

The blackfellow stared hard at Counihan. His dark eyes shone and his finger curled around the trigger of Frank's gun. He coughed, moved a little and the spurs on his boots gently rattled. His voice was steady.

'You, mister, busted our water tank at Bourke.' He turned on Sawtell. 'And you, boss, broke me brother's jaw at Wilcannia. I picked him up at the war memorial.'

'Who are you?' St John Jackson said. He wanted a cigarette, but dared not reach for his tobacco.

'I'm a blackfellow, boss.'

'Are there any more of you?'

'Nah.' He pulled his hat down a little lower over his face.

'I thought I'd lost you when you got that truck, but I seen you again at Four Mile Well.' He laughed. 'Shanks's pony, that's all we've got in the end. Your horses don't look too good. Are you blokes celebrating something?'

Frank Counihan watched the young blackfellow with his Luger submachine gun. Geoff's Webley was on top of the piano. When the time was right, he'd go for the little bastard. They all thought of the campfires behind them on the west bank of the Darling, Leonora Downs, Yanco Glen and the Dulingari Waterhole.

'You've come all this way on your own?' Sergius Donaldson said.

'Yeah, Father, I come all this way on me own.' He grinned. 'It was easy, all that stuff you ditched. No worries.'

'That was some ride,' Sawtell said. 'I have to hand it to you.' He stood up easily. Out of the corner of his eye, he could see the big service revolver.

'Yeah, it was some ride. You should've kept them first horses. What you picked was no good.'

'Why did you take this long?' Sergius Donaldson said.

417

'Aw, it's the first time I got all you blokes in the one place together. There's nowhere you can run to in here. I could have had you before, but I waited. I got loads of time.'

The flies buzzed and the young black man shifted slightly towards the piano. He coughed, wiped his nose again and held Frank Counihan's submachine gun on them all.

'You want some kind of compensation?' St John Jackson said. 'Is that it?'

'Yeah, you could say that.'

St John Jackson touched the studs on the holster of his Sam Browne belt. What compensation? What would Counihan and Sawtell do? Counihan especially. Extreme care was needed. He hoped young O'Donohue would keep his head. Where was he standing? He couldn't see.

'What do you want?' the Padre said. He remembered the blacks' camp at Bourke, the windmill, the old people by the fire, the trestles falling under Counihan's sledgehammer and the two young blacks standing in the shade of the she-oak. He also remembered Wilcannia: the blind black woman, the dog on the chain and St John Jackson waving his riding crop. *Thou hast shewn thy people heavy things.*

'I could do with a drink, Father, and a smoke. I'm almost out.'

'Give him one, Kevin,' Sawtell said. 'And roll him a cigarette.'

O'Donohue poured some port into a mug and passed it over. His hands shook as he rolled the cigarette. The blackfellow drained the mug.

'Do us a favour, mate,' he said to O'Donohue. 'Light the smoke. I don't want any of youse jumping me.'

'Have your drink and get out,' Sawtell said, 'we've got work to do.'

'I've had me drink. It don't look like you're working to me. More like a grog-up, I'd say.'

418

'Why don't you piss off?' Counihan said. 'And put that bloody gun down. We're the Australian army. What's one water tank? You've got the whole bloody country.'

'It was *our* tank, mister.' The blackfellow inhaled and blew the smoke slowly from his nostrils.

Sergius Donaldson stood at the back of the room. He felt old and tired and wanted to sit down. Outside, down at the creek, the ducks were flying, their wings cracking, drops of water spinning from their feathers. He heard the parakeets calling from the ruined Mission. What would the black man do? They had come a long way, and now this.

'We're soldiers,' St John Jackson said. 'The country's at war. Put that weapon down and be on your way.' He thought of the Munro brothers. 'Don't you understand?'

The blackfellow ground the butt of his cigarette under his boot and said: 'I don't see no war. All I see is some old soldiers on the piss and singing around the piano.'

He turned the Luger on Sawtell. 'After what you did, me brother didn't make it.'

All was silent and the six men stood in the small dining room. St John Jackson felt the lanyard of his Webley and sweated, the cheap port lay in his gut. What was happening? It was young O'Donohue's birthday. A bushfly was crawling on the keyboard of the old piano. Something moved outside and the blackfellow looked towards the window. Frank Counihan thought he saw his chance and jumped. He tackled strongly, but the black man fired five shots into Counihan's chest. The noise was deafening. Counihan was thrown back against the wall, grunted, fainted and fell. His braces were cut and his trousers slipped. Sawtell saw his mate fall but waited for his chance. St John Jackson managed to get out his Webley, but he fumbled with the lanyard and he, too, was shot in the heart and dropped against the keyboard of the piano. The room echoed discordantly with strange sounds of gunfire and piano strings; the Major tried to say something, slid, his

419

hat toppling, blood pulsing through his tunic. Sergius Donaldson moved toward St John Jackson, and the black-fellow turned again on Sawtell. O'Donohue sprang, they struggled, the submachine gun fell, Sawtell reached across the piano, grabbed the big Webley, flipped the safety and shot the black man squarely between the shoulders. He jerked forward, staggered, the blood ran down his shirt and he pitched to the floor. Sawtell fired again, threw the gun down, went to Frank Counihan and crouched by him; but his mate was speechless and dying. Blood oozed from his torn shirt and his lungs rattled. Sawtell went to speak and stopped, Counihan's blood running between his fingers.

Sergius Donaldson knelt by his old friend, looked upon his face and crossed himself; then he went to Counihan and blessed him as he lay dying. Sawtell sat on the floor and O'Donohue stood stock still and shaking. There was nothing they could do; there was no help now. The room reeked of gunfire and O'Donohue vomited.

'Lord Jesus Christ,' Sawtell said as he clutched Frank Counihan's hand. 'He was a Catholic, Padre, he went to my father's funeral.' Counihan breathed and died. Sawtell sat, his head in his hands.

'Lord Jesus Christ indeed,' Sergius Donaldson said. 'I only hope he can help us now.'

'Frank Counihan was a good man, Padre. He was a good man.'

'They both were, in their own ways. I've known Francis for a long time.' He thought. 'They were both courageous men.'

'And,' Sawtell said, 'St John Jackson saved my life.'

'Did he, indeed? Where?'

'At the mine.'

'He was a loyal soldier, too.' The Padre looked up and saw O'Donohue standing there, white-faced and shaking.

'You did your best, lad, a stout effort. Get the whisky, it's in my saddlebag.'

The boy got the Johnnie Walker, Sawtell pulled the cork and poured out three large measures, while Sergius Donaldson brought in the greatcoats and covered the bodies. There was now much blood on the floor and the flies clustered. They each drank and Sawtell picked up the Major's sheet music and the topee. Smashing that pump at Bourke had been their biggest military error. And Wilcannia, the blacks scattering in the street as they rode their horses. *Dump him on the war memorial, Frank.*

'Jesus Christ,' Sawtell said, 'after all this way I can't believe it.'

'We made an error, Mr Sawtell.'

'We did, and it's cost us plenty.'

'As Francis used to say, *c'est la guerre.*'

'It's more than that.' Sawtell looked at O'Donohue, who was standing there. 'Go and get the mules, Kevin, we haven't got much time. There's the heat and flies.'

'Okay.' The boy put his hat on and went outside to the yard.

'Have you any advice to offer, Padre?' Sawtell said.

'You asked me that once before, and I said God helps those who help themselves.'

'I prefer that to God moves in a mysterious way.'

'Indeed he may, but we have work to do. We have to bury our comrades. I've done it before.'

Sergius Donaldson looked at the greatcoats. He would pray long and hard tonight, and he would miss his friend, Francis St John Jackson. They were certainly in God's hands now. Outside the pub, Sawtell found the black-fellow's gun: it was an old pump-action Winchester .22.

They got the bodies on to the mules and took them down to the creek: the earth was softer there. The graves were dug under the coolibah trees by the lagoon where Counihan had caught the freshwater crayfish and the ducks and

421

pelicans swam. The work was hard, the birds screamed continually, the three of them took the shovel in turns and the work was not finished until after six. The sunset was crimson and purple and the light faded behind the western tablelands. Exhausted and sweating in the twilight, they rolled the bodies into the graves: Counihan with his slouch hat and St Christopher medal around his neck and St John Jackson with his topee, prayerbook and Sam Browne belt. In Counihan's grave, Sawtell tossed the Luger submachine gun; in St John Jackson's, the Padre tossed Kipling's poems and the sheet music from *HMS Pinafore*. The young blackfellow was buried with his Akubra hat and the Winchester.

They made three crosses from the branches of the trees and the Padre said a short service as the day ended and the moon and the evening star rose.

I am the resurrection and the life, saith the Lord: he that believeth in me, though he were dead, yet shall he live: and whosoever liveth and believeth in me shall never die.

The three of them stood bareheaded and Sawtell thought of Frank Counihan and Jack Hanrahan at his father's funeral. God bless the Irish. The earth was shovelled in by the light of the moon. Sawtell put his arm around O'Donohue's shoulder and they went back to the pub.

That night, they sat by the fire with the remains of the port. The frogs croaked and the bush rats ran. Sergius Donaldson got up.

'I'm going for a walk, I won't be long.'

'Take your shotgun, Padre,' Sawtell said.

'I shall. I've kept the Purdey, I'm sure he wouldn't mind.'

Sawtell and O'Donohue watched the Padre pick up the Major's Purdey and walk down to the Mission.

'He's not a bad old bloke,' O'Donohue said.

'He's not, he's a good soldier.' Sawtell drank, and rolled

a cigarette. 'We're leaving here in a day or two. I thought we might go to Innamincka Station tomorrow.'

'The horses are buggered.'

'I know. We'll take the mules.'

'I'm going to miss Frank Counihan.'

'Like your big black horse?'

'Yeah.'

'You've done well, Kevin.' The boy was silent and they sat by the fire. 'What did your father do?' Sawtell said.

'I told you: he was a cruel old bastard, a farmer at Mount Parnassus.' O'Donohue looked done in, and Sawtell thought of being with Smith when they had gone up to the front. *I been here before.* The greying hair and the Communion service with the makeshift altar.

'You go and get your head down, and I'll see you first thing in the morning.'

'Okay.'

Sawtell watched the boy go into the pub. He sat by the fire and thought of Frank Counihan and St John Jackson, the photographs pinned to the wall of the house at Bourke, his Bible. Where were they now? They hadn't gone through his saddlebags thoroughly, maybe the Padre had got them. He probably had: he wouldn't ask. He got up, threw more wood on the fire and waited for Sergius Donaldson. The Padre was his companion now.

In half an hour, Sergius Donaldson returned, propped the Major's shotgun on a verandah post and sat down.

'Do you want a drink, Padre?' Sawtell said.

'I do.'

'This time, we have a choice.' Sawtell laughed. 'Port or whisky?'

'A little whisky, I think.'

Sawtell got the bottle and poured out two measures. It was under half full.

'We should leave here in a day or two, Padre, and go north.'

'We should.'

'O'Donohue and I will probably go up to Innamincka Station tomorrow, if you can mind the camp.'

'Certainly.' The Padre proffered a Capstan cigarette. 'Have a tailor-made, these are the last, I've been saving them.'

'For occasions like these?'

'For occasions like these.'

Sawtell lit the cigarette and put on his greatcoat.

'Francis Xavier Counihan, an Irish Catholic from Ballarat.'

'Francis St John Jackson, a Protestant from Surrey. Did you ever go there?'

'I can't remember. I went to a military hospital in Berkshire once.' He thought of his mother knitting in the garden at Rotherwood Street, the standard roses, the forget-me-knots and the spring violets.

'You feel no bitterness, Mr Sawtell?'

'No, I've thought about it, I don't.'

'Why not?'

'We underestimated those people. There's more to them than empty wine flagons and quaint rock carvings. That young black rode 700 miles for his dues.'

'An eye for an eye?'

'No, just dues. We all got it wrong, Frank most of all. The young blackfellow came to collect, there's nothing wrong in that.' Sawtell threw his cigarette butt into the fire.

'Maybe they've got some rights and that young bugger tried to exercise them. It wasn't the Japs, it was the blackfellows we got wrong. In a day or two, it's the country to the north. I hope we've got that right.'

'We have?'

'I don't know, probably. It'll be a matter of judgement and care. I think we'll make it. As I've said before, other men have.'

'And God will provide.'

'Yes Padre, God will provide.' Sawtell was cold and very tired; he was sick of Innamincka, Cooper's Creek, the foraging and the killing. Lieutenant Atkins blown away, Smith in the sap, his old mate Frank Counihan and the Major, the boy on the road to Bourke and the shooting of the horses. 'Please excuse me, Padre, I'm going to bed.'

The night was long and cold and Sawtell could not sleep. He thought of Frank Counihan. *We'll just have to do what we can, one foot after another.*

Early next morning at dawn, Sawtell and O'Donohue left to find Innamincka Station. With the two mules, they walked north-east along a stony track away from the creek. After four hours, they stopped for a spell; the iron stone plain stretched fifty or sixty miles before them and there was no sign of life. Sawtell drank a little from his waterbottle and considered the landscape. The sky was cloudless and no birds flew.

'I don't like the look of this. What do you think?'

'It doesn't look too good.'

'Are you okay?'

'Yeah, I'm fine.'

'Right, we'll go until noon and if there's no sign of anything, we'll go back.'

'Okay.'

They continued north-east.

At noon, the plain still stretched before them and there was no sign of a windmill or tank. They had no thermometer, but Sawtell knew the temperature was well over one hundred degrees. He looked at the state of O'Donohue's boots, felt the heat on his back and lost his resolve. This trip would get them nowhere.

'Either the map's wrong or we're going the wrong way. We're turning back.'

'It's not worth a few more miles?' O'Donohue said. 'There could be feed at the next station.'

'But where's the bloody station?' Sawtell rubbed his eyes. 'There's no sign of anything. This country's lethal. Have you got a spare pair of boots?'

'No.'

'That settles it.' Sawtell stood on the iron stone. They turned back with the mules. This is one part to keep out of, Sawtell thought. This country unnerved him and he hoped it wasn't like this to the north-west. They marched back to Innamincka in complete silence and Sawtell couldn't get the iron stone plain out of his mind.

The evening fire burned. 'What do we do about feed for the horses?' O'Donohue said as they ate their tea.

'We'll have to keep to the creek for as long as possible. We'll look at the map in the morning.'

'When do you plan to leave?' the Padre said.

'I thought the day after tomorrow. I've got no great desire to stay here, despite the wildlife.'

'Nor have I.'

They sat by the fire. Sawtell looked over at the Mission building and thought he saw Frank Counihan walking up the track in the moonlight, his submachine gun over his shoulder. He picked up his rifle.

'I'm going down to the creek,' he said. 'I'll see you later.'

Sawtell went past the Mission, down to the edge of the billabong and sat on the bank. The birds, thank God, were asleep and the water gleamed. It was a good night for fishing and he wondered what happened when the creek dried up completely. Maybe it never did, and there was always wildlife here. Was the whole expedition insane? But there had never been any option after the Japanese had landed. The Japanese: he hadn't thought about them for some time. Maybe something had happened and they'd been thrown out. Maybe the Americans had returned and they were liberating the country. Had Tobruk been re-

426

lieved? What was happening in the Middle East and Russia? Should they go back and see? That was a trip of almost a thousand miles. It was most unlikely that Alice Springs was occupied. The war could last for bloody years. He remembered that many men were convinced that the Great War would never end. Wasn't there once a show called the Hundred Years War? His father would have known. He supposed there must be forced labour in Melbourne and Sydney. The whole thing was a nightmare, but he remembered the fiasco at Newcastle: that had been real enough. He and Frank had fought there and he could still hear the sound of the dive-bombers and the naval guns. They had seen the Japs at Wellington, Dubbo and Orange; and the Major and the Padre had been at Darwin. There were the corpses on the tennis courts. It was real enough. He stood up. They would go to the north. What was needed was perseverance and careful planning, and they would keep off that iron stone plain. Counihan and the Major. There was no real need to have smashed that bore at Bourke, they needn't have acted as they had at Wilcannia. They had got that wrong; but what was done, was done. *Forgive us, O Lord*. He walked over to the graves in the moonlight. There were the mounds and crosses. He took off his hat, stayed there a while and went back to the pub. With care and perseverance, they would make it.

They crouched over the maps on the verandah and Sawtell traced the route with his finger.

'Okay,' he said, 'there's the creek.'

'It's not a creek as I know it,' Sergius Donaldson said.

'It's not, it seems to be a series of channels and overflows, and there's a river called the Diamantina going north-east.'

Sawtell studied the maps. 'If we go north-west, we strike the Birdsville Track, we cross the Simpson Desert and go north to Alice. There's lots of stations on the way; with care, we can do it.'

'What food have we got?' the Padre said.

'There's plenty of grub,' O'Donohue said. 'We've got flour, rice, bully beef, sugar, some salt and lots of ammo.'

'Can you repair your boots, Kevin?' Sawtell said.

'Yeah, with leather from the Major's saddlebags.'

'And you, Padre?'

'I have a spare pair.'

'What about the horses?'

'They're buggered,' O'Donohue said. 'They need at least a month's rest.'

'We can't give them that, we'll keep to the creek as long as we can.'

'How long will the trip take, Mr Sawtell?' Sergius Donaldson said.

'A month, two months, it depends. There's a track to a station called King Lookout, that's our first objective.'

'We're in your hands, Mr Sawtell.'

'Yes, Padre, you are.'

They worked all the following day. O'Donohue cleaned the horses, patched up his boots and repaired the pack-frames. Sawtell and the Padre went out with their guns and came back with a wallaby and ducks. Sawtell slaughtered and cleaned the wallaby and hung the meat to dry in the sun. The guns were cleaned and the ammunition stored in pouches. They stacked the food carefully on the floor of the hotel and filled the waterbags. It seemed that nothing had been left to chance: their gear was in order and they were ready for the ride to the north, to King Lookout, then Birdsville and Alice Springs. At the end of the long day, they dined on cold roast duck and went to bed on the floor of the tiny, remote hotel.

They rose at dawn, watered the horses and mules, packed and went down the track past the Mission to the creek. When they got to the graves, they stopped, then splashed through the ford to the western side and struck north. The

428

dew was still on the ground, it was cold and the birds swarmed and flew over their heads. The creek ran in a series of wide, deep lagoons to the north-east; there were islands of green waterweeds and belts of eucalyptus, the feed was good for the horses and they browsed on the saltbush. Birds flew by the thousands and the morning became sultry, but there was no sign of rain. The trees were dark and red and looked like prehistoric animals. They walked for four hours, always to the north-east, and Sawtell knew that sooner or later, they would have to leave the creek and strike north-west to King Lookout and then Birdsville. Flies and mosquitoes plagued them, crawling into their mouths, ears and noses, and there was nothing they could do to stop them. From time to time, Sawtell walked out to the west and looked at the country beyond the trees only to find it barren and lifeless. There had to be a track to King Lookout. By noon it was 110 degrees.

They stopped to boil the billy and eat some cold meat. O'Donohue drank, but did not eat: his mouth was sore.

'Nothing to eat, Kevin?' Sawtell said.

'Got a few ulcers, I'll be okay.'

'Well, Padre?'

'Well, Mr Sawtell?'

'How do you feel?'

'Hot, and the insects don't help.'

'We'll rest for an hour. I'm going to cross the creek to have a look. There could be an outstation to the east. Who knows?'

Sawtell walked over the stones and through the channels to the other side. Then through the trees, he saw the grave. As he approached, he saw eight cast-iron plinths joined by steel hawsers surrounding a small monument of cement and stone. Sawtell read the small brass plate.

ROBERT O'HARA BURKE DIED HERE 28 JUNE 1861

RIP

429

He looked at the insignia on the plinths. They were made in England by Gilpin, Hedges & Mills, with Queen Boadicea stamped on the iron, her trident and her spear. There were the crossed axes of Albion. He thought of Major St John Jackson, turned away from the grave and sat in the shade of the old trees. Water hyacinth floated on the lagoon and a duck and ducklings swam. He wished he was sitting under the elm trees in the Fitzroy Gardens in Melbourne. Sawtell stayed by the grave for a while, then went back across the creek to the campfire.

'Was there anything to see?' Sergius Donaldson said.

Sawtell poured himself another mug of tea.

'No, Padre, there was nothing.'

The creek was now a sad, listless place and Sawtell was determined to leave it tomorrow. O'Donohue was stretched out, asleep: mouth ulcers were a sign of scurvy. After they had packed, Sawtell and the Padre rolled their cigarettes. It was the last of the papers and they stood by the horses.

'Well, Mr Sawtell,' Sergius Donaldson said, 'I shall have to give up smoking. Unlike you, I cannot use my prayer-book.'

'I'm not a religious man, Padre.'

There was no reply. They walked all day and, that night, set up camp by another large billabong. It was a dull, monotonous evening; they cooked some meat and sat around, resting their backs against the tree trunks. There was nothing to talk about and they watched the big grey moths flying into the flames and the centipedes crawling. Sawtell thought about a song or two, but O'Donohue's mouth was too sore to play the harmonica. The Padre went for his usual nocturnal walk and they settled down. Tomorrow, they faced the desert.

* * *

430

The treeless plain stretched before them, nothing grew, and sharp stones of flint covered the ground. They searched for small objects on the horizon, a low line of hills, a regular line of trees, or gums in a circle around a water tank. They needed some kind of goal for the day, but there was none. Within two hours, one of the horses cast a shoe and went lame. It was carrying the last Bren and ammunition. They stopped, Sawtell went back, threw the weapon off the packframe, smashed the breech and scattered the ammunition. There was no point in carrying weapons of war now. O'Donohue stood on the stones and looked at the horse: it wouldn't last the morning and he doubted if the others would make the end of the day. In all his travels so far, he had never seen such country and felt fear grow within him. His head ached and his limbs were stiff; his mouth was still sore and he could not eat at breakfast. What was happening to him? Should he tell the others? He stood by the mules and watched Sawtell come back. Sawtell stopped and looked at O'Donohue and the Padre.

'We never fired that bloody thing anyway.' Leave nothing to the enemy, Colonel Madigan had said. He cast about the red rock and looked for a hill or plateau. Where was the track for King Lookout? He came back and rolled a cigarette, using his prayerbook. The time by the gold hunter was eleven o'clock.

'Are you all right, Kevin?'

'Yeah, I'm fine.

'And you, Padre?'

'Satisfactory.'

'Right, two more hours and we'll have a breather.'

On they trudged, to the north-east, searching for some sign that other men had been here before them. Birds were flying high to the south-east and the creek, and somewhere they heard the sound of thunder. They watched the birds flying south to the lagoons; the tree line

431

was gone. The sun shone, and by noon, the thermometer registered 130 degrees: the summer was early in November, 1943.

At the end of the day, they saw an object on the red horizon and struggled toward it. Standing on the desert, was an old double-decker bus, a windmill and a tank. The bus was painted yellow and the blades of the windmill did not move. A bus, Sergius Donaldson thought, nothing more would surprise him now. He thought of Piccadilly, the fountains and the rumble of the West End traffic in the fog and rain. By the bus, there was a forty-four-gallon drum of empty wine flagons, a Lister diesel pump and old mattresses. Sawtell went over to the pump and found the tank was empty. Weatherbeaten stock rails stood upright in the stony ground.

'It's an out-station,' he said and pointed to the drum full of empty wine flagons. 'The blacks have been here.' He saw the rats running from the double-decker: they couldn't sleep in there tonight. 'It means we're close to King Lookout.' He looked north-west and all he saw was the sun on the horizon.

'Well, Mr Sawtell,' Sergius Donaldson said, 'I haven't seen one of those buses for some time.'

'And neither have I, Padre.'

'Where has it come from?'

'God knows, Adelaide perhaps. I think they have double-deckers down there. We Australians are careful people, nothing is thrown away.'

'We're throwing things away.'

'Padre, this is a lean and hungry trip.' Sawtell started to unpack the mules; he got out the ropes and strung up a picket line between the stock rails. At least, they wouldn't lose any horses tonight. It was a desolate place. O'Donohue gave the animals a drink from the waterbags and bucket and they lit a fire, using the timber from the broken fence posts. Sawtell had not counted on this stony desert;

432

he chewed the last of the jerked wallaby, they would have to shoot the old hack in the morning. That meant one day more on the track, but that couldn't be helped. The Padre sat reading his prayerbook by the fire and O'Donohue lay sleeping under his blankets, his head on his stock saddle. The boy had not eaten for twelve hours now, and he wondered about his prospects. He put the doubts aside: he was a strong Australian country lad, the cream of the Empire; lads like him had fought bravely in the trenches. The Padre finished reading, got up and came towards him by the fire.

'An odd scene, Mr Sawtell? A London bus in the desert.'

Sawtell wished that Frank Counihan and St John Jackson were with them: they could have helped. The Major would have argued, and that would have been something.

'Yeah, it's an odd scene, Padre. Would you care for a drink?'

'How much is left?'

'Half a bottle.'

'Why not, who knows what tomorrow will bring?'

Sawtell went to the saddlebag and got the bottle.

'You have your faith to sustain you, Padre, I have not.'

'That, Mr Sawtell, is your problem, not mine.'

They both drank one whisky and went to sleep upon the open ground by the bus, the Lister diesel, the forty-four-gallon drum and the verminous mattresses. The Padre prayed for them all and Sawtell lay in his blankets next to O'Donohue, trying to figure out the stars and the constellations. He was tired and could not think clearly; the Milky Way glowed, but he could not find Venus or the Southern Cross. Where was the Great Bear? The heavens were vast and he thought of the boys cheering on the troopship in the Indian Ocean. That was many years ago. They must find King Lookout tomorrow. And what about Kevin O'Donohue?

In the cold morning, there was the plain. There were no

433

birds, no laughing jackasses and no river lines. The dew was on the stones, the Padre and O'Donohue were still asleep. Sawtell stretched, got up and gathered wood for the fire. He knelt by the boy and listened for his breathing: it was shallow and his breath was foul. Where was Frank Counihan? Sawtell thought of the days on the road to Bourke, filled the billy from the waterbag and put it on the fire to boil. This was his routine. The moon was sinking and the sky was empty: it would be very hot today. He went over to the stock rail behind the bus; two of the horses had fallen during the night and Sawtell couldn't get them up. They were skin and bone now, and good for nothing. The Padre and O'Donohue slept and Sawtell looked at the fallen horses: they were ready for the knacker's. He went back to his bed-roll, picked up the Lee Enfield, returned to the horses and shot them both between the eyes. The Padre woke and saw the killing.

'Was that necessary, Mr Sawtell?'

'Don't question me, Padre, they were due for it.' He stood with the axe and Counihan's knife. 'I'll save you some liver for breakfast.'

O'Donohue had not woken and Sawtell started the butchery. The flies were already bad and it took him some time. He swung the axe, cut off the haunches and the rumps, split them into strips and put the meat on the rails to dry in the sun and wind. The air was black with flies, a piece of liver was saved for the Padre and he carried off the offal and threw it into the dry tank. Using one of the mules, Sawtell dragged the carcasses as far as he could away from the camp into the desert. The eagles and the crows appeared, and Sawtell washed himself the best he could. O'Donohue was awake. They had breakfast: the Padre, his liver; Sawtell, cold meat; and O'Donohue a cup of cold tea.

'How are you feeling, Kevin?' Sawtell said.

'Having trouble with me legs.'

434

Sawtell looked at the clergyman. 'Right, we'll stay here for a day and jerk the meat.'

'You can go on.'

'No, we'll need the meat.' Thank God, a wind was starting to blow: it would dry the meat and keep the flies away. The hot breeze was coming in from the west, into their faces. 'Take your blankets and doss down in the lee of the bus.'

They did as they were told; within an hour, the sky had darkened as the sandstorm approached. They sat through it, and by the end of the afternoon, the last horse had fallen. Sergius Donaldson crouched with Sawtell behind the bus. They had weighed O'Donohue's blankets down with saddles as the wind blew. At the end of the day, the Padre said:

'Mr Sawtell, I have disquieting news: I cannot see.'

The wind stopped during the night and, at dawn, Sawtell dumped the saddles, the bag of flour, half the rice, the harnesses and the excess ammunition. He kept the salt, the tea, the tins of bully beef, the sugar – and put the jerked meat into the torn and filthy muslin bags. The thermometer had broken, but he stuffed the bottle of whisky, the maps and compass into a saddlebag and loaded the mules. He oiled the Lee Enfield and the Major's Purdey: it was a fine gun, custom-made, and had brought down many plump waterfowl. Where was Cooper's Creek now? The ducks, the seagulls and the cormorants. Maybe they should return? He threw away the empty hurricane lamp and the glass smashed on the stones. They would have to travel light now.

'Do you need any help, Mr Sawtell?'

The Padre was awake, but O'Donohue was still asleep.

'No, I'm okay, you stay where you are, we leave in an hour.'

Sawtell looked at the plain and the clear sky. He considered climbing the narrow staircase to the top of the bus. He could sit in a seat and look out. He laughed. What was the point of that? He thought of his leave in London, the pretty girls in their flowery hats and the handsome young men strolling down Regent Street. The Australian soldiers in pubs, drinking Watney's Bitter and playing up: those were the days. The fire was lit, they had their tea and Sawtell picked up Kevin O'Donohue and placed him carefully on the back of the mule. He shouldered the Lee Enfield, put the Major's Purdey in the gun case and took Sergius Donaldson by the arm. They left the out-station and marched north-west. In the late morning, Kevin O'Donohue slipped from the mule. They stopped on the plain. Sawtell took the boy's hat off and found his hair was falling out; his fingernails were black and split and he could not speak. The Padre sat on the stones.

'What's happened, Mr Sawtell?'

'O'Donohue's in bad shape, we'll have to wait a while.'

He washed O'Donohue's face and mouth and stood there, powerless with the blind clergyman. Somewhere, far away, there was a thunderstorm and they waited. The heat was intense and they waited. Now and then, Sawtell looked at the gold hunter. He wound it. There was nothing to be done.

O'Donohue died just after half past two in the afternoon.

'You'd better say a prayer, Padre,' Sawtell said. 'The boy's dead.' He led Sergius Donaldson over.

I am the resurrection and the life, saith the Lord.

It took Sawtell two hours to scratch a two-foot grave in the stones and he piled the country rock into a mound. There was no timber to make a cross. The Padre conducted the short service from memory, and when it was over, they drank the last of the whisky.

'I fear our chances are slipping away,' the Padre said, 'and I regret I can't be of more assistance.'

436

'It's only a short walk now,' Sawtell said. 'If you're able, we'll go on until six.'

'I shall do my best.'

They washed their mouths from the waterbottles and walked on to the north with the two mules for two hours. Each was in his own private world now; there was only the sound of their boots and the mules' feet on the hard ground. Sergius Donaldson held Sawtell's arm: he was a weary traveller. Where was the river, the lock gates and the water running through the old timbers? He tripped and fell on the rocks. Sawtell helped him to his feet, he looked at the horizon and could not see clearly. He thought of taking a fix with the hand compass, but nothing was to be seen. Sawtell looked back. Where was O'Donohue's grave? It was lost already. Again, he heard the sound of thunder from the invisible tablelands. The sun was in the west, they walked and the Padre fell a second time into the red sand and stones. From time to time, Sawtell uncorked the water bottle and gave the clergyman a drink. He shook the flask and felt the canvas bags: there wasn't much left, and the mules, too, were shaking. Then Sawtell thought he saw a low plateau rising from the shimmering plains of rock. There was a lone emu running to the west and Sawtell changed direction for he thought that must be King Lookout. There would be a stone building, a Victorian homestead with shady verandahs, porticoes, a grand piano and a wine cellar. There would be hand-made parquet floors, beds and children's toys, a library and an orange grove. He thought of Sturt's Meadows and Kevin O'Donohue riding away on his big, black horse. *Robert O'Hara Burke died here.* Where were the young girls, throwing flowers, the crowded boulevards and the Cameron pipers? And Marcia? *You are my honey, honeysuckle, I am the bee.* There is a green hill far away.

Sergius Donaldson fell again, and this time could not

437

rise. It was getting dark. The Padre lay on the rocks and said:

'Mr Sawtell, leave me here and go on your own. You can come back. I'm quite comfortable and can last the night through.'

'No, Padre,' Sawtell said, 'you won't last the night by yourself. I'm taking you with me. We can manage.' The Padre was heavy as Sawtell got him to his feet. 'We'll go west, there's a creek where we can camp.'

They would follow the emu, but it had gone.

After half an hour more, Sawtell took out his watch. It was almost half past six. The Lee Enfield was burdensome on his shoulder. He was sure they could still make Alice Springs or even the Gulf of Carpentaria. The sky was empty and there were no enemy aircraft. Where were the Japanese? Did they ever exist? The evening breeze blew and darkness was settling down over the country. It seemed that darkness was coming down all over Australia. He still could not see the tree line, and as the night came upon them, they had nowhere to sleep. They stopped and Sergius Donaldson stood uncertain on the plain seeing nothing. He did not pray: he was too tired, and there was only the land. Sawtell looked for a vantage point, a hill, a tree, but there was none. He turned and led the Padre towards a small, shallow bed of stone. He settled him between the rocks; the clergyman touched him once and said nothing. He wished the Padre would speak: he didn't want a prayer or a Collect from the Gospel, he wanted to discuss the whereabouts of the creek. Two heads were better than one, but Sergius Donaldson was silent and lay upon the earth like an old and brittle tree, the Major's shotgun beside him. Sawtell threw off his haversack and put down the Lee Enfield. He walked thirty or forty steps across the plain, cast about in the gathering darkness, then walked back. They would have to bivouac where they were. Was that the sound of an aircraft? The clergyman was as still as the grave, his head upon his kit and his legs spreadeagled. Sawtell covered him with a blanket and weighed it down with stones. He must not forget to give the mules a drink this evening. Where were Colonel Madigan's orders? Counihan must have them. Where was Frank? He should be back by now. It took Sawtell a long time to roll a cigarette in the grimy, fragile pages of his prayerbook, and then he could not find the matches. He crouched in the lee of the rocks and stones as the west wind blew and felt very tired. He took out his father's watch, but it was now too dark to see the time. At last Sawtell went to sleep with the Padre. They would find King Lookout in the morning.

> My pulse is the clock of life;
> It shows how my moments are flying.
> It marks the departure of time,
> And tells me how fast I am dying.